Praise for Lucy Jane Bledsoe's other books published by the University of Wisconsin Press

A Thin Bright Line: A Novel

- Lambda Literary Award Finalist
- Publishing Triangle Ferro-Grumley Award Finalist

"Triumphs as an intimate and humane evocation of day-to-day life under inhumane circumstances."

New York Times Book Review

"Empowering and bold. . . . Bledsoe injects life and dimension through her often stunning dialogue."

Publishers Weekly

"Bledsoe's novel is an absolute wonder. Combining a McCullers-like facility in letting her settings tell half the story with characterization and dialogue worthy of Harper Lee, Bledsoe dives deep into the life of her protagonist."

New York Journal of Books

"Berkeley author Lucy Jane Bledsoe shows the sexy side of the 1950s in her new novel."

San Francisco Chronicle

"Author Lucy Jane Bledsoe is an impressively gifted novelist who in the pages of her latest epic, *A Thin Bright Line*, is able to consistently engage her readers' rapt and total attention from cover to cover."

Midwest Book Review

"A stirring and deeply felt story."

Kirkus Reviews

"Deftly weaves closeted sexuality, Cold War politics, and a mysterious death that haunts the author to this day."

San Jose Mercury News

"Gripping historical fiction about queer life at the height of the Cold War and the civil rights movement, and its grounding in fact really makes it sing."

Alison Bechdel, author of *Fun Home*

The Big Bang Symphony: A Novel of Antarctica

- Lambda Literary Award Finalist
- Publishing Triangle Ferro-Grumley Award Finalist
- Northern California Independent Booksellers Association, Fiction Award Finalist

"Captures the deadly beauty of the southernmost continent."
Kirkus Reviews

"Bledsoe uses the locale's incredible beauty and high potential for drama, danger, and self-discovery for insights small and great."
Booklist

"In the collision of art and science that is the novel, Bledsoe — part novelist, part science writer, and part intrepid adventurer — shows off a finely honed imagination and sensibility that, along with her deep passion for the wild places of the earth, inspire as they uplift."
Edge magazine

"A beautiful novel about living in that extreme space, vivid and suspenseful."
Kim Stanley Robinson

The Ice Cave: A Woman's Adventures from the Mojave to the Antarctic

"Guaranteed to give armchair naturalists and travelers a glorious ride from Alaska to Antarctica."
Library Journal

"An exhilarating read. . . . There's an aching beauty to her tales of travel."
Passport

"An honest — at times wrenchingly so — exploration of a personal relationship with wilderness, adrenaline and endorphins."
Portsmouth Herald

"A longing for spiritual release Bledsoe can find only in the wilderness is woven through these thoughtful essays."
Publishers Weekly

"Layered, literary, and unflinchingly honest."
World Hum: Travel Dispatches from a Shrinking Planet

Lava Falls

Also by Lucy Jane Bledsoe

Fiction

The Evolution of Love

A Thin Bright Line

The Big Bang Symphony: A Novel of Antarctica

Biting the Apple

This Wild Silence

Working Parts

Sweat: Stories and a Novella

Nonfiction

The Ice Cave: A Woman's Adventures from the Mojave to the Antarctic

Childrens

How to Survive in Antarctica

The Antarctic Scoop

Hoop Girlz

Cougar Canyon

Tracks in the Snow

The Big Bike Race

LAVA FALLS

LUCY JANE BLEDSOE

THE UNIVERSITY OF WISCONSIN PRESS

The University of Wisconsin Press
1930 Monroe Street, 3rd Floor
Madison, Wisconsin 53711-2059
uwpress.wisc.edu

3 Henrietta Street, Covent Garden
London WCE 8LU, United Kingdom
eurospanbookstore.com

Printed in the United States of America

This book may be available in a digital edition.

Library of Congress Cataloging-in-Publication Data

Names: Bledsoe, Lucy Jane, author.
Title: Lava Falls / Lucy Jane Bledsoe.
Description: Madison, Wisconsin: The University of Wisconsin Press, [2018]
Identifiers: LCCN 2018011132 | ISBN 9780299318505 (cloth: alk. paper)
Subjects: | LCGFT: Fiction.
Classification: LCC PS3552.L418 L38 2018 | DDC 813/.54—dc23
LC record available at https://lccn.loc.gov/2018011132

This is a work of fiction. While, as in all fiction, the literary perceptions and insights are based on experience and research, names, characters, places, and incidents are either products of the author's imagination or are used fictitiously.

For

Patricia

Contents

Lava Falls

Girl with Boat

So far as I know, they're all dead. I left in late autumn, four months after my mother died and a few days before the river froze up. I don't see how they could have continued on without her, though the twins were practically men by then. We all had depended so completely on her. Father was the dreamer, the one who launched our life up here, but she was the one who figured out how to till the frozen soil so we could plant early, how to dry berries so they didn't mold in the winter, how to stanch the flow of blood the time Derek sliced through his ankle with the axe. Father hadn't wanted to bring books with us. He said primitive men hadn't had books. He said the fun part was figuring out things for ourselves.

I am paddling upriver. I am returning after an absence of thirty-three years. I don't know what I'll find.

We moved to our inlet here on Sweet Creek, in eastern Alaska, when I was seven and the boys were five. Father and Mother must have been in their early thirties. He had a degree in political science and she in education. Until we left New England for the arctic, he worked construction and she taught junior high. I don't remember anything about the planning stages. My first memory of our Alaskan life is driving to the airport in the middle of the night.

Mother's enthusiasm held through the flight to Fairbanks but foundered as soon as she boarded the four-seater bush plane. We three children were left with the bush pilot's wife while they flew north on reconnaissance. Father cited the primacy of local knowledge as his rationale for letting the pilot choose the location for the rest of our lives. In hindsight, I have to admit that was wise. Had Father made the choice, I would probably be dead, too. He'd never been a practical man. I remember our night in the pilot's small home in Fairbanks as he and Father pored over maps. Father couldn't focus, didn't want to look, used his hands to wave away specifics. Over and over again, he repeated our requirements: a gentle creek, a flat place to build, good hunting, and complete isolation, a site where we would not encounter other people. The pilot would nod impatiently and try to draw Father's attention back to the map.

I also remember my extreme relief, the prospect of enormous grief sloughing away, when the pilot's wife drove me and my brothers to the airstrip. She said our parents had found the spot, and her husband would fly us there. Unlike my mother, I was all too glad to board that plane. Reunion with my parents was all that mattered back then.

I sat up front with the pilot and looked down at the frozen rivers and snowy forests. It was May, many weeks before the thaw. As we landed in a frosty meadow, the plane's skis sliding to a stop, I saw Mother and Father standing on the edge, next to heavy conifers, she hugging herself tightly, he filling his lungs with arctic air, as if he were breathing for the first time in his life.

I've resisted romanticizing my childhood. I've refused to use the stories to gain attention. I've kept my survivalist past—it's difficult even now as I paddle toward it to use that harsh word—hidden even from lovers. I don't know if I'm protecting myself or my father. The hold of a spiritual inheritance, a man's dream, especially when it's so fierce, can surprise you. Even if you see it as wrongheaded. I could hardly bring myself to tell my *guides* the location of the cabin. It was our family secret. Our security. Our only hope. Father's Eden. He had asked the bush pilot to not tell us the name of our creek, if it had one, so that we could never tell anyone where we were. After the pilot dropped me and my brothers off, we all watched him bank his plane toward the west, and then Father said, "Sweet Creek." And that was it.

Later I would learn that when we paddled downstream we reached another river with a name we also refused, merely calling it Big River. Another couple of long days' float down that and we came to the mighty Yukon. Once a year Father made this journey to Fort Yukon where he bought a few supplies. He'd return from these trips in a strange mood of combined elation and depression, as if the view of the outside world both greatly excited and deeply disappointed him. He felt weakened by our need to buy oats and nails and even boots. When the boys got older, they begged to be allowed to go along to Fort Yukon, but he never let them, claiming that there wouldn't be room in the boat for all the supplies. This wasn't true. He didn't want them to learn the way out.

It has taken me decades to realize that I never really did get out. From age seven to seventeen I lived here in isolation, with my mother and father and twin brothers, a girl growing up with the bear and river and aspen. I have sometimes wished I could find a way to tell my story. It's highly romantic. It could win me much. But it is both the heart of my loneliness and also my heart. It is my lifelong isolation. I am afraid that if I told it, I would be gutted, left with nothing at all.

Today, to make my return bearable, I tell myself that I am paddling up this river to visit my mother's grave. That's what I told my guides, too. It is the only way I can let myself come. Each paddle stroke brings me closer to that spot in the upper meadow, where she once flagged down a bush pilot to rescue her and where she is now buried. But I am coming back for so much more than a visit to my mother's grave. Now, just a couple of miles away, I realize that I am hoping that by visiting this mythic place I can release myself from its grip.

My guides, Gregory and Stuart, help in ways they don't know. They are sweet and young and handsome. So well meaning. They make me feel safe. It is true that they can't hide their admiration for my father. Their lust for his risk is fixed in their eyes, hangs in their open mouths. I am grateful for this and resentful of it. I don't break the spell by telling them how different they are from him. They have read many, many books on plants, mountains, rivers, and survival. They know how to tie dozens of knots, build good fires, roll a kayak. I am greatly comforted by their skills. Furthermore, they have evolved far past simple survival. They enjoy sipping scotch at dusk, the warmth of their expedition-weight sleeping bags, spinning long tales of their adventures. They make me want to tell my story at last. In fact, they make me want to start my love life over, to meet boys like them who might understand. Thirty-three years ago I delivered myself from this wilderness, but had I known how, had I known boys like Gregory and Stuart, I might have delivered my-self too from the emotional thicket in which I've spent my life roaming. Had I known not only how to tell my story but also why I must.

Please don't misunderstand. I've lived a happy life with good friends, fulfilling work, and lots of lovers. I couldn't ask for more. Yet I'm aware that I long for an intensity I wish I didn't long for. My early years gave me a wildness of heart that I have never been able to move beyond.

Mother wanted to leave even before the first snow fell. Over the years her requests took different forms. Begging. Demanding. With-holding sex, which we all knew about because we lived in one big room. There was a period, for about three years, starting when I was nine and the boys were seven, when she seemed to have finally given in. My parents were the happiest they'd ever been in those three years. There was lots of laughing. The weather was good. We lived like a family of bear.

Then she snapped, I guess. Or maybe the happiness had been faked all along. In late August of my twelfth year, she made a big SOS out of logs in the upper meadow. A pilot bringing in caribou hunters landed and found our cabin. That night Father hit mother. It was the only time. She lived another five years. Then, a high fever, from what we don't know, and she was gone in a matter of three days.

After she died that June, things went about how you'd expect. There was grief, enormous amounts of grief. Father expressed his philosophi-cally. The few times he spoke of her death, he mentioned the life cycle. He said her body was returning to the earth. As if she were compost. The twins expressed theirs physically. They felled trees and shot moose. They built an outbuilding for themselves, leaving me to sleep alone with my father in the cabin.

So far as I know, I was the only one who cried. My grief tore at me. At times I felt as if my flesh were being ripped from my bones. This is not hyperbole. It is what I felt. Other times it was as if the grief were a hand holding me underwater. Drowning in our own inlet where the water temperature is killer cold. I couldn't breathe. I couldn't get warm.

I imagined her everywhere. I saw her spirit in the retreating tracks of snowshoe hare, in eastward drifting clouds, in the Dopplered wails of wolves. I took these departures as messages from her, requests that I too leave. But I was seventeen years old and didn't want to die. I didn't know any other kind of leave-taking.

It took me four months. I didn't let myself think the word *abandon*. I couldn't have thought it and still left. Instead, I noted how the boys were already man-sized. I told myself that they didn't need me anymore. In fact, I went a few steps further. I let myself hate the boys. The way they trailed Father, helping, relentlessly helping. Derek still limping all those years later, and yet swinging that axe above his head, flying it down into the heart of a log. Dash better with a skinning knife than any of us, scraping the moose hide clean, working with such concentration you'd think he was painting a masterpiece. That's how I remembered him all these years, the skinning knife in his hand, straddling a great bloody kill, engrossed in the stench of moose blood, his eyes glazed with the work of survival.

It was Derek who heaped the dirt onto my mother, great shovelfuls of soil laced with bits of spring flowers. He worked with such strength and speed, as if he were afraid he might jump into the grave with her if he didn't fill the hole fast enough. In those months after her death, I did my best to ignore the traces of tenderness in Derek. He sometimes took my hand when walking. He paused in the course of his days, to watch bear cubs play or to listen to the papery rustle of aspen leaves. He taught himself to cook that summer, a hint of nurturance in his wild dishes. As if we didn't *all* hurt, I wanted to scream at him. As if there is time for staring at rain pelting the window glass. When I saw his pain, I became my father. I wanted to work. I wanted to make sense of things. I wanted to survive.

It was Mother who had secured my means for escaping, on a hot August afternoon, years earlier when I was ten. I like to think she knew what she was doing. The boys were off hunting with Father. Mother had sent me to get some water. It was a beautiful afternoon, the light making millions of diamond sparkles on the pale green water of our inlet. The bay was shaped like a rounded wave, and I liked to stand on the shore inside its curl. The main current of Sweet Creek was a good fifteen yards out from our beach.

The bright blue wooden kayak drifted languidly down the creek toward me. I almost shouted my excitement. Only rarely did we have visitors, adventurers who happened onto our stream, into our inlet. They'd all been young men who stared in awe at our cabin, our clothes, our homemade rowboat, our life. They would stop to talk, and every one of them openly expressed his desire to *be* us. Though Father had told our bush pilot that he wanted complete isolation, he liked these visits. They validated him. He was doing what these other men could only play at on their two-week escapades. He always used that word, *escapade*, emphasizing their circus act lives compared to our tooth-and-bone existence. When talking to these young men, he exaggerated our success, pretending that the meat and berries were plentiful, that the weather was ideal, that we enjoyed one another's company.

As the pretty blue boat drew closer, an eddy caught its bow and spun it around. The swirling bright blue on clear green, the prospect of outsiders, mesmerized me. Until I realized there was no one inside the kayak. I ran to get Mother.

She surprised me. I expected her to send me off to find Father and the boys. I assumed we'd launch a search for the missing kayaker. I was only ten, but I knew that a kayak without a paddler was bad news.

Mother saw it differently.

"Honey," she said. "Let's get it."

I glanced quickly up at her face. Her gaze was riveted on the still spinning boat, her thoughts a complete mystery to me at the time. That gaze, the sight of her determination, is my best memory of her. Even in midsummer, the water was numbingly cold. Yet Mother stripped off all her clothes and plunged in. Her hips swaying and her arms waving above the surface of the water, she waded out until she was navel deep, and then she swam. When she got halfway to the kayak, it bucked out of the eddy and started drifting downstream again. Tears swelled my chest as I watched her change course, begin stroking toward the boat. I didn't think she'd make it. But she kicked harder and windmilled her arms, moving faster than the current. When she reached the boat, she hooked her arms over the cockpit's lip and rested for as long as she dared, given that most of her body was still in the hypothermia-inducing creek. Then she hauled the boat back to shore, awkwardly holding it with one arm and fiercely kicking her legs, a very long, hard swim. I've often wondered how she survived that feat. It was a desperate act, and, I like to think, one of prescience. I like to think she risked her life for me, that she loved me that much.

I can still see the sparkling gems of creek water dripping off the ends of her nipples, the aching red of her pale skin, the way she held her mouth as she pulled the kayak along the shore to our beach. I kept expecting her to say something about the boat's rightful owner, or at least express concern about him, but she never did. It was ours now. It would eventually be mine.

I ran up the hill ahead of her and built a fire in the stove. I put on a kettle and, when she came in the door, wrapped her in blankets. I rubbed her wet head with a towel and dried her feet. She was too numb to dress herself, and so I did. Then, once she warmed up, we returned to our day's work.

I didn't know how Father would react to the kayak sitting on our beach. I watched for him all afternoon and caught sight of him coming out of the woods, the boys trailing a few yards behind. They had no game. Father strode right to the boat and examined it with his hands on his hips. Then he broke into a run up to the cabin, as if Mother and I were in danger. He assumed we had a visitor.

Father entered the cabin brusquely. Mother didn't tell him about her swim. She said the kayak had drifted to shore. He looked around suspiciously and then bolted back outside. I watched from the window, afraid that he'd shove the boat back into the current. He stood on the beach and looked at it for a long time. I wish I could guess what Father was thinking, but I never knew. Concern about the missing paddler? Paranoia about the same? Anxiety about any kind of input from the outside? Maybe he thought that keeping the boat was cheating.

In the morning, as soon as I got up, I ran outside and saw the pretty blue vessel still tipped on our beach. That very day Father began carving a paddle, and soon he and the boys used it regularly for fishing, alongside the crude rowboat Father had built himself.

This morning I left Gregory and Stuart in our camp on Sweet Creek. They promised, with much reluctance, to give me a full four hours lead time. I wanted to arrive alone. They tried citing last night's snowfall and my inexperience as reasons for not allowing this. I laughed at that. My inexperience! They laughed too, admitted the irony. But the truth is, Stuart had pointed out very gently, I'd lived in San Francisco for decades now. I hadn't slept outside since leaving Alaska. I liked nice restaurants and comfortable hotels. Stuart went so far as to point out that I wasn't a spring chicken. I laughed some more and told them both I'd be fine.

I *am* fine. The kayak I am paddling is much more comfortable than the one I made my escape in. It's plastic, so I don't have to worry about cracking its hull on rocks, and it's fitted out with a padded seat and backrest. It also has a rudder I control with foot pedals, so I don't waste lots of energy trying to stay on course. In fact, I surprise myself by feeling downright happy. The green-black trees look so familiar, as if I had been here last week. The sight of hard sunlight on glassy water jolts my heart. Even the dull pulse of working muscles feels like home.

Though my real home now includes a small white dog named Winston, a cappuccino maker, central heating, and walls lined with art prints. It seems like months ago that I left my flat, although it was only two weeks. I flew to Fairbanks on a commercial flight, arriving two days before Gregory and Stuart. I wanted time to find the diner, if it still existed. It does. I had breakfast there both mornings. Harold is long gone. The present owner had never heard of him. On the third day, I flew with Gregory and Stuart to Fort Yukon. I braced myself, thinking the sight of that muddy sprawl of a village would kick me in the stomach. Instead, it twisted my heart. I guess the place had become a part of me. I couldn't hate it any more than I can hate my own spleen. I walked out the mud road to find the plywood and tarpaper house where I had stayed with Ben and Susie. It was gone. Not a trace. Just dirt and grass.

My guides rented one double and one single kayak, and we floated down the Yukon River to the mouth of what my family called Big River. There we began paddling upstream, against the current, and it took us six long, hard days to reach the beginning of Sweet Creek. We camped there at the convergence and then paddled one more day to reach last night's camp. I'm within range now, a couple more hours. My arms and back have strengthened. The boys have shown me how to use my core, my abdomen muscles, to get more power. I am paddling upstream.

I've grown quite fond of Gregory and Stuart. At first I told them only the bare bones of my story. I showed them on a map where the cabin was. I asked them to take care of all the travel details. They did try asking questions, first over single-malt scotches that first night in Fairbanks. Then, tentatively, again in our camp at the meeting of Sweet Creek and Big River. Finally, last night, I relented.

They had surprised me by staging a celebration. They knew, even without having all the details, how important this journey was for me.

As a light, early autumn snow fell, they built a big fire and seared steaks. Gregory made his signature camp cake, a gooey chocolate concoction that seemed more pudding than cake. Stuart collected edible greens, but I spat out the first bite, saying edible was a subjective term. We passed around a bottle of cabernet.

I savored the lacy cold flakes, knowing that they didn't threaten my life, that I was safe. The baying of wolves came to my ears like a complex, rich music. I hadn't known that I missed their voices. The boys kept adding logs to the fire, long before it needed them.

Both are handsome in their own ways. Gregory is a bit hobbit-like with a puggish nose and rosy cheeks. He wears a full black beard, usually adorned with bits of oatmeal or drips of hot chocolate. His hair is self-cut, black, and pelt-like. Stuart is pale with full and childish red lips. His dark blond hair curls slightly at the ends. His hands are expressive and I imagine him to be a sensitive if awkward lover. He smiles every time I meet eyes with him. Both are conciliatory and try very hard. They are fascinated by my story.

I told them everything. About the bush pilot setting us down in the meadow, felling the trees and building our cabin, bear visitations, and even Mother's fever. I told them how Father had said he was grateful she'd died in the spring, after the thaw, so that we were able to bury her. I told them how I couldn't stop thinking, after he said that, about what it would have been like had she died in the winter, how we'd have had to store her body in the woodshed until the spring thaw, frozen solid, her hair breaking off and the fear in her eyes permanent. I told them about Mother's swim. Finally, about me leaving.

In early October of my seventeenth year, while the men were off hunting, I sat in the pebbles on our beach and stared at the blue kayak. For the millionth time I recalled the look of determination in my mother's eyes as she watched it spin in the bottle green eddy. That day, it sat next to me, landlocked, idle, ready. The river would freeze up soon.

A single gunshot released me. They had gotten another moose. It was the fourth that fall. They had food, far more than they needed. I could go. I knew they'd be several hours bringing the moose back. I could get far in that time.

I ran to our cabin and grabbed as much dried meat as I could carry. I stuffed it under the deck of the kayak and went back for more. I gathered up all my clothes, too, and what I didn't wear I shoved under the deck with the meat. I dragged the boat to the water's edge, climbed in, and launched.

I paddled down Sweet Creek, the current speeding me along, and when I came to Big River I pushed hard down that, too. I knew I had to beat the freeze, which could come instantly, any night now. I also knew that I was most likely racing my father. I was pretty sure he'd try to come after me, but he'd be in the much slower rowboat. So I paddled by starlight, late into the nights, and slept only briefly, when I absolutely had to, lying close to the kayak and shore so I could shove off quickly if needed. I ate the meat and drank the river water. I was not unhappy.

It took me only four days to reach the Yukon River, which I recognized by its sheer size. There was plenty of boat traffic and I waited for a vessel to come close enough for me to ask questions. I learned that Fort Yukon was about twenty-five miles upstream. But now I'd be paddling against the current. My father would be able to hitch a ride with a faster vessel and overtake me. I needed to find a hideaway for a few days, until the freeze, or until he gave up.

After paddling for a few hours along the Yukon's bank, I saw a plume of smoke coming out of the trees. I landed the boat and pulled it deep into the brush, well out of sight from the river. Then I hiked up a small trail to a clearing and a cabin. I knocked on the door.

The woman who answered reminded me of Mother. She wasn't as pretty and didn't look as capable. But she had that hard-eyed look, suspicious and tired and resourceful all at once. A man, jaunty and wiry, came to the door behind her. His whole body smiled.

"Who are you?" he asked.

I didn't know. I didn't have an answer to that question. I thought of Mother and Father. Of our cabin and the twins. I had left all that behind.

"I need work," I said. "For a few days." And then I made up a name.

The man didn't stop grinning. Behind him, two children started crying.

"No." The woman spoke quickly to beat her husband's yes. "We don't need anything."

"Sure," the man said. "Come on in."

"I said no," the woman repeated, but he grabbed my arm and pulled me into the cabin. Three children—two, three, and five years old—sat on the rough floorboards. The five-year-old got up and ran behind his mother.

For four days I was a nanny and all-around maid. I changed diapers and played peek-a-boo. I fried eggs and boiled coffee. I put up berries and mended clothes. I scrubbed the floor and shook out rugs. The woman hated me. Every hour I considered running back down the hill to my boat, but the prospect of being found, of being returned to the cabin on upper Sweet Creek, was an option I couldn't face. So I slept alone and cold in a tiny outbuilding. I got up before sunrise and followed orders. The man had had much less hunting luck than my father and brothers, and he left in a foul mood every morning in search of meat for the winter. In the evenings he ricocheted between nervous energy, when he'd bounce one of the children too hard on his knee or take things apart so he could put them back together, and passive sullenness, when he'd stare at the black stove for long stretches of time, barely blinking. I scurried with the wife to please him, bringing coffee and stoking the fire and keeping the children quiet. I prayed the freeze would come so I could travel again. I would walk the remaining miles to Fort Yukon.

On the fifth day, the man said I should come hunting with him, that he could use the help. The woman said no, that she needed me, but he tossed me a canteen and I followed him outside. We hiked for miles, the man who had been silent every night in the cabin now talking, talking, talking. I remember nothing of what he told me. I concentrated on containment, keeping myself in as small and compact a package as I could. He didn't touch me.

But, though I had no experience in such things, I knew he would soon.

That night the temperature dropped and I knew the inland streams would freeze. Slush had already started forming in the Yukon. I got up hours before dawn and crept down to the shore. I dragged my blue kayak out of the brush and pushed it into the crusted water. I began paddling upstream, ice crystals tinkling against my paddle and hull. Animals had eaten the last of my meat, stored in my kayak, and I had no food.

Yet a strange contentment came over me. I knew my father wouldn't risk getting caught away from the cabin and my brothers at freeze-up. I knew I was free. I began to consider the man's question, Who are you? I was a hungry girl with sore muscles. A grieving girl with nothing left of her mother but the memory of a steely gaze and a fierce swim. I was something very simple, alive, moving freely. I was a girl with boat.

A day and a half later, weak and dizzy and raw, I arrived at the mostly native town of Fort Yukon. To avoid drawing attention to myself, I pulled my hat with earflaps down as far as I could and stayed on the outskirts. I knocked on the door of the first cabin I came to and found Susie, a Gwich'in woman. I liked how she looked, so I told her my whole story, and that I needed to get to Fairbanks. Soon her husband Ben came home. They fed me and let me sleep on the floor of their front room, wrapped in blankets. In the morning, they showed me where I was, pulling out maps and using a finger to trace the Yukon River's two-thousand-mile route. The headwaters are in British Columbia, and from there the river travels northwest, crossing the border into Alaska. At Fort Yukon, it turns west and runs all the way to the Bering Sea. I was only about seventy-five miles north of Fairbanks, as the crow flies.

Ben and Susie asked me lots of questions about my journey and the number of hours I had been paddling. They figured out the exact location of our cabin and knew the name of our creek. Ben, who sat on the tribal council, argued that I should return to my father and brothers. Susie said that I was an adult at seventeen and should be able to make my own choices. In the end, they paid a bush pilot to fly me to Fairbanks.

I stayed in the big city, living in a boarding house and working at Harold's diner until I had paid Susie and Ben back for the flight. Each week I walked to the home of the bush pilot and gave him what cash I had. He made frequent trips to Fort Yukon and he delivered the money to Ben and Susie.

Then I kept working, saving for a plane ticket out of the state. But I didn't leave for another couple of years. I lost the fear of my father. Even if he had found me there, he couldn't have made me leave Fairbanks. Anyway, I met Sergey and thought about marrying him. I eventually figured out he hadn't been thinking about marrying me, and that's when I started saving for real. I liked what I read in the papers about San Francisco, and so when I had enough money for the ticket, I flew there and stayed.

Having heard my story, my guides wanted more than anything to witness my return. I could see it in their eyes. They were expecting something like *Into the Wild*, and frankly, so was I. Bleached human bones. Decades-old tins of chili. An open journal on the kitchen table scrawled with a few last desperate words. It would be a sight. I felt bad depriving them of it. But I had to do this alone.

So this morning they did a safety check on my kayak, more for show than anything else. They chipped out the ice cradled in the cockpit seat. They stuffed the hatches with food and warm clothes. They reviewed with me the route about six times until I laughed and pointed out that it was matter of paddling up the river, which by now was awfully narrow. It'd be difficult to get lost. They shifted their weight from one leg to the other, watched me carefully. What if I capsized, they wanted to know. What if I stopped for lunch and a brown bear approached. They pointed out that the cabin could be gone, that I might paddle right on by the site. I believe they'd grown fond of me, too. Both waded into the icy river to launch me. Sweet Stuart actually kissed me on the cheek.

"We'll see you in a few hours," Gregory said. "You have your radio?"

"I do." I tried to smile for their sake.

I didn't look back, just dug in the paddle and pushed aside the first load of water. Paddling upstream is hard work, but the boys have taught me to stay near the shore where there is often a countercurrent. Up here, the danger of bears is minimal, as long as I stay in my boat. They tell me it can be bad in more touristy areas, like Glacier Bay, where the brown bear have come to learn that kayaks mean human food. They tell stories of massive cinnamon-colored grizzlies swimming behind their boats, hoping to tip them and harvest the dried apricots and salami logs. Up here, as long as I stay on the water, I should be fine.

In any case, I don't intend to stop. The river's flow this late in the season is weak. I will be there in no time. A light snow, like last night's, fell for the first hour. But then the clouds flew west and the sky opened up blue.

As I draw close, I try to prepare myself for the possibilities. Maybe my brothers had found bush wives. For all I know, they'd sent for mail-order brides. I might find a thriving little community. The boys would be well into middle age. They might have grandchildren running around the little inlet. The one cabin might have blossomed into fifteen cabins.

On the other hand, the winter following the October I left was a particularly hard one. Breakup came very late that spring. In spite of having four moose, they could have all perished. Wolves could have gotten the meat or it could have rotted. A bear attack. Poisonous berries. Anything could have killed them. Bones, picked clean by scavengers, scattered about a rotting cabin.

I am paddling upstream, alone. Once again, a girl with boat. I am returning for the first time since I left when I was seventeen years old. I am not unhappy. The fireweed stalks are hot pink against the hard blue sky. Glaciated peaks soften the horizon in the far distance. I'm finding the paddling easier, despite my age, than it ever was then. Perhaps that's my willingness. I am, I realize, even eager.

I come around the last bend and see the cabin. It is whole and upright. Sunlight glints off the window. As I draw closer, the front door opens. A scrawny old man comes out holding a plate of food. He has white hair and a white beard, both crudely trimmed, as if with pruning shears. He sits on the same stump we put there our first season. He stabs the meat on his plate and takes a bite, chews. Then he looks downriver and sees me.

The old man doesn't even rise to his feet. He hardly squints. Later I'll learn that interlopers have become much more common than they were in our first years. Several parties of adventure seekers come through every summer and pilots fly dozens of hunters in for the fall season. I am nothing unusual, or so he thinks at first. He continues to concentrate on his meal until I start to land the boat on our beach. Then he sets the plate on the ground next to his stump and walks slowly toward me. He is bent and moves stiffly.

It is, of course, Father.

I can't bring myself to call him that, so instead I speak his Christian name.

That stops him. He looks about in confusion. I feel as if I have trapped him, caught him out, at long last. As if he's waited his entire life for someone to find him, and now someone has. But who?

He takes a step closer. Now he does squint. He speaks my mother's name. And that's when my heart breaks.

"No," I say. It's all I *can* say.

His knees buckle and he sits on the beach, legs splayed, eyes on me. I crawl out of the kayak and stand next to it, unable to move closer.

He struggles back to his feet, embarrassed by his weakness, and so now I make myself walk toward him. I stop a few feet away. Tears wet his whole face. He sits again, and so do I, there on the pebbled beach in the sun.

I speak first, telling him the short version of my life these past decades. I don't apologize for leaving. He listens, nodding as I speak.

Then I ask about the boys.

He looks across the river, across the trees, maybe even beyond the mountains. He says, "I don't know."

"You don't know?"

"They left two years after you."

"Did they take the rowboat?" It is sitting on the beach, not ten yards away. He shakes his head.

"They left on foot?"

"Must have."

I am stunned that the boys left, got out, and yet didn't ever try to contact me stateside. Maybe they hated me for leaving them. Or maybe they had only left *here*, the cabin on Sweet Creek. They could be anywhere in this wild state. Mother, Father, the twins, me, we are all devastatingly self-sufficient.

But, I know all too well, that doesn't mean not lonely.

I see in Father what I couldn't see as a girl. Grief. Huge rolling waves of it. As big as Alaska. As long as the Yukon. As far flung as the arctic terns. He sits on his beach, the one he's called home for over forty years, and tries to rest his eyes on his inlet. There is no rest. This place has not supported his family, after all. It has only supported him, one lonely man with an even lonelier dream.

Father rallies a bit that night in the cabin as he tells Gregory and Stuart stories about storms and hunger and wolves. They are rapt listeners. They nod in complete agreement when Father tells them that Alaska has been ruined, has become one big playground. He says he has no peace. The intruders arrive by boatloads and planeloads. Some come on foot. He claims to want nothing from them. But I can see that they have been keeping him alive. Surely he doesn't have the strength to hunt anymore. And all about his cabin are signs of the intruders' generosity: canned foods, a Gore-Tex jacket, a high-tech pair of snowshoes, even bags of chips. I easily picture these people coming upon the old man in his cabin and giving him everything they can spare.

We all sleep in the cabin that night. In the morning I take Gregory aside and tell him to call his contact in Fairbanks.

"Are you sure?" he asks. I may imagine it, but I think I see the accusation of betrayal in his eyes.

I nod. "I'm sure."

Then I tell Father to gather up anything he wants to take with him. The boys brace themselves, hands behind their backs, feet spread, watching the two of us, expecting his resistance, an outburst.

Father says, "I don't need anything."

"The helicopter will be here in an hour," I say.

Stuart actually tears up.

I ask my guides if one of them can handle the double kayak without me. I had been looking forward to drifting back down the rivers, the ease of leaving. It hadn't occurred to me that I would leave with more than an emotional souvenir, that my visiting Sweet Creek would be the beginning of a new, even more complex journey.

The chopper lands in the upper meadow. A ruddy redheaded pilot announces that he has another job, is doing us a favor by fitting in our run, and asks us to hurry. Gregory and Stuart stand on the edge of the meadow, just as Mother and Father had done when I first landed here. Father sits up front and the pilot helps him with his seatbelt. I press my forehead against the window and, as we fly away, take in the lay of the land from above. Our cabin quickly diminishes to a dark spot. Sweet Creek nothing more than a silvery ribbon. Big River the muscle of our geography, the attachment to the civilized Yukon, and then our life is gone.

Already I see Fairbanks. It had always been this close. I reach forward and take Father's hand off his thigh. I hold it against my cheek. He can't hear me over the roar of the helicopter's engine, but I say, "I'm sorry."

Life Drawing

Blair saw Charles most days on her walk home from school. He lived a block and a half away from her family, apparently by himself, and was usually watering his roses when she went by. He always looked at her. You might even say, studied her. As if he were—and this was a phrase she'd learned from her mother—undressing her with his eyes.

At his age, too. It made it dirtier.

Blair was proud of her solution to the problem. After a few weeks of this ogling, she started fetching her Bible from her backpack, as soon as she got off the school bus. She carried it prominently against her chest, like a shield, as she passed Charles's house.

The first time she did this, he smiled. It occurred to her then that she had been all wrong. Maybe he was a Christian, too. Maybe he knew her family and was only showing an interest. Blair was embarrassed that she'd thought the words *undressing* and *ogling*. She entertained the possibility that she, not he, had been the one having dirty thoughts. The truth was important to Blair, even if it made her uncomfortable.

That night at the dinner table she asked her parents if they knew the man who lived with all the roses in front of his house. They looked at her blankly, and then her father put down his knife and fork and asked, "Why?"

"His roses are such a beautiful example of God's presence," she said. "That's all."

Everyone nodded—her parents and her little sister Ruthie and big brother Joshua—and that was the end of it. She didn't mention Charles to her family again.

But she kept clutching her Bible as she passed by, and Charles kept looking. After that first time, though, he didn't smile anymore. Blair wondered if the word *sinister* would describe his interest in her. She couldn't help noticing that her walk loosened under his gaze.

On the Monday of the last week of school, he finally spoke to her.

"Do you read that?" he asked, gesturing with the running hose. The water came dangerously close to Blair's feet and she jumped back.

Charles laughed. "Sorry!"

"If you mean the Bible, yes I do."

"What does it tell you?"

"You haven't read it?"

Charles glanced down and then up again, meeting her purposefully challenging stare. "I have. Parts, anyway. It was a long time ago. Do you recommend it?"

Her father said to never let anyone mock the Bible or their faith. Smile, he said, and speak the words of the Savior. It didn't matter which words. Just be sure to always answer a disbeliever. Always defend God.

"I do recommend it."

"And it teaches you what?"

"To live chastely." Where did *that* come from? She was embarrassing herself again. So she added, "To love Jesus."

Charles nodded. "Thanks."

Blair stood still for a moment, watching him water his roses. Then she realized that she was pausing inappropriately, and so she walked on home.

The following day, Blair slowed her pace as she neared Charles's house. She'd thought about him a lot since their conversation, and it occurred to her that she had a responsibility as a Christian. She wanted another opportunity to talk to him. Today she held her Bible loosely in her hand, the one on his side of the street, and checked her outfit before coming into view. She wore tight jeans, like any fifteen-year-old, and two camisoles, a white one under a lace-trimmed, hot pink one. She tugged at the neckline of both, making sure she wasn't showing too much. She wanted to be very clear.

Blair stopped in front of his house, surprised to see that Charles wasn't watering his roses. When a moment later he stepped out the front door, she was mortified to be caught standing still, as if she were waiting for him.

"It's the young evangelist," Charles said and smiled more broadly than ever before.

"I take it," she said carefully, "you don't believe."

"Oh, I believe," he said.

His sincerity confused her. He believed in what?

He asked, "What's your favorite verse?"

Blair knew so many verses by heart, but her mind went blank. Or not so much blank, as it became filled with curiosity about this rose-tending man rather than with Bible verses. He was handsome, she realized, even if about three times her age. He was thin with gaunt cheeks and tousled brown hair, only a few strands of gray. His old skin looked pleasant, the way it rested softly against the muscles in his arms. He wore a faded dark green T-shirt and worn Levi's, a pair of sneakers on his feet. He looked so comfortable. What she had told her family was true, his roses were a testament to God's presence. The thorny bush he watered now, holding the hose end almost tenderly, letting the water gurgle onto the roots, had tight golden buds with orangey-red edges. She wanted to see them in full bloom.

He waited and so she blurted, "I like first Corinthians 13:13."

When he raised an eyebrow, she recited, "And now these three remain: faith, hope and love. But the greatest of these is love."

Then she felt the hot flush of blood in her face. This is the one Henry had quoted her just yesterday, but for the wrong reason. It was also the wrong version—his church used the King James.

Charles nodded and said, "Yes." As if he knew the verse. He moved the stream of water to the next rose bush. "Nice one."

"What's your favorite?" she asked back.

"Mainly I remember the not-so-nice ones."

Disbelievers loved doing this. They thought they could trip you up by quoting stuff out of context. This would be a good time for her to walk away. Her dad said to not listen to blasphemy. Even letting it enter your ears can taint you. But she waited.

Charles said, "How about this: 'For every one that curseth his father or his mother shall be surely put to death.' Leviticus 20:9."

The hose hung loosely in his hand, soaking the roots of yet another bush, as he quoted. Now he lifted it and sprayed the bush's leaves, almost as if he were angry.

Blair had never cursed her parents, and she never would.

"Put to death," he repeated, holding his thumb over the end of the hose to make the water squirt hard.

As Blair tried to think of the right thing to say, he continued. "Then there's this: 'But if this thing be true, and the tokens of virginity be not found for the damsel: Then they shall bring out the damsel to the door of her father's house, and the men of her city shall stone her with stones that she die.' Deuteronomy 22:20–21."

Shame pooled in the base of her belly. It was as if he knew. He was, after all, a man of her city. She imagined Charles, along with other neighbors, stoning her. But he only squinted at her, giving her one of those looks again, as if he were undressing her.

She left without saying goodbye or commenting on his verses. To-morrow she would tell Henry it was over. Better, she would leave the room right after band practice and not talk to him at all. She hadn't done anything irreversible yet. No one could stone her. She was a virgin. And not one of the reclaimed ones. She was a real virgin. No one could stone her, she repeated to herself, and as she did, a confusing rock pile of anger replaced the pool of shame in her belly.

That night when Blair said her prayers, she thanked God for in-troducing her to Charles. She realized He'd done so on purpose. Her neighbor was a test. And a reminder. She'd done nothing terrible yet. Not too terrible, anyway. She prayed for guidance and forgiveness and for pure thoughts. Then she prayed for her mother and father, for Ruthie and for Joshua. She climbed into bed and thought not about Charles but about his roses. They *were* lovely. He had deep red ones. And yellow ones that glowed. There were pale lavender ones too, dusty and strangely sad. Her favorites, though, were the yellow ones with orange edging on every petal.

Over the next couple of days, Blair tried to think of ways to reengage Charles in conversation about the Bible, but two things stopped her. One, he didn't speak first when she passed, and she didn't want to be bold. And two, she knew her intentions were not entirely spiritual.

Blair was only fifteen years old, but she knew a lie when she saw one, even when it was a lie she told only herself. She'd made a personal vow, not only to Jesus but to herself, to be rigorous about the truth. And the truth was: something about Charles attracted her. It wasn't a *sexual* attraction. God no, he was at least forty, probably older. But her heart did that flutter thing, and she felt hot in the face, and her bowels got all icy when she walked by him. It was different, totally different, from how she felt with Henry. Still. Whatever the feeling was, it didn't seem right, and until she understood what was going on, she thought she best ignore him.

But he kept looking, and with exaggerated daring. As if, as long as she didn't stop him, or take a different route home, he would filch everything he could get. Taking a different route home was exactly what she ought to do. Her continuing to let him look was, in a sense, agreeing to his nasty old man voyeurism, right?

Then, on the last day of school, Charles called out, "Hey."

Blair had rehearsed this moment many times in her mind. She didn't stop or even look in his direction. She kept walking, facing straight ahead. He laughed. It was not a mean laugh, just a short bellow. Like she'd surprised him, shown him something he hadn't realized. Her resolve maybe. But then her feet took over and, all on their own, stopped. She tried to order them to go on, but instead they turned to face Charles. Okay, so maybe this was God guiding her feet. She would tell him off. That's what she should do. Tell him to keep his filthy old eyes off of her body.

The words seemed so mean, though, when she saw his face. He was no longer laughing, but his lips remained parted, as if he wanted to say something but had no idea what. He hadn't shaved that day, so he had a bit of gray bristle, and the skin under his eyes sagged. She had this strange sense that looking at her sustained him in some way.

That thought was sinful, she knew that. It was the sin of pride to think that she had the power to sustain anyone. Only God could do that. It was also the sin of vanity. What made her think she was attractive enough for anyone to get anything from looking at her? She was fat. Had bad skin. Dull hair. She was duck footed.

And yet he kept staring, as if she were soaking his roots, nourishing the possibility of bloom.

"How old are you, anyway?" Charles asked.

"Fifteen."

He shrugged, as if that answered something, and said, "Okay."

"Okay, what?"

He didn't answer for a long time. Blair jutted out one hip, held the Bible against her breasts, pursed her lips. He smiled slowly and said, "You're very beautiful, do you know that?"

What happened next was shocking. A wave of tears surged up her throat, filled her eyes. She didn't know why. Every inch of her skin tingled with a sad ache. Like if she didn't hold onto this moment, it would never, ever come again.

Charles said, "I'd like to draw you."

"Draw me?" The tears made her voice scratchy.

He shrugged again. "You're too young, though."

Then the moment left, as if snatched away by God Himself. In its wake, she thought, this is a ruse. He wants to *draw* me? *Right.*

She swallowed back the remaining tears and wished there were an inconspicuous way to pull up the necklines of her two camisoles. They were aqua and black today, and especially low cut.

"You holding your Bible," Charles added. He walked over to the spigot and turned off the water, began rolling up the hose.

She couldn't help asking, "Why with my Bible?"

He thought for a moment and then shook his head. "It doesn't help to think about it too much. I just like the juxtaposition."

That meant contrast. Or even clash. This made her mad. Blair wasn't at odds with the Bible. It was her path and guide. She actually held it in front of her, like a steering wheel, and walked home.

Once school let out Blair had no reason to walk by Charles's house, and that was a relief. She put the man out of her mind. But pieces of him wouldn't go away, like his faded green T-shirt and the feeling behind his sagging eyes, the words *beautiful* and *juxtaposition*. She wanted to see how his roses were coming along.

On Friday night of the second week of summer vacation, Blair saw Henry at the mall. She was with her mom and Ruthie. He was with Chandra, another girl from school. His arm was draped over her shoulders so that his curled hand grazed her big boob. To make it even worse, Blair's mother noticed the couple and had to comment on them, saying something about their behavior being inappropriate. They were giggling and bumping hips and pointing in store windows.

Blair couldn't believe how much it hurt. His grin had seemed so sincere, for her alone. His kisses had seemed like they had love in them, not just lust. He'd quoted Bible verses to her!

Thinking about Henry kissing Chandra, his hand grazing her breast, made Blair want to throw everything she thought was true in the garbage. And stomp on it. She knew her feelings were extreme, crazy. She also knew—had known all along—that a relationship that takes place in the band room after band practice, and in no other place or time, was a false one.

It still hurt. A lot.

It was hot that second week of June, well into the nineties, so she wore her white shorts and navy blue halter top. The colors were modest, anyway. And of course she carried her Bible. She went barefoot, meaning she had to jump from one patch of weeds to the next, find pockets of shade to avoid the sun-scorched pavement. By the time she got to Charles's house, she wondered why she hadn't worn her flip-flops. She knocked on his door.

He looked very surprised to see her.

"Hi," she said. "Do you still want to draw me?"

She walked right by him and into the front room of his house. The place was a wreck, with newspapers and dirty dishes on all the surfaces. A pile of laundry, that may have been clean, filled a big armchair. He too was barefoot. She felt very puppyish in his dark and muddled dwelling. She liked how he seemed to be at a loss in her presence.

To remind him, Blair held the Bible against her breasts, and said, "Do you?"

"Sure. Come on out to my studio."

She followed him out a sliding glass door. They passed through an overgrown yard and entered the open door of a large one-room cottage. There were half a dozen house plants, and these were thriving, with lots of sunlight pouring in the high windows. A big wet-looking painting sat tilted against the back of an easel, the colors gooey and dark, and the air was rich with the smell of oily turpentine. There was also a royal blue settee, exactly as she might have expected, near the middle of the big room. Blair walked right to it and sat down.

"How do you want me?" she asked.

He paused a long time, looking at her, that sadness wilting his eyes. Then he said, "However you're comfortable."

Blair stretched out on the settee and crossed her ankles. She shook back her hair so that it draped over the settee top.

Charles laughed and said, "Kind of a cliché, but okay, I like it. Leave the Bible on your belly and let your hands and arms fall off either side of the chaise."

Blair embraced the new word. *Chaise.* It comforted her.

Charles moved the big canvas off his easel and propped up a sketch pad. Working with a piece of charcoal, he began at once. Not only the word but the chaise itself was comfortable, and Blair felt herself slacken. Outside of her own home, and all the reminders of who she was, Blair found that her mind tore off in a lot of unexpected directions. Her anger at Henry increased. The pleasure in her anticipation of the warm, expansive summer scared her. She felt pelted by a storm of questions.

"Have you ever been in love?" she asked Charles after several long minutes of silence.

He didn't answer. He'd entered some kind of zone as he drew. Blair wondered if he might fall in love with her. Or maybe he had already. He glanced at her with crisp little peeks, over and over again, each time returning to his sketch pad.

"I asked if you've ever been in love before."

"What do you think?" Charles asked.

"Probably. Maybe when you were young."

He still didn't answer, and it occurred to Blair that maybe he was a fag. Most male artists were. It would explain the roses and his sensitive hands. He obviously lived alone, too.

But then he wouldn't be undressing her with his eyes, if he were a fag.

Charles ripped the sheet of paper off the sketch pad and wadded it in both hands. He let the big ball of paper drop to the floor. He started again. Blair tried to keep quiet and still. A few minutes later, he ripped off another sheet, and this time he cursed.

"I guess it's not working," he said.

Blair didn't move. She liked the curve of the chaise against her backside. She liked the way the earthy smell of freshly watered green plants twined with the industrial reek of oil paints. She liked the hushed sound of charcoal on paper, knowing it traced her shape.

"You better go," Charles said.

The words reminded her of Henry. The ache of being dismissed. She sat up and put the Bible on the floor at her feet. "I saw my boyfriend at the mall with another girl."

Charles blinked, and she thought he probably didn't have a clue what that felt like. He was alone. He was a fag. Maybe he wished he wasn't, which explained why he looked at her that way. He was trying to go straight. She wondered if she ought to help him. Her church had sent two different boys to a special camp for this. One of her friends said they showed the boys dirty pictures of girls.

It occurred to her that Charles's homosexuality made her safe in his studio.

"Do you think," she asked, "it's wrong to kiss before marriage?"

Charles actually laughed, but then his face softened quickly. "No."

"What about more than kissing?"

Charles rubbed his bristly chin. "Look. I don't know."

"His name is Henry. He's a Christian, like me, but his church is so different from ours. Their Jesus says yes all the time. Our Jesus always says no."

Charles laughed again. He picked up his charcoal. "How do you know Henry?"

"We both play in the band at school. He plays cello. He's really cute. African American. Short-short hair. Big brown eyes with long lashes. He doesn't have any beard at all yet, kind of baby fat all over him, but under that he's really strong." Blair tried to keep herself in check, but continued anyway, saying, "He's a really good kisser."

"But you don't think Christian children should kiss." Charles was drawing quickly now, his hand sweeping across the pad, his eyes backlit by an emotion she couldn't name.

"We're not supposed to. Well. *Henry* says it's fine. He says even his pastor would say it's fine."

Charles nodded and kept drawing, as if he'd stopped listening.

"He has the softest lips imaginable."

When she didn't say anything more for a long time, Charles asked, "What do you play?"

"Flute."

"Where do the two of you go on your dates?"

"We don't. We just made out in the band rehearsal room. After practice. After everyone else had left."

Charles watched her face for a long moment, and she felt as if her sadness was naked. His hand holding the charcoal lowered, and he said,

"Look, Blair. Whatever you did with Henry was fine. It was good, even. Some people think sex is sacred."

Blair stood so quickly she almost lost her balance. She held the top of the chaise until she felt steady again, and then walked over to his easel. The way he'd drawn her sitting on the chaise with the Bible on the floor at her feet made it look as if she'd discarded the Book. As if she were about to kick it aside.

"How would *you* know?" she asked.

Suddenly she felt furious at everyone. Henry. Charles. Her parents. Maybe even Jesus. She glanced around the studio, as if she were trapped and looking for a way out, though the door was wide open. The walls were covered with charcoal sketches. She walked over to the nearest one, thinking she might rip it down. The woman was naked and so skinny each rib showed. Little sacks of skin hung off her butt. Her shoulder blades jutted like wings. Her head was bald, save a few patches of hair. She looked like someone in a concentration camp.

"Yuck," Blair said. "She's ugly."

She stepped to the next drawing, and saw that it was of the same woman, this time a frontal view. Again, the little sacks of skin, this time her breasts. An open mouth, like pain. The studio, she saw now, was filled with this skin-and-bones woman. Blair turned and saw Charles watching her, his own mouth set in a firm line.

"Who is it?" she asked.

"My wife."

Blair made herself hold his gaze. She tried to not hate herself.

"She died six months ago."

Blair swallowed. Her hands shook. "I'm sorry I called her ugly."

Charles smiled. "She would have liked that, to hear you call her ugly. She might have even liked the 'yuck.'"

Blair saw what had attracted her to Charles all along: he liked the truth, too. She felt it in the way he looked at things, including her. She reached up and touched one of the pictures. Just a knee and then her head. The picture wasn't ugly, after all. It was beautiful. Charles stood behind her.

Blair felt as if she were entering a vortex. Her entire world swirled. A gigantic toilet bowl, she at the center. All the pieces of her life were at odds. Making out with Henry, and letting him touch her breasts, was a sin. But it *had* felt sort of sacred, too. That's what hurt so much about him moving on. Their touching had held so much . . . beauty. But what was beauty? Here was a woman ravaged by illness and she was beautiful.

Blair went to fetch her Bible so she could leave.

"I'd like to draw you without your clothes." His voice was full, almost liquid.

She'd bent to pick up the Bible, and as she straightened, she kept her back to him. The words *contrast* and *juxtaposition* occurred to her. His wife's wasted body and her own plump, pink one. It might be the Christian thing to do. If it was in her power to ease the man's suffering, then shouldn't she?

By the time Blair turned to face Charles, she was telling herself the truth. She wanted his charcoal lines on her bare limbs, belly, and breasts. She untied her halter and dropped it on the floor. She pushed her shorts and panties down to her ankles, enduring a moment of shame, but that moment passed with scandalous speed.

The truth was, she didn't care that he watched her undress. She felt safe, whole, alive. The room filled with the feeling she got kissing Henry. But the feeling looked so much more complicated for Charles. There was—okay, just use the word—plain lust. But there was also something richer, deeper, more interesting. She stood, stark and full and now terribly sad herself, and waited for him to tell her what to do next.

"However you're comfortable," he said.

She thought of retrieving the Bible, for juxtaposition, but her pile of clothing covered it and she was more comfortable without it. Anyway, holding the Bible while naked might be a cliché. She sat in the trough of the chaise, cross-legged.

"That's good," Charles said and he went right to work.

He drew for a long time. She changed position whenever she felt like it, and he never complained. He simply tore off the paper and began again.

Blair loved how she felt beautiful under his gaze but confused by a certain detachment he seemed to possess. Occasionally he left his easel and crossed the short distance between them. She would wonder if he was going to kiss her, but he'd only suggest she move a foot or turn a shoulder. When he began asking questions about what it had been like kissing Henry in the band rehearsal room, she thought that talking about it, in this detailed way, was maybe more sinful than actually doing it. And yet, as she talked, he drew with even greater concentration, as if he listened to her only well enough to ask the next question. As if the response he wanted was in her body and not in her words.

The light shifted in the room, casting late afternoon shadows across the drawings of his emaciated wife and raising goose bumps on her own skin. Blair said, "You can touch me, if you want. I mean, just like my arms or something."

Just saying the words made her feel potent, opulent.

He paused and looked at her, as if tempted. At least she had broken his concentration. But then he returned to drawing with even greater absorption.

"Without faith," she asked, "how do you *not* touch someone?"

He smiled but didn't stop working. "Did your faith stop *you?*"

"No," she said. "It didn't."

"It doesn't stop anyone. Look at all those pastors, not to mention politicians, who get caught with their pants down. Sometimes with the wrong sex, too. I can't abide hypocrisy."

Neither could Blair. She realized that right then, for the first time. She couldn't abide hypocrisy.

She said, "I thought maybe you were a fag. I mean, before you told me about your wife."

Charles put down his charcoal, and a flash of anger crossed his face, like the time he'd sprayed the roses too hard. "Don't use that word."

"I thought you didn't like hypocrisy. I'm just saying—"

"Christians who hate are by definition hypocritical."

Shame burned from her throat down to the base of her belly, and this time it stayed. Still, she defended herself. "We don't hate them. We just hate the sin. It says right in Leviticus 20:13, 'If a man—'"

"I know what the Bible says. I'm tired. It's time for you to go."

Blair tried to think of a way to return to that feeling that had filled the studio just moments earlier. She wanted to talk about kissing Henry again, but Charles was tidying some canvasses on the other side of the room. He really was finished with her this time. She dressed quickly, catching her foot in the crotch of her panties and then a shank of her hair in the tie of her halter top. She picked up her Bible and hugged it to her chest, but didn't leave the side of the chaise. She was afraid of what she would be walking away from.

Charles turned and faced her. He said, "I was raised in a religious family, too. My brother was gay. My parents kicked him out of the house when he was just your age. I've never seen him since. I assume he's dead, though I've never found an obituary."

The vortex snatched up her mind again. All her thoughts swirled, making her nearly nauseous. The cancer-riddled body of Charles's wife. His brother standing in the flames of hell. The idea of losing Joshua, forever. Henry's fingertips on Chandra's breast. The word *beautiful*.

"Let yourself out," he said.

She stopped in his front yard to look at her favorite roses. They were in full bloom now, each flower a little fire, with yellow centers and orange edges. When her bare feet hit the hot tar on the street, she let them burn. She felt immeasurably sad, as if, like Charles, she'd lost everything.

Poker

I have moments, brief flashes, when I think I should have married you. You would *get* this. The ice, storms, science, seals. You would thrive here.

Only you never would have taken the risk. You wouldn't ever be here.

What risk? Tonight I sit in the galley with a glass of wine on the table next to my notebook. Brian is playing his guitar over by the wood-burning stove, and a couple of the girls are chatting on the couches. We get excellent South American wines on station and can buy them at cost. This one is full bodied and I can taste the Argentine steppes as the fruit slides across my tongue. But you, I'm betting, would scoff at wine talk, the silliness of claiming to taste minerals and soil. Perhaps you don't drink at all. Your dad, I remember, drank too much.

Twenty-five years ago you wanted me to marry you, and my mother begged me to do it. Now you're a superintendent of a national park. You live in a beautiful place, and your life is defined by protecting that beauty. That's a life I could get behind. If I were with you, I'd probably have a few kids. I'd be an excellent cook. I'd be in good shape, hiking trails with you every weekend, teaching the children how to tie knots, pitch tents, pace themselves on mountain climbs.

Instead I'm here at Palmer Station where by day I work as an assistant to the guy who manages hazardous materials. But my days are unimportant. It's the nights I want to tell you about. Maybe just last night.

The work day—I'll only say this—was long and exhausting. The *Laurence E. Gould*, the National Science Foundation ship, had come in.

They needed to get a team of paleontologists on some island up the peninsula, and so we had to offload and onload in one day. One very long day. I find I can't do physical labor as easily as I used to. That's a shock. Who would have thought I'd ever run out of strength? I'm learning what it means to need rest. Maybe you already know. Maybe having a daughter—I heard you had one—has given you a lesson in exhaustion. I hear children do that.

By seven o'clock we had finished and the *Gould* pulled away from the dock, its eager team of paleontologists on board. The ship, a mustard and orange hulk, moved away from us into the thick fog, pushing through the pancake ice that has crowded our bay for a week. While her shape was still visible, one of the mates came out on deck and yodeled, eerie and beautiful and plaintive notes riding the fog back to the station. Marty, one of our lines handlers, yodeled back. The *Gould* slid off into the Southern Ocean, its form blurring until only a patch of fog glowed yellow and orange. The two men exchanged song until there was no longer any visible trace of the ship.

I stood on Gamage Point, the small rocky piece of land next to the pier where the lines handlers had just let the ship go. They were leaving the point now, giving wide birth to an elephant seal who'd hauled out on the rocks to rest. She appeared undisturbed by the lines handlers, the yodeling, the behemoth orange and mustard beast slipping into the distant sea. Or maybe she *was* disturbed, but not enough to bother launching herself into the water. When all the other people were gone, I approached her slowly and took a seat on a rock very near her head.

She might have said, "Hi."

And so I answered, "Hi."

Her nostrils dilated and then quivered.

"Diesel," I told her. "It does stink."

She sighed and closed her eyes.

Brian shouted to me from the front door of the boathouse. "Poker, Jo."

I wanted to lie down next to the elephant seal. Her hide was scarred and tough looking, and though she was bulbous with fat, I imagined she'd feel as solid as the stones surrounding her patch of beach. Her face, though, was liquid with sweetness. From a circle of black dots above each eye grew short, bristly eyebrows. These were matched by many more black dots on either side of her nose, from which two sets of short whiskers grew. Her mouth curved up in a slight smile, or so it seemed from my human perspective, and her nose had a fold across the bridge, giving a pug effect. But her eyes—

Brian shouted again about the poker game and I wondered why he cared so much that I participate. I'd planned on going directly to bed. That yodeling had unhinged me. Like male sirens. I wanted to hear the music again, even if it broke my heart. Music can't break your heart, though. It can only remind you of a heart already broken. Not by you. Don't worry. I'm the one who said no. We haven't even talked in twenty-five years. It's only that I wanted to hear that shipboard music again, as if it could sear back together rifts long split open. Rifts that I sometimes imagine wouldn't have ever opened if I *had* married you. As if there is such thing as a safe harbor. As if there is a risk-free choice, the way the TV and magazines try to tell us. As if marriage is a big padded suit one wears against the ravages of life. These words make it seem as if I've been thinking of you these twenty-five years, but I haven't. Just once in a while.

When I stepped inside the boathouse, I saw why Brian had been so insistent about inviting me. Only three others had the energy for cards. The geezers, Harvey and Phil, were there. I'm not being disrespectful, that's what they call themselves. They're only in their fifties or maybe early sixties—you probably can't pass the medical much older than that—but most of the folks working here top off at around thirty-two. Except for the geezers and me.

The last card player in the boathouse was Caitlin. Ah, Caitlin. This was her first season on the Ice and she wasn't catching on to the culture very quickly. She'd been flirting with Brian all season, even though she knew, like everyone else knew, that he was devoted to a girlfriend back home in Washington State. Caitlin's a beautiful girl, but something about her efforts with regard to Brian just aren't pretty. In fact, I'd say she's a burden on the community. She doesn't understand about the Ice, how to carry on affairs here. It might look like high school, but it isn't. Talk to anyone here and you'll find they have a concrete dream, a life plan, and Antarctica is merely a part of it. Like Brian, closer to twenty than thirty, who is only having a lark before his real life begins. He isn't in limbo. He isn't free for the taking. This isn't adult camp. We're working. Most of us are trying, or had been trying, to get somewhere. Like Phil. This is his sixteenth season and he's here for one reason: money. He often brags about the home he and his wife have bought, how they never could have done so without his Ice money, about the things they will do in their retirement.

"You in?" Brian asked.

"Sure." I gave him a ten, and he counted me out a bank of red, blue, and white chips. No one complained that I'd come in the game late and was getting a full compliment of chips. I always play as long as my ten bucks lasts and then bail, have never presented a threat to more serious card players. Everyone relaxes when a woman reaches a certain age, and I find that very relaxing myself. You can do whatever you want. As long as you don't ask anyone for anything, you're set.

The boathouse smells of diesel and the sea, not fecund like coastal smells stateside, but the sharp tang of sea ice, the ocean at its freshest. A pile of orange life jackets fills one corner. A loft over Brian's desk is stacked high with survival duffels, each one containing sea rations, flares, matches in waterproof containers, a tent, a camp stove, everything anyone would need to survive if stranded on an Antarctic island. A bunch of spare motors for the Zodiacs hang from one wall, tipped as if they needed only priming and starting, and the whole boathouse would roar across the sea.

Harvey and Phil drank steadily, and Caitlin kept pace. Brian didn't drink at all. It occurs to me now that Brian is a lot like you were at his age. So cocksure of his life choices. It's a wonder to observe. He always holds his head a little too high, but he doesn't look arrogant, just darn pleased with his lot.

I quickly lost most of my chips. I always stay in a hand too long.

"Wife's taking a knitting class," Phil said.

"Good for her," I said.

"Says it calms her."

"Wasn't it gardening last season?" Harvey asked.

"Yep."

"Good to keep busy."

The group was not one for engaging conversation. Still, for Harvey to talk at all was something. He's one of the most silent men I've met. Brian is usually as chatty as you were, but Caitlin was making him nervous. His knee jiggled, bouncing on the spring of his foot and calf, in that way young men have. For all his apparent resolve and right living, he must have a dew point.

"Ha!" Caitlin cried, tossing down three nines. "Mine." She picked the chips from the center of the table one at a time and stacked them in her own cache. Then she threw an arm around Brian's neck and kissed his cheek. "I'm a lucky girl tonight."

I saw him soften. A place right at the center of his chest actually caved a little. The bouncing knee stilled. The geezers watched too, eyes dulled like war veterans, as if they were staring only at a blank wall. Brian drew his sweatshirt across his lap.

"Ha!" Caitlin repeated as Phil dealt. "Hit me again."

Then something in *me* caved, a tenderness toward the young woman. I know that pinball feeling of desire, the zinging crazy joy of flinging oneself. No one is immune. We all fling ourselves. Just in different directions.

I might as well come clean. Harvey and I had a short, and I mean probably three encounters, affair some ten years ago. Okay, that's out. It hardly means anything. It's not even a memory, more like a hitch in my memory. But when I enter a social situation and he's there, which isn't that often because usually the geezers just watch videos in the lounge at night, I notice. That's all.

Harvey is no bigger on eye contact than he is on conversation. Being around him is easy, even comforting sometimes. In the boathouse last night I pretended that he was a sunny boulder that I could lean against. Just in my imagination.

Harvey dealt me two pairs. Nothing much at all, just a couple of threes and sevens, but compared to my usual luck, it was something. My reasoning facility flooded with adrenaline. I refused to fold. After a few rounds of betting, the guys assumed I had a formidable hand and put down their cards. I stayed in, all revved up about my two pairs.

Caitlin was the last to fold. She figured she had nothing to lose.

Did I mention that Caitlin was a Stanford graduate? I think she thought that gave her an edge. Another cultural mistake. Artists and intellectuals are considered masturbators here. Traveling the highways of the mind is considered soft compared to the real labor of geographical and other physical knowledge.

I pulled eighty-six dollars worth of blue, red, and white chips toward me, using my forearms to corral the booty, laughing, having a good time.

"Look at that," Phil said.

Harvey clapped once, a gesture of generosity. The men were happy I'd won a big hand.

"Your deal," Harvey said. Something in him has given up. I wouldn't say it's sad to witness his surrender. I like his honesty. He watches videos. He plays cards. He repairs machinery. But I wouldn't sleep with him now. I wouldn't want to disturb the stillness that is Harvey.

The excitement of my big win wore off quickly, even as I shuffled the cards. I'd expected my usual run of a dozen hands and then, broke, I'd go up to my tent and sleep. With all these chips, I'd be playing half the night. It was bad form to win a big pot and then leave the game.

Luckily, I lost most of my chips in the next hour. The drinkers looked like they had settled into a long night of it, and Caitlin's hand anchored Brian to his folding chair. Such intense attachments, I thought, so much desire.

"Excuse me," I said. "Here." I quickly divided my remaining chips among the other players, pushing a pile in each of four directions.

"Don't do that," Brian said. "We don't care if you take a break for a few rounds."

Caitlin's hand lay on his forearm, her thumb sliding forward, back, like an accidental caress.

"You're coming back, right?" Brian asked when I stood up. As if I were his life raft. He gathered up the piles of chips I'd left for the other players and pushed them back to my spot at the table.

I don't know why, but I put a hand on Harvey's shoulder. Just briefly. "Sure," I said to Brian. "In a while."

It was still early enough in the season for the light to dim late at night, so that the sky was a pale orange. I picked my way out on the rocks to Gamage Point. She was still there, her animal self utterly, animally, plopped down on a patch of sand and stone.

"Hi," I said, sitting closer to her than the station biologists would have wanted me to. In fact, I could have scooted forward another foot and touched one of her eyelashes. Which reminds me: I wanted to tell you about her eyes. Such intelligence. That's a surprise, even when you know better. But what reached right in and grabbed my heart was the sadness in her eyes, an intelligence of heartbreak. Huge black irises. Only a bit of the white showing, and in that white ran rivers of red, as if she'd been crying and crying. I tried closing my eyes in the way that cats say I love you. She slow-blinked back.

Once, a neighbor of mine in Oregon, where I live in the off-season on my own piece of land with Douglas firs and a stream, had lost a cat. She hired an animal communicator to find the cat. I didn't judge my neighbor for this. I don't know if humans can communicate with animals. Obviously, we can make dogs sit and some people can make tigers jump through hoops. Chimps use American Sign Language. But the animal communicator, according to my neighbor, could carry on entire conversations with dogs, cats, birds, even lizards, about what they were feeling, what their surroundings looked like, what they wanted from the other creatures, usually humans, in their environment.

This animal communicator needed only a picture of Snookums, the lost cat, and she was able to telepathically talk to him. Snookums described his whereabouts—he mentioned a pond and grazing cattle, a red barn, an unusual fence made of a combination of stone and wood. It was the fence, in the end, that helped my neighbor locate Snookums. Ponds and grazing cattle and red barns are quite common in the rural part of Oregon where I live, but this fence was not. My neighbor drove the back roads until she saw a fence that matched Snookums's description. She found a pond and a red barn near this fence. She called and called for Snookums one day at dusk. Nothing. But she went back at dawn, and this time the cat came when he was called. The animal communicator spoke with him some more and learned that he'd chased a rabbit out of his own territory, and when a sudden storm came up he'd become disoriented. He couldn't find his way back home. He'd been living on field mice all those weeks. Finding the pond had saved his life, for he knew he needed to drink. He was very, very relieved to be home with my neighbor. She doesn't let him out of the house anymore. He spends his days on a cushion in the window, and my neighbor says he doesn't even want to go out anymore. He's had enough of the wild.

I wonder now why I haven't had enough of the wild. I wonder why I couldn't have had the domesticated wild with you.

"Love," I told the seal, "is something that comes to me rarely."

She blinked.

"Not at all in a long time."

Blink.

I got carried away and told the elephant seal all about the unending wars beyond this continent, and then of the absence I feel when I think of love. Her fur looked bristly, but quite comfortable, and her face pushed out from the fat of her elliptical body as if it were just emerging. I can only say that she listened.

When I finished telling her everything, she spoke of enough. For her, the rocky point was enough. Clearly, she'd had enough fish. Her posture, a softened blob, sighed comfort. Her solitariness suited her just fine.

When I returned to the boathouse and my waiting booty of chips, Caitlin was laughing too hard, as if she'd lost at more than cards.

"Deal me in," I said.

"Atta girl," Phil said.

The cards flashed from Harvey's hands onto the table.

"Give me another hand like the last one you dealt," I told him.

"Pair of threes," he snorted.

"We gotta watch Jo now," Brian said. A hint of patronizing, younger man to older woman. "She never used to bluff."

"Old dog, new tricks," I said.

Caitlin's face showed frustration. She didn't like my easy banter with the guys, the way I made it obvious it didn't matter to me one way or another if they found me attractive. She's a smart girl and I think she sensed what I know about Brian. That he lacks something essential. He's too sweet. No hide, no scars, no rivers of red in the whites of his eyes. He believes humans are separated from other animals by a divine line, that we have a higher capacity for morally correct behavior, for art, for reasoning.

"I have a neighbor at home," I said, fanning out my cards and having a look, "who hired an animal communicator."

"I believe in that," Phil said.

"Come *on*," Caitlin chastised.

"Her cat was three miles away and the animal communicator located him."

Busy with betting, no one said anything for a while. I had three aces. I turned in the other two other cards for two more, and got the fourth ace. "Ha!" I said, forgetting to bluff. "I'll raise you five."

"What do you got this time? Pair of twos?"

"I have four aces."

The men laughed. Caitlin tried laughing, too. I stared her down.

The pot was driven up to a hundred and twenty-six dollars this time. I scooped the chips my way. Then said, "Anyone see that elephant seal on Gamage Point?"

"Been there all day," Harvey said.

"I was communicating with her."

"Anything's possible," Phil said.

I omitted a bit about Harvey when I mentioned our affair earlier. I left out that we did it again two seasons ago. I guess I was already changing by then. It wasn't something wanton. It wasn't some drunken mistake. It's more that now, after these choices I've made and these years that have passed, I live closer to the planet. He and I found ourselves alone one day, quite by accident, in the aquarium, the cold, wet room where fish tanks hold anemones and krill and cod. I can't say who started it, or how long it took. Short, quick. Even sweet. I doubt he thought of a repeat any more than I have. The animal chance of it.

Suddenly I felt stifled by all of them—Brian and Caitlin, the geezers.

"I'm done," I said, again distributing my chips and ignoring Brian's protests.

I paused outside the boathouse and looked out to the edge of Gamage Point. She looked like a huge contented slug. I would leave my companion be for the night. I passed around the sides of the two buildings of Palmer Station and began climbing toward the glacier. When I'd reached the top of a slight rise, I turned. The geezers were just leaving the boathouse, making their way across the ice to the entrance of the building where they were housed. I waited a few moments for Caitlin to emerge, too, but she didn't. I imagined Brian fumbling with words of sincerity about why he couldn't.

Then, in the transcendent peachy light that I've known only in Antarctica, I saw Harvey turn and make his way to Gamage Point. I could tell, by the two triangles at his sides, that he stood with his hands on his hips, his elbows cocked out. I could have walked back down the hill to join him. But I didn't. I walked up the glacier to my tent. From there, I can see most of Arthur Harbor and the craggy wall of ice where the continent meets the sea.

Inside my tent, I undressed quickly and slid into the two sleeping bags. I listened to the glacier calve, the explosive crack of the ice splitting. I could see in my mind's eye the tilting block of ice and the slow motion collapse. Then the splash. Of course there were penguins too, squawking. Best of all were the wings of giant petrels thumping the air as they flew over me.

So many nests, so much chance. The cormorants build cake-like thrones on rocky buttes overhanging the sea. The silly penguins and their nests of stone. And my elephant seal on her own rocky beach. I thought of Brian, too, who in spite of his sincere protests surely now flailed on a bed of orange life jackets, dead center in the heat of himself.

My nest was a tent on the edge of a glacier, outfitted with a floor of woolen army blankets, two down sleeping bags, a pillow, and the comfort of books, a jug of water, and a bottle of ibuprofen. I had the ethereal music of an Antarctic summer night. Sometime after I fell asleep, my tent flew off the edge of the continent, out over the sea, with me in it. I dream a lot out here, but never of you. I save you for waking moments.

Tonight, I sit inside the station with my glass of wine, again contemplating my tent, but not yet going there. The two girls who were chatting on the couch have now opened a backgammon board. Brian still cradles his guitar, his fingers working hard to play out his melancholy. He won't meet my eyes. I want to tell him that it doesn't matter. Whatever hand you draw, however you bet on the cards. There are no safe harbors. There is only enough.

Wildcat

Leon could smell the wildcat. The windows gaped open at night and the ripe August air moved inside, carrying a trace of damp feline fur. He had smelled the cat every night this week. It came because of the deer, and the deer came because of the roses. They nosed the satin petals right off the stickery stalks. Leon had heard that roses were like ice cream to deer. These flowers, and other herbaceous treats, brought them out of the large regional park abutting the neighborhood and into people's yards. The wildcat followed.

"I smelled the wildcat again last night," Leon told his daughter while she made breakfast for Justin and lunch for herself. "I think we should keep the windows closed." He didn't really think that, he just wanted their reaction.

He was rewarded by a microscopic gasp from his grandson, so tiny it was audible only to him. His daughter would have missed it altogether. And even if she had heard it, she wouldn't have known it held awe as well as fear. In fact, that little expulsion of air expressed a perfect blending of the two. Meg missed it all.

She spoke too loudly, asserting, "The news said that Fish and Wildlife would catch it this week. It's too hot to keep the windows shut. Anyway, cougars don't come in houses. They want the deer."

Leon considered pointing out the tenderness of five-year-old boys, but thought that might be going too far. "I smelled him," Leon said. "He was in the yard."

His daughter made a huffing sound. The bank had been shedding workers all year, and now she had him to feed, too. She couldn't afford to think about a wildcat prowling the neighborhood. She had to close loans and proofread title papers. She had to make sure she was indispensable in her department. She had to hold onto her job at any cost. Though to his way of thinking, the cost had been very high.

Who needed the big city? The big bank. The clanging, metallic, tar-covered stench of it all.

He heard her slide the tuna sandwich into a plastic bag and drop this into her purse. There was the whiff of a soft peach passing from the bowl on the kitchen table into her purse as well. It would smash in there, juice up all her things. She was always in too much of a hurry. Her feet made soft puffing sounds as she walked across the kitchen floor in her fleece slippers, not unlike the sound the cat's paws made on the pavement outside at night, but lacking the grace and intention.

"Be good," she said to both of them. She kicked off the fleece slippers, and he listened to the clunk of her pumps fade to the door. Justin ran after her and slid the deadbolt. Meg's old Honda roared to life. She gave it way too much gas, like the scream she wouldn't allow herself. Off she went to work.

Justin was back in the kitchen asking, "Did you really smell the cougar last night?"

"Yes, sir."

"What does it smell like?"

"Trail dust. Wet hay. A slight bit of urine. Cat breath."

"Cat breath!" Justin squealed. "You didn't smell its breath! It didn't come that close."

He was right. Leon exaggerated. "Yes, sir. I did. I smelled that wildcat, from nose to anus."

Justin squealed again.

"I heard it, too."

Another small gasp. Leon didn't wait for the question. "Picture a regular cat's paw. Now think of one just like that, only the size of my hand." Leon spread his fingers and held up his hand, palm out. Then he pushed his open hand through two feet of air. "Hear that?" Leon was sure that Justin shook his head no. So he said, "Try again." He punched his open hand forward again. "The sound of air being displaced."

"Yeah," Justin breathed. "I heard it."

"Okay. That. And also the quietest possible mush sound. That paw stepping on the garden soil."

Justin was practically hyperventilating, so Leon let it go with, "Yes, sir. I smelled him good last night."

Every day grandfather and grandson ventured further from the house, despite Meg's explicit instructions to not set foot out the door. You can't cage a five-year-old boy any more than you can cage a sixty-six-year-old man. The more rules she laid out, the stronger Leon's impulse to break them. You just can't cage a person.

That was something Meg would probably never appreciate. She was afraid. Leon understood that. He also understood that most likely he himself had created the problem, all those years back, when he left Meg, her brother, and their mother. Meg was only three years old, and Peter was Justin's age, five. Over the years Meg had kept in touch, but barely. Peter hadn't spoken to Leon in decades. Refused to. Leon knew his son lived in Stockton, and lots of times he'd considered going there and making amends. But how do you do that? Years were like sand. They slid and dispersed. You couldn't pick them back up again. Anyway, you can't cage a man, and that's how it had felt, back then, like he was caged with two small children and a wife. Leon had been practically a boy himself.

It took guts for Meg to call him earlier this month. He'd hand her that. Guts and a big dose of desperation. He'd moved this spring when Gloria passed and her kids sold the house out from under him. But he was still in Pinedale, and Meg had found him. She didn't bother with hello, how are you, just laid out her situation. Scott had left in April. He had done the kind of leaving that doesn't include child support payments. Or even a divorce. The man was missing in action. Gone. She had the rent, groceries, health insurance, and childcare. She needed Leon to come out and take over the latter. At least until Justin started school in the fall.

"Anyway," she'd said. "I heard you're alone now."

A fireball under his breastbone. He missed Gloria desperately. Yes, desperately. Her bellowing laugh. Her self-deprecating humor. The heavy cushion of her in bed beside him.

"I get by fine," he'd told his daughter, playing his hand, pleased that she needed something from him.

"I doubt that. I don't have a lot of space. You'd have to share a room with Justin."

As if she were doing him a favor, rather than the other way around. He knew the situation had to be acute for her to be asking for his help. In fact, he knew the word "help" in association with his name was, in his daughter's mind, pretty much an oxymoron.

But he'd been curious. He'd never met his grandson. He hadn't seen Meg in about ten years. And now Scott had left pretty much the same way Leon had. That had to be tough on his daughter. Although, to be fair, Leon had always sent money when he had it. Not every month. Some years none at all. But when he could, he had. Now he had his social security, and though it barely covered the room he'd been renting since Gloria's kids had kicked him out of his own home, it was something. He could contribute to his grandson's upkeep.

Anyway, Gloria was gone now, and that hurt more than anything had ever hurt. He was sick to death of the fireball under his breastbone.

Meg and Justin fetched him from Pinedale, and as they drove back to the city she observed, "You look like a hobo, Dad. You're a mess."

Leon wanted to argue. But the ghost of Gloria's plump fingers smoothing his hair and brushing food off his shirt snuffed his anger. He gave in, saying, "True, that."

Meg sighed. He figured she was weighing what it meant to have an old man, a blind one no less, on her hands now, too. Maybe she was thinking she'd taken on a greater burden rather than lessening the one she had. That very first evening she lost her temper when she tripped over his cane, which he'd left propped against the couch, angling out onto the living room floor. He didn't like using the cane and had a habit of leaving it places. She told him he was in a new environment and that he had to use it. After recovering from her irritation, she placed the handle in his hand and for a brief moment closed her own hands around his.

Meg gave him a tour of the telephones, the cupboards, the bathrooms. She spoke with much clarity about her expectations. Regular and healthy meals. No daytime TV, but she would supply appropriate DVDs. She made both of them promise they wouldn't leave the house while she was at work.

"Okay," Justin said.

"Fine," Leon concurred. "Where would we go?"

So far they had walked down the street to the trailhead leading into the woods. They had visited the grounds of the school where Justin would start kindergarten in the fall. They rode the bus downtown and got burgers, fries, and milkshakes at the Foster Freeze. They caught the 67, which took them to the antique carousel in the park. That was the funnest day yet, and they planned to repeat it soon. It was a strain on the boy keeping secrets from his mom. Leon understood that. But a necessary strain.

That day of the tuna sandwich and soft peach, they snuck to the movies. The boy didn't read yet, but he knew what a movie theater marquee looked like. They got off the bus downtown and Justin led the way. Leon felt a measure of integrity when he learned the theater offered a Disney picture. Never mind that they stayed for a second feature that included a healthy dose of sex. And healthy it was. The sooner the boy understood, the better.

"Is that fucking?" Justin asked as they rode the bus back up the hill that afternoon.

"Not so loud," Leon said. He thought the bus was empty, but sometimes he missed lurkers. "Yes."

"Can we see it again?"

"No." Leon was a bit nervous. It was already past five. Meg usually got home around five-forty-five.

"What'd we do today?" Leon asked his grandson. It'd become their end-of-the-day drill.

After a long thoughtful silence, Justin said, "We watched the Shrek DVD. I made peanut butter and banana sandwiches for our lunch. Then we played catch with the Wiffle ball."

"Good man."

"Because you can hear the Wiffle ball moving through air. That's how you catch it."

"True, that."

The boy made a small sound of satisfaction.

Leon smelled the wildcat again that night. Its timing was all off. The deer had already been through the yard at dusk, checking for new blossoms, tender greens. They had lifted their dainty hooves—there were two of them—as they stepped around branches and over large clods of dirt. Justin had given Leon the blow-by-blow report, each descriptive word expressing his hope that the cougar would soon follow.

"It will," Leon promised. "It definitely will."

"Don't lead him on," Meg called from the kitchen. "The cougar won't come into our yard, Justin."

"Actually," Leon whispered to his grandson. "People who have nice yards fence them off. What you got here is an overgrown tangle of weeds and leftover perennials. Am I right?"

"What are perennials?" Justin whispered back.

"Plants that live forever and have flowers. But the point is the tangle and the lack of a fence. Good cover for wildcats."

Meg had told Leon that the landlord had given them a discounted rent on the condition that they take care of the yard. Scott was supposed to have done that, but he didn't, and now it was a veritable forest. The landlord had been threatening eviction.

Tonight the wildcat came up onto the cement walkway, just under the open bedroom window, and lingered there, its scent filling Leon's nostrils. He slept in Justin's bowed twin bed, and the boy used a camping pad with a sleeping bag on the floor. Leon reached out a hand and felt for the soft down on Justin's head.

"Grandpa?" he whispered.

"What?"

"You can't see the movies."

"True, that."

"You don't know what that man and woman were doing."

"Oh, yeah I do."

"How do you know?"

"I done it myself."

When the boy spoke again, his voice was high and girlish. "Fucking? You done that?"

"Of course," Leon said, now annoyed that Justin wouldn't just drop it. "You will too one day."

"But you can't see the movies."

"I don't need to see—" Leon paused and felt good about the word choice he made. "—intercourse to know what it is."

"Is the cougar out there tonight?"

"Yes, sir. Not ten yards away, I'd guess."

Now silence, as if Justin had quit breathing altogether. He'd probably gone too far again, entirely terrorized the child. Nothing for it, though. The boy would have to work things out on his own, fucking and the wildcat both.

Gloria liked fucking. She liked cats, too. Food and sleep. She liked just about anything that made her body feel good. That fireball pressed up through his chest again. Gloria, he thought. *Gloria*. No one could see him in the dark. So he let the tears fall out the corners of his eyes, slide down his temples, dampen the pillow.

In the morning, after Meg left for work, Justin said, "Grandpa, let's find it."

Leon thought for a moment, knowing exactly what the boy meant, and then said, "That had been my plan for the day, too."

"Good man," Justin said.

"What I figure," Leon said, "is that the cat hangs out in the woods during the day. It doesn't want to get seen in broad daylight."

"Because Fish and Wildlife is hunting it."

"Exactly."

"So," the boy whispered out of sheer excitement, "we need to go to the woods."

Justin made peanut butter and grape jelly sandwiches. He poured milk into small screw-top jugs. He packed these into the new book bag Meg had bought him for school. Then he handed Leon his cane and said, "Maybe you better take this."

Leon smiled, knowing the request came on account of their taking on a more ambitious adventure today. But he said, "Nah. It's just one more thing to keep track of. I got you to show me the way, don't I?"

"Um," in the high, girlish voice. "But—"

"Good man," Leon said and headed for the door.

Holding Justin's slight arm with its walnut-sized bicep was not easy. Leon had to stoop a bit. He imagined his grandson's face extra solemn with responsibility and concentration. All on his own accord, the boy started calling out changes in the terrain. "We're going off the curb here." And after a couple of blocks, "Off the street and onto the trail now. It's narrow."

"Good man."

"We're heading uphill now," Justin said, his thin little voice bulking up with authority. "There're trees on both sides. Big ones. We're in the woods now."

"I know that." The shade of the evergreen branches felt good, and so did the soles of his sneakers on the dirt path. He could smell the dusty blue sky. It was the happiest he'd felt since Gloria passed. He wished he could introduce his grandson to her.

"It's thick woods now," Justin said, and then Leon understood that the boy was describing for his own sake, not for his grandfather's. "It's cougar country, all right."

"True, that."

"Do you think he might be nearby."

"Don't smell nothing yet."

"We should go farther in, then."

"Yep."

A rustling in the underbrush sent the boy nearly out of his skin. His thin arm flew out of Leon's grasp. Then the boy grabbed with both fists onto Leon's shirt.

"Look around," Leon whispered. "I don't smell nothing. What do you see?"

"Ha!" Justin squealed. "A *bunny*, Grandpa. It's just a bunny."

"Little white tail, I reckon."

"Yeah," Justin breathed hard with relief. "It's just a rabbit. I saw it run right across the trail."

"Keep going."

There were more rustlings. Other rabbits. The flapping of wings. The scratching of tunneling mammals. Justin reported a snake. They sat on a big trailside stone to eat their sandwiches and drink the milk. They walked on through mostly eucalyptus now, with an underbrush of blackberry. It was hot and purple. A slight breeze kicked up.

"Okay," Leon said in a very quiet and deep voice. "I smell it."

Justin said nothing, but Leon felt the pulse of blood through the boy's arm, as if his heart was pumping overtime.

"You know the term 'scaredy cat'? That comes from wildcats. They don't like to be seen. They're extremely private. Loners. They do what they want and don't do what they don't want. Most times they don't want people."

"How close is he?" Justin whispered.

Leon sniffed audibly and then felt silly for the over-dramatization. "I'd say close. Otherwise I wouldn't be smelling him. I'd bet he's watching us. Deciding what to do."

"What are his choices?" the boy asked.

"You ever hear the expression, 'Curiosity killed the cat'? They like to look at things. So there's this conflict in every cat, this desire to see things, look at them, and that rubs against their desire for privacy, to stay hidden. He's got to choose which he wants right now."

Leon let go of the boy's arm and rested a hand on his little ball bearing shoulder. He felt a tensing there, a gathering of courage. They stood for several minutes in silence, waiting and listening. Then Justin said, "There it is. I see it."

The blue sky and dusty trail converged at a place in the center of Leon's chest. He felt suffocated by Gloria's absence, the confusion of his grief.

Justin said, "He's walking toward us. His tail is swishing. His eyes are bright and flashing. Can you smell his breath?"

"Yes," Leon said. "He had rabbit for lunch."

"He's not afraid of us," Justin whispered. "He's stopped and he's just looking. Curiosity won. He knows we won't hurt him. He knows we're not Fish and Wildlife."

Leon nodded.

"He's the best thing I've ever seen. He's tan with white and black tips. He's as big as you, Grandpa."

The clarity of the boy's imagination rang like a bell in his heart. The blue sky floated above him. The dusty trail held his weight. Leon took a quiet, long breath, and the fireball cooled. He smelled the wildcat all right. It was a few feet away, just standing there with its rabbit breath and feline sweat. A big musky grace. A presence so beautifully intense it made him feel almost whole.

"We should get going," Justin said in a regular voice and took Leon's hand, placing it through the crook of his elbow. "The path is wide enough here."

That night Meg slammed the door when she came in from work. She shouted, "I *asked* you. I *specifically* asked you. Why did I ever think you could be trusted? How stupid of me. How plain *stupid* of me."

Leon and Justin were in the kitchen making a salad. They thought they'd surprise Meg by making the dinner themselves. She dropped her purse on the kitchen table and kicked her pumps across the linoleum. "Ashley is home next door with her sick baby and two days in a row— *two days in a row*—she says she saw Justin marching off down the street with an old blind man. She said you were gone for over three hours yesterday and two hours today. Where?"

Leon sat down in a kitchen chair. "Well, now, Meg. You just can't keep a boy caged. Especially not in the summer."

"True, that," Justin said.

"He's a little, *little* boy. And you're a blind old man. This isn't Pinedale, Dad. This is a big city. No one's looking out for you."

"Apparently Ashley is."

"Where'd you go?"

"Just walking," Justin piped up. "We just walked."

"Go sit down in the front room," Leon said to his daughter. "We're making dinner tonight. Everyone is safe. Food soon."

"You haven't changed one iota," she said as she left the kitchen. Meg clicked on the TV news. A few minutes later, Leon and Justin brought in a dinner of spaghetti and salad on big plates. Meg turned up the volume.

When the anchor and reporters finished with the wars and economy, she hit the mute button and turned to her son. "You have to eat more than that." The little boy got up and sat next to his grandpa, taking the old man's hand.

"Great," Meg said. "This is just great."

"Turn it on!" Justin shrieked and grabbed the remote. He clicked up the volume in time to hear, "—just before dawn this morning. They treed the cougar here on Middlefield Road, where they attempted to tranquilize him with a dart. However, the cat was too fast for Fish and Wildlife. It crouched, poised for a leap from the tree, and an officer was forced to kill the cougar. No longer will this predator terrorize the residents in the homes adjacent to the wildlands."

Leon heard Justin catch his breath. The boy snuggled close, his knees bumping into Leon's thigh, his fists against his ribs. The reporter went on to interview a neighbor who expressed his outrage at this encroachment of the wild.

Meg burst into tears. Her plate and fork clanked as she dropped them on the coffee table. She ran to her room.

Leon put an arm around the boy and pulled him closer. Gloria liked to explain any rush of feeling by saying that it was her hormones acting up. Leon wasn't sure men had hormones, but if they did, his were acting up. He thought, I'll protect this child. He thought, I'm sorry it took me sixty-six years to get here. He thought, I want to alleviate my daughter's stress. He felt the bright awareness of love in his chest.

That night the boy slipped into bed next to Leon. Bird bones under satiny skin. Leon heard a muffled chirp-like sob.

"Yep," Leon said. "I can smell that cat again tonight."

The little boy stilled. Tensed. Sat up and said, "But they shot him this morning!"

"Nah. They just had to pretend they caught him to calm the public. Didn't we see him ourselves, at midday, alive and thriving?"

A long pause of discomfort. Justin didn't want to correct his grandfather. "But Grandpa, they *showed* the dead cougar on TV."

The sky, the trail, the fireball. This bowed bed and the night air. The pressure on his chest. The goddamn welling behind his eyes.

"On the other hand," Justin said cautiously, somberly. "You can't believe everything you see."

"True, that," Leon said as everything eased once again. "Good man."

Skylark

At three o'clock one morning in October of her senior year, Corey shoved open her bedroom window. The half-rotted wooden sash shuddered on its upward journey, making plenty of noise. She jumped out, landing in the crackly autumn leaves no one had raked, making even more noise. Any minute her mom would throw open the front door and drag her back inside. She paused at the front gate, looked back at the house, and then walked down the street. Five minutes later she arrived in front of the café where the Greyhound bus stopped two mornings a week. She was the only waiting passenger.

Corey heard the rumble of the approaching bus long before it rolled into view. Its brakes screeched to a stop, the exhaust pipe belching stink, and the doors sucked open. The street with its darkened storefronts was deserted. Not a soul came after her.

That wasn't surprising, given how hard her mom and stepdad had been partying last night. They probably didn't hit the sack until a couple of hours ago. But by the time she reached Little Rock, the school would call home, letting her mom know she hadn't shown up. The police would be waiting in the bus station, on the lookout for a seventeen-year-old girl with dark blond hair, straight and thick as a horse's mane, the ends of the bangs brushing her eyelashes, eczema reddening her hands, and a cellular level impatience. She twitched so much teachers thought she did meth. They were wrong. She didn't even smoke cigarettes.

Corey climbed the bus steps, gave the driver her ticket, and found a seat near the back. The behemoth vehicle coughed and farted out of town. She had no plan. She never dreamed she'd get this far. No one but herself now. She hugged her rucksack and concentrated her mind, the way she did when she was singing, the way that gave her intensity and swagger.

No, she couldn't even think of her song. Not now. She was still too close to home for that.

She'd do the girlfriends instead. If she did them all, did them thoroughly, it'd take her almost all the way to Little Rock. Kaylie, Emma, Angeline, Maggie, Tilda, and Lili. Their features were like musical notes—eyelashes, freckles, gestures, voices—that she'd memorized. Prisoners, she'd once read, recited poems in their cells. Instead, she had her girlfriends, every scrap of conversation she'd overheard, or in some cases even had with the girl herself, and the way they walked, talked, smiled. What made them blush or cringe. It would be creepy, if someone could read her mind. Like she was a stalker. But it was all in her head. No one got hurt or even embarrassed by undue attention. It was just a game that kept her close to her own heart. Tilda first.

Corey closed her eyes and brought up Tilda's fierce eyebrows. Her extra red lips. Her long, tangled black hair. Corey ran her fingers through the hair and let them get caught, the texture, both soft and coarse. She fell asleep before even starting the next girl.

In Little Rock, as she stepped off the bus, Corey felt her wrists tingle in anticipation of the handcuffs. Then she had to smile at her silliness; no one cuffed runaways. They'd just grasp her upper arm and guide her to the squad car. She waited just to the side of the bus door, looking around for the policewoman. She'd be both brusque and kind. "Come with me," she'd say and maybe they'd stop for a meal on the way to the station.

No one intercepted Corey in the Little Rock bus station, even though she had a full two-hour layover. She ate chips and drank a soda, which did little to mute her hunger, and then boarded her connecting ride. This bus was nearly full, but she found two seats to herself in the back.

As the bus lumbered westward, she had the strange feeling that she was acting against her own will. A crazy vim in her bloodstream had launched her out of the bedroom window, and she was still answering to it, riding the surge. She'd meant to stay and graduate. She had good grades. Prospects, Mrs. Sweeney the school counselor had said. Maybe a chance at a scholarship. As recently as yesterday, her silent chant had been just hold out, hold out, hold out.

But she'd bought the bus ticket, hadn't she? She'd gotten the tattoo. She'd meant it. She still meant it.

All through Arkansas and Oklahoma, Corey stared out the window, willed the ache in her stomach to morph into something useable, like hunger-strike strength. As they motored across the Texan panhandle she slumped low in her seat, as if the haters would see her escaping, drag her from the bus and down their dust-choked streets. She'd seen the stories on TV. New Mexico briefly brightened the view of her prospects, the strings of deep red chilis hanging from eaves and carports, anywhere they might dry in the clarifying sunshine. Then came the desert of Arizona, and Corey began to comprehend the gravity of what she'd done. She reached into the neck of her dress and touched her tattoo. *Skylark, have you anything to say to me?* She quickly withdrew her fingers. She couldn't awaken the song now. The music would shatter. Arizona was barren and dry, a long highway of ache.

Then, California: palm trees and farmland and big cities on the edge of the continent. Ha! Though she'd eaten too many pepperoni sticks and donuts, felt like a grime magnet, and her neck cricked audibly from sleeping in the bus seats, she'd done this ass-kicking thing: she came *here.*

They'd have found her phone by now. She left it on top of her bed, as clear and decisive as any written note. If she'd kept her phone, they'd be able to track her. Call her. Convince her. She'd meant it all right: the bus ticket, the tattoo, the left phone.

Corey disembarked in downtown Oakland, the early morning air fresh and sweet, with a hint of salt and rotted fruit, and thought maybe she was smelling the Pacific Ocean. She no longer expected police or social workers to nab her, but she waited on the street for a few minutes anyway. Nobody at all. Corey cleared her throat of the tears, shouldered her rucksack, and began walking toward the university campus, toward Mrs. Sweeney's stories. Telegraph Avenue was jammed with cafés, art galleries, convenience stores, bars, beauty shops, churches, and bail bond joints, each stacked right against the next, and she wanted to stop and look at everything. She did like being free. She liked the wide openness of her prospects. Movement felt like safety, especially with so many men checking her out.

Two hours later, Telegraph Avenue dead-ended at the university. Corey walked into Sproul Plaza and stopped at a fountain. Right here, on this very pavement, Mrs. Sweeney had been a part of the Free Speech Movement. That had happened a thousand years ago, but Corey liked the old woman's stories, the idea that every voice mattered. She touched her tattoo. *Skylark, have you seen a valley green with spring, where my heart can go a journeying?*

Three years ago, Corey won the statewide junior high school singing contest and a solo with the Arkansas Symphony Orchestra in Little Rock. The lead-up to the event was the happiest time in her life. Sure, her mom and stepdad argued nonstop about whether she should be on *American Idol* or *America's Got Talent*, how exactly they could cash in on her gift, but they agreed on her value. Her worth. Her beauty. They'd gone to Memphis to buy the blue satin gown and matching heels. They visited a doctor who prescribed a lotion to relieve the eczema on her cracked hands. On the day of the concert, her mom made her hot tea and buttered cinnamon toast in the morning, took her for a manicure and pedicure, and then to the beauty parlor to have her hair highlighted and curled into long ringlets. Hideous, in retrospect, but at the time Corey thought the springs of bright blond hair helped seal her future. Right before the concert, a fresh argument broke out between her mom and stepdad as they stood in front of Robinson Center Music Hall. The grand architecture, the six stone pillars, terrified the adults. Her mother gripped Corey's shoulders too hard and brought her face too close, told her to sing as if she were in the shower or the backyard, that was all, *just sing*. But Corey wasn't afraid. Not in the least. She felt bolstered by the muscular building, its stone gray beauty, and when she stepped out on stage, by the hot bright lights, the symphony seated behind her and the audience seated before her, everyone waiting for her to sing.

Oh, Skylark, my heart is riding on your wings.

"You look like you're fresh off the bus." The tall skinny boy who spoke to Corey sat four feet away on the rim of the fountain, shirtless. His clavicle spanned his shoulders, straining the skin, like some prehistoric musical instrument. A short upper lip kept his mouth open, even when he wasn't speaking, and the gap between his two front teeth made him look sweet. His Afro had a diameter of about a foot, radiating out around his head like a black halo. At his feet sat a grubby backpack. "What's your name?"

"Corinne." They'd put her full name on the program at Robinson Center Music Hall.

"Where you from?"

"Arkansas."

He laughed, like the whole state was a joke. "You a long way from home."

"This is home." Corey tapped the left side of her chest, her skylark. *Oh, won't you lead me there?*

"You seem pretty green. My advice is you find Michelle."

"I have plans." Who was Michelle?

"Sure. I can tell." He laughed again. "I like your getup."

She'd taken scissors to the blue satin dress, cut it short, let out the back seam and sewn in a panel of blue fabric she bought in Dottie's Sewing Corner. The frayed, uneven bottom of the dress, which used to hang to her ankles, now barely covered her upper thighs. The combat boots were supposed to be ironic with the dress, as was the green and black lumberjack jacket. The navy beanie held her bangs in place.

"Thank you," she said.

He smiled, that tooth gap so innocent. She had to trust someone.

After an hour of random conversation, Corey walked with Leonard to his camp. He had food, he said, and she was starving. Anyway, she couldn't sleep on the street.

On the ridge above the city of Berkeley, they took a trail into a forest of eucalyptus and redwood trees. Leonard said there were mountain lions and coyotes. She said she wasn't afraid of wild animals. "Or anything at all, for that matter," she added. The trail was dark and she had no weapon. She tried not to think of Mrs. Sweeney and her prospects, nor did she touch her tattoo. These woods would haunt the song right out of her.

Leonard stepped off the trail and she followed him for another twenty yards, heading straight into the chaos of wilderness. Corey had expected a clearing, a picnic table, a fire ring, but he stopped at a place that looked more like a nest, just a bowl of thick forest duff surrounded by soaring tree trunks.

"Home," he said. "For tonight, anyway." He opened his backpack and pulled out a jar of peanut butter and half a loaf of bread. "Are you hungry?" She lunged for the food, and he laughed as he dug a folding knife out of his pocket and tossed it to her. Corey made sandwiches while he put up his tent. They climbed inside to eat.

"Where are you from?" she asked.

"My grandma lives in Oakland. She raised me."

Corey understood. Leonard was too beautiful with his long limbs and sweet smile, the gap and full lips. He'd had to leave. Corey couldn't help wondering about the details: Who was the man, when and where and how many times? Did his grandma know?

With her stepdad, it was all eyes for the year after her Little Rock debut, and she'd misunderstood the looks. The lust, she'd thought, was all about her voice. His belief that it would bring him money.

"If I were a girl," Leonard said, his mouth full of peanut butter and bread, "I'd go stay with Michelle."

His tone, the way he said her name, made Michelle sound like a compromise.

"She killed her husband," he added.

That sentence, those four words, thudded in Corey's eardrums. She tucked it away to think about later.

"Some say she's a sergeant at lesbian boot camp."

Corey kept her poker face.

"But a nicer way to put it, she's a girl scout den mother."

"If she's so great, why aren't you staying with her?"

"I don't like rules and she's got a lot. Anyway, the first one is no cisgender males." Leonard reached out a hand, his fingers curled, and brushed Corey's cheek with his knuckles. She didn't know what cisgender male meant, but apparently Leonard was one. Best to just get this part over with. Corey shucked off her lumberjack jacket, crossed her arms, grabbed the hem of her blue satin dress, and lifted it over her head. Her bra was the same royal blue as the dress. Both of her skylark's feet and most of the right wing were tucked inside the bra, but its left wing and head flew above the lace trim.

Leonard touched the skylark, so gently it tickled, and then he kissed the bird. Those plum lips on the small swell of her breast.

She swallowed back her voice, the way it rose in her throat: not now, not now.

"This means something," Leonard said. He used the light on his phone to look at her tattoo more carefully. He was the third person, counting the artist who'd made the bird but not herself, to see her skylark. "Taking flight," he said. "I like the streaky browns. It's beautiful."

She couldn't quite bear the way his touching the skylark made her need to sing, not here and with this boy, not in these dark woods, so she held his ears and pulled his head to hers, kissed his mouth, scooted her hips under his. He reared up, quizzical, and she tried to sound playful, even experienced, when she said, "Oh, I'm on the pill." But her voice hissed a bit and he looked doubtful. She batted his muscled arm and said, "Seriously! Jeez!" Leonard shook his head and found a condom in his backpack. She clutched the balled up blue satin dress in her left hand as he entered her. Tears welled and flowed down her cheeks; she turned her head so he wouldn't see. The song she held back snarled into a sob. She didn't know if she could control it, the pressure growing in her chest, right under the skylark, and pushing up her throat.

Leonard rolled off of her and saw the tears, the scrunched face. "What. I thought. You okay?"

She nodded. "Yeah." Added, "Absolutely."

Leonard flipped onto his back and stared up at the taffeta.

"Sorry," she said. "I'm not very good at that."

"You're fine."

"I like girls."

He turned his head so fast that she braced herself to be hit.

No one had stopped her from leaving the house in the middle of the night, taking the Greyhound out of town, rolling across two-thirds of the country, disembarking in Oakland, walking to Berkeley. She wasn't a missing person. She was lying in the dark woods with a boy she'd met a few hours ago, no one within earshot, even if she screamed.

"You didn't say. I thought—"

She bit her bottom lip hard to cut off the tears, to hold in the sobs, and tasted blood as the skin broke between her teeth. She tried to popu-late her mind, the tent, with Tilda, Lili, Angeline, an army of girlfriends, none of whom she'd ever touched, all of whom she'd thought, at one time or another, that she loved.

Leonard propped himself up on an elbow, his head in his hand, and used his other hand to brush the bangs out of her face. Then he combed his fingers through her hair, his fingertips running lightly along her scalp. She bawled then, cried hard for a long time, and thought, when she finally quieted, that she could go straight for Leonard, give up girls, girls she'd never even had yet. Maybe that's what she'd do. The thought caused her tears to morph into laughter. That would be more ironic than combat boots with a blue satin dress: run away to California to go straight.

Leonard slept with his hands curled, his mouth parted, his Afro smashed where his head lay on his folded T-shirt. Corey lay awake for hours, listening to swishing tree boughs, scratchy critter feet, unidentified sighs. She pressed her open palm over her skylark. *In your lonely flight, haven't you heard the music of the night?*

"I got business to do," Leonard said in the morning when she thought maybe they'd hang out for the day. He told her where she could get a free shower and how to check her email at the library. "Best thing you could do is go see Michelle."

After a hot shower at the public swim center, Corey found the library. She waited her turn and then sat facing the monitor. If she logged on, wouldn't they be able to trace her location? She'd been gone for three and a half days. By now they would have sobered up, contacted the authorities, maybe even driven out to the quarry, up to the national forest, into Memphis and Little Rock. Tracking her via a remote computer would be too costly, too complicated. It wouldn't hurt to open her email.

First she deleted the junk messages. Then she read the one from Mrs. Sweeney, who scolded her for not coming to school, as if Corey were just watching TV on the couch at home.

There were three messages from her mom. Three was a lot. A sign of concern. A fist clenched in Corey's stomach.

She read them in the order they were sent. The subject line of the first was a bunch of question marks: ???????? Corey opened the email and read, "Where the fuck are you?" Given the profanity, probably written while inebriated. As in, drunk.

The second message read, "Tell me you're safe." Corey bit her raw bottom lip and swallowed hard.

She opened the last email and read, "You did good to leave. Bonkers here. Some day I'll see you on American Idol. Fly, girl. Fly and sing."

Corey shoved back the wooden library chair so hard it toppled. She ran down the stairs and out the front door, where she huddled into herself on the sidewalk, back against the stucco exterior of the library, and cried. An older woman who looked like a teacher or a librarian or a nun, with short gray hair and purple glasses, crouched down and asked if she was okay. Corey told her to please go away. Then not wanting to keep on blubbering in public, she pushed herself up, thinking she'd go look for Leonard. He'd been pretty clear about the two of them splitting this morning, but maybe he'd want company again tonight. Corey was hungry.

"Hey girl in blue satin dress."

The person speaking to her wore a pair of red Vans, clean tan chinos, a red T-shirt, and a kickass haircut. The sides of her head were nearly shaved, leaving the top shock long, glossy, and black. Her cheeks, and the place directly below her bottom lip, were plump. Mexican, maybe, with swimmable brown eyes and toasty skin.

"Saw you lose it in there. Bad email?"

Corey nodded.

"Boyfriend? Girlfriend?"

"Mom."

"Oh, man, that's the worst. What'd she say?"

Corey shook her head.

"I get it." The girl reached a hand toward Corey's shoulder. "You look kind of disoriented. New in town?"

Was it stamped on her forehead?

"I'm gonna write down an address. Come by. You look like you need some stabilizing." The girl smiled, like that was okay, like everybody needed stabilizing. "Ask for Michelle."

Michelle again! Corey took the piece of paper. It was probably some kind of cult, Michelle the abusive prophet. They'd shave her head, brainwash her. She'd spend her days handing out pamphlets. She'd seen them at the mall in Little Rock.

"I'm Albatross," the girl said.

Corey wondered why you'd take that name. Surely her parents hadn't given it to her. Never mind the insane name, Albatross was the cutest girl she'd ever seen in her life. Corey's hand migrated to her chest. *Is there a meadow in the mist, where someone's waiting to be kissed?* She felt so flustered, she forgot to protect herself with her formal name. "I'm just Corey. Corey from Arkansas."

Albatross smiled, those cheeks rounding out, the eyes brimming warmth. "So Corey of Arkansas. You're kinda beautiful. You know that?"

As the girl walked away, Corey wrangled the circus in her chest, the feeling of crazy clown sadness and happiness all performing at once. *Hey,* she said quietly, or maybe not at all, just thought the word, as the chubby Mexican girl in baggy chinos and a red T-shirt disappeared around the corner. *Come back.*

Kaylie, Emma, Angeline, Maggie, Tilda, Lili, and Albatross.

She tucked the scrap of paper in the outer pocket of her rucksack and walked over to the campus to look for Leonard. He wasn't at the fountain. It'd be dark in a couple of hours, and she had nowhere to sleep. She did have ten dollars left, but that might have to last the rest of her life. She walked back up to his camp, arriving at the beginning of dusk. He wasn't there, so she sat on the forest floor to wait. It grew cold. The night swirled in, blacked out the edges, and still she sat, cross-legged, by herself. She tried to concentrate on her girlfriends for distraction, but couldn't conjure them, not with her mom's words running through her head: *Where the fuck are you? Tell me you're safe. You did good to leave. Bonkers here. Some day I'll see you on American Idol. Fly, girl. Fly and sing.*

Corey curled up in the tightest ball possible, pulled her green and black lumberjack jacket over her head, to wait out the night. After a while the terror passed and even her hunger toughened into a kind of sinew. The smell of the fir needles and soil, the roughness of them on her cheek, the low whoosh of the moon passing overhead. She could not run from this place. She had no choice but to slide her hand over her heart, on top of the skylark, and listen.

It was hard to believe that only three years had passed since she stood on that stage, fearless. Cool satin and warm light on her skin. An audience of hundreds, wishing her well, expecting nothing more from her than a beautiful song. The symphony's pianist flapped out his tux tails, nodded as he sat at the gleaming black grand piano. He played the prelude as she brought her mouth up to the microphone. She began singing, oh so softly, *Skylark, have you anything to say to me? Won't you tell me where my love can be?*

Corey brought the house down. They were on their feet. Uproarious applauding. A sea of teeth, happy, happy, happy smiles. Even some two-fingered whistling. They heard her prayer. Her voice.

Corey's joy lasted for about a week. Then her mom and stepdad went into overdrive sending out CDs of her performance to all the recording studios, talent scouts, and random famous people they could find online. They spent their paychecks on clothes they expected her to wear in upcoming performances. They drank more expensive brands of gin. They took a trip to Nashville, set her up on a prominent street corner where she sang all weekend, the adults fully expecting her to be discovered any moment. She wasn't. As the months went by, and nothing came of their efforts, her stepdad became more and more frustrated. And angry at the money they'd spent. When he looked at her, and he did all the time, it seemed like he wanted to reach down her throat and grab her voice in his own two hands.

Corey stopped singing. So he tried to fuck it out of her.

Lying on the forest floor in the woods above Berkeley, Corey eventually realized that she didn't mind being alone. It was a kind of relief. The air was cold and opaque, but velvety. The smell of the evergreen needles was a balm. The song in her chest loosened, as if it too sensed the absence, at long last, of danger.

At first light Corey returned to the public swim center and waited there on the street, shivering in the dawn cold. When the locker room opened, she undressed, showered, and then wrapped a towel she found on the wooden bench around her waist. She covered her top half with the lumberjack jacket. Then she washed out her blue dress, bra, and underwear with soap and hot water. She changed back into the wet clothes and headed for the library.

A warm sun dried her dress as she walked. She bought a quart of milk and a sandwich at the Stop-N-Go, drank and ate it all standing on the sidewalk, and then crossed the street to the library, planning what she might write back to her mother.

First she sat in the reading room, where they had comfy chairs, and read a magazine. The food in her stomach made her feel better, even if she now only had a total of three dollars and change. She'd have to join that cult for a while, just so she could eat. Maybe she could resist the brainwashing part. She'd handled worse than Michelle.

"Corey from Arkansas!" Albatross shouted, drawing the attention of the librarian, who with her bird-bright eyes and strict mouth looked like a Chinese Mrs. Sweeney.

A white girl, if the term applied to someone whose skin was covered with black and red ink, approached with Albatross. It wasn't like Corey wanted to look at the tattooed girl's breasts, but how could you not? Besides bulging out of the tight camisole, they were covered with black thorny vines and red roses. The same motif—which technically didn't make sense because roses have stalks, not vines—sleeved the girl's arms. Her gold hoop earrings were nearly as big as her face.

"You know this chick?" asked thorny vines and roses, putting an arm around Albatross, right there in the library reading room. Okay, so they were girlfriends. Corey glanced at the watchful librarian.

"Corey, Hannah. Hannah, Corey." Albatross sunk her hands in the front pockets of her tan chinos, that fat-cheeked grin directed right at Corey. *So Corey of Arkansas. You're kinda beautiful. You know that?*

Corey raised a tentative hand. "Hi."

"Let's go," Hannah said to Albatross. "We got stuff to do."

"I didn't stop by that address yet," Corey said.

"What she talking about?" Hannah asked, slitting up her eyes.

"I thought she might take your place at Michelle's," Albatross said.

"*My* place?" Hannah cocked her hips and braced her fists on them. "Your place is opening up, too."

"But I was wondering," Corey said, even as the word *caution* pulsed through her nervous system. "Who's Michelle?"

Hannah huffed. "A royal bitch, that's who."

"You're mad 'cause she asked you to leave." Albatross spoke softly.

Hannah reared back, her eyes piss hot. "This chick wants to jump through her hoops, fine. It don't have nothing to do with us. Let's go."

"I'm not going to New York with you," Albatross said, and Corey had the feeling it was the first time she'd said this to Hannah. More, she had the feeling, liked the feeling, that maybe her own presence gave Albatross a kind of courage.

Hannah glared at Albatross, her lips twitching like she had a mouthful of venom. "Yeah, you are."

"No. I'm not." Albatross planted her feet apart, crossed her arms over her chest. "I'm staying here."

A new strategy dawned on Hannah's cellophane face. She slimed all fake mellow, dropped into the chair next to Corey, took her hand. "Albatross is right. This is a real opportunity for you. Places don't open up all that often at Michelle's. True, I got kicked out. The bitch is rigid. But some girls need the structure. I'm guessing that's your story." Hannah paused. "So, like, what *is* your story?"

Corey pulled her hand away.

"Mm hm." Hannah cooed like a fake shrink. "Father? Uncle? Teacher?"

"Shut the fuck up," Albatross said. "Leave her alone."

Corey wobbled to her feet and grabbed her rucksack. She looked down a long black wormhole, as if she stood in one universe and needed to pass through an impossible portal to get to another one. She wouldn't survive the journey, even if she could get through that opening. Still, Corey willed her feet to move, to go somewhere, anywhere. As she slung on her rucksack, her hand grazed the skylark. *And in your lonely flight, have you heard the music?*

"Ain't nobody coming after you, is there?" Hannah said.

"Excuse me," Corey whispered. "I'm going to email my mom."

"Your mom. There's a joke."

"What is wrong with you?" Albatross said to Hannah, her voice way too loud for a library. The man with rolled blankets at his feet put down his book. The pair of teenagers doing math nudged each other, giggled. A mom with twin boys dragged them out of the reading room.

"Seriously? You *like* this hillbilly chick? I just know you're not so stupid that you'd choose this piece of white trash over New York." Right there in the library, Hannah spat to the side of Corey.

The librarian picked up the phone. "Send security to the reading room. Yes. Immediately."

"No," Albatross said carefully, as if speaking to something bigger than the spitting. "I want my GED."

"You could get that in New York. You're just chicken. Scared shitless. You *like* Michelle's rules."

"Who's Michelle?" Corey shouted to be heard. She needed to know.

"Michelle is a maniacal bitch who killed her husband. Shot him dead. Did time. Got out. Collects runaway girls."

"No," Albatross said.

"Oh, *yeah*," Hannah said. "You go there and be her slave, Arkansas. You cute enough, maybe you can service her, too."

"That's pure slander," Albatross shouted. "Michelle's husband abused her for years. She keeps a house for runaway girls because when she was inside she thought long and hard about the cycles of violence. How they start. How they don't stop. She got a lot of rules, but they're about keeping us safe, breaking those cycles." It was as if Albatross were addressing everyone in the reading room, as if what she was trying to say was the most important message possible. She was trembling all over.

"Look who's brainwashed." Hannah paraded out of the reading room, her butt rolling in her tight jeans, the vines swirling around her shoulders and neck. Corey wished they'd strangle her.

Then Hannah pivoted and lunged back, put her nose and cigarette breath right up in Corey's face. "Touch my girl and you're dead meat."

"I'm not your girl," Albatross said.

Hannah's hand swept up fast, but Albatross caught the wrist before it hit her. Beyond the two girls, Corey saw the security guard lope into the reading room, hitching up the belted pants of his uniform. Hannah got Albatross in a headlock, the latter's neck hooked in her elbow. Albatross kicked hard but caught only air.

Some of the library patrons gathered around to watch. A young woman with dreadlocks shouted for the girls to stop fighting, and then she leapt forward, wrapped her arms around Hannah's waist and tried to pull her off of Albatross. The librarian shouted for the dreadlocked girl to get away from the fight. The security guard didn't move any closer; instead he made a call, as if he were afraid of the fighting girls and needed backup.

Corey touched her skylark tattoo. Her voice was right there, just under her fingertips, a tangle of danger and joy, entwined just like Hannah and Albatross. No one was coming after her. That hurt so much. It also meant she was free. *Fly, girl. Fly and sing.*

Corey reached to the very bottom of her belly and pulled up the first note, the first word. "*Skylark.*" She sang it so softly that only Hannah, who'd wrestled Albatross to the cold hard floor at Corey's feet, could hear. "*Have you anything to say to me?*"

Now Albatross heard, too. The girls' holds on each other loosened.

Corey kept singing as she climbed up on the long wooden tabletop. She liked that she was wearing her blue satin dress, hacked off, with combat boots and her hair naturally straight. The acoustics in the book-lined room were excellent, and her voice took flight. Hannah and Alba-tross panted, knotted in a now motionless embrace. Corey sang the song all the way through, repeating the last verse, her favorite, three times. *Skylark, I don't know if you can find these things, but my heart is riding on your wings. So if you see them anywhere, won't you lead me there?*

When she finished, silence filled the library. The security guard stood halfway across the room, hands dangled at his sides, his shoulders loosened and chest caved, as if protecting something soft inside. The librarian held her clasped hands at her throat, as if she too wanted to sing. Hannah moved away first, took slow steps backwards, as if Corey were an alien beast, as if the song pierced her anger. Albatross listened for more song in the silence, tears wetting her round cheeks.

Corey didn't know where she'd go. In the next month, week, or even minute. She didn't know if she'd ever see her mom again. If her mom would leave her stepdad. If Corey would graduate from high school or live on the street for the rest of her life. She didn't know if she'd go see about a spot in Michelle's house, if Michelle was benevolent or predatory. If Hannah would leave for New York, if Albatross would go with her. Corey didn't know if Albatross would stay here and kiss her.

Corey knew nothing at all about her prospects. But she knew she had her voice, right here under her skylark. She knew she could sing.

The Found Child

John and Ray found the baby on a Sunday morning, a few hours before their flight back to New York. They had been on a long weekend in Wyoming, of all places. Ray wanted nature. John said fine, if the package included good food. A couple of their more westerly inclined friends suggested the dude ranch, and it *had* been fun, even restorative. They'd liked the elderly couple who ran the ranch, the horseback riding was novel, and the scenery stunning. John read an entire book, and Ray walked for hours through the tall grasses. They made love twice, which they didn't really do all that much anymore.

In their minds, the lovemaking somehow got tangled up with finding the baby. Of course they knew they hadn't made the baby. And neither man was particularly sentimental, so it's not like they coddled the notion by purposely placing the lovemaking side by side with the baby-finding. But they did feel close. Their intimacy had created a field of hope. Ray was forty-three and John had turned forty earlier that year. They'd been together for eleven years and had talked about having children for most of that time. Their best lesbian couple friends wanted to bear the child, and it would have been perfect because they were also an interracial couple. But while the women liked the idea of an agreement that included lots of fatherly involvement, they didn't want to share legal custody. The friendship actually ended over that disagreement. Ray thought adoption was a good idea, particularly since biracial babies were easier to come by. But every time they started down the adoption path, they ran into smothering worries about DNA and inherited problems. Then, too, it was the eighties, and so many of their friends had died. How could anyone think of ushering a child into this cruel world? Yet they also thought that maybe a child was exactly what they needed to help them believe once again in life.

Their friends held the opinion, after a few years of this waffling, that the couple didn't really want children, they only wanted to talk about them. This wasn't true. They did want children. Desperately. Which added to the feeling, which developed into a belief, that a found baby belonged to them.

They were driving back to the Cheyenne airport in their rental car and stopped in Rawlins to look for a good bakery and some coffee. Rawlins is a scruffy, angry little town with nothing in it but dead storefronts and, on the outskirts, a couple of big box stores. Dry snarls of tumbleweed rolled down the main drag. There was no nice bakery, no decent-looking restaurant, pretty much no cup of coffee either of them would consider drinking. They went into a diner and got to-go cups of tea, despite a stale smell and the waitress's mean squint. As they walked back to the car, John snarkily commented that everyone they'd encountered in Rawlins appeared to have fetal alcohol syndrome. Who wouldn't drink to excess, he carried on, if forced to live in a town like that?

And there, on a bus bench, was the baby.

The strangest part, at the very first, was how well cared for he looked. He was strapped tightly into a car seat. His head was covered with a blue knit cap, his body trundled up in a matching blue blanket. He was quiet, his eyes open, and he stared unblinkingly up at the two men. Later, John would tell anyone who would listen that the first time he met eyes with his son, he saw a great degree of intelligence and a clear determination. Both men felt the baby drink in their kindness, felt him fix his infant spirit onto their warm, responsible, adult bodies. He did seem to welcome John and Ray, unconditionally, into his life.

The men looked all around, but they saw no one who could have deposited the baby on the bench. Ray went back inside the diner to make inquiries. John stayed outside and stared at the little apparition. He eased off its cap and discovered, as he expected from the coffee ice cream tone of the baby's skin, a head of black fuzz, already curling into perfect loops. Ray returned and said no one knew anything about the infant. There were no cars driving down the main drag, no pedestrians lingering on street corners. Only the waitress saw the two men take the baby.

As he grew into a little boy, the fathers tried to imagine his story. They'd start down different narrative paths and get stopped by heartbreak or confusion. One way or another, they always concluded that some white girl got herself knocked up by some black dude, and she abandoned her baby. John consistently ended these conversations with a sentence his disbelief wouldn't let him finish. "Anyone who . . ." he'd say, shaking his head, feeling his heart squeeze tight. His outrage fueled his love for Akasha and never left him. Sometimes Ray patted his partner's hand or knee and cautioned against such anger. Akasha was safe now. He was loved. He was thriving.

Meanwhile, they told all their friends and acquaintances that they had adopted Akasha through regular channels, that they'd been quiet about it because they hadn't wanted to get anyone's hopes up, least of all theirs. With a couple of their nosier friends, the lie became a bit more elaborate, but in the end no one had reason to question their story. Still, there were times, usually in the middle of the night, when Ray worried. What if a mistake had been made? What if there was some reasonable explanation for why the baby had been left, maybe temporarily, on the bus bench? These paths of thought led Ray to moments of actual horror: What had they done?

"It's possible," he'd say quietly to John, "that someone is heartbroken." John would chuff, roll over. "Anyone who . . ." And Ray knew he was right. There could be no good excuse, not a single one, for abandoning a baby. "A bus stop," John would add. "In Rawlins, Wyoming. Eight o'clock on a Sunday morning. No 'mistake' is that cruel."

John was an attorney in Manhattan with Weinraub, Smythe, and Kingsley. He came from Richmond, Virginia, where his father had worked his entire life in a cigarette factory. John believed deeply in the American Dream, that his successes were earned and therefore due him. Ray, too, had worked very hard for his cello seat with the string quartet, but he thought he was more lucky than deserving. Ray believed in chance and knew that beauty could be shattered at any moment.

The logistics of raising a child worked particularly well for the couple, especially since they could afford help. Ray traveled a lot with the quartet, but when he was in town he always picked up Akasha from school. John made time, as many nights as possible, to do homework with his son, insisting on the boy achieving at least as much as he had, preferably more. Akasha started piano lessons at the age of four and pleased them enormously with his aptitude.

But it was Akasha's nanny, Mindy, who was the cornerstone of their life. After hiring and firing two others in Akasha's first year, John considered moving his mother up from Richmond, an idea that pleased no one but felt like the only option. Then the quartet's violinist suggested his sister, a middle-aged woman who wanted to emigrate from Uzbekistan.

"Mindy's very bright," the violinist said. "You won't find a more responsible nanny." Here he paused, narrowed his eyes in deliberation, nodded hard and added, "She's had a bit of a bad patch recently. She needs a change."

None of this sounded promising. They told the violinist no. He argued, brought it up at every rehearsal, offered to pay her airfare if they promised employment for a minimum of six months. He began to wear them down, especially after John's mother changed her mind about coming. Semi-relieved, Ray asked for more details about the "bad patch."

"That's not important. Trust me," the violinist said. "Mindy is fierce. She protects what she loves."

Those last two sentences were curiously compelling. Ray and John negotiated down to a promised three-month trial and braced themselves for the Uzbekistani nanny.

Mindy worked out magnificently. She didn't speak a word of English when she arrived, but Akasha instantly adored her. They couldn't stop her from cleaning the house and making vats of borscht, all while singing to and playing with Akasha. Mindy learned English along with her charge, and loved him nearly as much as John and Ray did. Some might have considered her overly involved in the family, but the men were grateful. Her loyalty was prodigious. They didn't worry about keeping secrets from her, and she was the only other person in the world who knew about Akasha's provenance.

So, after the rocky beginning with the bad nannies, all went well for the first years of Akasha's childhood. Then, when he was nine years old, the boy's mother returned to Rawlins. She walked the block with the bus stop bench, stopping in at every storefront to question the clerks. Despite the futility of her search, her hope roared. The diner sat directly behind the bus stop bench. She pulled open the door. The waitress who was wiping tables immediately divulged all she remembered: Ray coming back in to ask about the baby and watching the men load the little bundle into their car. She'd figured they were taking the baby to the police or fire station. They'd hardly looked like kidnappers with their shiny loafers and pressed blue jeans. Even so, she'd written down the car's license plate number, as well as its color and make, and then stuffed the piece of paper into her purse. She never heard a thing on the TV about a lost baby, and no one came looking in the diner, so she'd figured that was that. She didn't try to disguise her judgment as she told the girl who said she was the child's mother that she was a few years late, and that she had no idea if that slip of paper still existed. It did, though, and she knew exactly where she'd tucked it, inside her *Joy of Cooking* at home. She figured she'd make the girl wait, as a test, and if she came back the next day, she'd give it to her.

The mother did return the next day. The rental agency had records, and the mother found someone willing to track down that specific transaction. She showed up in the lobby of Weinraub, Smythe, and Kingsley on a Tuesday afternoon and asked to see John.

John was the only African American member of the firm, and this young woman was also black. The receptionist assumed that she must be a relative of John's and buzzed his office to say that someone was here to see him. John assumed, because of the receptionist's chummy tone, that it was Ray and Akasha. Once in a while they stopped by at this hour, around four o'clock, if they had some good news, like an A+ on a paper or a part in a school performance.

But the young woman who entered his office was a stranger. She was twenty-something, dark-skinned, and very frightened. Even her shoulders were trembling. He saw that she was beautiful with long hands and big eyes and a plum-like mouth.

"Are you John Washington?"

He nodded.

"My name is Francine Wynne."

He thought of buzzing his secretary and asking her to usher the woman out. It was entirely inappropriate that she should show up without an appointment. But something in her demeanor, a fear so raw it ran through his blood, too, caused him to gesture toward the big leather chair across from his desk. She glanced at it and dismissed the seat immediately, as if it were far too grand for her. She remained standing.

"How can I help you?"

When she took a breath, it was as if she inhaled pure courage. Her eyes blazed up and her mouth opened wide, the words more than ready. "I left my baby outside a diner in Rawlins, Wyoming."

He wanted to knock her down. Snap his fingers and make her disappear. Use language that would cut her to the quick. His mind scanned, lightning fast, over his privileges and the options they offered. He thought of calling the police, and then thought better of it. He stood. The words *Anyone who* skidded across his mind, over and over again, but while they usually quieted Ray, they didn't do much for John now.

"It was you, wasn't it?" she said. "You and some white man."

"Where are you from?"

"Cheyenne. I—"

"No." John held up a hand. "No. I'm sorry, I can't help you."

"It's my baby."

He couldn't believe he was having to face this moment without Ray. Overwhelmed, thrown off balance, John made his first mistake. He said, "Okay. Wait. I'll hear you out. But not here. Can you come by our apartment? Tomorrow."

"Tomorrow?" Her face said, *Are you crazy? I just told you I'm the mother of the baby you stole.* "What did you do with him?"

A door, an opportunity. It hadn't occurred to him that she would assume they hadn't kept the baby. Good. They had some time. The enormous relief of this reprieve caused him to make another mistake. Another indirect concession. He opened his wallet, took out a credit card, and handed it to her. "Look," he said. "We can talk. But not now and not here. Find a hotel. We'll talk tomorrow."

"Why not tonight?" she asked, holding the credit card between two fingertips as if it were the tail of a rat.

"We're busy." It was true. Ray had rehearsal.

"This is useless to me," she said, wagging the piece of plastic. "Do I look like John Washington?"

"Just call a hotel. Say I'm your husband. People use other people's credit cards all the time."

He was behaving desperately. Why would he go to these lengths, give her his *credit card*, if he weren't guilty? He saw that realization dawn on her face. She exhaled a long toxic sigh and her whole body loosened with a hope so visceral he felt it radiating from her core, saw it glowing on her skin, filling the room.

"I don't have your baby," he lied dully. "But we can talk."

She set the credit card on his desk. "Keep your card."

"No," he said quickly. Already he was thinking of how Akasha would feel, ten years down the road, if he found out about this encounter. How John had denied his mother, forced her to sleep in the train station, or worse. It wouldn't matter that it was she who had abandoned him. Akasha would blame John. That's how these things worked. So he called the Larchmont, a nice place near their apartment in the Village, and booked her a room for the night. A big one, too, as they were out of anything modest. Then he called the restaurant down the street and gave the maître d' his credit card number and said that Francine Wynne could order whatever she liked.

When he hung up the phone, she asked, "Is he safe? Is he happy?"

John grabbed his overcoat and walked out, leaving Francine standing in his office and his secretary in the dark about what had just happened.

That evening, Akasha had a lot of homework, and they spent two hours doing math and writing a paper on Sojourner Truth. Perhaps the latter's influence, her name alone, affected the outcome of the situation. When Ray came home, they put Akasha to bed and Ray read him a story. Mindy, having overheard John tell Ray they had to talk, and noting the high level of anxiety in his voice, did not go out that evening, nor did she retreat to her room. Instead, she busied herself in the kitchen, well within earshot, while John told Ray what had happened. Shocked at the news, Mindy gave up any pretense of housekeeping and leaned against the doorjamb to listen. Ray looked physically ill. He reached for a pillow and held it against his stomach.

"I've been working it through," John said. "Look. What's she going to do? Let's say she goes to the police. They're going to believe her? Or do anything about it if they do? Even if she managed to use the right channels and got someone to officially challenge our parenthood, who's going to give Akasha back to a woman who left her baby at a bus stop? *Who?* I say we tell her we have Akasha and that we aren't giving him up. We shame her, right here, tomorrow night. Let her scuttle right back to that stanky state of Wyoming."

Ray looked at John with an expression that said he expected more of his partner. To willingly shame someone? No.

"I am Akasha's mother," came a heavily accented voice from the kitchen doorway.

Both men turned to see a red-in-the-face Mindy standing boldly with her hands on her hips. "No one will take him away. I will swear it in a court of law! I have an Ethiopian friend who will say he is the father. I am sure of it. We give him a little money, maybe. But it is done."

Mindy's love of Akasha flowed right into their own. They were moved by her offer. "Come sit with us," John said. She marched into the living room as if they were taking her up on her plan.

"DNA," Ray said. "If this were ever officially challenged, DNA would settle everything in a nanosecond."

"He looks just like her," John said. "No one would need DNA."

"Then we will move," Mindy said with so much feeling her voice was guttural. "California," she suggested. "Or Chicago. Somewhere big."

John looked at Mindy for a long time, taking her proposition seriously. He would do it. He'd give up the firm, the money. He was pretty sure Ray would give up the quartet, too. They'd go into hiding. At least for a few years. Until Akasha was out of college. After all, Francine Wynne was just a girl herself. There was plenty of time for her to know her biological son, but later, when Akasha could decide for himself. Anyway, John and Ray were the boy's parents now. She obviously couldn't begin to give Akasha what they were able to provide. It would be unethical to turn a child over to this woman who . . .

"Tomorrow night," Ray said to Mindy. "Do you have somewhere you can take him?"

"Yes. Oh, yes." She nodded vigorously, a very willing accomplice.

The next day, Ray helped Mindy clear away all traces of Akasha from the apartment. It wasn't enough to shove his baseball bat and books into a closet. What if she came with something like a search warrant? They stuffed the boy's possessions into the car and carried a vase of flowers into Akasha's bedroom, replacing his sea creature curtains with taupe ones. Detail by detail, they transformed the place into a vacant guest room. John picked up Chinese food on his way home from the office. They decided against wine.

Francine Wynne showed up right on time, at seven o'clock. She wore a pale green dress and black pumps, nylons too, as if she were coming for a job interview, though she covered the outfit with a ridiculously bright pink polyester parka. Still, Ray was struck by her beauty. She wore her hair short. Her eyes were keen. Her mouth looked just like Akasha's. Actually, every inch of her looked just like Akasha, including her thin, elegant build.

John braced himself against any possibility of sympathy. He saw her eyes scan the room, tripping on the paintings and pausing on the leather furniture. Assessing, he was sure, how well she could take them to the cleaners.

"Come in," Ray said, waving a hand at the dining room table. "Have a seat."

"I want to see him."

"We don't have him," John said. "He's not here."

"What did you do with him?" Later, much later, both men would remember fondly her expression right then. She embodied the capacity to kill. The ferocity of her love, even in absentia, was like a seed she planted in the heart of their family. It would take years to sprout and bloom, but for now, they clung to their plan of resistance.

Ray waited for John to deliver the lie. It wasn't that John was less truthful than Ray. He certainly wasn't a liar. But he *was* an attorney. He was adept at using language to achieve his own ends. As a musician, Ray stayed closer to the visceral truth in a moment. John had a much greater ability to see gradations and shadings.

But John was strangely silent. And when he did speak, his voice was uncharacteristically tinny. He said, "We turned him over to the police in Rawlins. Of course."

"They have no record of that."

John warmed up a bit. "That doesn't surprise me. Rawlins, after all."

Ray fumbled with the cartons of Chinese food and poured green tea into three white ceramic cups. "Please," he said, gesturing for Francine to sit. "Help yourself." She did, and for a few minutes, they ate in silence. The fork trembled in Francine's hand as she lifted bites to her mouth. She was hungry. The thought of their son's mother being hungry upset John. He tried to put the feeling aside. She'd made her choices. When she took a sip of the green tea, she made a little face. Ray wished they'd bought some Coke or at least made iced tea.

When she finished half her plate, Francine set down her fork and studied John's face. Then she turned her scrutiny onto Ray. He actually squirmed a bit as she seemed to search for a handle on his soul.

She stood up and pushed back her chair. She got her jacket out of the closet and put it on. She took a long last look around at their artwork and colorful walls and plush rugs and cushy couches. She sighed in the exact same way Akasha sighed when he felt defeated. It always made John want to crush his son to his chest and promise him that abandonment was in his past, that there was nothing in his future that wasn't possible. He couldn't help noticing that Francine was young enough to be his daughter. He also couldn't help noting her vulnerability. And resourcefulness. He swallowed back the softening, though. Out of necessity.

Ray stood, too. He said, "Francine, wait."

Every cell in her body seemed to pause. She waited.

Ray said, "Oh, shit."

John said, "I'll make drinks. Do you drink, Francine?"

"No," she said, "But under the circumstances . . ."

They laughed together for the first time. John poured short shots of scotch. It wouldn't do to get loopy.

"Maybe if you were willing to listen," Francine said.

"Of course," Ray said. "Of course we're willing to listen."

They settled on the couches. She touched her lips to the scotch and made the same face she'd made at the green tea. She set the tumbler down and explained. When she was fifteen years old, she got involved with her high school principal. She was doing very well academically and he offered to help. He took her to a special college prep class on Saturdays. Her parents were happy she was getting the extra attention, and since she had a boyfriend, it didn't occur to them that the man was anything but decent with their daughter. And the truth was, he didn't force himself on her. She would have said, if anyone had asked, that she was in love. He wasn't *that* old. He was funny. He was gentle. He taught her about sex. He promised her college. When she got pregnant, she protected him and told her parents that her boyfriend was the father. Francine dropped the boyfriend, and thankfully her parents weren't interested in confronting him about the pregnancy. The principal tried to convince her to get an abortion, but she knew her parents would forbid that, and anyway, she wanted the baby. She was elated, and not surprised—their relationship seemed that real to her—when the principal said they would get married. They would go somewhere far away, maybe Los Angeles. He said he was conducting a nationwide search for a new job. In the meantime, he continued pressing for an abortion. They couldn't get married yet, he argued, and if she had the baby, they would take it away from her. Still she refused, and so he convinced her to run away. It would keep both her and the baby safe, he said. He paid for the room in Laramie and visited on weekends. When the baby was born, he came right away. She was touched because he'd bought a car seat and baby clothes. As they drove down the highway, the baby in her arms, she let herself believe they were going to Los Angeles right then. At five o'clock in the morning, he pulled off the highway and into the town of Rawlins. Francine didn't think to ask what he was doing. Holding and nursing her baby was a kind of bliss she'd never known before. Even *thoughts* were intrusions. He pulled up to the bus stop and said that he was going to set up the new car seat so that they could strap in the baby. He said it wasn't safe for her to hold the infant in her arms. She kissed her baby, snookered his neck, talked to him while the child's father wrestled with the car seat. When she turned and saw him put it on the bus stop bench, she assumed it was for some assembly purpose. When he took the baby from her, she handed him over willingly, wanting him to have every measure of safety. Then, realizing that she was very hungry, she reached for an orange and peeled it. A few moments later, as she was about to turn to check on their progress, the principal threw himself into the driver's seat. His agitation, and the way he accelerated into the quiet Sunday morning, startled her. She asked what he was doing. As he sped onto the freeway, she turned and saw the empty backseat. Her disbelief paralyzed her. She doubted her vision, not him. She begged him to tell her what was happening. He began talking in cool, measured sentences that he'd obviously rehearsed.

"Where is my son?" Francine asked now, her face rigid with calcified sorrow. "Where is he?"

No, was all Ray could think. *No, no, no.*

Anyone who, John chanted silently to himself.

"I've never touched an orange since," Francine said, took a gulp of the scotch, and finished her story. The baby's father drove too fast for her to jump out of the car, although she'd wished a million times that that's what she had done. He told her it was the very best thing for the baby, that no one would let her keep him, that some nice couple would adopt him and that he'd have everything he needed, much more than she could ever give him, including a measure of dignity. He asked her what she thought she — a black teenage girl, those were his words — could ever give a child?

He drove them back to the room in Laramie and stayed with her for twenty-four hours. He held her while she cried. He talked and talked and talked. He wove long stories about the baby's life and how good it would be.

She knew now that he was only protecting himself. It worked. He was still principal at the Cheyenne high school, and she hadn't seen him since, nor had she ever exposed him. She got a job in Laramie and eventually reconciled with her family, telling them that she'd given the baby up for adoption. A smothering shame kept her from ever returning to the bus stop.

"Now I'm ashamed of my shame," she finished quietly. "If I had gone back to Rawlins then, even a week later, maybe I would have found my son sooner."

She knew they had Akasha.

"We love him," Ray said softly.

Her face crumpled and the sobs loosened.

"He's our whole life," John said.

They waited while she cried, and when she could finally lift her face out of her hands, she said, "I don't know what's making me cry harder. Knowing that I'll see him again soon. Or that he's been safe all this while." And she cried some more.

Ray nodded at John, who picked up the phone. Getting Mindy to agree to bring Akasha home was next to impossible. She refused. Ray watched John open and close his eyes as he endured Mindy's storm of words. They were loud enough that he heard some of them. "Never again . . . you don't know women . . . I won't." But John used his most lawyerly voice to tell her that if she didn't show up in half an hour with Akasha, she could consider herself fired.

Francine washed and dried her face. She arranged herself on the couch to look relaxed. She wanted to be as beautiful as possible for her son. While they waited, Ray and John told her the highlights of Akasha's nine years, and she listened with intense concentration.

Thirty minutes later, Mindy unlocked the front door and brought in the boy. She stood pressed behind him with her arm held down across his shoulder and stomach. She glowered at Francine.

Francine didn't lunge at Akasha. Nor did she cry out or claim him in any way. She controlled her demeanor, sitting with her legs crossed, hands in her lap. Only her eyes touched his face. He looked back.

"Come in," John said. "Mindy. Akasha. Sit down."

They did.

"This is Francine Wynne."

Akasha shrugged, and everyone but Mindy laughed.

"She's a new friend of ours."

"Hi." Confused by the emotion thickening the air, Akasha raised a hand and gave a little wave, and then glanced at his dads.

"It's very nice to meet you," Francine said, trying not to frighten the boy with her wonderment.

"Can I use the computer?" Akasha asked.

"Sure," Ray said. "Go on. You're free to go, too, Mindy."

Akasha ran off to John and Ray's room, but Mindy stayed put.

"Actually," John said. "We need to talk to Francine—"

Ray put a hand on John's knee. "Mindy can stay."

John nodded, a feeling of doom ballooning inside him. Everyone, even Mindy, seemed to have more power in this situation than he did.

"I want," Francine whispered, "the very best for my son."

Ray wished he'd heeded John's warnings. Francine's intelligence hadn't been a surprise. After all, she was Akasha's mother. Her ferocity, too, could be expected, from a biological point of view. But the grace in her conduct was downright threatening. Ray cleared his throat, preparing to take control of the situation.

Francine said, "You're going to think I'm bribing you."

Mindy narrowed her eyes.

"You might not believe I want what is best for him." She paused and said, "Akasha," holding the name in her mouth.

"You actually don't have any rights here." John took the offensive. "No court would back you. Ever."

John's attempt to shame her away from Akasha made Ray uneasy. But the tactic was necessary. He nodded hard in agreement.

"Two gay guys?" Francine said, folding her arms. "Huh."

Her threat shocked them for a moment, but then Ray actually smiled. He realized he was glad that she could no longer be shamed. Not only for her, but for Akasha.

But John charged forward. "Two gay guys with good jobs who have given him *everything*. Don't even try—"

"I'm his birth mom."

"Oh, right. Anyone who—"

Ray put a hand on John's arm. "Let's listen."

"I got my GED while waitressing in Laramie. That took me two years. I've been working as an aide in the hospital since then. I want to go to nursing school," she said. "Tuition and an apartment until I'm through. Full visitation rights with Akasha. Once I have my nursing license, nothing more financially. I'm willing to put this all in writing."

"You're *willing*?" John was incredulous.

Mindy made her hissing sound—*Sss, sss*—the one she used to veto words, behaviors, ideas.

"He lives with us," Ray said. "That's not negotiable."

John swung around and looked at him like he was crazy, like he was bargaining with a terrorist.

Francine's tears flowed freely again. "I only had him for a few hours. But I've lived with my son for nine years, too. I love him. I love Akasha."

John said, "But hey, if you can profit off him, all the better, right?"

Mindy stood up as if she were going to drag Francine out of the apartment herself. Ray grabbed her wrist and pulled her back onto the couch.

Francine repeated, "I want him to have the best."

Ray nodded, getting it. "Including the best mother."

John shook his head, refusing to buy in. "You gotta be kidding," he said to his partner. "No. The answer is no."

"Why don't you think about it," Francine said, standing up. "I want to be in my son's life. And not as some girl who made a very big mistake, a high school dropout who cleans toilets for a living. I want to be someone he can be proud of. And I know I can be." She took a deep breath. "I'll be in town through the weekend." She looked at John. "On my own dime. Please keep your credit card in your wallet."

John tried to smirk, but couldn't. Ray tried to think of a way to give her some money, but that would be like trying to put out a burning building by spitting on it.

She was just a girl herself, from Wyoming, of all places, and yet she sounded commanding as she said, "I'd like to say goodnight to him."

Akasha was asleep on John and Ray's bed. He looked exposed and helpless sprawled on the king-size mattress. His hands were loose, open cups. His lips were slightly parted, as if he'd fallen asleep midsentence. Francine took a couple of steps toward him, reached out to touch him, and then changed her mind. She didn't say another word as she gathered her pink parka and let herself out.

Ray and John fought for two days straight. Ray struggled to overcome his fear of losing Akasha and took the position that it would be good for him to have his mother in his life. He wasn't sure he trusted Francine, but he had to admit that her story changed everything. Working with her just seemed smarter than working against her, even though her proposal would cost tens of thousands of dollars and who knew how much in emotional currency. John argued that he'd had no more advantages than she'd had, probably fewer. When he was fifteen, he knew what was at stake when he had sex with someone, and he also knew exactly how hard he would have to work to get himself to where he is today. She'd made her choices a long time ago, and she'd have to live with the consequences.

John didn't think of himself as hardhearted. But he couldn't bear the risk. They didn't know Francine. They didn't know what she'd do if they let her into their lives. Shutting her out, completely, was the only safe option. Akasha sat in the balance.

As the week progressed and they didn't hear from her, both men became uneasy. Ray was curious, and John was suspicious, but they agreed they needed to talk with her. Away from the house and excluding Akasha. She didn't answer the messages they left at the Larchmont. When they stopped by the hotel, they learned that she'd checked out. Francine had left their lives as suddenly as she'd come.

For the next couple of years, they nervously awaited letters from lawyers, or worse, some bureaucratic seizure of Akasha from their home. Both Ray and John felt a twist in their gut when they thought of

Francine. Neither knew if they'd done right or wrong. They didn't even know what their choices had been.

John had the first sighting, three years later, when Akasha was twelve. A winter storm canceled school, and all the neighbor kids were sliding on pieces of cardboard down stairways packed with snow. Akasha smacked his head on the iron railing surrounding the trunk of an elm. His blood soaked the white snow. Mindy raced him to the hospital. Ray was in Baltimore with the quartet, but John left work and got there as they were stitching him up.

Francine sat in the hospital waiting area. At first, John assumed it had to be an uncanny resemblance. But when she raised her eyes and met his, the defiance was unmistakable. Claiming her right to be there for Akasha's medical emergency. John was astonished. He felt leveled, outdone. Like before, his first impulse was to call the police. And say what? That his son's mother was stalking them? Clearly she'd witnessed the accident and made her way to the hospital. Clearly she was watching their family. How often? From where?

John ignored her. And he didn't tell Ray. Maybe that made her bolder, because he saw her again, just a few months later. He arrived late to a school concert in which Akasha was playing the piano. She stood in the very back of the auditorium, holding her coat tight around her body. If she saw him, she pretended she didn't. He didn't tell Ray about that time, either.

Nor did Ray tell John about the times *he'd* sighted Francine walking down their street, then once in their neighborhood grocery. She frightened both men, but like a ghost, she seemed less harmful if unacknowledged. The last time they saw her was at Akasha's high school graduation. Of course they were together this time, but each still pretended he didn't know the woman who looked exactly like their son.

Akasha attended John's alma mater and graduated with honors and a degree in art history. He won a Fulbright to study post–Cultural Revolution Chinese art and went off to Beijing for two years. Ray and John couldn't have been more proud.

In Beijing, Akasha fell in love with another Fulbright scholar, Megan, and when they returned to the States, both got into graduate programs in New England. The fathers thought they married rather young, but they were twenty-five, and anyway, Megan was pregnant.

When their daughter, Zoey, was born, Ray and John went up to stay for a week. That's when Akasha announced his intention to find his biological parents. Both fathers strongly advised against this. When he was twenty-one, they had told Akasha about the bus stop bench, the Cheyenne principal, and a bare minimum about Francine's visit years earlier. They did not mention the stalking. In theory, they believed he should have as much information about his life as possible, but they didn't want him getting hurt. At least that's the excuse they gave themselves.

That night, whispering in bed in Akasha and Megan's guest room, John said that he couldn't stand the idea of the principal experiencing some sort of redemption based on how well Akasha had turned out, that this man might take their son's beautiful character and outstanding accomplishments as proof of his right action. In the morning, over coffee at the kitchen table, he told Akasha that he forbade him from going to Cheyenne. Akasha got up and pulled John's head against his chest, saying, "It's okay, Dad. Everything turned out all right, didn't it?" Megan put a hand on Ray's shoulder and squeezed gently. They were grandparents now, old men who apparently needed comforting. Ray reached for his granddaughter and Megan handed her over. This, he thought, is what an abundance of love will do for you. Such forgiveness. In moments like this, he could practically see the walls behind which he and John had lived.

Akasha didn't call ahead. Megan and Zoey traveled with him to Cheyenne, but they stayed in the motel while he went out to the house, which he'd found easily using an online people-search site. The principal's wife opened the door. Thinking quickly, not wanting to drop a bomb in the middle of their lives, Akasha said that he was a former student. The man who came to the door was balding but robust looking. He came across as the kind of person who thought physical fitness equated moral fitness. He had a readymade public smile, probably from years of being a principal in a smallish town, but it wilted as he recognized Akasha. His mouth puckered. The veins in his neck bulged. Loudly, so that his wife could hear, he said, "Hey, how's it going? Glad you stopped by." And he shut the door in Akasha's face.

Akasha cried when he told the story to his dads on the phone later that night. "I think it's fair to say he had hate in his eyes. *Hate.*"

"That's not hate, son," John said. "That's fear. They can look just the same."

"I almost took Zoey with me. I'm so glad I didn't. It would have been like exposing her to toxic radiation."

"I'm sorry," John said.

"We love you," Ray said. "Megan loves you. And our miraculous granddaughter thinks you make the sun and moon rise."

John and Ray were relieved, in a way, by how the experiment had turned out. Akasha had been hurt, but in a quick, surgical way. The principal had shown his colors immediately. It was over now. He and Megan and Zoey could get on with their lives.

But Akasha wasn't finished. Next he found Francine. She was listed everywhere a person could be listed, including the phone book. She shared lots of information about her life on a couple of social media sites. She lived in Brooklyn and was a nurse at St. Vincent's.

"A nurse? A real one?" Ray asked.

"What other kind is there?"

"An aide or something."

"No, a real nurse."

"She made her choices," John said.

"I want you to be a part of this," Akasha said.

"You don't want to do this," John countered.

"Okay," Ray said.

Akasha, Megan, and Zoey came to New York for the weekend. On Friday night they all had dinner with Mindy, who now lived in her own apartment and clerked for a high-end bath products store. Years ago, John and Ray had set up a retirement account for her, but though she was pushing seventy, she refused to retire. She loved her job. The eastern European accent, coupled with her assertive personality, had helped her win several sales awards. Mindy had intensified rather than mellowed over the years. Megan found the woman frightening.

"Here, here, here!" Mindy barked, clapping her hands with each word, and then thrusting her arms at the baby. Megan instinctively shrank back, clutching Zoey.

Akasha said, "Let go, sweetie," and transferred Zoey from Megan to Mindy. No one else got to hold the baby the rest of that evening.

By prior agreement, they did not tell Mindy about the following night's meeting with Francine. "Just don't," John had told Akasha earlier in the week. "It wouldn't be fair to her."

"Trust us," Ray said. "You'd give her a heart attack."

On Saturday morning, John claimed he had work to do and retreated to the office. Ray shooed Akasha and his family out to the park and obsessively cleaned the already clean apartment. John thought the meeting should be businesslike with nothing more than coffee and cookies. But Akasha bought enough hors d'oeuvres to make dinner for ten and laid them carefully out on the coffee table.

Francine arrived a few minutes early, wearing a pair of nice jeans and a pale yellow cashmere sweater. She had a good winter coat, which Ray took from her. Megan was still in the bedroom nursing Zoey. Akasha did not hug Francine or even extend a hand. He said, "Thank you for coming."

She nodded, tried to speak and couldn't.

Ray ushered everyone into the living room while John got drinks.

Akasha sat blinking, staring.

Francine said, "So. Thank you."

"It's okay?" Akasha asked.

Ray closed his eyes, unable to shut out the picture of Akasha in the car seat, on the bus bench.

John bustled in with glasses of wine and handed them out. He said, "Okay, so let's start with why you never followed through seventeen years ago."

"Dad."

"This is awkward, son. We may as well do facts first."

"He's a lawyer," Akasha said to Francine.

She smiled and said, "I know."

Ray dredged his mind for something softer to say, for a way to steer them onto an easier path of getting to know one another.

"He's right, though," Francine said. "I'd welcome the opportunity to explain a few things. It's a good place to start."

"Shoot," John said.

"Dad," Akasha said. "Lighten up."

"So John and Ray told you I found you when you were nine?"

Akasha nodded.

"I was . . . I guess desperate *is* the right word . . . to be in your life. And to make whatever amends I could make. I wanted to be your mother. On the spot, right here in this living room, I came up with an idea. I'd finish my education here in the city. I'd get a chance to be in your life. I asked them to pay for this."

Akasha looked at Ray and then John. "You didn't tell me this. You left stuff out." The anger in his voice pissed John off. He stood up.

Francine ignored John and spoke directly to Akasha. "Of course, it sounded entirely self-interested. Like I was using them. The more I thought about it, the more I realized that they would never believe that my motives were anything other than selfish. And they *were* selfish. I wanted you."

Francine took a sip of her wine. "I might have been able to get past worrying about their misunderstanding me. But after that evening, seeing everything you had, especially all the love you had, I realized that the selfish part would be my intruding in your life. You were safe. And happy. You are so loved. I realized I would be an obligation. Or worse, an anchor."

Ray reached for John's hand and pulled him back onto the couch.

"But," Akasha said, already visibly awed by his mother. "You moved to New York and got your nursing degree, anyway."

She nodded. "I wanted to be available. Completely available. For this moment." Her face spasmed. She regained control and said, "I have a nice apartment. I live alone, but I've been seeing Sterling for nine years. He's a community college teacher. Life is, for the most part, good."

Zoey, still in the bedroom with Megan, shrieked.

"You're a grandmother," Akasha said.

Francine nodded, and both Ray and John wondered if her stalking had reached all the way up into New England these past years.

Akasha stood to go get Megan and Zoey, and that's when the key turned in the front door lock.

"Oh, shit," John said. "Mindy. How many times have I asked you to get the key back from her?"

"Right. You try."

"She still has a key?" Akasha asked.

Ray shrugged. "She likes to do stuff like drop off cakes on our birthdays."

Mindy shut the door behind her, threw the deadbolt, and unwrapped her scarf. "So! Good evening, everyone!" she said with too much bluster.

Francine got up and gave Mindy a hug.

John leapt back to his feet.

Ray closed his eyes and shook his head.

Francine escorted the older woman to the couch and helped her sit.

"What's going on?" Akasha asked.

"*You*—?" John glanced around himself as if looking for an object to hurl at Mindy.

Ray sat back and laughed out loud. Already he looked forward to hearing how this alliance came about.

"She once lost a baby, too," Francine said. "Before she came to this country."

Mindy made her shushing sound. "*Sss. Sss.*"

"Okay," Francine said, taking Mindy's hand. "Another story for another time."

"You had a baby?" Akasha said.

"*Sss. Sss.*"

Megan came shyly into the living room holding Zoey, who gurgled and then shrieked again. Akasha's face lit up with his beautiful smile, and everyone looked at him looking at Zoey.

John remained standing, swaying a bit with the weightlessness of shock. Mindy's betrayal undermined everything, including his own curdling lies. "How dare you—" he breathed into the room, but everyone ignored him. He stepped around the coffee table and reached for the baby, prying her away from Megan. Finally, John had everyone's attention.

"Anyone who—" he said for the thousandth time.

"Loved Akasha that much?" Ray asked.

The words sluiced away John's indignation. He stood in the middle of the room, a man holding his granddaughter, nothing more, nothing less. His lies on Akasha's behalf hadn't been half as potent as Francine's patience or Mindy's arbitration.

John carried the infant to Francine and gently handed her over. He'd never seen arms so full.

The Antarctic

The fight left both sisters drained, sad, and confused about the future of their relationship. Each realized in its wake that for half a century they'd been each other's bedrock, the assumption upon which their lives rested. Together they'd navigated girlhood in their small northern Illinois town, found and lost adulthood loves, managed their mother's Alzheimer's, their father's stroke, and now they lived together, along with the menagerie of three dogs, eight cats, four birds, and whatever other beasts needed shelter at the moment. The animals were technically Regina's province, and Janet had a small wing of her own in the back of the house, with a bathroom and its own entrance, where she could and did take refuge, but practically speaking, she shared responsibility for the animals. After all, Regina had taken her in, too.

As children they'd had squabbles, as all siblings do, and of course there were irritations as adults. Regina's tendency to deny and control, for example, could irk Janet, and Janet's recent inclination toward impulsiveness, random behaviors that had no purpose, rankled her sister. But the deep truth of the matter was that they loved, and even liked, one another. The living situation was companionable and surprisingly easy. The fight seemed to erupt out of the blue.

It had been eleven years since the truck had hit and killed Janet's husband, and she realized with a start one morning that not only did she no longer feel any grief—to be truthful, she hadn't in about ten years—she was getting bored. She'd turned fifty this year, and for so long the loss of her husband had been the defining moment of her life, the primary lens through which she saw herself. Others, too, viewed her through Doug's death. A tragedy. If she never heard that word again, she wouldn't mind. He left her with an unexpectedly large financial debt, a tangle of feelings, including, yes, grief, but also a shameful sense of liberation. Rebuilding her life—an expression she also wouldn't mind losing—had consumed this decade. She'd learned about managing finances, developed a robust roster of clients who used her science writing skills, and made new friends, primarily online since their town rarely offered anything new on that front. She was considering joining a gym.

Regina, for her part, had bucked up under the responsibility of sheltering her sister. She'd lived alone since the end of a brief, early marriage, and in any case, she wouldn't have considered saying no. She viewed it not too differently from how she viewed taking in injured and otherwise unwanted animals. Someone had to do it.

As it turned out, the arrangement proved more than satisfactory. Practically speaking, it was nice to share the household chores, and since Janet worked from home, she was available to care for the animals during the day. Regina became especially glad for her sister's companionship, a human voice amid the cawing and barking and mewling, when seven months ago Maury left the clinic and her at the same time. They had been coworkers for fifteen years, and lovers for twelve.

Regina sometimes lay awake in the earliest hours of the morning, thinking about Maury, his fresh pink cheeks, his sandy curls, his long, pale limbs. His haunted eyes. Of late she'd spent as much time in these darkest moments thinking about her sister. Her impulsiveness had become more pronounced. Demanding might be too strong a word, but she expressed her views more forcefully and seemingly without forethought. She brought exotic fruits home from the grocery store and went to movies in the afternoon. She'd begun talking to strangers in public, about nothing whatsoever, like whether or not they used the clumping kind of cat litter, which the sisters absolutely did not in their household, and for good reason, so why would Janet discuss it with a stranger, other than a desire to engage that person in conversation about anything? In the stillest part of the night, Regina feared that Janet might move out.

Then, in November of last year, when the sky was flat and gray, and only a few red apples hung hard and near-frozen from the tree in their backyard, they had the fight.

"I've had the most disturbing thought," Janet said at the breakfast table. It was their custom to eat a boiled egg each, and with that Regina had toast with butter and jam, while Janet had a bowl of Raisin Bran. They did not usually speak at this hour, other than an exchange of information necessary to the day. So Regina simply ignored Janet's mention of a disturbing thought. Certainly it could wait for the evening.

Janet continued anyway. "It occurred to me that I could see the end of my life. A straight shot through, like looking out a window and there, a short distance ahead, was The End. Capital T and capital E."

Regina put down her half piece of toast and took a sip of coffee, regretting that it was still too hot to drink quickly. She could carry the cup into her bedroom, but she wanted to finish the toast. And anyway, she tried always to choose kindness, so she said, "I find that image comforting, not disturbing."

"I was sure you'd say that. But I don't. The idea that there won't be a single surprise from here to the end . . . Oh!" she wailed, causing Regina to set down her coffee cup and pay closer attention.

"Well, what *is* it?" she asked.

"The idea. That this is it. You and me—and you know I love you, Regina—but this routine life of ours. Breakfast, work, dinner, bed. Endlessly, unchangingly, for another, say twenty or thirty years. I can't *bear* it."

Regina thought that a person who'd lost her husband to a drunk running a red light would have more sense than to think there were no surprises in life. In fact, Regina had thought that she was doing her sister a favor by providing constancy, that very "routine life of ours," to assuage the trauma Janet had suffered eleven years ago. She knew that Janet was grateful, but there was something irritating about her dissatisfaction. After all, there were so many in need. Maybe, Regina thought, she *would* bring home that cockatoo someone had left on the clinic porch. Janet would enjoy him.

Janet watched her sister's face, and with growing consternation saw that she was not getting through to her. Of course Regina enjoyed the certainty, the solid footing. She probably thought of her own death with satisfaction, the same way one might think of one's bed at four in the afternoon, savoring the thought of getting into it at the day's end. More,

Janet could just hear Regina saying in the not too distant future that she'd had quite enough of this adventure called life, thank you very much, and turning off her own light. Yes, suicide. After all, she'd euthanized any number of animals in her practice, and Regina was zealous in her belief that there is no distinction between humans and the rest of the animal kingdom. "We are animals," she liked to remind people, annoyed at the human race's incessant need to think of ourselves as higher.

It was aggravating. She used this insistence on being an animal to keep distance between herself and other people. To keep herself cloistered here at home with the beasts.

"The mail carrier accidentally delivered the McAllisters' mail to us yesterday," Janet carried on, and Regina was glad that she'd changed the subject. "There was a brochure for a voyage to Antarctica."

Maybe Janet just needed to chat more. Since Maury had left, Regina knew she'd sunk into a silent melancholy, taken advantage of her sister's comfortable presence. Maybe she'd been selfish, blind to Janet's need for a bit more interaction. And yet, Regina drew the line at early morning conversation. She poured out the rest of her coffee and rinsed the cup, shoved her uneaten toast down the disposal.

"I think we should go," Janet said.

Regina pretended she hadn't heard and picked up her keys.

"Regina!" Janet nearly shouted. "You don't need to leave for work for another fifteen minutes. I insist you talk to me about this."

Regina turned slowly, a hot flash rising on the word "insist."

"You work too hard," Janet said. "You never take a break, have any fun."

"Paying good money to be locked up with a bunch of strangers and heaved about on the open sea is my idea of hell."

"Imagine seeing real penguins and seals!"

"Imagine crossing the Drake Passage at our age."

"I'm fifty and you're fifty-two," Janet said in a low and slow voice. "We're not dead."

"Go!" Regina said. "Go! Leave me here in peace. I would *love* a bit of time to myself."

"You've become a drudge, Regina. No one will want to be around you. You only know how to relate to animals."

"And animals are all I *want* to relate to."

"Well, that's obvious. You've nearly lost touch with the English language altogether. You grunt and, perhaps if you're happy, which you haven't been in months, chirp a bit. You're becoming downright misanthropic."

"And you're becoming one of those silly women who will talk to *anyone* about anything at all, even when you have nothing to say, as if the sound of your own voice is all that keeps you alive. You look desperate, Janet. To a plain *stranger* you look desperate."

"Well, at least I'm honest in my appearance then, because I *feel* desperate. You live this subterranean life, refusing human comforts, pretending that all you need are the beasts. You're *becoming* a beast."

"Don't be stupid. I've been a beast since the day I was born, as have you. If you think there is any difference, any difference at all, between you and the rest of the animals on Earth, then—"

"Oh, for crying out loud. *This* again. Yes, yes, *yes*. I know. Ninety-eight percent and the chimps. Oh, yes, and seventy percent with the mice. I *know*, Regina. But truly, I don't care how much my DNA resembles a hippopotamus's, I'm not going to wallow in mud."

The words were harsh enough, and the tones of their voices even more severe, but the feeling that they had hit rock bottom, each on her own and in their relationship to one another, was palpable. They had reached cold places, separately and together, from which they could not return.

Regina left for the clinic, knowing now for sure that her sister would be making plans to move out. She felt heartsick.

Janet too felt devastated, and yet, after a short walk with the dogs, she found within her thicket of upset a tiny heart of excitement in the frisson of it all. Something had broken, and speaking strictly from a physics perspective, that meant energy had been released. Janet used it, after putting the dogs back in the fenced yard, to call Orca Expeditions. She gave the nice lady on the phone her credit card information to reserve two places in an upgraded cabin. For the first time since Doug's death, she had a bit of extra money, and she saw no reason to hoard it away in a bank account. Especially when she glimpsed out that window to the wall she knew to be the end of her life.

When Regina came home that evening, Janet said nothing about having booked the trip. To her immense surprise, Regina brought it up herself, saying that okay, she would go. Janet knew that this was an apology for her hard words this morning, but still, it was a whopping big apology. Janet still said nothing about having booked the trip already, and didn't apologize for her own hard words, although she wished she knew how to. Both sisters pretended nothing had happened.

When, two weeks later, the thick packet of vouchers from Orca Expeditions arrived, Janet simply left it out on the kitchen table. Another two weeks passed before either sister mentioned the trip again, and when Regina did, it was to suggest they shop for parkas and long underwear. Janet told herself that Regina was secretly excited about the trip.

The night before their flight to Ushuaia, the town on the southern-most tip of Argentina, a spit away from the deathtrap called Cape Horn, Regina worked late. She checked in on every single boarder at the clinic and reviewed all her patients' files, double-checking that she'd made every necessary arrangement for her two-week absence. They hadn't yet replaced Maury, but George and Cecelia were more than happy to cover for her. Regina had always been the one most willing to come in on weekends, or in the middle of the night, when there were emergencies, and she never complained about covering for her colleagues when they went on vacations with their families. Their enthusiasm to reciprocate made Regina a little uneasy, an echo of Janet's acid assessment of her life.

None of them—not George nor Cecelia, and certainly not Janet—knew about Maury, that she had in fact experienced an enormous and reciprocal love for these many years, limited in practical terms as it was. She didn't like them feeling sorry for her. She *hated* them feeling sorry for her. But she was deeply grateful that she and Maury had never hurt anyone else. With their impeccable secrecy, they had managed that much.

Dreading the trip, Regina stayed at the clinic for as long as she could that night. Agreeing to Antarctica was the only way she could think of to make amends to Janet for her mean words. She might not have even minded enduring the miserable trip if she thought it would make Janet happy, but of course it wouldn't. How could it? It would only last for two weeks, and then they would return to their lives, which Janet ap-parently now found intolerable. The trip would only forestall more dramatic changes.

After leaving the clinic, Regina drove by Maury's house. She hadn't done this in over a year, not once since he'd ended it. She had only ever done it a handful of times. Now she parked in the dark across the street, thinking that she had nothing to lose. Maury had made a clean break, and now she was going to Antarctica. She had a right to view this part of her life, from the outside, one last time.

Maury lived with his wife and remaining child—the other two were in college—in this pleasant ranch-style house. Tonight the windows were buttery with light, only darkened now and then by a passing figure. She couldn't tell if it was Maury, his wife Susan, or their sixteen-year-old Thomas moving about the house. She sat there in her car until someone turned off the downstairs lights, and then the upstairs ones, all but one bedroom. That, she suspected, would be the boy's. Even though it seemed too early for Maury and Susan to be going to bed.

Regina started the engine of her car and drove home. When she came in the front door unwrapping her scarf, Janet—still cautious in her triumph about this impending trip—said, "I thought you'd gone AWOL."

"I'm worried about the animals," Regina said and dodged a particularly penetrating look from her sister by rushing to her bedroom. She had a hard, silent cry and then lay awake most of the night.

Two days later, Janet knelt in front of the toilet heaving up her last two meals while Regina held her head. The bent-over position hurt Regina's back, and she was angry because she had known all along that this voyage would be hell. And here, not five hours out, it was indeed.

More heaving and moaning from Janet.

Unfortunately, there is no possibility of bailing when you're on a ship. They were onboard for the duration. Regina missed the beasts already.

Janet raised her head and sat back on her heels. She wiped her mouth with the back of her hand. "Perhaps," she said, "that'll be the end of it."

Regina sincerely doubted it. She helped Janet move onto the bunk, where she whimpered and closed her eyes. Regina patted her knee. It was all she could do to not state the obvious, out loud, that this trip was a mistake.

"Go look at the sea." Janet spoke as if her mouth was full of marbles.

To keep herself from saying something irretrievable, she took her sister's suggestion, suited up, and made her way through the labyrinth of close corridors and stairwells, until she managed to emerge onto one of the decks. A cold spitting rain struck her face, and she welcomed it. The only other passengers hale enough, and stupid enough, to be on deck were two women, perhaps also sisters as they looked alike with their dark hair and rosy mouths, walking brisk laps. They laughed their hellos each time they passed Regina, as if this voyage was a hilarious joke. It was a more sensible response, Regina supposed, than any other one, short of staying home. If Janet was so intent on noting the difference between humans and other beasts, then this was one perhaps Regina should mention to her: our ridiculous pursuits. Rockets to the moon. Treks, strapped to oxygen tanks, to summits towering above our atmosphere. Voyages in steel tanks across the roughest stretch of sea, this passage named after Sir Francis Drake. Regina was in the business of comfort. She reduced pain, healed illness, and yes, ended lives when they became unbearable. Only humans, so far as she knew, engaged in behaviors that *increased* pain and called it fun.

She stopped and looked over the edge of the railing. The water was cold and turbulent, tossing them about, and gunmetal gray. She hoped the neighbor girl was as responsible as her references said she was. She'd only ever left the beasts for three or four days at a time, never for two weeks. They would be sick with worry, and the neighbor girl didn't know their habits. Regina had given her a twelve-page set of instructions, well in advance of their leaving, so that the girl could study it, and when she questioned her the day before their departure, she did seem to have grasped most of the content. Still, it was imperative that Willa have her own water bowl, in the downstairs bathroom, and that it was filled daily, and preferably twice daily. That Dendur be watched carefully for any weakness in his back legs. That Sugar be groomed regularly because he's too old to do it himself anymore. That the birds' cages were covered *at dusk*, not before and not after. That Florence—well, the list goes on. They were certainly paying the girl well enough. Regina had assumed a place to live for two weeks was recompense enough, but Janet looked into it, and apparently it's customary to pay house sitters. The girl actually argued for a particularly high rate because of the beasts' special needs.

Regina sighed, wishing she were a bit nicer of a person. At least she tried to be scrupulously honest, Maury notwithstanding, even when she was the only one who knew the difference. So a couple of hours later, when the seas suddenly calmed and her sister recovered from seasickness, she admitted to herself the ugly truth that she might prefer Janet remaining bedridden for the duration of this voyage.

Janet lifted her head and declared, "It's calmed, hasn't it!" Before Regina could answer, Janet was up brushing her teeth and dressing for dinner. Regina thought she might skip the meal, but Janet insisted, and so they went to the dining room and found two places at an empty table. She was relieved that no one joined them.

"Who's that silver fox?" Janet asked.

Regina breathed deeply and removed her reading glasses. She'd brought the information packet from the cabin to read at dinner, and now put the tip of her index finger on her place in the text. She followed Janet's far too obvious gaze to see an utter stereotype of a cruise gentleman sitting at a table much too close to theirs. He actually nodded slowly, raising two fingers to his brow in what Regina assumed was an attempt at a suave greeting. She felt stabbed by an ache of missing Maury, his fresh genuineness.

"I think he's looking at you," Janet said.

Had Regina answered at all, she would have said *oh, shut up.* Their first night at sea, and her vow of patience had stretched to gossamer strands. A hot flash washed the back of her neck and dripped between her breasts. She forced herself to return to reading the information packet, although she couldn't concentrate after her sister had used that ridiculous term "silver fox." If she closed the reading material, it would signal an openness to conversation, which would be erroneous, and so she kept her glazed eyes on the page until a plate of food arrived.

"Handsome," Janet said. She was still looking at the man.

"He's eighty if he's a day," Regina commented.

"Not yet sixty-five," Janet returned.

"And you're fifty."

"It's you he's looking at."

Regina lowered her glasses and examined her sister's face for signs of impending dementia. For someone who spent her life reporting on scientific fact, she sure could summon some doozy fantasies. Janet carved up her chicken breast and forked it into her mouth as if she hadn't been vomiting into the head, as they call the toilet on a ship, just hours ago. Regina pushed her chicken—dry as an old rag—away and signaled for the waiter. She asked for a glass of wine. And didn't Janet grin at that. She thought Regina was loosening up. Her mission, apparently. No, Regina was simply anesthetizing herself.

She noticed the two dark-haired, rosy-mouthed sisters sitting with two other women. Who wouldn't notice them? They were howling with laughter. Two empty wine bottles already littered their tabletop. The four women were probably in their thirties. One had prematurely gray hair, cut short, and bright blue eyes. The fourth in their group was thin and mousy, with straggly hair and a pinched nose, and every time the laughter erupted she looked shocked for a moment and then, as if she got the joke a bit late, joined in. When she laughed, her face became merry like a pixie. Regina had an inexplicable urge to tell that table of women about Maury.

The seas were rough again the next day, and Janet passed a few hours, after throwing up her large breakfast, lying in her bunk. But like the day before, she was fine by dinnertime. Downright festive, in fact. She put on a new pair of jeans and an also new royal blue silk shirt. The silver fox sat down at their table, right next to Regina and across from Janet.

"What's brought you two ladies to the ice continent," he asked, apparently thinking himself witty.

Janet didn't even begin with niceties. She launched, "I woke up one morning and realized I could see the end of my life. Barring unforeseen circumstances, I pretty much know what will happen between here and there."

Regina interrupted to say, "The words 'barring unforeseen circumstances' negate your whole point, Janet."

The silver fox grinned at Regina as if *she'd* been witty.

Janet barely gave her sister a glance and continued. "The thought was *horrifying* to me. I told this to the checker at our grocery store, and she gave me this *look*. Like a cross between pity and disapproval. Because, you see, my husband was killed by a drunk driver eleven years ago. Of course I know perfectly well that I haven't a clue what's around the next corner. *No* one knows that better than me, because of what happened to Doug, and yet I couldn't shake the feeling. Then, I thought, why should I shake it? Or, maybe it was more that I *should* shake it, as in, shake up my life. So I booked the trip for me and my sister Regina. I'm Janet, by the way."

Regina shook the silver fox's hand—he said his name but she didn't listen—and looked for the four women. There they were. Laughing again, although more quietly this evening. Regina wondered what their occasion was. Certainly none of them thought she could see the end of her life.

When Clayton invited the sisters for an after-dinner drink, Janet readily agreed. She could tell that he was more interested in Regina, and she tried to subtly cajole her sister into coming along. One of Regina's charms was that she remained entirely unaware that she held sway with some men. Not most men, but Janet had seen it a few times, the exceptional man who found the force of Regina's personality, alongside her stark kind of beauty, irresistible. She projected both autonomy and sorrow, setting up a lovely dissonance, her own energy field. Janet liked men who were drawn to her sister; it was a sign of intelligence, of complexity.

Though the sisters actually looked a lot alike, Janet did not have the same effect on men. It was probably true that she attracted *more* men — though we're not talking big numbers here — but she felt they were an inferior sort. She always felt plain and flat next to Regina. Her sister's hair looked passion blown while hers merely messy. Regina inhabited her extra fifteen pounds, as if she needed them to house her love for the beasts, while Janet just felt fat. And yes, as Regina had pointed out, Janet came off as slightly desperate.

So be it. Off she went to the bar with Clayton, while Regina opted for yet another walk on the deck. Clayton wasn't bad looking. His silver hair was plentiful and coifed. His face a little too red. He had a generous smile and wide eyes, grayish-green. His blocky build had the appearance of conscientious maintenance. There was a gold chain, but if — and she was embarrassed to have this thought even privately — things ever developed, she could certainly find a way to get him to lose the jewelry. In any case, Janet was delighted to sit at one of the small round tables with him and order a white Russian. Clayton had scotch. He told pleasantly boring stories about his life, and Janet enjoyed herself immensely.

Regina walked around and around the upper deck, breathing the cold, wet salt. She liked the silvery light. She liked how the vast sky floated atop the vast sea, the clean line of the horizon, its burnished shimmer. She cast her thoughts farther and farther out, the expanse a balm.

On her eighth lap, she saw, off the bow, perhaps a hundred and fifty yards away, a disturbance in the sea. A froth. No, a spray. Yes, it was a spray! She'd never seen whales before. Regina gripped the railing and strained her eyes, and there it was again, a seawater fountain spouting high into the silver sky. Two! Regina caught a glimpse of both shiny black hides, mounding out of the water, side by side, and then rolling back into the immense sea of tears.

She longed to tell Maury. She tried to imagine what he was doing at that very moment, but she couldn't remember the complicated time difference between northern Illinois and the Antarctic, nor did she know what his life looked like now. Maybe his eyes were no longer haunted. He had suffered so much. No one believes affairs like theirs can happen innocently, but they can and do. And once love happens, how can anyone turn their back? Who on Earth can give up the one thing worth living for?

Yet she admired him for leaving. Love can be a gigantic paradox. No use thinking there is something to understand. Other than people do what they have to do. He loved his wife. He'd never stopped loving her. Their three children had been four, six, and seven when the affair began. Regina never ever expected him to leave his family. Slowly, over the years, what he lost was himself, and once that happened, there was no one there to love anyone else. He'd become a ghost of guilt.

Maury must have been applying for other positions for some time. He'd figured out, and rightly, that changing clinics would be the only way to make a clean break. He had a much longer commute to work now, and she wondered how he had explained the change to Susan.

When the four rowdy young women approached, Regina tried to point out the whales. But they must have dived deep and swum away, because they were no longer visible. The women introduced themselves. They'd met and traveled together, over a decade ago, during a college year in Spain. The two dark-haired ones were indeed sisters, in fact, twins. By sheer coincidence, all four friends had experienced devastating break-ups last year. The twins came up with the idea of taking a trip together.

"Well, me, too," Regina said. "Although I can't say that's why I'm on this trip."

"Details," Pixie said.

"His name was Maury and he was married." A couple of "Ahs" and two of them pointed at the short-haired, blue-eyed one, apparently part of her story, too.

"Don't mention this in front of my sister," Regina said. "She never knew about Maury."

Janet didn't return to the cabin until after ten o'clock, and while she could tell that Regina wasn't interested in hearing about her evening, she was compelled to share the details anyway. She said Clayton owned a picture-framing business and had been married twice. He never planned to marry again, he'd been clear about that, and Janet laughed merrily. "The *idea*," she crowed, "that he thought he had to warn me!"

"He looks like an aging Ken doll."

Janet looked shocked that Regina had spoken so meanly. But not as shocked as Regina was herself. "Oh, god, I'm sorry. I don't know what's wrong with me." She knew exactly what was wrong with her. She closed her eyes. She had to let Janet go. She had to bear her grief alone. Everyone does.

Janet thought Regina was jealous. This made her angry. After all, Clayton could have happened to Regina. Janet had tried to step aside. But her sister preferred taking bracing walks alone, sucking in the frigid air. That was her choice. And this was Janet's. She wanted this. Whatever it was. She said, "You have nerve judging me. I know about Maury."

Regina could barely contain her welling sorrow. It washed right over her surprise at Janet's knowing. She felt as if she were drowning.

"At least Clayton's available," Janet said quietly. "At least I'm not lying to anyone."

Regina nodded again and held her sister's hot gaze. "I'm sorry," she managed to say and then stood. Of course Janet had known. There are no secrets; our lives are as plain as biology. She longed to fill her lungs with that cold salt air. She left Janet in the cabin.

At the end of the following day, they glimpsed the continent for the first time. The entire group of passengers stood shivering at the bow, their eyes straining for the ice-crusted landmass. Regina stayed on deck half the night as they chugged south, that wall of ice getting closer and closer. Around midnight, they came upon their first iceberg, soon followed by many others, and Regina went to get Janet, thinking she really should see this. She wasn't in the cabin, so Regina checked the bar, and found that room dark and empty. A mirror ball swayed with the motion of the ship, glinting.

Janet felt no fear or even ambivalence. Going with Clayton to his cabin, after checking to make sure his cabin mate was on deck with the rest of the passengers, felt straightforward and beautifully simple. She did wonder how she might justify the liaison to her sister. She was a beast, she'd tell Regina, a hundred percent animal. The thought made Janet laugh, which made Clayton laugh, and then they were both holding their stomachs in a giant release of mirth. A man who saw the humor in sex! And she hadn't even shared her beastly thoughts out loud. She liked Clayton very much. In any case, by the time her shirt was off, Janet didn't care one whit what her sister would think. Clayton was tender and kind, his eyes expressing the same gratitude she felt. She didn't think she'd ever love him, but oh she loved this moment. The next one, too, and then the one after that. The ship rocked the small cabin, her insides going liquid like the sea, Clayton's hands fearless.

The next morning, Regina got up and left the cabin very early, not wanting to be there when Janet returned. They were scheduled to make their first landfall today and the zodiacs were leaving at eight. Regina planned to stay onboard, but she wanted to watch the launch. At breakfast, the four women who were celebrating their breakups invited her to join their boat, and Regina surprised herself by saying yes.

A few minutes later, she bumped along in the front spot of the zodiac, the rubber bow riding high on the crests of sea chop and slamming down in the troughs, jarring her bones. Pixie looked as frightened as Regina felt, and the bright blue-eyed woman looked simply startled, but the twins were hollering with laughter once again. Sisters can make you feel brave, Regina thought. She swallowed hard and willed this day over soon.

The young blond-bearded guide at the helm of the zodiac searched the sea ahead, a scowl squeezing his brow. He eased the motor down to a quiet purr and shouted, "Don't think we're going to make it!"

Regina's heart plummeted to the pit of her stomach. Death by a quick lethal injection was one thing. Dog-paddling in the Southern Ocean until one lost strength, or simply got too cold and sunk, was quite another. Even the twins sobered up.

Then the young man shut off the motor altogether. "It's just too choppy to go ashore," he said, and Regina realized that that was all he had meant about not making it. "We'll try again later today. But it looks like we have a pretty nice consolation prize for you." He nodded to a spot in the sea beyond Regina's head. She didn't bother turning. Her neck hurt. But everyone else strained to see, the twins actually standing in the boat until the guide told them to sit.

Then the pixie gasped. Instinct took over, and Regina pivoted on the hard bench to look at the rough sea. Not thirty yards away, the glistening black tail of a humpback whale sunk into the water, a spray flying off the tips. Then, not much farther out, another gleaming black hide, studded with barnacles, arched out of the water. And another and yet another. They were surrounded by humpback whales. One swam right for their small rubber boat, its back barely breaking the surface of the water. When it was merely feet away, it raised its massive head and looked at her. Looked at Regina. Yes, the humpback whale made eye contact and held her gaze. Cool and easy. Curious.

The whale dove right under the zodiac, without disturbing the boat's stability, and was gone, leaving Regina with an overwhelming feeling of peace.

The sisters found each other in the dining room at lunch and sat at a table by themselves. They didn't need to say a word. Janet was phosphorescent and Regina was a deep blue-green.

My Beautiful Awakening

Jurek looks mean. Sinewy and red faced. Squinty eyed, as if he's perennially suspicious. That scraggly blond ponytail. I can only imagine that Dong Mei wanted to flee from the first moment she laid eyes on him.

But then neither of their looks were a secret. She would have seen his picture on the website, just as he'd seen hers. I have no idea how the process works or the deals are made, but I do know she accepted his offer, including the paid plane tickets for not only herself but her two sons.

Jurek bought Dong Mei. That part is not debatable.

But nothing else about our story is simple. I knew Jurek first by the sound of his labor, long before meeting him, and this permanently colored my impression of the man.

I moved to central Alaska in September and for the first few days I was overwhelmed by the extremity of what I'd done. I'd traded in my urban life, full of friends and amenities, for a one-room cabin a mile outside a small town in the arctic. During the first week, as I unpacked kitchen utensils, cleaned windows, and looked for a job, any job, I felt like the world's biggest fool. I was a thorough and unadulterated cliché. Middle-aged and heartbroken, I thought I could find solace in the coldest, darkest, most remote place I could get to. Some friend of a friend had a teaching gig for the academic year in New York and I had thought the coincidence—his need for a cabin-sitter and my need for retreat— breathtakingly serendipitous. When in fact it was a random coincidence that would undoubtedly plunge me into a despair from which I would never return.

That's the state toward which I was hurtling when I first noticed Jurek. After a few days of constant activity, I finally sat outside, on the porch of my cabin, and looked around. The surrounding birch trees were an inferno of gold, and the sky a contrasting harsh blue. Late autumn roared in my ears. I was afraid to breathe, as if the air would scour my lungs.

I had moved as far away from Lindsay as I could get and even so, I found myself looking down the dirt road leading to my cabin as if she might come walking toward me with her long limbs and toothy grin. Over and over again, I imagined the whole scenario, how she would learn my whereabouts from a mutual friend, how she'd buy a plane ticket, how she'd find me. It was a childish fantasy, unbecoming to a woman of my age. But then the entire love affair had been a shock, and for all the reasons it couldn't continue, my one vow to myself was that I'd hold onto that wild astonishment of love. I would let her go, but not the tenderness she'd inspired.

Sitting on my porch that afternoon, I realized that I'd heard the sound of chopping wood ever since I arrived. It had been incessant, beginning early in the mornings and going late into the nights. It was the sound of impending winter—*whoosh, thunk, zip*—and seemed to be in cahoots with the molting leaves and frigid sky.

I have always been deathly afraid of chopping wood. The way you have to swing the axe over your head and bring it flying, with force, in a great arc back toward your own body. The only way to prevent hacking yourself in half is to accurately hit the chunk of wood on the chopping block. I can't imagine possessing that kind of confidence in precision.

The longer I listened, the more Jurek's wood chopping became a kind of mantra. *Whoosh, thunk, zip.* It was a sound of danger, but also of potential warmth. It began to resonate with my sorrow, touch me too intimately. Before long, I'd eroticized that axe swinging and wood splitting. The danger, rhythm, and comfort.

When he arrived with the first offering of firewood, I felt as if I had willed him. I worried that he saw my attraction to his labor. His ugliness intrigued me.

"Welcome, neighbor," he said without a smile. "What brings you?"

The directness of his question threw me off. But I saw his point. You didn't just happen to get to a small town in central Alaska, say, because your company transferred you. You decide. You have a reason.

"Broken heart," I said.

He nodded and stepped across my threshold uninvited. I put on water for coffee and watched him inspect my things. He continued nodding as he did, as if he were gathering information, making an inventory. Then he sat in my one chair, a wooden rocker, and said, "I'll bring you a full supply of firewood later. I'm clearing my land for a cabin, so I have a surplus."

"Thank you. That's very kind." I was relieved to have my fuel problem solved, but also already worried about payback.

"I heard the guy is just renting his cabin."

"He has a teaching gig in New York. I have the cabin until June."

"Winter."

"Yes."

"You like darkness."

Not particularly, I thought, but only shrugged.

"And then?"

He asked too many questions, but this landscape didn't allow any fat, so I answered them. "I gave up my apartment and job. So I don't know."

I handed him his coffee and sat cross-legged on my bed. He said, "My wife will be arriving in a few weeks. Her name is Dong Mei and she has two sons, Roger and Seth, nine and seven."

"Where are they now?"

"China."

"You've . . . uh . . . been to China?"

"No. I ordered her." He raised his eyes to mine and challenged me to object. He was right: I heartily disapproved. The practice, I'd heard, was rife with abuse.

He leaned forward and put his elbows on his thighs, held the coffee cup with two hands in front of his pointy knees. "Life is about work. Getting things done. Food on the table and a fire in the stove. Love isn't a meal. It's a brown bear shaking you in its jaws and tossing you aside."

I meant to sound sarcastic, at least ironic, when I said, "Your heart's been broken, too."

"Nope," he lied. "Love is one big fucking vortex. A man just has to work." He paused, shifted, and then added, "I guess a woman has to work, too, but I don't know nothing about that."

"So you're going for a business arrangement."

"Yep."

I was curious what that arrangement looked like. Sex for food? Housecleaning for wood chopping? When I thought of the eroticism in the sounds of his work, my distaste at his buying a mail-order bride withered a bit. Up here, beyond the reach of everyday civility, it was difficult to hold onto common judgments.

"What about the sons?" I asked.

"I see them as collateral. She's not going anywhere with two young sons, right? She'll be grateful for my support." Jurek reached into his back pocket and pulled out a wallet. He withdrew a photograph and handed it to me.

Dong Mei was beautiful. She smiled with her mouth closed, her lips plump and moist, as if she sucked on a secret. Her hair flew off to the right, giving the impression that her image had been captured on a windy day, and yet the purplish-gray background was obviously that of a studio shot. The model girl details put me off, made me distrustful, but her gaze was surprisingly direct, especially for someone as young as she was, at least half my and Jurek's age. What struck me the hardest were her thick eyebrows. They reminded me of Lindsay's. I had loved the furry vulnerability of them.

I handed the picture back and stood up. "I better get back to work."

Jurek laughed. "You were sitting on your porch doing nothing." He didn't make any move to get up from my rocking chair. When I didn't move either, he said, "I know what you're thinking. What's a beautiful woman like Dong Mei going to do with a man like me. I'll tell you what. We're going to have a family."

"She has two sons," I found myself saying, defending her already.

"I want a bunch more."

"Does she?"

"Sure."

That week I got a job in the Java Luv Café making cappuccinos and heating up muffins and bowls of soup in the microwave. I wiped down tables and answered the phone, too. The café had a public computer and that's where Jurek communicated with Dong Mei. He liked to read me her emails, translated by Google, which he found rich and inviting and I thought were chilly and enterprising. She detailed her needs—clothes, food, and school for her two boys—and asked questions about his job and housing. She mentioned once that she had a choice of men and that she was still deciding. Jurek laughed at that one and said he doubted it, not with two young children.

A couple of times, when Jurek wasn't in the café, I thought of looking at the computer's browser history, finding the site where he'd met Dong Mei, logging on, and warning her. There was no cabin. Jurek lived in a tent. He had a compulsion for chopping wood. And Alaska was a place soon to be snuffed out by snow. But it was none of my business, and anyway, who was I to judge anyone by how they bargained with loneliness?

The weeks passed and Jurek kept chopping wood. By November when it began snowing in earnest, he'd built a wood stack next to my cabin that would carry me through three winters.

Each day brought only a few short hours of murky daylight, but I tried to adapt, venturing out in the dark to explore my new territory. A small and already frozen river passed between my cabin and town, and this made a nice winter thoroughfare. I could ski for as long as I liked along its course and not worry about route finding or getting lost. After work and supper, I would click into my backcountry skis, snap a head-lamp around my fleece cap, and head out the road, turning either north or south to ski up or down the river. On the northern route, about a mile out, there was a tall spruce, spindly with a spiked top. The entire tree tipped slightly toward the river—a crisply black silhouette—and as I skied toward it I could see the night sky through the sparse layers of branches.

Lindsay had said, when we were deciding to part, that she didn't know if she could do love—she'd said intimacy, not love, but what's the difference?—because she needed to preserve her own view of the sky. Relationships, for her, were like storms that blew dark and billowy clouds across her aerial landscape. They blinded her.

I named this spruce the Grief Tree. For her. And because of its proud height and short, drooping branches. I always paused there and reconfirmed my vow of tenderness. In spite of my painful longing, I wished her well.

Then, back in my cabin, I'd make tea and open a novel. If the book was satisfying, my life felt full enough, doable. If the story was poorly told, everything seemed wrong—the café, my cabin, the cold and cease-less snow. Yet I never put a book down until I finished the last page.

On occasional nights, rather late, there would be a knock at my door. I never failed to start, be jolted by a quick fleeting stab of hope. But of course it was never her. It was always Jurek, who would enter wordlessly and take his place in the rocking chair. I thought I should mind, but I didn't. I liked the way that he was so cruelly not her. I tried to see his visits as corrective measures, minor surgeries to cut away my longing. I liked the unpleasant way he would squint around my cabin and never quite look at *me*. I would make coffee, and we would talk until the silences between topics became too long even for him. Then he would push up from the rocker, rinse his mug in the sink, and walk out my door without saying goodbye.

One night, I found myself telling him about Lindsay. I told him everything. Her full name. Where she lived. Where and what she taught. Her stride and smile. Her fears. He stared at a spot on the floor in front of my feet as I spoke, showing no sign of understanding, as if he were merely waiting for me to finish so he could speak again of Dong Mei. I persisted anyway, my need to talk about her driving me to tell him even how I sometimes looked for her on the road and listened for her knock on the door. My vulnerability, alongside his apparent indifference, made me feel testy. I finished by saying, "I don't know which of us is more delusional, you or me."

He looked up then and at last made eye contact. He paused, maybe considering my feelings, but his direct honesty won out and he said, "You are." Then he rinsed his mug and left.

Not long after this conversation, at three o'clock one morning, a hollow rapping woke me from a deep sleep. I swung my feet to the floor and sat still for a moment, listening, and there it was again, insistent and growing louder. Knocking. It was not a dream. I was trembling as I opened the door.

Jurek stood on my porch, with his broad-legged stance, grinning hard. I nearly hit him.

He said, "I have a surprise."

"It's the middle of the night."

He turned toward the darkness behind him and said, "Come. Come. *Come!*" He gestured exaggeratedly, and out of the northern night came a woman and behind her, like two cubs, a pair of boys.

"Dong Mei," Jurek said. "Roger and Seth."

The boys each held fistfuls of their mother's cotton jacket. The black sky poured in the cabin door. There were a couple of feet of snow on the ground, and the temperature was in the teens. The newcomers were dressed lightly and all three were shivering.

Jurek reached out an arm, laid it across my middle, and pushed me to the side. Then he ushered in his new family. He led Dong Mei to the rocking chair and nudged her into it. The boys ran to her side.

Jurek said, "I figure they can sleep here a night or two, until I'm ready for them."

I shook my head.

"I'll get a sleeping bag. You have extra blankets? They're used to hardship. They'll be fine on the floor. This may be the fanciest place they've ever slept. It's warm!" He was giddy with excitement, his skinny limbs twitching like a marionette's.

"You have to get them a room in the motel," I said.

Jurek scowled. "I won't put my family in a motel. That place is a flea palace." He stared hard at Dong Mei, and then turned back to me. "Besides, you're lonely."

"No," I said.

And with that, Jurek left, leaving the cabin door swinging on its hinges. I walked slowly over and took a long look at the sky—the beginning of the aurora borealis flared purple across the velvety black—and said Lindsay's name once, as if I knew it would be a long while before I had time to even think of her again.

I shut the door and turned to my houseguests. Dong Mei sat with her head ducked and her hands folded in her lap. She refused to look at me, though the boys gaped.

"Does anyone speak English?" When I got no answer, I foolishly asked the question louder. I heard myself nearly chanting, "English? English?" until I counseled myself to calm down.

As it happened, I didn't have extra blankets or pillows. I'd come to Alaska with nothing but what I'd need myself. I had intended solitude. So I opened the drawers of my dresser and pulled out any warm clothes I could find—fleece pullovers, a down vest, and a couple of wool sweaters. I handed these out. Then I tossed my own pillow off the bed and yanked away the down comforter. I laid the sheets out on the wooden floorboards, positioned and fluffed the pillow, and gestured to the family. They looked very frightened as they scurried onto the sheet. I handed Dong Mei the comforter and she pulled it over herself and her children. They fanned out their legs so that all three heads could fit on the one pillow. They must have been exhausted, or maybe scared to death, because they lay motionless.

When, a couple of minutes later, Jurek burst back in the door, Dong Mei cried out in fright. He smiled at the sight of them in the makeshift bed, a papa bird inspecting his nesting family, and didn't even look at me as he handed over a sleeping bag. He said he'd see us in the morning.

I put the sleeping bag on my mattress and crawled in. It smelled like dirty man and I wanted to gag. I hardly slept that first night.

The next day, Jurek collected a load of bedding in town and brought it by the cabin. I told him again that his crew could not stay with me. He said only until he got a place for them to live. For the next three days, Jurek worked at leveling a small plot in the clearing on his land. I watched in disbelief. Did he think he could build a cabin during the winter? Did he think Dong Mei, Roger, and Seth could stay with me while he did? Every time I tried to ask, he brushed me off, refused to talk. His focus was extraordinary.

Meanwhile, I couldn't stop Dong Mei from working. I'd come home from my shift at the café and find her on her hands and knees, scrubbing the floor with Ajax, which bleached the wood, made the place smell like a swimming pool, and left a powdery residue which she kept pointing at proudly, as if proof of her labor and the floor's sanitation. Or she'd cook, once making a soup with ferns she'd dug up from under the snow, a can of tuna, peanut butter, and hot pepper flakes. She and her sons ate the soup with slurpy relish and she looked hurt that I would not eat the bowl she placed in front of me when I sat at the table with my own quesadilla. I begged her to stop trying to be useful, but she didn't understand a word I said. I tried shouting the word, "No!" as I pointed at the ruined floorboards or the pot of soup, and I hated how it sounded, like I was trying to communicate with a dog. I also tried the subliminal approach, hoping she'd catch my meaning even if she didn't know the actual words, when I quietly explained, "You don't have to work, Dong Mei. Just make yourself and your sons comfortable."

She and the boys spoke only in whispers, to each other, the entire time they stayed in my cabin.

Meanwhile, her sons had dismantled the perfectly neat woodpile and restacked it with military precision. They shoveled the snow away from the perimeter of my cabin, making an ugly, ten-foot-wide band of bare frozen ground. They found their way into town the third day and returned with some ingredients from which Dong Mei made a stew that, I admit, smelled delicious. I still refused to eat any, though, on principal. For one, with me, she didn't have to work for her keep. For another, I didn't want her thinking she could in any way pay for her stay. I know, the two thoughts conflicted, but both were true. I wasn't Jurek. I wasn't buying a companion or even a domestic worker. Nothing she could do would make the arrangement okay with me.

Jurek visited each night but only briefly, grinning hard at his recent purchases and barely acknowledging my existence. Then, on the fifth day, he pulled a small Airstream onto the clearing on his lot, and came to fetch them.

I was relieved to see them go, and yet, in the vacuum, my loneliness rushed back in. Jurek never thanked me and never came to my cabin for late-night talks anymore. Nor did he stop by the Java Luv Café to check his email. I sometimes saw his pickup truck in town, his blond head and their three black ones all squeezed into the heated cabin. Once there was an armchair in the bed of the truck. Another time a barbeque grill. After that, the smell of roasting meat sometimes drifted all the way to my porch. Her Chinese words, staccato to my ears, also began drifting my way as she became comfortable enough to speak up, claim her new home, communicate freely with her sons. The little boys' voices rang out through the white birch branches as they threw snowballs and played chase.

I did, once, take a pan of brownies over to the Airstream. The rounded pod looked homey from the outside, the windows yellow squares of light, the snow silently sliding off the silver siding. Jurek shouted for me to come on in. He sat at the tiny Formica table, holding a mug of coffee, and the two boys sat across from him, quietly drawing on paper with crayons. Dong Mei sat on the bed, turning the pages of a magazine.

There was something slightly different in her demeanor that night. Later I'd call it a defiance, but then I only thought she'd become more present in her body. I was glad to see she wasn't scrubbing the stove or mending his shirts. She watched me talking to Jurek from under those handsome eyebrows, but if I glanced her way, she quickly looked back down at the magazine.

Jurek, for his part, was delighted. He said the boys were exceptionally smart for their ages, and that they loved sleeping in the tent. I asked him how he knew that. Jurek said that this life, full-time camping, was a boy's dream come true. They would start school right after the holidays. In the spring, he would begin building a house—not a cabin, he said, a *house*. When he got the money, he was going to get braces for Dong Mei's teeth.

If Jurek was disappointed that she wasn't as pretty as her picture, he didn't show it. The closed-mouth smile in her photograph covered a set of very crooked teeth. She was a good ten years older than when the picture had been taken, but then that still made her at least fifteen years younger than Jurek.

His mouth gummy with a chocolate smile, he said, "Maybe they have ladies for, you know, ladies." I shook my head, uncomprehending. "I highly recommend the arrangement. Everything is contractual, on paper." He leaned forward and bore down on me with his gaze. "No endless discussion and no emotional garbage."

Not only did I now get his meaning—he thought I should find my own mail-order bride—I felt nailed by his edict. My emotional life was about as purple as the aurora borealis, or had been anyway, until I traded it in for northern austerity. Maybe I was on the same path as Jurek, after all. I got up and returned to my cabin.

I resumed my nightly skis to the Grief Tree. My views of the sky were grand and unobstructed, the northern lights now making nightly statements, as if to affirm my overwrought ideas about love. Bars of lime green pulsed overhead, followed by giant whirling eddies of purple. That's what it had felt like to have her inside me, my core touched and lit.

I don't blame Lindsay for being unable to bear the intensity. Who can? Having my loneliness relieved by her had been strenuous, like a too-long hike at high altitude. It was shockingly beautiful, but I couldn't really live there. Could I?

Jurek was absolutely right. You should endure life alone or find a partner in the true sense of the word, a companion in sex and work. As the solstice came and went, the broad sweeping strokes of my skis on the snow-crusted ice righted me. The bracing cold soothed. The asceticism of my cabin began, again, to feel just right.

Then, one night when I returned from my ski, I found Jurek inside.

"They're gone," he said, his desperation palpable.

"What do you mean, gone?"

"I went to get supplies in town late this afternoon. When I got back, they weren't in the Airstream. I figured they'd gone for a walk, or to pick stuff. She's always digging up plants and stuff. But they didn't come back. I've been all over town. I've been all over the woods." His voice clawed at the air. He bit back something much more fierce than tears when he said, "I hoped they'd be *here*, in your cabin."

I was suddenly furious. She took his money. She entered into an agreement. How dare she break Jurek's heart. His loss swept into the atmospheric high of my own, and I was a storm of righteousness.

I jumped into the truck with Jurek and we began combing the roads leading away from town. He drove slowly, and I looked for shadows in the trees. I scanned the snow for tracks. We returned to town, and I banged on the door of unit six in the motel, where the owner lived. When the man said he hadn't seen them, Jurek grabbed the front of his T-shirt and threatened violence if he was lying. I pulled Jurek off the man and we got back in the truck. It was two in the morning by then, but I convinced him we had to drive to the Fairbanks airport. When we arrived, hours later, we walked bleary eyed by the ticket counters, checking the customers in line, looking for Dong Mei, Roger, and Seth. It was there that I began to be ashamed of my behavior. I was hunting a woman and her children, who had, by all appearances, chosen to leave a man.

Later that morning, when Jurek dropped me off at my cabin, our eyes met briefly before I got out of the dark truck. Sometime during the night he must have made some emotional adjustment, because now he seemed to look at me with pity, as if I were the one who had been betrayed. He quietly said, "There's no such thing."

I slept for most of that day. I didn't even call in to the Java Luv Café. When I woke up, I rolled onto my back and looked at the wooden ceiling. I had no idea what losses Dong Mei had endured over the course of her life. Nor did I know what living with Jurek had been like. At the very least, he'd wildly misrepresented himself and his circumstances. I had no right to judge her.

I got up and made myself a good dinner. Then I skied to my Grief Tree. I was hoping for the aurora borealis — now I *wanted* to be reminded of Lindsay, of the possibility of love — but there was just the black, black sky with a sparkle of stars. After stopping and paying homage to the tree, I decided to ski farther down the frozen river.

Not much beyond, maybe a couple hundred yards, their tracks came down the bank and headed upstream. It was obviously them, three sets of tracks, those of one adult and two children. I stopped, listened, and looked around. They'd been gone over twenty-four hours. They could be in danger. I pictured the three runaways somewhere in advance of me, laying down tracks, fleeing.

I didn't know what to do. If I let them go, they might die out here. If I found them, would I return them to Jurek? Take them to the airport? I didn't have the money to buy them plane tickets, and I'm sure they didn't either. Slowly at first, I skied after the tracks, heading straight up the river. Then my worry grew and accelerated my speed, until I was sprint-skiing, gasping for breath, desperate to overtake them.

They had built a small fire on the western bank. The boys crouched next to it, knees jutting, hands turned out like cowboys. Dong Mei paced on the perimeter of firelight, tossing small twigs into the flames. She stood taller as I approached, held her ground. There was something harsh about her now, as if she were guarding against a low-grade anger.

I stopped and looked. We were like four wild animals caught in an uncertain encounter. Something told me to not disturb them. I had nothing to offer. And yet, I snapped out of my skis and climbed the snowy bank. Dong Mei bent and poured something from a tin pot sitting in the coals into a plastic mug. She held this out to me, and I tasted the steaming liquid. It was an odd, rooty tea that I hoped wasn't poisonous. The earthy flavor made me think of sex.

I didn't know what to do next. The fire, the tea, her posture, these things led me to believe that maybe she knew exactly what she was doing. Anyway, their lives weren't my jurisdiction. Still, I couldn't help having an opinion. Two opinions, actually. A big part of me wanted to shout, "Run, girl!" A smaller but more reasonable part knew they had little chance in an Alaskan winter — despite the ability to make hot tea and fire — without shelter. They were lucky to have made it through one night. And apparently, Dong Mei knew it. When I gestured for them to follow me, she spoke briefly to her sons, and they kicked snow onto the fire. The family followed me.

Walking rather than skiing, it took us well over an hour to get back to my cabin, and the boys were stumbling with exhaustion. I fed them crackers with peanut butter and hot soup from cans, and gave them my bed. Dong Mei allowed Roger and Seth to take it, but refused herself, curling up on the floor, at a distance from the now roaring wood stove, which she pointed at, meaning for me to sleep close to the fire. I gave her Jurek's stinky sleeping bag.

In the morning, I awoke to find Dong Mei filling the kitchen sink and stuffing the down bag into the hot sudsy water. She squished and sloshed the feathers and nylon with vigorous arm motions, doing her best, I supposed, to eradicate the noxious smell. When I returned from work that evening, it had been wrung out and hung from a rafter, drying. A dinner of pasta with tomato sauce and hamburger meat was waiting for me, and it was delicious. The four of us ate at the table like a family.

I said, "Dong Mei, we have to figure out what to do about you and the boys."

She spoke in brisk Chinese, looking right at me, as if I might have picked up the language in the few weeks she'd been here.

I was shocked when the older boy, Roger, interpreted. "He make tent for us with bear. No safe."

Dong Mei spoke again.

Roger said, "He want babies. No."

Wide eyed, Seth tried to join in, but Dong Mei shushed him each time he repeated his brother's English. However, as it turned out, the younger boy had a better command of the language, and over the next couple of days, I usually turned to him when I wanted information.

"Did he hit you or the boys?" I asked. It was a crude question, and I felt intrusive, especially when I had to mime the question because no one understood the words, but how else was I going to find out what I needed to know to make them safe?

"No," Roger and Seth told me in unison.

"Did he feed you enough?"

"Yes."

"Did he scare you in any way?"

The boys translated and all three looked at each other with what seemed like utter incomprehension. In the end, I surmised that Jurek scared them a great deal—who wouldn't be scared by the squinty, hyper man?—but he hadn't mistreated them. I supposed that this would make it more difficult to get help for them, but I did go online at the Java Luv Café and search for organizations that rescued mail-order brides who'd changed their minds.

In the meantime, I tried to come to terms with the plain fact that I was hiding them. From Jurek. Who lived a mere hundred and fifty yards away. This truth was hard to square with the fact that not forty-eight hours earlier I'd been hunting for them with Jurek, and also that he was my friend.

On the up side, this all distracted me from mucking about in my own pool of loss, at least until the third day when there was a knock on my door. It was faint, not the usual pounding, and I hardly heard it at first. My fantasy of Lindsay tracking me down was absurd. I knew that. But the quality of this knocking had a quiet resonance. Like something destined.

This moment of foolishness on my part was quickly smashed by Dong Mei flinging herself across the room to slap a hand over Seth's mouth and to gesture with her other for Roger to keep silent. She grabbed their wrists and dragged them to the bathroom, the only place in the cabin with a shutting door. I made my heavy way toward the knocking.

The door swung open before I could get there. Jurek paced to the rocker and sat. I forced myself to not look at the closed bathroom door. I also counseled myself to not make him suspicious by hurrying him off.

He glanced at the stove where there was in fact some coffee already made, not to mention too many cereal bowls in the sink. I lit a burner and heated up the coffee.

As Jurek swallowed, his Adam's apple slid up and down his throat like a knife. He leaned forward, elbows on his knees, and held the mug loosely in his hands.

"How do you know you love her?" he asked.

"Jurek," I said. "You forgot. There's no such thing."

His eyes were shining as he lifted his gaze to hold mine. "How?"

So I pretended to think about it. Then I said, "Because I can tell you every single one of her faults and I don't care."

"So why'd you leave?"

Again I pretended to not readily know the answer. I couldn't tell him that that kind of intimacy and joy are like too harsh a light, unbearable. So I said, "It's better to turn away while it's still pure."

He looked up at me again, eyes narrowed with suspicion. "But you told me you're waiting for her to come find you."

"There were circumstances I haven't told you about. She agreed that it was unworkable. I didn't run out on her. She wanted to keep her view of the sky."

"Maybe you need to go find *her*."

He stood and strode toward the bathroom.

"No!" I cried.

Jurek turned and changed course. He paced back toward me, scrutinizing my few possessions as he had the first time he'd come to the cabin, as if looking for a clue to life. Then he sat again, apparently finding nothing worthwhile. He looked lost.

Maybe Lindsay did want to be found. Maybe even Dong Mei hoped Jurek would bust down the bathroom door. But he never even noticed that it was atypically shut. He slunk out of the cabin a couple of minutes later, leaving the coffee cup on the floor by the rocker.

At dinner that night, I told the boys to tell their mother that they couldn't stay any longer. Seth translated and then gave me her response. "She clean and cook."

"No," I said firmly. "You all have to leave tomorrow. I'm sorry."

A rapid-fire discussion took place in Chinese, and then Roger spoke up in as manly a voice as the nine-year-old could muster. "We make money. We make very big money and give you."

I shook my head, which they misinterpreted, or maybe just blatantly ignored, because all three smiled.

"No!" I shouted. "No money. No work. No staying here in my cabin. You must be gone tomorrow."

But of course they didn't leave the next day. When I returned from work, all three sat at my small table. Before them was a small amount of cash. They were counting the dollars and stacking the coins. Seth proudly explained that the boys had gone to town and found a couple of odd jobs.

"But Jurek will see you," I blurted.

"We here safe," Roger explained to me.

In direct retort, the door flew open, and Jurek entered, carrying an axe. He raised it over his head and roared, not at them, but at me, "You dirty lying bitch."

I think he meant to kill me. I saw the axe blade come my way. The same one that chopped wood would now split open my head. Dong Mei screamed at the boys, and they fled to the bathroom. She threw herself at Jurek, lifted her thin arms, and took hold of the axe handle.

"Go," she said to him. It was the first English I heard her speak.

He wrenched the axe away and stepped around her, coming for me once again. There was nowhere for me to go, so I waited for the first hack. But Dong Mei leapt onto his back, wrapped her arms around his neck and her legs around his waist. She shouted in English, "YOU! NOW! STOP!"

His entire body softened, as if he experienced her interception as an embrace. The axe slowly lowered. She slid off his back and took it from his hand. Then she used it to gesture toward the door, again saying, "Go!"

"Why did you leave?" he asked her. "I love you."

"No love," she said, and he looked flattened. "You go. No love."

He cast me one last crushing look and did leave. Dong Mei put the axe on the kitchen table and called her boys out of the bathroom. She hugged them both and then told me, through Seth, "We danger you."

She stuffed their tin pot and plastic mugs in her canvas duffel. The boys zipped up the parkas that Jurek had bought them. And the family left, not ten minutes after Jurek had. I knew I should stop them. Where were they going to go? I heard the crunching of their footsteps as they walked away from my cabin.

I didn't see any of them—Dong Mei, Roger, Seth, or Jurek—for a whole week. Then one day after work, as I was walking to the grocery store in town, I saw the two boys entering unit three of the motel. A couple of days later, I heard that Dong Mei was housekeeping for the owner in exchange for the room. The boys had begun school and were also offering themselves for every possible kind of job—running errands, washing cars, shoveling snow, even selling cups of hot coffee they made by running an extension cord from their motel room to a hot plate set up on a card table on the sidewalk in front of the motel, until the motel owner shut that operation down. I didn't know when they had time to do their schoolwork, but their English improved rapidly. I was relieved I didn't have to worry about them anymore. Clearly they could take care of themselves.

As for Jurek, he'd stopped talking to me. He wouldn't even meet eyes or say hi if we passed on the sidewalk, and he never came into the Java Luv Café anymore. I did hear a lot of gossip about him. People said that while the boys' coffee business was up and running, Jurek bought more cups than anyone. They said that he had the boys wash his truck weekly and that he invented errands for them to run.

But when I started noticing that he had the two little boys working on the construction site next door, actually hammering nails and hoisting two-by-fours, that they worked ten-hour days on the weekends, many of those hours in the arctic dark, building the cabin their mother was no longer interested in living in, I got angry.

I counseled myself to not butt in—the axe incident was still fresh in my memory—but when Dong Mei came in the café one day to use the computer, I couldn't help commenting. "Dong Mei," I said. "Don't let Jurek use your sons."

"Use?" she said quizzically. "What you mean, use?"

Of course by now she knew the common meaning of the word, so I explained *my* meaning. "In this country there are child labor laws. He's making Roger and Seth work far too many hours. He's using them for labor he'd have to pay adults much, much more for. It's called exploitation."

I misinterpreted the shocked look on her face. I thought she was experiencing that feeling of being slapped when you learn someone has taken advantage of you.

She spoke emphatically. "He pay much. Too much. He try twenty buck an hour." She laughed now, her crooked teeth making a merry mockery of me. "I tell him, minimum wage only. Boys learn skill. Very, very good."

I know she saw the confusion on my face, because she hurriedly closed her lips around the crazy teeth, and reached out a hand. It hovered for a moment in the space between us, and then alighted on my forearm, a very gentle touch. Now she, too, was looking at me with pity. Apparently, I didn't have a clue about love *or* work. She said quietly, "Jurek sweet man. He wait." She withdrew her hand and rubbed it with her other in a sensual gesture of anticipation. "Very sweet."

In late March, there was a knock on my door in the evening. It had been weeks since anyone had knocked. "Hello?" I called out. "Who's there?"

"Me." The door opened, and Jurek walked straight to the rocker and sat, as if he'd never threatened me with an axe. I made coffee.

"She said she doesn't want a money arrangement. She wants to pay me back for the plane tickets. That could takes *years*."

"I heard she got a job cooking at the diner."

"Yeah. But only minimum wage, plus two meals a day for all three of them. And she cleans the motel for their room. I pay the boys as much as she'll let me for hanging out at the construction site. She's saving all their wages. But still."

"Then what? After she pays you back for the plane tickets?"

He shrugged. "She said no promises. She wants a real house with bedrooms. She's angry I had the boys sleeping in the tent."

"I can understand that."

"Boys like to camp."

"Not if they don't have a comfortable home to return to."

"She says she doesn't want any more children."

"I guess that would be her prerogative."

"She won't even see me. Not even to go to a movie or out to dinner."

Jurek looked miserable, consumed. I probably should have told him about Dong Mei calling him sweet. Instead, I said, "It was stupid to send all your money and expect them to love you in exchange."

I thought he'd bat the word love aside. But he said, "I didn't expect anything. That's what seemed so perfect about the arrangement. I met her on the computer, so I thought she'd *be* like a computer. Somehow I knew the boys would have personalities that I would like or dislike, but I thought of her as a blank." He breathed and swallowed and blinked. "She's not a blank. She's . . . she's fierce. And beautiful. And maddening."

"You love her."

"Per your definition. All her faults. And still."

His admission blasted something open inside me. I smiled as goofily as if I were the one in love.

"The world is in a deeper 3-D," he said. "Colors everywhere are more intense. It's like I never heard birds sing before. All that. She's my beautiful awakening."

That night I skied to the Grief Tree and looked hard at the open spaces between the dark branches. It was a new moon and the sky was black, opaque. Then, as I watched, a smudge of chartreuse warmed the blackness. It spread and brightened to bottle green, began dancing. A rosy luster twirled through the green, eddied and sunk into itself. Bars of purple light pulsed across the sky. Her hand inside me, lit.

By April, Dong Mei had paid Jurek back for only one of the plane tickets, but she agreed to have tea with him anyway, on the condition that the date take place in the Java Luv Café during my shift. The boys each had muffins with butter, and Jurek had a latte with a double shot of espresso. They all conversed in English, although the boys had to translate lots of words for their mother, and she endearingly pronounced his name, "Jerk." Sometimes Jurek tried to pantomime the meaning of a word, and twice I saw Dong Mei laugh at his antics.

Soon they were dating regularly, and my presence was no longer necessary. She still refused to move back in with him until she'd paid back all of the money for the plane tickets. As she explained to me one day on the street, "I no want business marriage. Also, I want house for boys."

Jurek worked night and day on the house. He never visited me in my cabin or at the café, but occasionally I strolled over to check on his progress. The stone chimney went in, the walls went up, and the windows were installed. He'd started much earlier than was advisable, and had to keep the entire project covered with plastic sheeting, which made the work worse than awkward. But finally he put on the roof.

That's when Jurek came over to tell me he was taking the family to Palm Springs, where he and Dong Mei would get remarried. This time with flowers and a cake, he said. He'd booked them into a hotel with three swimming pools and a Jacuzzi. The grounds were planted with hibiscus and palms. His happiness was as palpable as his desperation had been the day they disappeared.

"One other thing," he said, still standing on my porch.

I gestured into the cabin, toward the rocker.

He shook his head. He didn't have time. My native loneliness settled over me as I waited to hear his one other thing.

I could see him considering his words. Jurek had never been one to speak unless he had something to say, but I'd never seen him visibly thinking. Finally, "I emailed her."

"Who?"

He only nodded.

Words cannot describe the incredulity I felt.

"I told her that she'd have the most enormous view of the sky possible up here. Black and starry in winter. I didn't tell her about the northern lights. Sounds like they might scare her. But I said that in the summer she could study the clouds and blue twenty-four-seven, if she wanted."

Jurek was crazy. Why hadn't I admitted that earlier? I breathed relief at the realization that he couldn't possibly have contacted Lindsay, and leaned back against the doorjamb, crossed my arms, waited for him to finish this nonsense.

He saw that I didn't believe him. He said, "There are search engines, you know, where you can find anyone. Handful of keystrokes."

"You're not serious."

He was. He really was.

"I told her your exact whereabouts. And that you're pining. I gave details to make sure she believed me."

"You have no right."

He shrugged. "To the contrary. I had to. I know I told you there's no such thing. But." He swallowed, blinked, looked away. "Dong Mei and Seth and Roger. They walked right in." He tapped his breastbone.

He turned and stepped off my porch.

The days were full of light now, and the ice on the river had mostly melted. There was enough patchy snow on the banks to make my way to the Grief Tree, and sometimes I did. I had to decide soon whether I would find another place to live up here or return to the lower forty-eight. With the insulating snow rapidly melting, I began to feel ridiculous again, holing myself up in the north as if I were some kind of hibernating mammal. The bright light of the returned northern sun exposed me. A slight and vulnerable human being, after all.

One night, while my neighbors were still on their honeymoon in Palm Springs, there was a knock on my door. It was dark, and the aurora was making a late spring appearance. I stared at the door, and then over my shoulder at the kitchen window where the colors swirled against the sky.

And so, why not, I opened the door.

Wolf

I wasn't exactly happy with Jim wanting to change his name to Anatoly, but I tried to roll with it. Change is good in a relationship, right? That was the whole reason we went to Yellowstone in the first place, to zest up our marriage, have a little fun, do something new.

I didn't think we needed an overhaul, though. Nor did I think the change needed to bleed outside our marriage. But after the first trip to the park, he started asking our neighbors to call him Anatoly. It was embarrassing.

"Been reading our Dostoevsky, have we?" said our next door neighbor Clarence, pleased with himself for thinking he'd dredged up a literary reference. The other next door neighbor, Walter, narrowed his eyes, assessed, and then shrugged, neither agreeing nor disagreeing, pretty much just dismissing. I imagined both of them telling their wives, Cathy and Shawna, and having a good laugh on our behalf. Little did I know back then that I needn't have worried about the neighbors, that we'd soon be selling the house.

Still, in the beginning, I tried to find the humor myself. My complaints for the thirty-plus years we'd been together clustered around sameness, a hazy boredom that occasionally drifted through our otherwise happy marriage. So a new name? Why not? It didn't occur to me that it might signify an entire identity change.

Anatoly means east or sunrise. Fitting, I suppose. But how did he know that? Had he been researching wild names before we even visited the park and met the wolf watchers? I heard him tell them his name was Anatoly that very first morning. He removed his mitten and thrust out his hand, and the reluctant recipient of his greeting ignored the hand but nodded when Jim said, "Anatoly." Barely awake, I decided I'd misheard, that Jim had probably only made some obscure joke the other man didn't get. I got back in the car and unscrewed the thermos lid, poured myself some coffee.

The ranger had told us that the wolves were most active at dawn and dusk, and that the best way to view them was to look for the cluster of people beside the road with viewing scopes. It was the dead of January, but sure enough that morning as we drove out the northern park road and entered the Lamar Valley, we found seven people in one of the pullouts, standing with alert expectation in front of fat cylinders on long legs.

Clouds obscured the stars. The sky was black and the snow a deep lavender. We parked our Ford Fiesta next to the fleet of SUVs, and that's when Jim introduced himself as Anatoly. Forgive me for repeating that moment; it's the part of this life shift I can't explain. The name must have come to him in the way dreams lay out whole stories we don't even know exist in our unconscious. A wild name, Anatoly, parked in the recesses of Jim's psyche, perhaps for years, waiting for the right mix of circumstances to surface. Or maybe the sight of that black sky and lavender snow, the promise of those long-legged scopes, birthed the name right then and there.

For a few minutes I watched my husband from the car. He asked questions and received brief answers from some of the wolf watchers. Others ignored him. A couple pointedly never even looked at him. I saw him tamp down his eagerness, realize that there was a culture here, that he best observe rather than blunder.

This was my first moment of capitulation, although I certainly didn't recognize it as such at the time. Viewing my husband through the windshield, as if it were a lens that allowed me to see him objectively, I saw a man in longing. For what, I couldn't have said, but my annoyance at his enthusiasm for a predawn adventure dissolved. He was thrilled to be there, lured by the mystery of wolves, hoping to experience something new. I couldn't fault him on that. Whatever malaise had settled over our life together, Jim himself had always had a childlike curiosity that I loved. I opened the door and stepped back into the bitter cold air.

The ridge to the east darkened and the sky directly above it lightened. The mustard yellow burgeoned into a tangerine orange, and then came the first rays of the sun, sheer daggers of light.

A wolf howled.

The wolf watchers aligned themselves with their scopes and began scanning. Jim opened his mouth to ask a question, and I put my mitten against his lips and shook my head. He nodded his thanks, knew that I was right about silence now. The wolf howled again.

Jim looked over his shoulder, as if the animal were about to pounce on him, and then did a quick 360 degree search. I thought he was startled, maybe frightened, but then I realized that the look on his face was deep calm, intense concentration. That howling wolf spoke to his heart more directly than the cries of our babies had.

That night, while Jim was in the shower, I called Barbara from our room at the Mammoth Hot Springs Hotel and told her, "Your father has fallen in love with a female alpha wolf."

"Meaning?" I could hear the background clanking of dinner pots.

"There's this culture of people who go into the park every single day, and they stay *all* day, looking for the wolf packs."

"Why?"

"I don't know."

"And this has what to do with Dad?"

"I think he *does* know."

"Call Mark. Have him talk to Dad."

"Mark," I said a few moments later, "I think your dad is considering joining a wolf pack."

Mark laughed. "Sounds about right."

"It does? How so?"

"He has that wandering in him."

This almost offended me. "He's never wandered from *us*."

"No. But essentially he's a nomad."

Separate. Quiet. Restless. Yes, the word fit, but I didn't like it.

"That's crazy," I said. "What are you talking about?"

"It just always seemed like he needed a passion." Mark hesitated, not wanting to hurt my feelings. "He's always been a little bit sad. Not a lot. But a little bit."

"And a wolf pack is going to make him not sad?"

"It might."

Clearly there would be no advantage to putting Mark on the phone with his father. Nor could I make myself tell him that I think Jim had introduced himself to the wolf watchers as Anatoly.

"Hey, it's not another woman," Mark laughed. "Not a human one, anyway."

"That's very comforting."

"What did Barbara say?"

"She said to call you."

Two hours after sunrise that first morning, the Lamar Canyon pack was spotted. "Got 'em," said one of the three gray-bearded observers. Later I'd know them as Joe, Gregory, and Zack, but it wasn't until the next trip that I could tell them apart. He spoke quietly, but with a load of triumph.

"Where?" everyone asked in unison, and the man identified a ridge in the distance, began describing clusters of trees, shapes of long shadows on the snow, and snags that could not be seen with the naked eye.

Jim literally squirmed with the desire to see. One of the gray beards motioned him over to his scope. He spoke quietly, explaining that the alpha female was to the far left, out in front, and that four other pack members were running along behind her.

"Let me adjust the scope," he said. "They've probably run out of view already." I saw the others slide their scope handles to the right, following the running wolves. Jim looked again after the adjustment and almost cried out in his joy. He held back the cry, though, and won points, I'm sure, with the viewing pack.

"Did you see?" the gray beard asked, and Jim nodded.

What *I* saw was my husband's relationship to those wolves. It was visceral, visual and audible both, as if I could see and hear his heart bursting out of his chest and whizzing out to that pack of freely running canines.

"She . . ." he said to me later in the car. "She . . ." So moved he couldn't finish his sentence, but I knew he was talking about the alpha female, her silvery coat and sprightly legs, her clarity of purpose.

The next morning we returned to the Lamar Valley well before sunrise, and this time the pack was in the valley itself, playing and resting, only a few hundred yards away. The wolf watchers saw my husband's serious caring, and they began to feed him tidbits of information about this particular pack, and especially about the alpha female. Eventually the pack headed at a trot over the ridge to the west, and in under ten seconds the watchers had loaded their scopes into the backs of their vehicles and took off down the road. Jim and I looked at each other in dismay, confused for a moment, but he caught right on.

"They're going to the next pullout where they hope to see them come over the ridge toward them." He was at the wheel of the Ford Fiesta before I'd even lowered my binoculars. I swear he might have driven off without me if I hadn't hopped to, so eager he was to see the pack crest the ridge with the rest of the watchers.

Thankfully our short holiday ended. We were both expected back at work on Monday. I chose to think of the whole experience as a positive infusion of joy and adventure, especially for Jim. He told everyone about the wolves. He also told everyone to please call him Anatoly.

I snapped after about two weeks of this. "Tell me," I begged. "What's wrong with the name Jim? It's been good enough for fifty-two years."

My question brought on what I soon learned to call The Look. His gaze slid past me, *way* past me, over the buildings of town, beyond the meadows and hills of the parklands near our home, far beyond. Is it possible to look farther away than a horizon? Jim did. Anatoly did.

We returned to Yellowstone a month later. In the meantime, he'd read every book there was to read and had followed the ten park packs—and the two loners—on the websites of the wolf watchers. He knew how to identify the alpha males and females, the names and ranges of the packs. The Mollies, he told me, lived just north of the lake, while the Canyon, Blacktail, and Agate packs had territories to the west of the Lamar Canyon Pack.

"Eleven packs," I told him as we approached the park. He glanced at me, knowing I was adding the odd group of people who organized their entire lives around viewing the wolves in Yellowstone, but he was immune to criticism on this front. He merely nodded at my comment. It was like he was a lone wolf on the periphery, looking for a way to be admitted to the pack. Knowledge was always valuable, and he'd armed himself with lots. So was acquiescent behavior, and he greeted the group quietly our first morning of this second trip, nodding like they did, setting up his scope, scanning the ridge tops with his binoculars. He pretended he'd already been accepted.

I'm surprised he brought me along. Couldn't I be considered a liability? Sure, one astute male who was apparently willing to buy into every single rule had a chance, but I was a dubious female, suspicious, circling on the outside, quite ready to attack from a psychological point of view. I granted these people what I thought was a generous assessment: they were passionate. But where is the line between passion and obsession?

Take Michelle, maybe forty-five years old, evidently unemployed, she rose before the sun each and every morning and drove into the park to view wolves. At least Louise and Gregory were retired, or so I assumed by their ages, and they shared the fixation with each other. Another couple, Ashley and Neil, were not old enough to be retired, nor did they exhibit a shared delight in the wolf pursuit. In fact, their quiet and infrequent—but forceful nonetheless—banter revealed a deep competitiveness.

"Got her," Neil said on our first morning back in the park.

"Oh, you mean 54?" Ashley responded with strained cheeriness. "I've been watching her for five minutes."

After an irritated pause, Neil said, "That would be impossible, dear. She came over the ridge seventeen seconds ago."

"Hon?" Syrupy. "You're talking about 31. *He*—" the pronoun emphasis pointing out that Neil had gotten even the sex of the animal wrong— "is right there next to the closest tree. You're right about *that*."

"Oh, 31?" Neil retorted. "He's been there since before sunrise. I recognized his voice, which made it quite clear that he was somewhere in that stand of alders."

Ashley swung her scope forty-five degrees to the right, as if she'd suddenly become aware of a whole new wolf situation and Neil, who'd pulled back from his scope for the argument, couldn't resist pushing his eye back against the eyepiece and swinging his that way, too. I bet there was nothing there at all. Ashley was just messing with Neil.

The entire group usually stayed all day, until the last possible chance of a sighting at dusk. "See you in the morning!" they'd call out quietly at the end of the day, packing up their scopes. On our last night in the park that second trip, Jim and I overheard them making arrangements to have dinner together. Michelle was cooking spaghetti for everyone at her place just outside Silver Gate. Jim was hurt that we hadn't been invited.

"Why would we be?" I asked him, appalled at his feeling of belonging. "We don't know these people. We have lives two hundred miles away, a house, grown children, and grandchildren. We have jobs."

After dinner in our hotel, while Jim interrogated a wildlife tour guide he'd found in the lobby, I sat on a nearby couch and called Barbara. I felt as if I shouldn't let him out of my sight, though I couldn't name what it was I feared.

"Mom, it's late. I'm trying to get the kids to bed."

"I know," I whispered, feeling as if I were betraying Jim by telling on him to our children. "We're back in the park."

"You mean Yellowstone?"

"*Yes.*"

Barbara paused, and I was gratified that she was finally *getting* the situation. "So that Dad can look for wolves again?"

"Yes."

In her silence I heard her decide that she couldn't do anything about my problem. "Girls," she called to her daughters. "You want to say hi to Grandma?"

After she put them each on an extension, I greeted my two grand-daughters, three and five years old, by telling them, "Your grandpa wants to become a wolf."

The older one, Bella, giggled, but Heidi said nothing. I may have scared her. Bella said, "Grandma, that's not possible. That only happens in fairytales."

"True," I forced myself to admit. There was no call for frightening my grandchildren. Nor was it fair to hope for support from five- and three-year-olds. But children can sometimes believe the unbelievable, and I needed someone to witness this change in my husband. Bella snickered again, and Heidi started to ask a question, but Barbara took the phones away from them and announced bedtime. I heard shrieking, and Barbara hung up without saying goodbye. She often assumed rudeness was okay in the wake of parenting, and that I'd understand having had two children myself, but I could have used a "goodbye" and "I love you."

Two weeks later, we were back in Yellowstone, and this time Anatoly had me drop him off in Lamar Valley. We both doubted very much that the Park Service condoned camping in the backcountry, at least not here in the most common wolf territory, but there was no talking him out of it. I tried the tactic of telling him that if Joe, Gregory, Zack, Michelle, Ashley, Louise, or Neil found out, he'd be shunned. Not disturbing the wolves in their habitat was the supreme rule.

Never mind the fact that he'd never camped a day in his life. Here we were, though, in the Lamar Valley, in the pitch black of extreme early morning, so he could get out of sight before the wolf watchers arrived. He'd outfitted himself with a backpack, tent, stove, and snowshoes. I insisted on no meat products in his pack, which he agreed was a good idea, but nothing else I suggested held any weight.

I love my husband and I feared for his life, I truly did, but after thirty years of marriage you do learn that you can't stop anyone from doing something they want to do. You really can't. And in the case of my husband sleeping with the wolves, "want" wasn't even a close approximation to the verb needed to describe what Anatoly was after.

The problem was getting him out, and hopefully back, without anyone seeing him. Even though he was setting out well before the wolf watchers' arrival, I dropped him far from any of the pullouts, and then he had to hoof it fast, headlamp strapped to his forehead, to get out of sight of the road. How he'd get back to the road the next day, without being spotted, I didn't know. Or even care. By this time I thought his arrest might be the best outcome.

I lay in bed that night, back in the Mammoth Hot Springs Hotel, reading a book. I'd already gone to the ranger talk and eaten a multicourse dinner to pass the time, but there was no television reception out there, so I was left with a book and my thoughts. I'll spare you the gratuitous details of those. I did sleep for a couple of hours.

The next day I sat in the Ford Fiesta, the engine running so that I could have heat, and scanned the landscape with my binoculars. Earlier, as I scraped the ice off the windows of the car in the dark, I felt like a fool. Why I had allowed this, I didn't know. I should have insisted on a counselor. I could have refused to be an accomplice. He wouldn't have been able to get anyone else to help him. I could have put a stop to the whole enterprise.

Instead I had dropped the man off in the soul of February, temperatures barely hovering above zero, in wolf country. My own husband. Seriously, I was the one who should have made an appointment with a counselor.

"You're enabling," Barbara had told me a few days earlier.

Mark only laughed, angering me with his blithe reaction. Men supporting men's harebrained schemes.

What had I done? Introducing my husband as Anatoly was an embarrassment. But explaining that he'd lost his life because I left him off in wolf country in the middle of a winter night was probably criminal.

I saw a dot on the snowy ridge. A moving dot. Just one, with two legs. I trained my binoculars on the animal and whispered, "Got 'im."

As my husband loped toward me, I checked his gait for a limp. None. As he drew even closer, I looked for blood or pain on his face. Again, none.

I'd wanted him to live, of course, but I realized then that I'd hoped for pain, for a terrifying experience that would cure him of this newfound love of the wild. Hope and expectation are two different things, though, and seeing that he was fine, just fine, I shifted into the latter. I knew what I would see when he reached the car. A hard wolfish stare. Maybe a growl. Claims of spiritual visitations. I half-expected him to have found a downed animal and be hauling the pelt, maybe wearing it draped across his shoulders. We'd gone past the chance of a counselor helping us. We'd need an intervention.

Jim pulled the door of the passenger seat open and stuck in his head. "Open the trunk?" I heard him dump his sodden backpack on top of the extra jackets and boots, followed by a clacking of snowshoes, and then he was back at the passenger door, opening it and dropping into the seat. Would he howl at me?

For the first time I wished for the company of Joe, Gregory, Zack, Michelle, Ashley, Louise, and Neil. Unfortunately, the wolf watchers were in a different part of the park that day, but if they'd been there, they surely would have reported my husband to the Park Service and every other wildlife protection agency. They would never again allow him to set up his scope alongside theirs. He would be a pariah, this man who would disturb the wolves, who believed that he alone could beat his own DNA, join even for a night a different species. But they weren't there, so I was left on my own to accept my husband's experience.

After settling into the seat, he turned and looked at me. His eyes were soft. Actually, his entire body was soft, almost slumped, loose and happy, like after the best sex. I looked for the part of him that yearned back toward the ridge, but it wasn't there. He was looking at *me*.

"Sweetie," he said. "Thank you."

"Thank you?"

"I mean, *wow*. That was fucking scary. And beautiful. And awesome. And here you are, to pick me up. Thank you."

"Did you see them?"

He shook his head. "No. But I heard them. A lot. And just being there. With them, within their range, in their habitat. I know they smelled me, knew I was there."

"I suppose so."

"They did."

I nodded and wondered if I could start driving now.

"I don't think any of the others saw me."

He meant others, as in the others in his own group. His pack.

"They wouldn't approve, Jim. They'd be very angry."

"I know. It was wrong of me. It was just something I had to do. And I knew I had to do it soon, and fast, before I realized the full wrongness of it. Do you know what I mean?"

Understanding came to me in a flash, maybe in the same way the name Anatoly came to Jim, something I'd known all along, a willingness that just needed the right set of conditions to emerge. His gray eyes were still looking at me, directly, and they were full of love. For me, yes, but I saw that the love also encompassed much more: the mountains and wolves, himself. It made me think how we were just two people making a life in a vast world that we barely glimpsed. I thought of how our marriage had sometimes felt like a tar pit: jobs, illnesses, housework, difficult communication sucking us ever deeper into a thick, gooey place. But all along, beyond the pit, was this open wildness infused with love.

"You do know what I mean, don't you?" he said.

I did.

He took my hand. "Please."

"Okay," I said.

We bought the four-wheel drive so we could manage icy roads. On our fourth trip, we got invited to dinner with the others. The look on my husband's face was more biological satisfaction than happiness; it was as if they'd thrown a chunk of raw elk at his feet. But the thing was, these people turned out to be more regular than I'd expected. Everyone shared stories over the beers and spaghetti, but not just wolf stories. They had children and grandchildren. Some had traveled all over the world. Most had left jobs that had pinned them to lives that had become untenable. Each of them now pursued wolves fulltime, pretty much every day, winter, spring, summer, and fall.

At the end of the evening they said, "See you in the morning."

Within the year, we took early retirements and bought a house just outside the park. Our son Mark finally became concerned. I supposed he was worried about having to support us in our dotage. He should have thought of that at the beginning, when there might have been a chance of talking his father out of the new lifestyle. Barbara surprised me by cheering us on. She and Jason brought the kids out right away, and while they didn't have the patience for wolves, they loved seeing the bison and elk and coyotes.

I've never let myself forget how crazy it looks from the outside. And I'll never be as devoted as Jim. Some days I stay home. In fact, I found a part-time job in Gardiner, to give us a bit of cash to supplement our retirement income.

Jim dropped the Russian name. That was just a portal, he said. He couldn't enter the wild as an aging man from suburbia. He had needed to slip out of the jumpsuit of his life, but he was afraid to stand naked. Anatoly was a costume, he said, one that conjured wailing winds and cold snow, a distraction that would allow his transformation.

"So now you're naked?" our son asked, smirking, no longer male bonding.

"Yes," Jim answered. "You don't know until you've heard them howl."

The End of Jesus

Mac had been gone for more than thirty years. So when I found her little book in Powell's I collapsed in shock, dropped right there onto the bookstore's wood plank floor in a dusty splotch of sunlight coming from a high window. In my trembling hands I held the book that had failed to save Mac's life, though it had saved mine.

I'd come back to Oregon for my mother's memorial service, which would be taking place in under an hour, and I'd walked to the bookstore in a kind of trance that was a combination of grief and dread. The city of books was a comfort, all those words, all that knowledge, the vast diversity of human experience. I strolled through the store's many rooms as an antidote to the service I was about to attend, where everyone would believe in one, and only one, truth. I considered staying in the bookstore, skipping my mother's memorial service. That blasphemous thought made me touch the books for grounding, for random guidance, and I dragged my hand along a row of bumpy spines.

And there it was. I would have known it anywhere. The unassuming slim girth. The short red spine with the white lettering. Mac's book.

It wasn't just the same title, it was the very book, *her copy*. I knew this because when I opened it up and flipped through, I found a section of blank pages in the back. On the first of these pages was the printed word "Notes." Here the book owner was supposed to write down her own observations, and Mac had, with brief discretion. She'd written:

June 10: Sylvia.
June 14: Sylvia. Sylvia.

June 30: Sylvia. Sylvia. Sylvia.
August 9: Robin's rocks.
August 18: Hell.
September 9: How to survive.
October 12: The end of Jesus.

The August 9 entry? That's me, Robin. I'd lived under an entire rock pile of guilt ever since, but apparently it hadn't been misplaced. I was one of three people she named in the season of her demise: Sylvia, me, Jesus.

I bought the book and took it back to my hotel, where I packed and checked out. Yes, my mother had died. And yes, I felt an enormous and tangled sadness. But that didn't mean I had to subject myself to her most recent pastor and congregation who, I'd been informed many times, prayed for me regularly.

Instead, I drove to the scene of my thirty-year-old crime, Armpit, Oregon, a small town three hours from Portland. I wish I could say all those years provided me with a kind of armor, but they didn't. What happens to you at that dawn-of-adolescence age is like a dream, the way it penetrates your entire psyche, floods you with feelings as bright as sky, as wet as water, as blunt as rocks. You can't lift an arm without lifting the weight of that dream, too. As I drove into town through the Douglas firs that line the highway, I once again became that tender twelve-year-old girl whose geography had a radius of about ten miles. Who knew how to read but hadn't ventured beyond the Bible. Who believed Jesus was everyone's savior. And why not? His picture alone looked like a way out. The thin, defenseless chest and skinny arms. Scraggly but clean, even pretty, hair. Sorrowful eyes. He didn't hunt or belch as a joke. He shared his food and washed bad women's feet. A model for love.

The church was exactly as I remembered it, two big prefab structures, attached like an L. An early autumn drizzle made the place even more dreary, but I got out of my truck to brave the dampness. The confusing thing about returning to a place that so warped your existence is that you simultaneously can't believe you've let it have so much power over you even as it exerts its force all over again.

New Day Church of Jesus Christ had youth events on most Saturday evenings, which were pretty much mandatory. Movies, karaoke, even some early version of Christian speed-dating for the teens. The community room is large and the little kids were kept on one side, drawing pictures or listening to stories. Age was the only beyond I could imagine, and so I always watched the big kids.

One warm July evening, I saw Mac leave the community room, and not by the door that led to the bathrooms. It was pizza night. The big boys threw wadded napkins, shouted insults, chugged sodas. Trevor, who already shaved a dark beard daily, decked a skinny boy and was "wrestling" him, but the other kid didn't look like he was having fun. As the mayhem escalated, Mac slipped out. I stepped out right behind her.

Mac walked across the church parking lot and straight into the woods. I hesitated because there wasn't any path, just trees and who knew what animals. But it was still bright out, and Mac didn't seem afraid. I followed quietly.

Mac was fifteen years old and unlike all the other teen girls at New Day. Lanky and awkward, she wore boyish clothes and her long brown hair pulled back in a ponytail. I thought she got away with dressing like that because she was so smart. Mac knew the Bible inside and out. She could quote verses by heart. Yet she refused to flaunt it. This frustrated Pastor Evans, how if he called out the chapter and verse, she'd deliver the words, but if he asked her to supply a passage that illustrated some point, she'd shake her head. She wasn't willing to twist the meanings of Bible stories to flesh out anyone's agenda. Sometimes, though, she'd spontaneously recite a verse, simply setting the words, verbatim, alongside life. She always carried a small Bible right in her back pocket. The word against the body.

On that warm evening she moved through the woods with the ease of an elk. As she ducked under a downed tree, the mossy log leaning against the upright trunk of another, she ran her hand along the cushion of green. Soon she emerged from the woods and onto the cut-off road that led to the dump. She walked slowly, tossing stones at trees. Sometimes she stopped and looked up at the sky, and I'd look too, expecting a plane or a bird, but there was only the blue. At the top of the small hill overlooking the dump, she turned and said, "Why are you following me?"

I shrugged.

She looked at me for a long time and I looked right back. The jeans, bright white boy's tee, and blue and green plaid flannel shirt looked good on her. She seemed so comfortable. I coveted her high-top sneakers.

"Why did you leave the church?" I asked.

Mac sat down on the hill's small summit, and I climbed up to sit next to her, regretting the stupid question. The dump had baked in the sun all day, and the stench was ripe, a cross between burnt rubber and rotted banana peels.

She said, "I have things I want to think about."

"Yeah, me too."

She looked at me again, and I felt exposed, like in those dreams where you realize you accidentally went to school naked. And yet, it felt strangely good, like deep honesty. Even the stench felt necessary right then. She asked, "You ever been out here?"

"Once to drop off our old refrigerator."

"Watch," she said, and nodded toward the pile of car parts, cut grass, carpet scraps, television hulls. There were four crows, their wings shiny black, flapping around the trash, picking at anything edible.

"The crows?"

"Them. For starters."

We sat in silence for a few minutes and watched the crows. They had their own personalities. Some were funny. Some, mean. One kept chasing the others away, like it deserved an advantage.

The sun set and I worried about walking back in the dark, but something kept me seated next to Mac, and I was sure glad I stayed, because at late dusk, a black bear came out of the woods and climbed up on the garbage. The crows screamed and leapt into the air, circled over the bear, as if they could drive it away, and then alighted on a different part of the garbage heap. The bear snoofed around until it found a relatively fresh dump of potatoes and cabbage and orange rinds. It scarfed all that down.

After the bear finished eating, it lifted its head and looked right at us. I grabbed Mac's arm.

"Won't hurt ya," she said. "He only wants to eat."

There was a fortifying calm about Mac. Like she knew a really good secret. I thought about all the other kids back in the church, shouting bad jokes and burping pepperoni breath, and how extraordinary it was that I got to be here, with the crows, bear, and Mac. Deep in my gut I felt a glow, and it spread all around us. I swear, I felt as if something lifted me right off the ground and floated me. I whispered, "Thank you, Jesus," and Mac smiled at me. She got it.

Mac let me walk back to the church with her and we went right through the murky woods. It was as if she had cat eyes, could see in the dark. I held onto the tail of her flannel shirt. The glowing and floating stayed with me the whole time I was with her.

That week I walked out to the dump every chance I got, hoping to find her. Finally, late Thursday afternoon, I saw her sitting on top of the hill. I was afraid she wouldn't be happy to see me, so I hid in the woods and watched. After about five minutes, she shouted, "I see you." At first I wanted to run in shame. But as I stepped into the sunshine, the shame was replaced by that Jesus feeling, levitating me to Mac. She got up, shook out each leg, and met me halfway. "I'm walking back now," she said and let me fall in step beside her.

This time, instead of going directly through the woods to the church parking lot, she headed off toward the creek. When we got near, she crouched down and said, "You know this plant?" She held her open hand under a whorl of fuzzy, serrated leaves as if presenting something sacred.

I shook my head.

"Nettles. They'll sting you. But you can also eat them." She reached into her back pocket and pulled out what I had always thought was a Bible. She flipped through the pages until she found the one she wanted, used a splay of fingers to hold up the book and show me the drawing. She spoke from memorized knowledge. "The whole plant is edible but it tastes best when it's young. If you cook it, the stingers mush out. You can also put the whole plant in a blender. It's good for joint and muscle pain." She handed me the little red book so I could read for myself, like maybe I wouldn't believe her. I looked at the cover: *How to Survive in the Wilderness.*

"Watch," she said. Mac scraped away a layer of forest floor. She pinched some of the black soil between two fingers, placed it on her tongue and swallowed. I kept my eyes on her face, awed.

"The difference between dirt and soil," she said. "Dirt is just dirt. Stuff you don't want to touch. But soil is completely clean. It's old trees and plants all broken down. It's perfectly fine to eat."

"Like the bear eating at the dump?"

"No, not like that at all. That bear shouldn't eat at the dump. He does it because it's easy. He should find his own roots, berries, and gophers."

The next Saturday night she once again walked right out of the church, the little square book in her back pocket, its shape discernable under her flannel shirt, moving against her butt as she walked. I knew what I'd seen: *How to Survive in the Wilderness*. Yet somehow my mind did a trick and pretended it was the Bible, after all. When she'd been gone a few minutes, I pictured her ducking under the mossy log.

I would have followed her again if I could have. No one had missed *her* the previous week. Pastor Evans liked working with kids who pushed the envelope: girls who showed too much skin or boys who smoked pot. He enjoyed wrestling with people's souls. With Mac's sensible clothes and quiet intelligence, she usually flew under his radar. But I was only twelve years old. Carly, the assistant pastor in charge of the little kids, had conniptions when I'd turned up missing. I lied and said I'd left the community room to take a nap in the lounge. Now she watched me like a hawk.

But I continued my weekday pilgrimages to the dump, sometimes checking once in the morning and again in the afternoon. I'd noticed the way the other teen girls ignored Mac and the teen boys, if they paid her any attention at all, snickered at her clothes and voice and stride. I thought of myself as the only person on Earth who appreciated Mac, probably her only true friend. I imagined her to be lonely, lonely enough to not mind the companionship of a little kid.

On a hot midsummer day, I was stunned to find Mac sitting on the hill above the dump with someone else. I stayed in the woods where I could watch, and this time she was too busy with that other person to notice me.

This would be August 9. Mac described that day's events with two words: *Robin's rocks*.

Mac's companion was a pretty girl, her own age, with brown skin and wavy black hair. Her close-fitting cool lime tank top showed a lot of her breasts, and tight jeans sheathed her full hips. Her feet were bare and her toenails painted a dark color, maybe blue. The two girls laughed and pulled at tufts of grass. Mac laid her arms across her drawn up knees and hid her face in them. Then she peeked at the girl out the side of her self-made mask. The girl pulled one of Mac's hands away from her face and held it in her own lap. She tickled Mac's palm with her fingers, as if writing words there. Mac's expression became very serious. The girl leaned in so that their faces were about two inches apart.

Mac kissed her. Right on the mouth.

That was okay. Jesus is love, right? This looked like love.

But the kiss didn't end. It just kept going. They looked like they were mashing each other's faces. The girl leaned back and pulled Mac down with her. They scooched their entire bodies against each other.

That white light I had felt with Mac? The glow I thought was Jesus? It popped and hissed like firecrackers now. It burnt and scorched, turned to hot, dry coals.

I bent down and found a rock. It was the size of a golf ball, with sharp edges. I fired it at the two girls. It landed near their feet, but they didn't even notice. I felt angry and helpless. I didn't think I could breathe. I picked up a bigger rock and fired it, too. This one landed a few feet away from their heads, and now they sat up, startled, looking around. I began pelting them with stones, throwing as hard and fast as I could. Mac leapt to her feet and picked up a rock herself. She threw it back at me and shouted, "Get out of here!"

That's when I saw the bear. It lumbered toward the dump, but stopped when it saw the human crossfire. Mac and her friend were up on the hill, but I was in the woods, in the bear's territory, and this only increased my fear. I meant to shout the words, but they came out in a hoarse whisper. "I'm telling," I said. "I'm gonna tell."

I ran all the way to the church, tripping on sticks, once falling so hard I scraped both forearms. I got right up, though, and ran so fiercely that by the time I got to the church parking lot I was wet with tears and sweat. Pastor Evans always said that he was there for us, that we could come and talk any time. I went directly to his office.

The door was locked. A dry mark board hung from a nail on the door and a marker dangled from a string. Across the top of the board were the words: *I want to see you! Leave a note.* I gripped the marker and wrote, "Robin was here."

I never told.

I never told.

I never told.

But Mac stopped sneaking out of church. She lost weight, as well as her purposeful gait. She stopped objecting when Pastor Evans or Carly called her Mackenzie. Her gaze, rather than searching out worthy subjects, seemed to land just anywhere. Mac's suffering was like bait for the ministry. Pastor Evans called on her more often, asked her to pass out the cupcakes or say the closing prayer.

I checked the dump daily, badly wanting to tell her I'd never told. Always the crows were there. Sometimes the bear showed up. I'd sit on the hill and think nonstop about that kiss between Mac and Sylvia, and then grow hot with chagrin at the memory of my rock throwing. Sometimes, when my despair became unbearable, I pretended Mac sat next to me. That way I could see the crows and bear and sky and woods through her eyes. Shimmering with light. I pretended to know that secret her whole body had seemed to hold. Before.

Each time I left the dump, I stopped in the woods near the creek, scratched away a layer of the forest floor, and ate a taste of soil.

I stalked her at church, too, but she looked right through me, as if I were invisible. She always moved away before I could say a word. Once I slid into the pew behind her in the chapel and, talking in a desperate whisper, said, "I didn't tell, Mac. I swear it." But she was gone before the first words left my mouth.

I saw the other girl everywhere. At the grocery. Waiting at the bus stop. In the library. She always wore gigantic gold hoop earrings that tangled and glinted in her dark hair. She was really pretty, even though her face was badly broken out with acne. I liked her mouth. It was asymmetrical and her smile was like cocking a gun, quick and then released. She worked in the Arco convenience store, and so I asked Gregory, whose dad owned the station, her name.

"You mean Sylvia?" he said. "That Indian chick?"

I shrugged and walked away, as if he'd misheard my question.

On a Saturday night in early September, after the opening prayer, while the little kids were still corralled with the big ones, Pastor Evans rested his hand on her shoulder with a restraining chumminess. "Mackenzie, I know the other kids would love to hear about wilderness survival. Go on up front and share a bit of what you know."

"I don't know about that," she said.

"Why, you're never without your book." It sounded like a reprimand, like she was never without the wrong book. He caught himself and smiled hard.

Carly moved to Mac's side, took hold of her arm, and lifted her out of the folding chair. The older boys slid low in their seats, smirking.

"Yeah, sure, okay," Mac said, as if she were making a choice. She walked to the front of the group and quickly said the stuff about nettles. As she spoke she shifted her weight from one foot to the other, kept her hands stuffed in her pockets. She listed three other plants you can eat, too. Then she tried to take her seat, but Pastor Evans smiled hard again and said, "A bit more, please. This is fascinating."

Mac talked about building a shelter against rain and wind. She said that a hat was the best protection against hypothermia because you lose ninety percent of your body heat from your head. She didn't tell them anything about crows, bears, or soil.

"Thank you, Mackenzie," Pastor Evans said when at last he let her sit down. "It fills my heart with joy when pretty girls like you take an interest in the works of God."

A couple of the big boys cracked up, elbowed each other. Carly shook her head at them. Later that evening, Pastor Evans took those boys aside and gave them a talking to. He did this in front of everyone, and I understood that the reproach was meant not only for the boys but for the girl who'd triggered their behavior. That was *September 9: How to survive.*

The next Saturday night the teens had a dance. Mac's notes in the back of her book lists her talk, how to survive, as having taken place *after* the *Hell* entry. I would have reversed those two. Surely *Hell* refers to the events I'm about to relate.

The little kids got to sit against the far wall and watch the dance. I rooted for Mac to slip out, to go spend the evening with the bear on the dump, but she was being watched too closely now. Several of the boys asked her to dance, and it was obvious even to me that the staff had made them. Seeing that big strong girl, who knew how to survive in the wilderness, and more, the difference between soil and dirt, in the arms of a pallid, spineless boy made me want to throw up.

But here's what broke my heart: I remembered what she had said about the bear, how it should be hunting its own good food, not eating garbage when it didn't have to. It ate the garbage anyway, voluntarily. So did Mac. I could see it: she was *trying*. She wore black slacks instead of her jeans. She had on a yellow blouse rather than her T-shirt and plaid flannel. Stupid flats on her feet. She waited between dances, staring straight ahead, some false pride propping her up.

Pastor Evans and Carly milled among the dancing couples to make sure the teens didn't touch too much. Most of the little kids fell asleep, sinking into sugar comas after all the cookies and juice. I stayed alert, felt as if I had to, not unlike the circulating ministry.

Then I saw her slip out, after all. I wanted to cheer.

Until Trevor stepped out right behind her.

I asked to go to the restroom and then raced down the hallway to another door to the outside. Mac and Trevor walked together now, crossing the parking lot, heading for the woods. I couldn't believe my eyes. The woods belonged to Mac. The soft green mosses and joint-healing nettles. Why would she show them to *him*?

A hand clamped around my upper arm and a rough female voice said, "Get back inside." It was Carly.

"But Mac and—"

"Mind your business."

"No!" I cried, bursting into tears. I went limp as she dragged me back inside the church.

Now, decades later, standing in that very same parking lot getting pelted by rain, I imagined Mac going limp, too, out in the woods with Trevor. I now understood that theirs had been a sanctioned excursion to the woods. Where some kids needed to be restrained, others needed encouragement. Pastor Evans might have considered it a compassionate correction. Just a kiss, he might have suggested to the boy. Trevor needed to learn kindness. Mac needed to be unlocked. How I wished, standing there in the rain as an adult, I could have found a way, back then, to rescue Mac.

School started that week, and I had a hard teacher, lots of homework. It got dark earlier in the afternoons, and I never walked to the dump again.

But sometimes, if I had some money, I stopped in at the Arco convenience store in the late afternoon during Sylvia's shift. I spent as long as I dared browsing the chips and candy, the beautiful girl a hot presence at my back. Then I'd carry the chosen snack to the counter and set it down with my dollar. I was afraid of her. Her face aflame with acne, her gaze scraped across me. Her tight clothes and big hoop earrings said fuck you. Still, I kept coming.

On about my tenth visit, she said, "You're the girl who threw rocks."

I quaked so hard I had to hold onto the edge of the counter. That day she wore a fuchsia sweater and skinny jeans tucked into high boots, a big belt.

"Little tattler," she said. "Rat."

"I didn't tell," I whispered.

"Right." She crossed her arms and her breasts squooshed up. "Get lost."

A guy plunked a six-pack of Coke down on the counter and she waved me aside. I stood outside the Arco station the rest of the afternoon, until the end of her shift, and when she came out, I said, speaking loudly and clearly this time, "I didn't tell."

"Go home," she said. "Don't come back."

The way I felt about Sylvia wasn't the Jesus feeling. There was no glow, no levitation. I admired Mac. I wanted to be her. Sylvia was gorgeous. I wanted to touch her.

One day, in the middle of math, my teacher got a call from the school office. After she hung up the phone, she said, "Your sister Sylvia is here for you, Robin. You have a dental appointment in fifteen minutes."

An icy fear blatted in my stomach. I could have told my teacher that I didn't have a sister, nor a dental appointment. But I packed up my books, all of them, my notebooks as well, as if leaving school for good, and then got my jacket out of the closet. I walked down the hall and entered the school office. An older girl I'd never seen before stood up from the row of visitor chairs and scolded, "So you, like, forgot, Robin? Mom's really mad. Hurry up. Let's go."

I followed her out the door and into the cold, rainy day. She didn't say another word and neither did I, though I snuck glances at her. She was tall and athletic, wore her dark blond hair short, and popped her knuckles continuously. We walked to the end of the block, and then around the corner, where the real Sylvia was waiting.

"Ha. It worked," Sylvia said. To me she explained, "This is Lynne. With the color of my skin, they weren't going to buy my being your sister." She put a hand on my shoulder and nodded at the gold Mustang parked at the curb. "Get in."

Lynne got behind the wheel, and Sylvia climbed in the front passenger seat and then cranked around to face me in the backseat. She looked cold, wearing just a sweater, and she crossed her arms, squooshing her breasts. Lynne looked straight ahead.

"Mac's in trouble," Sylvia said. "She tried to kill herself. She's in the hospital."

Lynne turned the key in the ignition, pulled the Mustang away from the curb.

A sound of anguish shot out of me, as rank as vomit, and I clamped my mouth shut. My fault. It was my fault. Her fortifying calm. Her glow. Gone. Because of me.

Sylvia welled up, too, her eyes full and her broken skin red. "I tried to see her but that pervert of a pastor of yours is in the room with her, won't let me in. You're in their church. He'll let you in."

"What am I supposed to do?" I croaked.

"Get her out of there."

Of course Sylvia and Lynne, at ages fifteen and sixteen, were children, too. They didn't have a real plan. They felt as desperate as I did. But I didn't know any of this at the time. So far as I was concerned, they were more savvy than true adults. They handed me the job of getting Mac out of the hospital, and I strained under the weight of that grave responsibility. Not only had I caused Mac's fall, her chances for life were now in my hands.

I got out of the Mustang and walked, alone, down the long corridors of the hospital. Nothing says despair better than a hospital room. The white. The tubes and instruments. The drips and astringent smells. The flickering of hope, like a flashing taunt. Maybe it'll be okay, but probably not.

Mac was on her back, the bed propping her up. Her eyes were open and she stared at the wall below the mounted television. She looked so lost.

"Mac!" I cried and started into the room, but Pastor Evans stood abruptly and blocked my entrance.

"Please," I told him as he pushed me into the corridor and shut the door behind us. "I need to see her."

"Not now, Robin. Mackenzie is in critical condition. She needs your prayers. And you can do that at home."

"I need to see her," I wailed and tried to step around him.

"I know your heart is heavy," he said. "Shall we pray together?"

The words of his prayer wrapped around me like a rope. The wail continued inside me but his "Amen" was like a gag. After praying, he gave me a little shove down the corridor, and I went like a zombie back toward the exit and the Mustang in the parking lot. I got in the backseat and Lynne started the engine. They didn't ask for an explanation and I didn't have one to give. We were all frozen in our grief.

The next day I skipped school and walked the three miles out to the hospital. I arrived a little after ten o'clock, and Pastor Evans was just coming out the front door of the main entrance. He took hold of my arm, gripping it in the same way Carly had outside the dance that night, and looked closely at my face, as if detecting the same disease in me that had been discovered in Mac. "What are you doing out here? How did you find out about Mackenzie, anyway?"

I tried to shake him off, but he held on tight.

"I'll drive you back to school."

"Let *go*," I said and kicked him in the shin.

"She's gone," Pastor Evans said angrily. "Mackenzie is gone."

More than thirty years have passed since that day. Pastor Evans might be sixty. He might be sitting in the church office a few yards away, writing this Sunday's sermon. I didn't need to find out. I didn't trust myself to behave honorably, not with my mother's death fresh in my heart, opening up all the other complicated wounds, too. Instead I drove to the Arco station. Of course Sylvia wouldn't still work there, but I went inside anyway. I recognized the man behind the counter. It was Gregory, the boy-now-man whose father owned the station. This would be the second time I asked him about Sylvia.

"Sure, I remember her. She's in Portland now. Runs a shelter for runaway kids. She comes back all the time to see her folks. They still live out on Walker Road."

I drove all the way back to Portland that same day and checked back into the same hotel. My mother's service would have been over by then, and no doubt the mourners had clucked about my absence. Well, I gave them something to be sanctimonious about. My gift to my mother's congregation.

In the morning, I found the shelter for runaway kids and, moments later, found Sylvia herself. I like to think I'm handsome enough. My short brown hair is lightened by gray, and my face is lined and brightened by a life in the outdoors. I try to hold inside me that glow I first discovered with Mac, a love of the bear and crows and forest. Though I've been haunted by my part in Mac's death, I've also survived because of what she showed me. I don't know what Sylvia saw when I stepped into her office.

She said, "Can I help you?"

Her smile was still quick and asymmetrical. She crossed her arms, that same gesture all these years later, and yes, it still squooshed her breasts. She'd plumped up quite a bit, and her acne had cleared, leaving scars. Her hair was still black and glossy as crow feathers, and she wore it shoulder length. She was still gorgeous.

"I'm Robin," I said. "The girl who threw rocks."

I watched her face as the memory came into focus. "Oh, my god."

"Yeah," I said. "Wow." I talked fast, wanting to establish a connection, and so I told her about my work organizing wilderness adventures for girls to learn self-esteem and build confidence, how maybe our programs could partner. Then I blushed.

"Awesome. Yeah, we should talk." She looked down, crossed and uncrossed her arms, and said, "It's because of Mac, isn't it? That you do this work?"

"Absolutely," I said, grateful that she had spoken her name.

The quick, asymmetrical smile. "Me, too. Let's have dinner tonight. Are you free?"

"Very."

She laughed and I realized that she was no longer the older girl. I wasn't twelve to her fifteen anymore; I was forty-five to her forty-eight.

"Okay, look," she said and glanced at her watch as if it were almost dinnertime rather than midmorning. "I've had two crises already today. More surely to come. But I should be able to get out of here by eight o'clock. Is that too late?"

"That's fine."

"Good. I have an idea. Meet me here, okay?"

At eight o'clock sharp, I parked on the street, a block away from the shelter, and walked down to get Sylvia. She locked her office, a fat ring of keys jangling in her hands, and waved goodbye to the kids and attending adults remaining for the night.

"It's raining," I said as she headed outside without a coat.

She shrugged. "I'm lucky to get out of the house with underwear on, let alone outerwear."

There was a lovely recklessness about Sylvia. Drops of rain caught in her hair as we walked down Burnside, passing Powell's Books. When she stopped at the door of a bar and pulled it open, I felt disappointed. I would have preferred somewhere more upscale, some roasted halibut and field greens, maybe a crème brulée, rather than a bar burger with rancid fries. We stepped into the dark interior and climbed a set of stairs. At the top, she grinned at me, as if delighted by our destination.

It was a lesbian joint. I mean, big deal, right? Maybe she wanted to confirm that she was in fact queer. But why so super pleased? She sashayed right up to the bar and kissed the cheek of a woman holding a beer and watching the television. The woman looked at Sylvia, then looked at me.

Mac. It was Mac.

She shouted, "Fucking A! It's the kid. Sylvia! It's the kid, isn't it?" She jumped off the barstool and grabbed me in a headlock, mussed my hair with her knuckles, as if I were still twelve years old. "How the hell are you?" she asked, releasing me.

Speechless.

"I wanted to surprise you," Sylvia said.

Thunderstruck.

"Can I get you a beer?" Mac asked. "Whiskey? Whadda ya want? It's on me."

This was a dream. It had to be. So I treated it like one. I jumped right to the heart of the matter, before I woke up and lost my opportunity. "Mac, I never told."

She frowned, smiled, frowned. She looked at Sylvia, and then back at me. "Say what?"

"That day at the dump. When I threw rocks at you and Sylvia. I never told anyone." I was talking to a dead person. This had to be some surreal manifestation of angst about my mother's death.

Mac slammed a palm down on the bar top and shouted, "Ha! I remember that! That was fucking hilarious!" She looked at Sylvia again and then bent over laughing. "God, that was funny," she said, straightening. "That was so funny."

"I thought you thought I told the pastor."

"*You* tell? That would have been rich. Baby butch that you were? You would have only implicated yourself." She punched my arm.

"That's not why I didn't tell," I said.

But she'd turned to order another beer from the bartender and drank half of it before looking at me again. This wasn't a dream. Mac was alive. Had been, all these years. She looked the same, thin and angular, though now her hair was short and her arms were covered with tattoos.

"We're going to get a bite," Sylvia said. "Come with us."

"Game's on," Mac said, nodding toward the mounted television. It reminded me of the one in her hospital room. "But it's great to see you," she said to me, and for a moment her eyes softened, lingered, so that I could hope those couple of times sitting on the hill above the dump, walking through the woods, had meant something to her, too.

Sylvia and I did go somewhere upscale for dinner, and I even ordered halibut. When our glasses of wine arrived, she said, "You look really shook up. I'm sorry I sprung Mac as a surprise. I guess I've had time to assimilate everything and didn't think how it'd be for you." She pushed her wild hair off her face, sipped her wine, pressed her lips together. "Actually, I should apologize for back then, as well. You were even younger than we were, just a little girl. I'm sorry we involved you in our drama."

"Your drama?"

"It took me years," she said, "to understand that it wasn't me who caused Mac's suicide attempt."

"*You?*"

"Yeah." She was wistful now, twisting a strand of hair in her fingers. Half a lifetime of emotion skidded across her face.

I shook my head, signaling my incomprehension.

"Me and Lynne. That big tall basketball chick with the gold Mustang. Who can resist that?" She laughed. "We were just kids. We didn't know our mouths from our feet. Seriously. But I did love Mac. We were each other's first, and it was so intense. But that sick church you all were in. Shit. It wreaked havoc with Mac's sweet soul. Know what I mean?"

Oh yeah.

"She couldn't handle it. What was happening between me and her, and how that played with her Jesus thing. And *I* couldn't handle the conflict tearing her up. I was only fifteen! I wanted to have fun. So I did. With Lynne. Mac found out and went apeshit."

"August 18?" I asked. The day marked *Hell*.

Sylvia squinted, looked at the ceiling for a long calculation, and then, "You know, that's probably about right."

All these years I had thought her dissolution had been my fault.

"But it wasn't my fault," Sylvia said. "It was that sick church. It'd been *years* in the making, her inability to reconcile who she thought she was supposed to be with who she really was. Our falling in love—" She paused and laughed. "Even if only for a couple of months at age fifteen. That was just the crisis that tipped the whole cart."

Pastor Evans's words had been thrumming in my ears all evening. *She's gone. Mackenzie is gone.*

"I thought she died."

"Died? You mean . . ."

"Yes. All these years I thought Mac was dead. Until I saw her in the bar an hour ago."

"Oh, Robin." Sylvia reached across the table for my hand. "God. I'm so, so sorry. I never would have . . . Why would you have thought . . . ?"

I held her hand tight, twelve years old, after all.

"Jesus," Sylvia said, understanding coming into her face. "No one tells kids anything." She took a gulp of wine. "She ran away. She left from the hospital that night."

I had been sobbing into my pillow as Mac ran through the darkness, her stomach pumped, her lungs and legs no doubt aching. Mac survived.

"What was the date?" I asked.

Sylvia shook her head. "I don't know. October something."

I knew. *October 12: The end of Jesus.* The same day I kicked Pastor Evans in the shin. Mac and I lost our faith on the exact same day. That was enormously comforting to me.

"Where'd she go?" I asked. Maybe Pastor Evans felt beat by Mac, one upped, because no one ever mentioned her at church, at least not around me. He must have needed her gone.

"All over. She tells wild stories from those years. Eventually she ended up here in Portland. She got a good job doing park maintenance for the city, until she hurt her back. Now she's on disability." Sylvia began twisting her hair again. "She's okay. Nice little house in northeast.

Single. Unless you count the three dogs and two cats." She shrugged. "She drinks too much." Then she laughed. "Mac dead? You couldn't kill her with a lead pipe."

It felt good to laugh, and afterward we met eyes across the table, held each other that way. That felt good, too. Reckless good.

When we said goodbye, we exchanged contact information and re-confirmed our intentions to get our programs together. I asked her for Mac's address, too. After I wrote down the street and number, Sylvia leaned forward and kissed me on the mouth. Then she shrugged, as if she'd surprised herself, and walked away.

In the morning I drove over to Mac's house and parked in front. It was the sweetest place, the yard a tangle of squashes, lettuces, purple lobelia, and orange nasturtium. Three bird houses, homemade from the looks of them, hung from different low branches of a huge willow. The house was small and needed paint. A stone path led to the front door.

How ludicrous we are at twelve years old, living our dreamlike lives, iconic moments looming. Floating in bubbles of silence. A few months after Mac's hospitalization and disappearance, my family moved to another town in Oregon, and then again the following year, until eventually we landed in Portland, where my mother just died.

Mac had survived and my mother was gone. The one truly gone. There are no words for a loss this big, against a backdrop this, in the end, small. I would perhaps spend another few decades trying to understand my new loss. I needed to go clean out my mother's apartment.

First I would return Mac's book. I opened it up and reread her notes, beginning with Sylvia and ending with Jesus. I found a pen and wrote, at the bottom of the list, today's date, followed by a colon. Then, *Mac, Mac, Mac.*

I put the book in my back pocket, wondering if I would really relinquish it, and walked up the path to knock on her door.

Lava Falls

Night and day the river flows. If time is the mind of space, the River is the soul of the desert. Brave boatmen come, they go, they die, the voyage flows on forever. We are all canyoneers. We are all passengers on this little living mossy ship, this delicate dory sailing round the sun that humans call the Earth. Joy, shipmates, joy.

Edward Abbey, *Desert Solitaire*

Nearly a thousand years ago, Renny rose in the dark, before anyone else had awakened, and silently, quickly made her way to the canyon rim. The sky sparkled with cool starlight as the beginning of daylight tinged the eastern horizon. She let herself over the lip of the canyon wall.

As Renny descended the cliff, her feet found tiny ledges and her hands grasped knobs of rock. She'd watched her brothers make the descent, studying their moves, memorizing the exact angle in the bend of their legs, their elbows. She'd listened to their concentrated breathing so she could replicate it, exactly.

She didn't dare look down, far below into the chasm where the muddy waters of the river flowed weak with drought. Up on the rim where they lived, the streams had been nearly dry for a few seasons, and there was no way to haul water from the big river up these cliffs. She'd thought they all ought to leave, find another home, even though the journey and search might be grueling.

154

The elders criticized her for voicing any opinion at all, but she hadn't been able to stop, and now that she had a child in her belly, her thoughts burst fuchsia and cerulean, as loud and bright as the pre-drought cacti blooms. She just couldn't shut up. She guessed that someone had decided that a baby would be the solution to her.

It didn't matter anymore. She didn't have to worry about talking too much. About the dry streambeds and empty bellies. The arguments over how best to survive. She and her child were leaving.

The people stored clay pots of seeds in caves partway down the cliff face, away from other animals and the hot sun. She wouldn't take much, just enough to grind into meal for her journey, with some left over to plant at her new home. She pictured trees for shade, a stream for drinking and bathing and wetting the seeds. She'd supplement the seeds with pinyon nuts and grass rice. She'd snare rabbits and roast agave.

Renny's feet touched down on a narrow level ledge. She made it! She'd heard her brothers laugh at the jolt of safety they always felt when their feet reached the path. She allowed herself to let go of the rock face with one hand and spread her fingers across her belly, but she didn't dare look down at the river still far below. Keeping one hand on the rock wall, she walked along the route until she came to the bridge.

A rock slide had carved a gulley through the path. The distance across this breach, miniscule in comparison to the grand canyon, was only the length of a tall man's body. Slim tree trunks had been lashed together and laid from one side to the other, the ends secured with piles of rock. The passage would be wobbly. She had to place her feet just so.

Renny set a foot on the sticks, curling her toes around the wood. She took deep breaths as she crossed the bridge and reached the other side with just a couple of inhalations and exhalations.

From there, she knew from careful listening, it wasn't far to the granaries. When she reached the two caves in the side of the cliff, she climbed up and into the mouth of the first one. She entered the darkness by feel, on her hands and knees, the rocks cutting into her skin. Here she could sit, away from the drop-off, and rest. But she didn't rest for long. Waving her arms in front of her, using her hands as eyes in the dark, she found the first pot. Reaching in, her hands sunk into the dry seeds. She let them run through her fingers several times before filling her pouch.

She would have liked to rest longer inside the stony cavern, but she knew she had to start her climb back up to the rim before anyone noticed her gone. She stepped out of the mouth of the cave. The light of dawn pearled the sky, washing away the last stars. She'd hide the pouch of seeds, bury it in a shallow hole, until tomorrow night when she would leave for good.

The river below, though diminished, still tore through the canyon. She could see it clearly now, the water an opaque, creamy brown, like a mother's milk mixed with mashed beans. The streams up on the rim, back when they still flowed freely, did so clear as the sky. But the big river moved so fast, pitched downhill so steeply, that it scoured the earth away from its bed and churned mud into its flow, prompting her people to joke that the big river was just very wet mud.

She crossed back over the bridge and scooted along the narrow ledge, her confidence blooming, until she couldn't find the matrix of handholds and toeholds leading to the top. She'd studied the route from above, not from below. She'd not thought to stop on her way down, once she'd reached the path, to mark the climbing route. The rock wall above her, in every direction, looked sheer, impossible to scale.

Sunlight now splashed against the top of the opposing canyon wall. She had to get back, couldn't afford to be caught stealing from the cache. Renny picked the most likely spot and began climbing. Sweat drenched her face and neck as the heat of the morning intensified. Her breath came in gasps. She clung to the crumbs of rock.

When she fell, the terror lasted for only a brief span of time, no longer than a scream, but it was the most intense fear possible, tumbled with boulders and slammed by waves of whitewater, and bursting with love for the daughter growing inside her.

Then the fear evaporated. And she began to dream.

Well into the twenty-first century, six women gathered at Lees Ferry, packing up their two bright yellow inflatable oar boats in preparation for rafting through the Grand Canyon.

Marylou, who'd organized this expedition, had flown into Flagstaff early that morning, looking down from her plane at the deep gash in the continent, glowing russet red in the morning sun, framed by two dams, the Glen Canyon upstream and the Hoover downstream. From so far above, the Glen Canyon Dam looked elegant, a pale slice of moon. Marylou knew this appearance of delicacy was deceptive. Holding back a river, and one so mighty as the Colorado, was a Herculean task, an undertaking that required outsized arrogance by the men who thought it possible. But, astonishingly, it *was* possible. Behind the dam wallowed the immense Lake Mead storing untold megawatts of energy for the hot, dry cities of the West. Sitting in her airplane seat, she'd laughed out loud at the breathtaking ambition of human beings.

Now at river's edge, Marylou was the one with lit gray eyes and messy medium-length matching gray hair. A high school language arts teacher, fifty years old and freshly divorced, she'd convinced her daughter, Paige, twenty-one, a coffeehouse barista, to come along, as well as her best friend since childhood, Laurie, fifty-two, a psychotherapist. Thinking it'd be nice for Paige if there were at least one other young person, she'd also invited Kara, thirty-two, a favorite prior student who now worked as a firefighter in a small town in the Southwest. Maeve, seventy-three, a retired philosophy professor, had once, briefly, been married to Marylou's father and was probably a bad idea, but the older woman had been insistent when she heard about the trip. And really, why not? Marylou hoped that twenty-three years down the road, she'd be fully recovered from the trauma of Joe leaving her and embarking on new adventures herself. Finally, Marylou had been delighted to get a yes from Josie, forty-one, a woman who did workshops on survival skills at the high school from time to time. A real coup, given that Josie worked as a river guide and had run the Grand Canyon several times.

Marylou waved goodbye to the outfitter, a guy named Raymond, a member of the Hualapai tribe who owned the land at the takeout 226 miles downstream. Raymond had rented them the boats, as well as most of the gear, and would meet them at trip's end. Then she put her hands on her hips and faced the river. The sound of Raymond's truck rumbling back out the road to the highway faded and the swish of moving water came into the foreground of her consciousness. She smiled and congratulated herself on dreaming up — and fully executing! — this trip. She needed this big river, these good friends, so badly right now. How stupid of Joe to leave the sanctuary — at least *she* had thought of it as a sanctuary—of their home in this horrific moment in history, when the fabric of the entire country was being ripped apart, when everything they held dear was being dismantled. Then again, why should she expect his behavior to be logical? Nothing about human beings was logical. It might well have been his terror that caused him to bail. *Oh, stop*, she told herself. Trying to make sense of what Joe did, any thoughts of him at all, threatened to destroy her excitement about the next two weeks. So she hummed the Dixie Chicks' "Wide Open Spaces" to keep him at bay.

Laurie was the first of the six women to take an interest in the only other party at the Lees Ferry put-in. The man, somewhere in his young sixties, wore chocolate brown board shorts, a tan T-shirt, and bright blue Chacos on his feet. Flyaway wisps of graying hair barely covered his scalp and his bent wire-rim glasses sat askew on his face. The young woman had pink skin, freckled all over, and bright strawberry blond hair, knotted on top of her head. She wore big white plastic-framed sunglasses and a short flowered sundress. She moved like a cat, lithe and supple, with a purposeful intelligence. Even the way she strode to their pile of gear, pawing through it until she extracted two hats, embodied a double message, one of cute youth (the bare legs and twitchy butt, jaunty smile) and another of intention, maybe even calculation. She popped on an oversized straw cowboy hat, grinning under the shade of the wide brim, and handed him one of those goofy synthetic jobs with the skirt hanging from the back brim to protect his neck. She didn't rub in, or even comment on, the sunscreen smeared unevenly all over his face, which suggested to Laurie that the pair didn't know each other well. In fact, it became evident that he was a geology professor and she his student because as he worked the foot pump to inflate their raft, he began his field lectures, his arms waving toward the cliffs upstream. Laurie caught words like "Triassic" and "sandstone" and "Chinle Formation." The blue casing of their rubber boat lofted a bit with each word.

Laurie decided she didn't much like the student. The young woman listened to her prof's open air lecture with a cold concentration. The word shrewd might apply. It was as if she had an abundance of confidence that she kept under wraps. She was smart *and* cute, and she knew it, but for some reason protected the smart while flaunting the cute. Annoying. Of course Laurie couldn't assess an IQ from afar, or any other personality traits for that matter, and yet you'd be surprised at how much about a person was obvious from minute one. She had to put those snap observations aside, always, in her work as a psychotherapist. But now she was on vacation. Couldn't she just this once allow herself to make a slew of assumptions about this stranger couple? It was fun. She smiled at her freedom.

Laurie forgave the man his needlessly loud voice in favor of admiring his obvious passion. He gesticulated, expounded, his heart racing—this last part she guessed, of course, but what thrilled a geologist more than the Grand Canyon?

"The Grand Canyon," the man nearly shouted, "is neither the deepest nor the longest canyon on Earth, but what makes it magnificent is its extraordinarily intact geological history—its strata dating back more than *1.8 billion* years with many intervening periods of geologic history represented in its exposed cliffs and slopes. Stacked in sequence! Ancient deserts, mountains, even *seas*. All in evidence right here in these cliffs."

His voice squeaked once or twice with excitement. In fact, the man was practically glowing. Who could blame Laurie for noticing that he was also quite fit for his age? His legs were muscled and his shoulders broad, as if he'd rowed many a mile and hefted thousands of ancient rocks. Even his stomach was flat, and Laurie rarely saw that on men of his years. She enjoyed the frisson of pleasure shivering up from her pelvis and into her breasts.

Good for him, she rallied on silently, for mentoring a female grad student. It had to be difficult in geology, what many would consider a man's field, even today, or especially today, in this so-called post-feminist era, where the obstacles women encountered were said to be imagined. Laurie knew differently from her clients, especially in traditionally male fields.

Nothing lit Laurie's erotic core more than personal passion, and his was evident. But equally appealing to her was evidence of just action. This man—she heard the young woman call him Howard—was opening the crown jewel of geological fieldwork, the Grand Canyon, to a female student. That was admirable. Laurie liked him very much. Since they were launching from Lees Ferry on the same day, their two expeditions would likely see more of each other along the journey. This too pleased Laurie.

For the next two hours, she helped the other five women in her group pack up their two boats with the boxes and coolers of gear and food. She decided, while dragging two dry bags full of tents to the boats, that she'd concentrate on herself this trip. She didn't have to take care of a soul. Her mother had died six months ago, after a long illness in Laurie's spare bedroom; this loss prompted her to break up with Alan after a three-year tepid affair; and she wouldn't have a single client for two weeks. Surely with six women there'd be drama. But it didn't have to be *her* drama. She'd keep distance, keep quiet, open herself to the air and water and rock of the canyon. Think of herself for once. What a novel idea.

Did that mean she was allowed to fantasize about the geologist or did it mean she should *not* fantasize about the geologist? She'd vowed, just last month, that she was done with men. Alan, after all, was handsome, gainfully employed, and loved the outdoors as much as she did. Giving him up was a big statement. In her younger years, he might have been more than enough. But she found his deafness (or did he choose not to listen?) beyond irksome, his two daughters insufferable, and in fact she never had loved him enough. He became a placeholder. A distraction while her mother died. What if she left that place open, let in the breeze of possibility, or simply filled the space with herself?

Laurie caught the geologist's eye and smiled. He turned away. Maybe he was married. All the better. She could flirt without consequences.

Josie noticed the shrink—what was her name again?—staring at the couple also launching today and wondered if she too was irritated by his loud lecturing. He seemed to be shouting everything he knew about the geology of the region.

"The upper part of the canyon is known as Marble Canyon. The rocks upstream from here, in Glen Canyon, belong to a much younger group. But ahead!" He clapped his hands, as if to summon the attention of everyone at Lees Ferry. "We're going to see the great plunging fold called the East Kaibab Monocline, not to mention the Grand Canyon Supergroup and Great Unconformity."

Josie knew exactly why the guy annoyed her so much. He reminded her of her dad, him extemporizing, talking nonstop, his enthusiasms bigger, grander, louder, brighter than anyone else's could ever be. And

Josie, as a little girl, as a teenager even, trying to keep up, to understand his wild joy. When she was five years old, he built her a child-sized kayak and taught her to paddle on a trip down the Rogue River in Oregon. "You're an otter!" he shouted from his own boat. "The kayak is an extension of your torso. Feel the water in your thighs. In your *feet*." She wheeled the paddle, dipping the blades, for all she was worth through stretches of flat water until he decided she was skilled enough to try a small rapid. "You're not afraid," he told her. "Fear is impossible when you know how to read the river."

She would never tell him, even then as a little girl, how that whitewater made her feel. Yes, fear, the most intense fear ever, but also thrill. Even then, in a little girl kind of way, she knew that she was her father's daughter, that she was doomed to love a wilderness that many didn't even know existed. She did rebel, but silently, in her own language, knowing that she was a salmon, not an otter, feeling the froth in her head, not her thighs. But her father's brand of love was in her DNA and any real rebellion was impossible. He'd ruined her for life, bequeathing her his longing for transcendence, a longing that rendered regular experience dull. Anything short of endorphins-drenched joy made her impatient.

She knew now at age forty-one that she was just like him. At least a lot like him. But that didn't mean she didn't still resent him for the inheritance. It didn't mean that he wasn't still an arrogant jerk. His own personal walls were as hard and magnificent as these canyon walls. Between them he let flow his own private Colorado, pure and fierce and guarded. Only for him.

Which is what *she* should be focusing on, too. The river. Just the river. Always the river. She let her gaze travel as far as it would go downstream, and then climbed it up the northern cliffs. How did she even get here? Born into the late twentieth century, yet stuck like her father in this centuries-old rock sandwich. Time seemed to have entered its own whitewater rapid lately, the years surging, wrecking all the beaches and harbors, smashing boats against rocks. So much of this country's wilderness was being destroyed, and so quickly, in the human desperation for resources. At least for the profits those resources delivered. Maybe that was why she'd agreed to this trip. Maybe spending two weeks in Earth's deep history would be instructive.

Ah, cut the drama. Face the truth. This wasn't about Earth's history. It was about her own history. That was why she was here, why she'd said yes to Marylou's invitation.

Exactly twenty-five years ago, Josie ran the Grand Canyon for the first time. It was far from her dad's first time. He was one of the famed wooden dory rowers from the early days and had already navigated the big waters of the Colorado, and dozens of other rivers all over the West, many, many times. He outfitted her in her own rowboat, adult-sized this time, and he paddled a kayak. They launched, just the two of them, on her sixteenth birthday. She wasn't afraid. Not anymore. Fear, she knew by then, was a luxury, and one she couldn't afford, not with a dad like hers. He'd taught her that you took risks to get places you wanted to get to, and he applied that agenda to emotional, mental, and physical journeys. If you failed, you experienced pain. So what. Maybe, someday, you'd experience premature death.

Not yet, not for Josie and not for him, either. He and her mom lived in their hippie abode, a ramshackle wooden dwelling, not unlike a tree house only it sat on the ground, with loads of skylights and flowering trees, in the hills above Berkeley. They drank copious red wine and played stringed instruments, and though both approached seventy, they still climbed mountains, though smaller ones, and ran rivers, albeit slower ones. Her father was a legend in his own circle. He didn't even know there were other circles.

Josie remembered every drop of time from those fast days during her first time on the river. She piloted her rowboat expertly through House Rock Rapid, the Roaring Twenties and Georgie Rapid, even Hance, Sockdolager, Horn Creek, and Hermit rapids. Her confidence soared, matching her father's, as she pulled the long oars through the water, her legs stretched out in front of her, her back nearly resting on the rim of the stern before lunging forward with all her might for another stroke. At sixteen she'd bought into her father's myth of invincibility. If possible, she had become even more arrogant than he was. A river running a fast life. Already.

Then they came to Crystal Rapid just past Mile 98, one of the most feared and respected rapids in the canyon. In the whole damned country, for that matter. Two debris fans enter the river at that point, colliding and turning the flow into a massive, roiling chaos of giant waves. Her dad shot through in his kayak, expertly paddling like a fool through the ten-foot waves coming at him from all directions, whooping his childlike laughter of ecstasy.

Josie waited upstream in her rowboat, pausing in the tongue of the rapid, the smooth green water that funnels into the whitewater. She heard his jubilant hollering, saw the red blades of his paddle flashing in and out of the white, and then saw him get spit out the bottom, still upright, always successful when he pitted himself against the elements.

A pleasurable hubris coursed through her blood. She knew she was supposed to have carefully watched the route he took through the rapid, and also that it was her job to not just replicate what he did but to assess for herself whether it was the best way. Take into account her size, the kind of boat she piloted, the second by second changes in the water's behavior. Rule number one of reading rivers was to not assume anyone, not even your legendary father, knew the best line to take. Anyhow, he paddled a kayak and she rowed a rowboat. All of this considering had to happen in an instant because the river ferried her boat along the tongue, into the V, and sucked her into the turbulence.

A moment later, she was swimming. Or drowning. Water swamped her from above, from every direction, and she thrashed for air, drank too much river. She felt hands gripping her ankles, dragging her down to the river bed, more hands pinning her there on the bottom. She opened her eyes and saw the bubbles, the mud and rocks, and heard an eerie hissing. Whatever held her ankles let go and she got tumbled, as if in a massive washing machine, head over heels, snorting in water, the hissing morphing into a siren, a high-pitched scream in her ears. She thought it was the call of death.

To this day, she doesn't know if she lost consciousness. She just knows that, besides the hands pulling her under, there were two more hands, strong ones, grabbing the shoulder straps of her life jacket and hoisting her, like a dead river otter, onto the top of the kayak. Somehow her dad managed to paddle, with her draped across the bow, to an eddy at the side of the current. There he thumped her back and, she'll never forget, said, "You lost the boat."

She flung herself off the deck of his kayak, well aware that she was committing herself back to the river, and thereby probably committing suicide — Tuna Creek Rapid was less than a mile downstream and she'd be swept into that liquid entropy—but she wanted only to get away from him. Hypothermic, exhausted, maybe already dead. Fine. That would teach him. The eddy was calm, however, and she only bobbed for a moment in the ice cold water before she swam a couple of strokes to the riverbank where she crawled out, sat on the rocks heaving for breath, and used every ounce of will she possessed to not cry. She did not cry.

Her father dragged his kayak onto the rocks and fumbled in the hatch where he found a thermos. He poured her a cup of hot chocolate. Which she wanted to refuse but couldn't. Then he dug back into the hatch and retrieved the bag of gorp, a disgusting mix of raisins, M&Ms, and peanuts, a concoction she'd always hated, and hated to this day. He'd insisted, though, throughout her childhood, on every wilderness trip, that she eat it. There had been some short trips where gorp was the *only* food they ate. That morning on the rocks just below Crystal Rapid, she threw back handfuls of the cloyingly dense fare, her survival instinct kicking in big time. Her body knew it needed calories, even if she thought, for a few minutes anyway, that she didn't want to live.

"You're in luck," her father commented. "Look."

Josie raised her eyes. He held her paddle aloft. "I grabbed it right before I grabbed you. I managed to toss it like a spear to shore. Brilliant!"

She looked away.

"The thing is," he carried on.

"I *know*," she cried. "Whatever you do, don't lose your paddle or your boat. I *know*."

He'd told her a thousand times: if a rapid flips you, you're supposed to grab onto the boat. It might save your life in the immediate moment. But it will also greatly increase your chances of survival in the near future as you'll need a boat, never mind the supplies in the boat, to finish the trip.

As if grabbing onto a boat that has flipped you in a rapid is even remotely possible. She squeezed her eyes shut, wanting to ward off the coming lecture on the best practices for doing just that, a lesson he'd given her many times already. But he surprised her by remaining quiet for a moment. Then he said, "Double lucky. The boat is just downstream, I can see it, in another eddy. Do you think you can swim to it?"

Swim. The man was insane. She was so exhausted, she couldn't even lift her arms. And she was seriously cold.

"Or," he said, his voice softening. "You could paddle the kayak and I could swim. Let's do that."

Later that night at their campfire, he told her that she'd done well so far and that capsizing the boat was the best possible thing because now she wouldn't be afraid of flipping. "There are only two kinds of boatmen," he told her, the firelight accentuating the golden flecks in his devilish eyes. "Those who have flipped and those who *will* flip." He used his bare hands to take the can of tinned beef stew from its place in the coals and, in a show of indulgence, wrapped his kerchief around the hot metal before handing it to her. "I'm proud of you, Josie."

Her father was a legend. But he was old now. She'd been working as a river guide herself for nearly twenty years. She'd never intended that. She refused the cliché that she was trying to prove something, to herself or to her father, but she knew that was what it looked like. She'd meant to move on a long time ago. Maybe have kids. Or do *something* normal. But rivers, they were better than spouses, she couldn't deny that. And maybe she'd one-upped her father by pronouncing them better even than kids. She hadn't saddled herself as he'd done. She was free as an undammed river. Once you got used to that intoxicating connection, that oneness with something so wild and fierce, regular life paled.

She knew from hours and hours of riverside conversations that this was true for all river guides. Even him. But he'd compromised.

Not her.

Sure, at some point, maybe at several points, you got to a place in your life where you thought you were done. Especially with *this* river. How many times did you have to prove to yourself that you could navigate the biggest water? But you weren't done. You came back. Even if you stayed away for a long while, as Josie had now for several years, ever since the Park Service stopped patrolling and the culture in the river corridor went rogue. You came back.

The truth was, when Marylou emailed her with the invitation, she wrote back yes within five minutes. "I just turned fifty," the teacher had written. "I'm menopausal. My marriage has ended. The world is going to hell in a handbasket. I'm scared. We're all scared. And somehow I've been thinking of you and your workshop. Survival, yes. But connecting with the true power on this planet, rock and water. You're so matter-of-fact when you talk to the kids, but I feel your plain words as love. This is way too much personal information! Just this: I'm planning a Grand Canyon rafting trip. Please join us."

Josie knew Marylou relatively well, in a work kind of way, having done at least five workshops at the high school. She knew the woman was a lot crunchier than she was, loved kids and loved to sing. She admired Marylou's practical approach to the national nightmare, meaning she taught high school, surely the most difficult job in existence, and one that required an inexplicable capacity for hope. Josie had said yes because, as different as they were, she trusted Marylou. And more, she couldn't resist the siren song of the Grand Canyon.

Josie hadn't even asked who else was coming along. She just said yes—yes, yes, *yes!*—swamped by a longing to see the river again. She relished the idea of running the Colorado without responsibility, a private trip, one where she wasn't accountable to anyone. No reports to write at trip's end. No false politeness to a group of crass clients. No sixteen-hour work days, from morning coffee at five a.m. to bandaging strangers' blisters at nine p.m. The Grand Canyon, the Colorado River, on her own terms.

But she realized now, as they finished packing up the boats, that she'd been foolish. Of *course* she'd be guiding this trip. Josie had the most experience by far with her nine runs. And it wasn't like she could just sit back and let people make stupid decisions. So not only would she be the de facto trip leader, she'd have to do the work without the acknowledgment, without the buy-in by the "clients," and without the pay.

An eerie stasis shimmered the hot air at Lees Ferry, the aura of the place so different from the last time Josie had been there. In the interim, the government had sold off so much public land to private mining interests. The Arizona uranium mines had devastated the water supplies for many of the native people living in the region and threatened to contaminate the water flowing into the Grand Canyon. The Park Service had been all but gutted, leaving a skeletal budget for only the most famous parks. Even at Lees Ferry's parking lot, cracked pavement hosted weeds as tall as Josie herself. Graffiti covered the cinderblock walls of the restrooms and the locks on the doors had been broken, though no one would want to use the overflowing toilets anyway. There wasn't a ranger in sight. Josie was eager to get going, to commit herself to the deep canyon where there would be no reminders of the nation spiraling out of the control. For the next two weeks, anyway, she'd be free. This was why she'd said yes.

"You okay taking the helm of one boat?" Marylou asked, right on cue. Yeah. Sure. Of course.

"We can take turns," Marylou said, reading Josie's face, "but for today, starting out, it'd be good if someone who knew what she was doing took charge."

Josie nodded.

As the six women found seats in the two fully loaded oar boats, Josie took one last look at the father and daughter pair, also about to launch. The girl, she'd heard the name Brynn, somewhere in her thirties, placated her father, Howard, nodding at his ongoing discourse, pretending to listen. Josie detected an anger in the young woman's body. Not on the surface, not even below the skin, but deeper, as if an organic rage inhabited her viscera, intensified their functions, resided patiently, waiting for release.

Maybe Josie was projecting.

"Good luck," she said to the girl under her breath.

Josie shoved her boat into the current and hopped on the stern tube, climbed over the cross tube, and took hold of the two long oars. She leaned all the way forward, let the skinny wooden blades drop into the water behind her, and began pulling. Marylou, who rowed the other boat, hailed Josie with a big full arm wave, and began singing, in her throaty but forceful alto, Libby Roderick's "Low to the Ground." The four passengers whooped their excitement.

They were off.

For the next two days, Laurie looked for the handsome professor and his student to no avail. Perhaps they were doing the trip in a more leisurely fashion so that Howard could show Brynn up-close-and-personal views of the rock. Laurie wouldn't mind up-close-and-personal views of *him*. She could entertain herself with fantasies, in any case. She was deep into one of these, the professor and herself swimming *au naturel* in one of the river's deep jade pools, the hot midday sun a luscious contrast to the icy water, when Maeve interrupted her musing with, "Oh, how I would love to have seen the river when it was wild and free."

Annoyed with the intrusion, Laurie eyed the older woman's lumpy, veiny legs suspiciously, as if they spoke to Laurie's own imminent demise.

Laurie cared a lot about how she looked and prided herself on a healthy libido at fifty-two. She knew to not dress like a twenty-year-old, but she wouldn't be caught dead in those homely shorts, balloony and a hideous mustard color. Maeve wore her smoke-colored, curly hair in the style of a mop and had a propensity to grin at nothing.

Laurie knew it was shallow of her to be hypercritical of another woman's physical presentation. But was it so wrong to take pride in one's appearance? A good haircut went a long way toward mediating the effects of age.

Laurie leaned over the boat's inflated tube and dragged a hand in the water. "Feels pretty wild and free to me."

"Hardly," Maeve countered. "Every drop is rationed. The dams have eliminated the great seasonal floods that once swept through the Grand Canyon."

Laurie let the older woman have the last word.

But later that day, as they floated through a narrow and spectacular stretch of the Marble Canyon, Maeve felt it necessary to provide the history of the aborted Marble Canyon Dam. She pointed out the bore holes, which had been driven into the canyon walls, before environmentalists David Brower, Martin Litton, and others managed to stop the project.

"Well, and they *did* stop it," Laurie said, hoping to make the point that they should enjoy what had been saved rather than mourn what might have been lost.

"The Marble Canyon Dam, yes," Maeve said in her calm philosopher voice. "But of course the river is hardly free. Our entire trip is framed by—indeed, controlled by—the Glen Canyon Dam upstream and the Hoover Dam downstream."

"The dams were built," Laurie snapped. "It's done."

"You can't just harness a river!"

"Apparently you can." Laurie was ashamed of herself for digging in.

"One day," Maeve replied, undaunted and unoffended by Laurie's retorts, "the dams will crumble away. I wonder how many years from now. A hundred? Five thousand? We don't know. But we do know, with certainty, that the dams imprisoning the Colorado River are just a blip on its history. The river *will* be free again one day."

"Yes." Laurie forced herself to speak the conciliatory word.

"Imagine," Maeve said, in reference to who knew what, that goofy old lady's smile on her face.

Marylou, who rowed the boat in which Laurie and Maeve rode, launched into a lusty protest song about dams. She'd had this need to sing for as long as Laurie could remember. They'd been best friends since their mothers were in the PTA together, all the way through grammar and high school, despite the two years difference in their ages, and now their entire adulthood, and Laurie had come to admire her friend's unwavering optimism. Even now, just a year after her husband had left her for another woman, completely shocking her heart, Marylou responded by organizing an epic journey and singing through the first couple of days.

If Laurie was honest with herself, and she tried to be always, she had to admit that a part of her welcomed Marylou's newfound wider view of life. Not her heartbreak, of course not that, but there'd always been a gap in their friendship between Laurie's clear-eyed view of relationships and Marylou's rose-tinted one. How Marylou could have missed Joe's desperation, his itchiness, his foot which had been out the door for years, was beyond her. Laurie herself had been married three times. Of course there was no pride in that. But there *was* knowledge. Wisdom? Perhaps too strong a word, and perhaps not.

It was just that she now felt she and Marylou could be closer, and what was the harm in celebrating that?

Laurie pivoted around to give her friend's knee a squeeze. Just before turning back to face forward again, Laurie glimpsed a spot of blue upstream. The professor and his student! It cheered her instantly and she wished she hadn't tangled with Maeve. She didn't mind *his* musings on the earthly timelines. Maybe she was sexist. After all, Maeve's PhD was as valid as his. No, that wasn't it. He was passionately appreciative, forward looking, and Maeve was full of doomsday, crumbling dams, enslaved rivers. Not to mention her bad shorts and haircut. Well, then too, Laurie just liked a man, that's all. She smiled at herself.

A hard jostle almost sent her over the side of the boat and she realized she hadn't even noticed the upcoming riffle. She grabbed two of the straps holding down their gear and rode out the bouncy waves, a few washing into her lap, wetting her orange and red and yellow sarong. Once the ride smoothed out again, she turned to watch the cheery blue raft fly through the riffle. Howard's boat caught a speedy current and swept it right smack into the women's boat. The collision of inflated rubber caused a big jolt, and they all shared a laugh. Laurie tried to think of something clever to say, but Howard rowed hard, pulling away quickly before she thought of anything. Sometimes keeping silent was the most advisable course of action, especially with men, and she was pleased she'd been sparing in her attention during the interaction. The pair took the lead, remained visible for a couple of hours, but then disappeared altogether by late afternoon.

Laurie saw their camp late that day, next to a trickling waterfall, and longed to stop as well. The young blond Brynn stood under the waterfall in her athletic bra and shorts, letting the water sluice over her head and face, and seemed to not even notice the two yellow boats skimming past. Howard, who was arranging their gear on the beach, waved. All six women waved back and Laurie felt irrationally disappointed that he'd become not just hers, but all of theirs.

On the morning of day three, the river made a swirling S, from Mile 41 to Mile 45, and midway through that meander a raven drew Kara's attention to a place high up on the canyon wall. The bird flew in circles, each one bigger than the one before, its glossy black wings soaring against the red rock. In the center of those loops of flight, at a spot on the side of the vertical cliff, Kara spotted a few sticks placed horizontally across a wash. She squinted, thinking she maybe didn't see them at all, because how would sticks, probably actually small logs, get placed on a ledge way up there? Before the Glen Canyon Dam went live in 1963, the volume of the river grew enormously with spring snowmelt, but even then the river wouldn't have flooded anywhere near that high.

The sticks spanned a gap in the stone wall, as if bridging a route across the face of the rock. There was a figure on the sticks, lithe legs crisscrossing their way along the length. A flow of raven hair, long and uneven, swished out from her shoulders as the woman tilted, almost lost her balance. Then she lunged, made the far side, where she squatted, as if in the relief of safety. But none of that was possible. Kara couldn't have seen a human figure on the side of the cliff.

"It's an Anasazi bridge." Josie's voice startled Kara.

"Really?" She twisted around to look at Josie, who for the third day in a row was piloting one of their boats. She was such a solid girl with tight clear skin and a tighter ponytail, more just a stub of light brown hair. Her ears, in full view with the hair pulled so completely back, nearly came to a point at the top. Her eyes were a tawny color, like a mountain lion's.

"Hundreds of years old," Josie said. "The Anasazi had granaries in the sides of the cliffs."

Kara didn't say she'd seen a girl walking across the bridge, because of course she hadn't. As their boat floated swiftly downstream, she turned for one last look. There: tiny sticks across a rock fall, far above the river and far below the rim. No figure. Just very old sticks, a red face of rock, topped by a blue sky and circling ravens.

"But how did they even get down to the bridge? And the granaries?"

"Hold tight," Josie said. "Rapid coming up."

Kara liked Josie's voice, the quiet confidence backed by a reserve of deep vulnerability. It was a compelling combination. *Hold tight. Rapid coming up.* Kara let the words tremble through her and was shocked by the pleasure.

As they slid into the rapid, romped on the big waves, she felt her resolve to resist that pleasure jostle free. She gave up. Gave in. The hot, dry desert air laid bare the essence of herself as a body, no more, no less. The walls of radiant rock crumbling. The often-interrupted but never-ending migration of the green river. Her thoughts unmoored, flowing loose and fast, easy and serendipitous. The heat and clarity.

Maeve, the other passenger in her boat that day, made an *mmm* sound, as if she'd just bitten into a ripe peach. Alarmed that her thoughts had been read—though that was as impossible as there being a girl on the side of the cliff—Kara jerked around to look at Maeve, who smiled happily at seemingly nothing. Kara laughed out loud.

Paige wished she were in the boat with Kara. She thought she might have a crush on her, which kind of surprised her because even though all her friends had dated girls, at least once, she never had. Anyway, she was currently dating Justin and found him quite captivating. For one thing, he was four years older. So refreshing! He knew a *lot* about sex, which they had in the supply closet at work, as often as possible, deep in the aroma of coffee beans. She liked his calloused hands, his inscrutable eyes, which were always bruised looking, like he never slept. Life tortured Justin. He made no bones about that, all his difficulties with employment and family, and she knew she'd never want to, like, *marry* him, but it was the best sex she'd ever had in her life. His need for her was so great, and his, well frankly, skills, were off the charts. She even asked her mom if he could come on this trip, knowing full well he wouldn't want to come, and also knowing her mom would say no, which she did. She supposed she just wanted to make the challenge to both of them. Would Justin give her a whole two weeks, not to mention his vacation days? And was her mom willing to see, really see, Paige's life, her real life? Also, just making the request became a way to bring him along in her mind, and she did think of him all the time, and how they could be fucking in the tent or in the sand or even maybe in the shallow pools along the shore. He told her she was a nymphomaniac and she'd said, hell yeah she was.

So this possible crush. Kind of a surprise. Kara was tall and lanky, with shoulder-length black hair, currently tangled because whose wasn't out here, and a meditative approach to everything. She didn't speak quickly. She spent more time alone than the others did, sitting by the river while the rest of the women gathered around the camp kitchen, or taking walks up side canyons by herself. Nah, Paige decided, the girl really wasn't her type, and anyway, she did like the equipment on Justin. Quite a bit.

Still, she wanted to be closer to Kara, wanted to know how she achieved that peacefulness, that calm independence. What Paige had, she realized, was a powerful friend crush.

Over the next few days, Paige's curiosity about Kara grew, but her enthusiasm for every other aspect of the trip ebbed. In fact, things just got worse and worse, including a bout of diarrhea, protracted dinner conversations on topics that interested her not at all, hellishly hot weather, and her mom's endless singing. Oh, and there was the time Maeve accidentally let go of an oar and the end smacked Paige in the face.

On the sixth afternoon, the women battled a fierce upstream wind. The strong gusts splashed waves in their faces and made downstream travel nearly impossible. Paige had been stuck at the oars for most of the day, rowing and rowing and rowing. If she stopped for even a second, the wind pushed them back upstream. The current accounted for nothing against this gale. Her arms and back ached, and she was starving. There'd been a few "jokes" about her youth making her responsible for more rowing than the other women, and she resented it. Today, during the brutal windstorm, Kara and Josie had taken turns rowing the other boat, but her two passengers, Maeve and Laurie, lasted five minutes each when they took turns, and then they handed the oars back to Paige. Her mom, riding in the other boat, had sung all the verses of "Blowing in the Wind" a couple of times, and then remembered "Wind Beneath My Wings," a song right up her alley, and sang that one with too much passion and not enough skill. It took an enormous amount of self control for Paige to not scream, "You are not Bette Fucking Midler!" Her mom's attempt to blanket all difficulty with music had gotten much worse since Paige's dad left. It was as if Marylou thought she could sing herself to happiness.

Thankfully, long before their usual stopping time, Josie shouted, to be heard above the noisy squalls, that they should just make camp for the day. They were unnecessarily exhausting themselves. No kidding. Genius call. Once the boats were tied to stakes on the beach, Paige collapsed on the sand, every muscle vibrating with fatigue, and stared up at the hard blue sky. The wind blasted sand across her face, stinging her eyes and filling her nostrils.

She tried but couldn't stanch the fury she felt toward her mom, the stoic way Marylou endured the hardships of this trip, unwilling to just admit, flat out state the truth, that this was not fun. It was, in fact, a brutal way to spend two weeks. Sand folded into every crevice of Paige's body, including, she'd discovered while wiping, her labia. No, she wasn't going to wade into the ice cold, not to mention sweep-you-away swift, Colorado River to rinse off, either. She just wanted someone to set up her tent and give her a plate of food.

Fat chance. These older women expected her to wait on them, again the jolly jokes about the decades they had on her and how they remembered what it was like to have unending energy at her age. They were the ones who ordered coffees so specifically you'd think they were a cocktail of meds. Exact amounts of nonfat milk, one-third caffeinated and two-thirds decaf, and topped with a quarter teaspoon of cinnamon. God forbid if your hand slipped and you did a half teaspoon. Dump the drink and start over. That was the problem with getting old, she supposed, you kept fine-tuning your desires until you had these elaborate, and frankly preposterous, formulas for every tiny thing in life. Of course on this trip, for these two weeks, these women were drinking cowboy coffee, the grounds boiled right with the water, and liking it just fine.

Okay, so she was twenty-one and in the prime of life, but they'd had their salad days, as her mom liked to call them, and so let her have hers. Leave her alone. She could hear her mom calling her name right now, probably to help unload these barely floating excuses for boats. As if she hadn't done more than her share of the labor already.

Paige dragged herself off the ground and carried dry bags, coolers, the toilet bucket, cook stoves, and bags of tents up the hill to the camp, the whole while shouldering against the wind. It blew and blew and blew, as hot and foul as bad breath.

Once they'd unloaded the boats and were finally free to do as they pleased, Paige trudged her tent to the very back of the beach, away from the snorers, and hauled it out of its sheath. *Boom.* A big fiery blast of wind exploded onto the beach and nearly ripped the tent from her hands. The fabric buffeted into the air as she held on, the tent flapping like an environmentalist's pride flag. She heard the shouts of the other women as they tried to secure the gear back in camp, the wind ravaging everything. Paige gripped tight, hoping the tent wouldn't function as a powerful kite and carry her up into the air, maybe over the torrents and then drop her. A moment later, the air quieted. She shook out her tent, inserted the poles, and popped it up.

She heard the next big gust blasting through the mesquite trees before she felt it. She stopped what she was doing, rummaging in the tent bag for the stakes, and turned to look at the swirling cloud of dust and sand headed her way. She threw an arm across her eyes just as the gust arrived. It snatched up her tent and lofted it into the air.

"Hey!" Paige shouted as the wind carried the tent high over the camp kitchen, over the heads of the women setting up their own tents. Like a billowy wingless bird, the tent gained altitude as it sailed upstream over the river. A moment later the air stilled and the tent dropped into the water where it changed course, now conveyed by the current rather than the wind, and floated downstream, still fully erected and zipped.

Paige had run down to the beach, under her flying tent, and now stood watching it float away. She turned to look for Kara, who after all was a firefighter and knew how to rescue things, but the tall woman did not dive into the river to nab the floating tent. Of course she didn't. The tent rode down the center of the fast-moving flow, and anyway, the windstorm kicked up yet another notch and everyone clung to her own partially erected and wafting tent, trying to hold on.

Right then, as if things weren't bad enough, that creepy couple came into view, the old guy pulling hard on the oars to beat the wind, and headed right for their beach. A moment later, Howard leapt ashore, handing Paige the bowline. He ran up the bank, and right past all the women clutching their blowing tents, to the rocky hillside backing the beach. He hefted a large rock and hauled it back to camp, dropping it on a corner of Laurie's tent. Meanwhile, Brynn disembarked and took the bowline from Paige. She drove a metal stake into the sand and tied off the raft. She smiled at Paige and said, "Thanks." Then Brynn helped Howard secure everyone's tent. Back and forth they hustled, making multiple trips to the hillside, carrying loads of rocks like prison laborers and setting them on the inside corners of all the tents. A few of the women joined the effort, once their own tents were secured. Paige's was totally gone.

The wind stopped as abruptly as it had started earlier in the afternoon, and a stillness softened the camp. The women breathed sighs of relief, finished setting up their tents, began filling pots with water and chopping vegetables for pasta. Of course someone invited Howard and Brynn to join them for supper.

"Sorry to crowd your camp," Howard said once they were all seated in camp chairs with full plates. "But the wind was killing us. And Hance is a difficult rapid. Big standing waves. Treacherous boulders and ledges. Best to tackle it in the morning and in calmer weather."

"Oh, heavens," Laurie crooned. "If you hadn't shown up, we would all be tentless at this point."

Ew, Paige thought. Actual bile rose from her belly. A small gag reflex. The age spots on top of his head, clearly visible through the sparse gray hair, the matching wiry gray hair on his arms and legs. The saggy skin under his chin. The visible black nose hairs. She'd known Laurie, her mom's best friend, literally her whole life and knew she was what Marylou affectionately termed man-crazy, but Paige rarely had witnessed that part of Laurie. Anyway, obviously Brynn and Howard were together. At least that's what her mom thought: that he'd left his age-appropriate wife for Brynn. Then again, that's what Marylou *would* think. As if everyone else's life mirrored hers.

Which it didn't. In fact, Paige didn't buy her mom's story that Howard and Brynn were a legit couple. Nothing in Brynn's body language suggested that she enjoyed the old man. She definitely didn't want to be fucking him, that much was clear. And yet. It was as if they were playing out a charade of being a couple.

Something was wrong. Radically askew. Paige couldn't quite put her finger on it, but this wasn't the same old story of an older guy falling for a younger woman. Or if it was, there was a serious twist in the narrative.

Which brought Paige back to what annoyed her so much about her mom's generation. There was so much they just didn't see. Didn't *want* to see. They clung to the old rules. They refused to acknowledge that chaos reigned, even in personal relationships, especially in personal relationships. That was the thing about Armageddon—okay, a dramatic word, but she didn't think it was a big stretch—it didn't just ravage the planet, it also infected hearts and souls. It was a cancer. The human race was fucked. Only a few exceptional people escaped the rot. People like Kara. Maybe Maeve, too. Marylou, on the other hand, didn't even realize there was something to rise above. She believed deeply in human decency. She *still* did. Okay, yeah, it kind of made Paige tear up, this sweetness on her mom's part, this clinging to the life raft of a reality no longer in play.

But no, this "professor," if you bought Laurie's story about the pair, was taking advantage of the pink girl. Howard could be some kind of sophisticated kidnapper. What did he have on Brynn? *Something.* Or she could be swirling in the vortex of a victim's mentality, somehow believing that she wanted to be with him, that he was going to save her from . . . what? *Something.*

Laurie was a freaking shrink. Couldn't she see this?

God, Paige hated this trip. No one had said word one about where she was going to sleep now that her tent had liberated itself. What, on a rock like a coyote? And tomorrow morning: Hance Rapid. Howard had said treacherous ledges. What were "big standing waves"?

After finishing a second plate of pasta, Paige put a handful of Oreos in her shorts pocket and walked away from the circle of campers, who were happily reviewing their days on the river so far. She found a big rock out of earshot and took a seat to eat the cookies.

She wondered what Justin was doing. He wasn't really her boyfriend. They'd never done anything outside of work. Her mom would predictably say he was using her, meaning the fucking in the supply room. As if it couldn't be the case that Paige was using *him*. Which was really more like it. Paige ought to tell her mother that she was a nymphomaniac. It'd be a kind of coming out. Anyway, Paige was definitely into Justin and wouldn't mind hanging out sometime, outside of work, but truly, the sex got her through shifts and you couldn't ask for more than that. Well, of course you *could*. But it was better to not tie herself to someone as depressed as Justin. She was free if someone better came along. Like a male Kara. She'd like that, someone confident and beautiful and kind, but not in a saccharine way.

To her surprise, Brynn sauntered in her direction.

"Hey," Brynn said. Her straw cowboy hat was hella dope. So were her mirrored aviator sunglasses. So were her blue toenails. Her freckled skin had tanned over the past week and she looked like a model on the cover of a health magazine. "I ran out of sunscreen. I know it's a lot to ask, but do you think you have any extra?"

Paige liked that she had asked *her*. Besides Kara, there were no other young people out here. Well, Josie was young*ish*, but she was more like an old person in a young person's body. Probably Brynn also wanted an excuse to walk away from the deadly boring dinner conversation.

Brynn smiled when Paige didn't answer right away. "I know, sunscreen is as valuable as gold down here. You don't just ask for it lightly. The exchange rate's gotta be high. Name your price."

She had a flirtatious smile. Paige wondered if she'd ever be interested in Justin. Probably not. She'd see him as a whiner, which he was. She should break up with him.

"What I really want," Paige said, "is out of this hellhole of a canyon. Can you do that for me?"

Brynn laughed a loud and genuine laugh. "Seriously?"

"Seriously," Paige said. Then she thought of something else she'd like: the girl's story. What *was* the deal between her and Howard? "I have a whole extra tube of sunscreen. You can have it."

"Oh, dude, thanks. That would be so helpful. I don't know what I was thinking bringing just one tube."

"Is he your boyfriend?"

Brynn removed the mirrored sunglasses and looked at Paige. For a quick moment, Paige thought she saw fear in her eyes, like tiny flashing SOS signs, but just as quickly the eyes flattened in defiance. Brynn squinted at the setting sun and said, "Howard's my husband."

"For real?".

She nodded.

"Are you in love?"

"Do I, like, know you?" Brynn's pink skin darkened. She seemed indignant, but not *very* indignant.

"Because," Paige continued, "you don't seem like you are."

Brynn put one fist on her hip and cocked the forefinger of her other hand at Paige. "You're mouthy, girl, you know that?"

Paige nodded. "Were you, like, trying to get back at your parents or something?"

Brynn laughed, but it sounded forced, and she shook her head. "Plus, that's rude. That's so rude."

Maybe she figured he'd die soon. But he wouldn't necessarily. Paige's great-grandma was ninety-six. With Alzheimer's. Brynn could be changing Howard's diapers and spoon-feeding him a few years down the road.

"I just honestly want to know. You can trust me." Paige surprised even herself with the ballsy inquiry. It just seemed like Brynn had a secret and, since there was nothing else to do down here in this hot, sandy, claustrophobic canyon, she wanted to hear it.

"I don't trust you. I don't even know you. Can I get that sunscreen?"

Maybe Paige had the story all wrong. Instead of an actual or psychological kidnapping, maybe it went the other way. Maybe Brynn was the one taking the old man for some kind of ride. He thought Brynn wanted the Grand Canyon. He thought Brynn wanted him. It was probably as simple and stupid as money. He might just have a little mishap down here where there was no law enforcement, where simple accidents like falling off of cliffs were as common as mud.

Paige shivered despite the air temperature of 91 degrees Fahrenheit. She slid off the boulder and said, "Wait here."

After retrieving the sunscreen from her dry bag and hiking back up the beach to the boulder, she tossed the tube to Brynn, who pocketed it and walked away without even saying thank you.

The encounter made Paige miss Justin. At least miss the sex. It was so straightforward: retreat to the supply room, lock the door, do it fast before anyone noticed they were missing. The only times she really had to listen to his rambling troubles were when they were both assigned to the front of the house, making coffee drinks together, and the other employees were on other tasks, which wasn't all that often.

The sun blazed orange as it dropped over the rim, leaving Paige overwhelmed by the complexity of this place with its hot wind and cold water, with the complexity, for that matter, of all of Earth and its crazy inhabitants, especially the humans, the crazy fucking humans.

Kara was glad that the couple were camped with them that night. It was a nice break from the ongoing group dynamics, which were impossible to block out when you ate, slept, and shat in such close proximity. Paige wasn't speaking to her mother Marylou, apparently because she felt the trip had been misrepresented to her. The pair already had had a public row over the makeshift toilet, which Paige thought too primitive, and the blowing sand, which Page claimed blinded her. For reasons Kara couldn't detect, Laurie seemed annoyed with Maeve, snipping whenever the lovely older woman made an observation. Marylou drove everyone nuts with her constant singing; she knew a song to go with every task, be it dishwashing, rowing, cleaning the sand from her tent, or bathing in the river. She was super cheerful, which didn't make sense, given the recent breakup of her marriage.

Kara wanted only to focus on the jeweled river, the brilliantly hued canyon walls, the feel of the velvety sand on the soles of her feet, the feast of pink, yellow, and orange blossoms on the cacti, the ethereal music of the canyon wrens. She wanted only to rest her mind.

Her job had been hell the past year. She worked as a firefighter in a small southwestern town and she loved the high-stakes moments, the endorphins-spiked action. She loved entering burning houses. Saving, rescuing. So many families still had their dogs and photo albums because of her team. Last year she'd jumped out of a second story house, into a waiting net, with a Maine coon cat in her arms.

There were the failures, too. The times they arrived too late, the houses nothing but black crisps. Human lives lost. Once, even children. She'd spent hours in therapy over some of those lives, the ones where she believed that if she'd done something differently she could have saved them. She had moments when she felt those losses like asphyxiation, as if the oxygen had been drawn from *her* room.

But nothing had prepared her for the challenges of being named lieutenant. Men she'd worked alongside, quite cordially for years, did not take well to her new supervisory role. Their insubordination took the form of jokes, ones she should be able to take if she had a sense of humor, and deafness, an inability to hear directives she gave. There were really only one and a half problem guys (the half someone was a problem only intermittently). What hurt were the others who, though they seemed fine with her leadership and did not crack the "jokes" or feign deafness, didn't intervene. Their silence was its own form of insubordination. She knew she couldn't complain. She knew she had to persevere. Stay the course. Prove, through as perfect work and decision-making as she could accomplish, her right to being lieutenant. But it had been a bitch of a year.

What a pleasure to sit in a boat powered by the competent Josie, to witness her stroking through the rapids like a water dancer, to listen to her spellbinding explanations about how to read the river. Kara loved how much she was learning about the history of the whole planet, as evidenced in the rock layers. She loved the thrilling splashy rapids. She loved how for two weeks, no one questioned her own qualifications. She didn't have to prove anything; she just had to listen, see, smell, and touch, follow orders and do her share of the work.

Also, Kara was falling in love with Josie. The power of the feeling stunned her. The intensity of sensation drugged out her whole world, as if everything were an hallucination. The viridian water. The swirling millennia of rock in the canyon walls. The sweet mesquite breath in the air. The melodies of the wrens. It was all almost too much.

The thing was, Kara knew better than to fall for someone like Josie. The woman's outer toughness protected an inner vulnerability, a raw tenderness that people like Josie didn't like to acknowledge. That dissonance appealed to Kara enormously. She viewed it as a sweetness, that internal longing doing battle with the armored exterior. But she'd learned long ago that whatever sweetness occasionally resulted in relationships with people like that, for example those first times making love when the sex overcame the armor, it was a deadly combination over time. When there was a big discord between a person's outer self and inner self, the result could only be conflict. Those people often had tempers. Or intimacy issues—either too many lovers or refusing to have any (after letting you fall in love with them). It was so tempting to think you could flip a person like that, show her how to manage the tenderness, that it wouldn't kill her. But Kara hadn't had a lot of success in that endeavor and she'd vowed to stop trying.

So Kara focused on the maps, the passing geological landmarks, and the startling scenery to distract herself from what would surely be a romantic misstep—no, a face plant—should she take it. She tried to convince herself that she was experiencing the powerful delusion of a situational crush: the joys of vacation, of a breathtaking landscape, confusing her sexual synapses. She resisted. The rigorous schedule—rising at dawn and rowing all day, setting up camp and making dinner, crashing into hard sleeps at dusk—aided her resistance.

But then there were the long days on the water, Kara doing her best to get in Josie's boat, where there was time to talk about everything: families, jobs, friends, and of course the river and canyon itself. The talk was as absorbing as lovemaking.

The morning after the windstorm, Paige asked Kara if the two of them could ride in the same boat that day, and Kara had looked at her blankly, as if she barely knew who Paige was, and said, "Oh, I think Josie, Marylou, and I are going together today." Paige rode with Maeve and Laurie again, and it was another torturous day, one terrifying rapid after another. They finally stopped, in the early evening, just upstream from Crystal Rapid.

At dinner, Paige sat in the camp chair next to Kara, but a minute later Josie showed up carrying her own camp chair and said, "Is there room here?"

There was an entire beach of room. And about five open spaces in the circle of camp chairs. What Josie wanted was for Paige to move, so she could sit next to Kara. She stood abruptly, knocking over her camp chair. She left it toppled in the sand and walked her plate to the trash receptacle. As she scraped away her food, she looked back at Josie and Kara, neither of whom had noticed her huffy exit, both of whom were bent over laughing at some shared joke.

Paige left camp, following a dry creek bed leading up a narrow side canyon. Maybe she could hike all the way to the rim. How far to the closest town? She walked and walked and walked, sweating and crying both, draining her body of all its fluids. She carried no water, wore no hat. Maybe she could trigger an evacuation event. She imagined a helicopter swooping in overhead, hovering as the rescuers lowered a ladder, herself clutching the bottom rung, swinging freely over the river, between the walls of rock, as the rescue team reeled her up. Then off she'd go to a hot shower, a real mattress, the sanity of people her own age. But of course none of that would happen because none of their phones worked down here, not even for an instant, not anywhere.

The pink coil looked like a huge fresh turd deposited on the black rock. As she stood staring, one end of the coil rose up, revealing a diamond-shaped head, two little beady eyes. Paige couldn't move away, mesmerized by its geometric pattern of scales, the thick whorl of its body. The snake flicked its tail, shaking the packets on the tip. There was no mistaking the sound, dry and hollow like seeds in a pod. Paige was paralyzed not just by her fear but also by her attraction to the fear. Did anything matter at all? She was tentless, exhausted, hungry, thirsty, angry, and sad. The only person on this trip close to her age was a super-accomplished firefighter, someone she'd overheard Laurie say was wise beyond her years. Of course she'd barely given Paige the time of day. Let the snake strike.

The rattler raised its head even more, along with the first four inches of its body, making a thick oozing approach. A forked tongue flicked in and out, in and out. Paige stuck her own tongue out in response. Josie had said something about a rattlesnake found only here called the Grand Canyon Pink.

It struck, uncoiling and shooting forward, lightning quick.

Paige screamed, fell backwards, pain exploding in her shoulder and right arm. Colors swirled in her vision, blue and green and brown, and most of all hot pink. The fuchsia bloom of a barrel cactus shouted an inch from her nose. She scrambled as fast as she could, scuttling away on her butt, bumping into more cacti, setting off dozens more tiny explosions of pain. She managed to get to her feet, the radiating pain acute. The snake was gone. How long did she have before the poisons attacked her vital organs?

Paige stumbled back toward camp, tears and snot flowing. When she thought she could hear voices, she called, "Help!"

All five women came running. Marylou unwrapped her sarong, spread it on the ground, and they laid Paige down. She screamed with pain as her skin made contact with the fabric and she bolted upright again.

"Cactus spines," Josie said. "She fell onto a cactus."

"Hold still," Kara said.

"They're barbed," Josie said. "Tweezers and glue."

"Glue?" Paige squeaked.

Josie, who'd brought some just for this purpose, told Marylou where to find it. Marylou ran, wearing just her sports bra and panties, back to the camp to get the tools.

All five women worked their way over Paige's skin, locating the cactus spines. Kara pulled them out with the tweezers, her other hand finding thorn-free places on Paige's skin to steady the girl who sobbed openly. It hurt so much she didn't know if she could endure it. They found barbed spines in her hip, butt cheeks, and even one in her neck. They didn't find a rattlesnake bite because there hadn't been one. Just a foolish, clumsy fall onto not one but several cacti. Josie dotted glue onto the miniscule spines that Kara hadn't been able to remove with the tweezers. After ten minutes, she peeled off the glue patches and the tiny little needles came out.

Maeve handed Paige a full water bottle and she drank that down. Laurie gave her three ibuprofen and she swallowed those. Marylou dabbed antibiotic ointment on all the red spots where the cactus spines had been removed. And yes, her mom knew a song about cacti, and yes, she began singing it. Clad just in her cotton underpants and big white sports bra.

"Shut up!" Paige screamed.

Marylou stopped mid-lyric, looking as if her daughter had slapped her.

"Hey, come on, Paige," Laurie said.

"If you weren't so fucking checked out," Paige raved on, "Dad wouldn't have left. How can you *sing* all the fucking time? I mean, I practically died. A fucking rattlesnake struck me. And you're *singing*. We're all practically dying of dehydration, and you're singing. We're running a river that kills people for *fun*. You're checked out, Mom. You sing all the time so you don't have to think about anything. You are so fucking cheerful all the fucking time. I can't stand it. I just can't. THIS IS NOT FUN. This trip is an ordeal. JUST STOP SINGING."

Marylou burst into tears and ran to her tent. They all listened to the sound of her zipping it up tight. Laurie stood looking at Paige for a moment, decided she could do nothing for her, and walked down to tend Marylou.

"Just go," Paige said looking right at Kara. She turned to Josie. "You too."

"But wait," Kara said to Josie. "She said rattlesnake bite."

"We checked her all over. There was no rattlesnake bite."

Paige had never felt more foolish in her life. She knew the snake had missed. She knew that the pain came from her stupid stumble into the cacti. She shook her head hard and repeated, "Just *go*."

Maeve nodded at the two younger women. They exchanged looks and left. Maeve sat in the sand next to the sarong on which Paige sat, now sobbing into her arms folded on her knees. Maeve didn't say a word, didn't touch her, just sat beside her in silence for an hour. At dusk she stood and left as well.

Paige watched the full moon rise. Then she rose herself and shook out her mom's sarong, making sure to get it completely free of sand. She walked back to camp and found her bags of stuff, dug out her lotion, and applied it to her sore skin. The rest of the women were all in their tents, a couple already snoring.

Paige walked over to her mom's tent.

"Can I come in?"

Marylou didn't answer with words, but she unzipped the tent partway. Paige unzipped it the rest of the way and crawled in.

"Here's your sarong. I'm sorry. I was a jerk."

Her mom's face scared her, the extremity of sadness. She'd obviously been crying, the skin around her eyes swollen and damp. But worse, her entire face sagged, as if she had given up. Her mom never gave up. Paige hoped she wasn't giving up on her. She hugged Marylou. "I'm sorry. I didn't mean what I said. I miss Dad."

"I miss him too."

"I don't even know why he left." Paige paused and added, "I mean, I know it's not because of your singing."

Marylou widened her eyes theatrically, as in, she couldn't believe Paige was actually saying that, but then she burst out laughing. Paige laughed too.

"It probably *was* because of my singing," Marylou said once they quieted. "I mean, Dad is depressed. You know that. He's always been depressed. I'm not. I don't want to pretend that I am."

"But what about . . . I mean . . . that woman . . ."

"That lasted about three weeks."

"Really?"

"Yeah, really. Of course, really."

"So why don't—"

"We get back together?"

"Yeah. I guess. I mean, he made a mistake."

Marylou sighed. How many details do you share with your daughter about her father's abandonment? The truth was, Marylou might have forgiven him if it hadn't been for that first conversation, the one in which he told her about his new girlfriend.

"Just leave," Marylou had said after his initial confession, once she had the gist. "I don't want any details."

"But we've been together for twenty-three years." He actually said that to her, as if it were his right to cash in on what he considered an ongoing intimacy. He wanted to share. Didn't she want to know?

She did not. Besides, she already knew what he'd say. Something about this woman finally making him happy, how he couldn't turn his back on that. He had a duty to himself. This was his one shot. He might have used words like that.

But more than anything, she didn't need to hear more from him because she had her own burst of insight in that moment, despite her rightful rage. Maybe it was the rage that triggered the epiphany. What she saw then was that he'd abandoned her years ago. He'd been in a primary relationship with his depression all this time, not with her. His breaking up with the girlfriend just three weeks later only proved her point.

She loved Joe. She did. And she experienced his absence as an anguish.

But she also loved getting to know herself again, herself not in the service of trying to make someone else happy, someone who would never be happy.

Marylou brushed Paige's bangs off her forehead. "I'm done, honey. I'm done with your father."

"So *you* left *him*?"

"No. You know that's not how it went. He broke all trust. He acted more foolishly than I can forget, even if I could forgive. But mostly, you're right, I'm a singer, I love life, even when it hurts like hell, and he doesn't. Call me shallow, I—"

"You're not shallow."

"Well, your dad thinks I am. That if I'm not mortally depressed like him, I don't see clearly what's happening in the world. I see it."

They both let a long silence go by. Paige realized that she'd adopted her dad's criticism, and she also realized that it wasn't fair. Maybe her mom was one of those people who escaped the rot. Who remained intact, body and soul, in desperate times.

"Is it okay if I sleep here with you tonight?"

"Of course it is."

Paige snuggled up next to her mom. Last night she'd slept on a tarp out in the open. The moon glaring. This was much nicer.

"Sing the one about the moon."

Marylou raised her head and gave her daughter a look of exaggerated disbelief.

So Paige started singing on her own. *It's that old devil moon, that you stole from the sky.*

It only took one line and Marylou joined in. Their two voices, Marylou's alto and Paige's soprano, fluttered over the silent camp as they sang through all the verses. The rest of the women listened, the full moon beaming in the windows of their tents.

Josie couldn't sleep. It was nice hearing Marylou and her kid sing together. They must have made up. Sweet. But she felt uneasy, twitchy. Surely the prospect of running Crystal in the morning wasn't causing the imbalance. She'd never capsized there again, not in all the runs she'd done since the one with her dad twenty-five years ago.

But that stretch of river commanded her respect, always. She crawled out of the tent and slid into her flip flips. The moon flooded their beach with a light like polished wedding gown satin, elegant and formal. Josie shivered with a strange, strong feeling, almost like a premonition, as if she were on the brink of something important.

Maybe it was just the eeriness of the river corridor devoid of other travelers. They'd encountered even fewer than Josie had expected. For a few years after the collapse of the National Park Service permit system, which regulated how many boaters could be on the water, the river became one big party, with thousands celebrating the open access, or so she'd heard. Josie had stayed away, not wanting to see the place getting trashed. But then everything quieted way down again, as fewer and fewer people had the resources or appetite for nonessential adventure, as mere survival became the number one goal for most Americans.

Josie credited Marylou for wanting to do this trip anyway, for a kind of clear-sighted insistence on connecting to this iconic American landscape, at a time when America hurt so badly. Josie was grateful to be here now, especially now.

She walked along the shore until she came to the path leading up to the scouting location. She climbed quickly and felt immediate relief from her uneasiness once she attained a good view of Crystal Rapid. She sat on a rock and meditated on the monster waves, silver in the moonlight, letting herself drift into a river zone. Her father liked to say that moonlight was the best illumination for seeing, truly seeing, the detail in a river current. The hard light of the sun cast too many shadows, bounced off the high places. The soft light of the moon captured the visual nuances. Even so, she'd have to come back up to the scouting location again in the morning because the configuration of waves and holes changed almost hourly depending on how much water they were releasing or withholding from the Glen Canyon Dam. The quiet wild of the spot was perfect for now. She allowed herself memories of that trip with her dad, just sixteen years old, writhing underwater at this very place in the river, his words that night in the firelight over canned beef stew. She had to admit: he'd given her the gift of a unique kind of joy.

"Hey."

Josie startled so hard she almost fell off her rock. That girl Brynn stood just down the trail, her pale hair luminous in the moonlight. Josie hadn't heard anyone's tread on the rocky path.

"Sorry. I didn't mean to scare you. We're camped just below, in the willow. An unpleasant little camp, but Howard didn't want to crowd you guys again."

"It would have been fine."

"Mind if I sit?"

Josie gestured at the surrounding rocks, indicating a range of choices, and Brynn sat on one, saying, "It's too bright to sleep."

Josie nodded.

"One of the others told me you're a professional river guide."

Josie nodded again. She noted an impatience in Brynn, a carefully managed one, as if she were trying to get at something important but bided her time.

"I'm kind of afraid of doing Crystal in the morning," Brynn said. They both looked down at the silvery sparkles on the raging froth below. "It's supposed to be one of the most dangerous."

Josie didn't know if she should respond as a guide did to a client, with an honest and calm assessment of the challenges, or as one relative stranger to another, with a shrug. She was leaning toward a brief version of the former—pointing out the two holes, one on the left and one on the right, perfectly visible in the light of the full moon, and telling how you had to thread between them, a tricky maneuver that required skill, but was doable—when she saw something odd.

A boat approached Crystal Rapid. The dusky yellow raft spun gently in the glassy black water, a picture of perfect serenity. Only it was midnight. There ought not be any craft on the river.

Josie stared harder, tried to bring the scene into crisper focus. The rubber oar boat was a deeper yellow than either of their two boats, more egg yolk than sunshine. There were dry bags and a cooler lashed to the metal frame. But there were no people on board. No crew. Not even a single rower at the oars. No one. She heard Brynn catch her breath.

"A ghost boat," Josie whispered. She'd learned the term from her dad, but she'd never seen one.

"Oh my god." Brynn moved closer to the edge to get a better look.

The dark yellow disc of a boat slipped into the silken tongue of the rapid. It seemed to hang there for a moment, to pause as if it had will of its own, and in that atom of time, Josie was in the wooden rowboat, just a girl, about to be baptized. She remembered perfectly her first experiences of that blissful intersection between safety and danger, the deep satisfaction in attaining the skills needed to occupy that slim territory of ecstasy. They were skills everyone needed, especially now, and maybe *that* was why she'd said yes to Marylou. It was what she could do: show a small group of women, using the metaphor of the river, how to navigate the dramatic changes in the courses of our intertwined lives. She couldn't wait to tell her dad about how she was finding the Colorado River corridor now. He'd be eager to hear.

Josie and Brynn watched the unmanned boat make a perfect run through the rapid, sliding between the holes, shooting out the foot, and dancing on downstream.

"Are they dead?" Brynn asked.

"Could be. Or maybe they hiked out. Hard to say."

"Guides usually know about other parties on the river," Brynn said.

Josie wondered how Brynn would know that. She'd said she was a novice, hadn't ever been here, didn't know anything about the Grand Canyon or the Colorado River. The two women made eye contact and held each other's gazes, as if assessing trust. Brynn looked away first.

"Not anymore," Josie said. "Anyway, I'm not guiding this trip. We're just a group of friends. Loosely connected."

Brynn nodded and stood looking down at Crystal, one fist on her hip, too much intelligence in her gaze to be who she said she was. Brynn had knowledge. Knowledge of the canyon.

"That's some crazy shit," she said, nodding downstream where the ghost boat had disappeared. "See you on the river."

In the morning, all three boats slid artfully through Crystal and whooshed on downstream, running the string of rapids called the Gems. After that, the women lost track of Howard and Brynn and didn't see them at all for the next few days as they flew through Fossil, Specter, Deubendorff, Tapeats, and Upset rapids. Laurie was disappointed because, as she put it to herself, it was always nice to have a man on the horizon.

Lava Falls was the last major challenge of the trip. As they washed toward that chaotic maelstrom, tears of fear filled Paige's eyes. The boom and bellow of the rapid could be heard long before any visual clues could be discerned. The auditory input was terrifying. Lava Falls was reported to be giant, and its voice confirmed this reputation.

The roar grew louder and louder as they approached. When Josie announced the necessity of pulling over to scout the rapid, Paige thought she'd faint from the delay. Couldn't they just *go*? Just run the freaking monster and get it over with? Both boats pulled onto a tiny patch of sand just above the deafening roar. Even from here, all that could be seen was flat, undisturbed water. That was because they were above the lip of the rapid, the place where the riverbed dropped precipitously, causing the liquid riot in the first place. Josie, Kara, and Marylou climbed the hillside to assess the route through the treachery. Paige stayed in the boat, guzzling water from a bottle. Water was life. And she wanted to live.

Then she had an idea. If there were a trail up to the scouting location, then it ought to be possible to simply hike around Lava Falls! They could pick her up below.

When the three women returned, ominously silent, and jumped into the boats, Paige began climbing out.

"Do you have to pee?" Josie asked, obviously annoyed to have her concentration broken.

"I'm walking around the rapid."

"Not possible."

"Come on, sweetie," her mom said, grabbing her wrist and yanking her back into the boat.

Paige wanted more than anything to say no, to refuse, to throw a tantrum. But she'd already done that a few nights ago, acted the fool, and she couldn't do it again. She glanced at Kara, who said, "Hold on tight. You'll be fine."

The two boats—one piloted by Josie, with Laurie and Maeve as passengers, and the other piloted by Marylou, with Kara and Paige— shoved off. As they drifted back out into the river's main current, Paige squeezed her eyes shut and imagined Kara holding a giant fire hose, her entire body shaking with the intensity of the water pressure, spraying the upper windows of a burning house. Kara knew how to rescue people. She did. Kara said she'd be fine.

In a spurt of courage, Paige decided to do this with her eyes open. She looked around, marveling at how slow they were moving now, knowing that very soon the face of the river would change from peaceful to violent. Thirty seconds. Twenty. Ten. She glanced at the northern riverbank, wondering if there *was* a trail, and that's when she noticed a wide dry gully, littered with red gravel and black cinders. Walking down the gully toward the river she saw, she's certain she saw, although god knows she might well have been hallucinating from fear, two women. Each wore a pack on her back and a rifle slung across her chest. The guns looked crude and unfamiliar, a strange innovation from another time. Their pants and shirts were torn and filthy. The sole on one of the girl's boots flapped loose. They held hands as they stumbled forward through the rocks, looking both grim and beatific. Yes, it had to be an hallucination. One tripped on a rock and fell to a knee. Her shoulders buckled, but her friend grabbed her under the armpits and hoisted her. Why did they keep holding hands in such rough terrain?

Paige turned and shouted at Kara, to be heard over the thunder of the river, wanting her to look up the gully. She flailed wildly with her arm, pointing. Kara did glance, briefly, but then looked away because she was much more interested in the flight of a snowy egret sailing right above their heads in the downstream draft. Kara smiled.

Again Paige tried to get her to see the women, and again Kara looked, but obviously saw nothing. She scowled a little, not wanting to be distracted from watching the lovely bird. She craned her neck and followed the egret's flight until it was nothing more than a white speck before disappearing altogether.

Paige stared up the gully, waiting for the mirage of the two traveling women to evaporate. She didn't actually want to die, and seeing this vision, shimmering in the heat of day, convinced her that she had in fact already died. Or was on the brink of death, already entering an in-between realm.

The thunderous din intensified, overtook all of her senses. Now she could see the spray shooting above the waterline just ahead, but still not the giant waves beyond the drop-off. She gripped the boat straps so hard her knuckles hurt. Both her mom and Kara appeared to have entered zones of deep concentration. Fucking shit, her mom was brave! At the oars, about to steer this yellow rubber raft through one of America's fiercest stretches of water. Paige wanted to tell her mom she loved her. She wanted Kara to notice her. She wanted another drink of water. She wanted, wanted, wanted.

Kara knew that fear was a healthy response to adversity. She wasn't immune to it, as many of her friends assumed because of the work she did. She was terrified on every fire. And that was a good thing: fear called up the deep cellular attentiveness needed to do her job.

So she also knew that her lack of fear this morning approaching Lava Falls was not normal and it occurred to her that she should be worried. Worried about the absence of jitters, dread, alarm. Fear fueled the precision response necessary in calamities, and who knew what Lava Falls would deliver? She knew jackshit about running rivers, and here she was about to tackle one of the craziest waterways anywhere, and she blithely felt nothing but a floaty elation. Nearly invincible. So much joy.

They went first.

Moments before sliding into Lava Falls, Kara smiled at the sky. No, not the sky. She tracked a snowy egret, its bright yellow feet pointed in perfect dancer form behind its flight, the fluff of feathers in the wind off its neck, the white wings in crisp aerial perfection against the blue. Kara flew with the bird.

"Here we go!" Marylou sang out.

Kara looked back at Josie at the helm of the other raft, queuing up for its run, and gripped the purple straps holding down the dry bags.

A hole to the left, Josie had said, and then immediately one to the right, and Marylou had to thread the oar boat, using just these two long partially flattened sticks, as if it were possible to steer in that furious wet tumult between the two.

After the raft slid along the polished jade water and into the V of the tongue, the waves pounded over their heads, fully submerging the raft and all three passengers. They plunged into the hole, swallowed by green water, bubbles fizzing everywhere, plugging their mouths. They sunk, going down into the forever deep flow. The raft bucked hard. The back end heaved up, collapsing the two ends together like a sandwich before popping open again. A lateral wave smashed across the deck of the boat, ripping Kara's hands from the straps and knocking her back against the cooler. The boat spun a full 360 degrees as another massive wave slammed into their faces.

Wait. The next wave lapped at the portside tube. They spun gently in the eddy below the rapid. Just like that. All three passengers were still on board. One of the oars rocked in its oarlock, attached to the boat, but not in Marylou's grip. Kara reached into the river and grabbed the handle, passed it to Marylou. They'd made it through Lava Falls.

Josie! The thought sprung in full glory like Athena from Zeus's head! Oh, the hyperbole of love, but Kara didn't care.

She turned to watch the other boat make its run. Josie rowed through expertly, as Laurie and Maeve shrieked with glee. As if this were fun. Of course it was fun! They too went completely underwater but resurfaced quickly. They heehawed their way out the bottom of the rapid, sliding into a spot in the gentle eddy right next to their companions' boat. Marylou and Josie each raised an oar over her head and tapped the tips of the blades, as if they were toasting with champagne glasses. Everyone laughed, and laughed hard, at surviving the biggest rapid of the canyon.

"Look!" Laurie cried.

The sight of Howard and Brynn's blue raft, poised at the top of the falls, aborted the chorus of laughter. The women hadn't seen the couple in several days and they seemed unreal, as if appearing out of nowhere. The boat hovered at the top of the rapid for an unnaturally long period of time, as if that were even possible, trapped in a bubble of anticipation.

The blue boat seemed to almost levitate briefly before dropping into Lava. Unlike the previous boatload of women, Howard and Brynn were utterly silent as the water wrapped the boat, sunk it, disappearing the two humans, leaving just the violence of water slamming over rocks, churning so much air the upheaval was as white as clouds.

They were in the hole.

The boat popped to the surface, upside down, surging in the spot just below the tongue where the river magnificently flipped back on itself. Then the boat twisted, caromed all the way out of the water, and landed right side up again, spun in circles. The passengers were gone.

The women sat bobbing in their peaceful eddy, studying the stretch of whitewater and calm green below, searching, searching, searching.

Her head appeared first, bright strawberry blond hair plastered over her face, her mouth a red gasping O, her hands wheeling the air rather than the water. She washed headfirst downstream, maybe in shock, completely forgetting to turn onto her back and travel feet first.

"I got her!" Josie boomed in a deep commanding voice, thrusting the oars in the water and committing her entire body to rowing, the focus on her face compelling and beautiful, heading straight for the swimmer.

Marylou, Kara, and Paige stayed behind, looking for Howard. He hadn't surfaced and Kara feared that he was trapped underwater in the cement mixer turbulence of the hole.

There! He emerged swimming ferociously, his glasses gone, but his eyes scanning like an eagle's. "Brynn!" he choked out, not once, but two and then three times, sucking down more water in his desperate attempt to reach her with his voice.

When Josie got to Brynn, she tossed the oar handles at Laurie and leaned over the fat lip of the raft. Brynn flailed in the water, gulping too much, slapping the slippery rubber of the boat as if she could gain purchase on her own. Once she realized Josie was trying to help, she grasped wildly for *her* instead of the boat. Brynn thrashed desperately, heaving and gurgling, out of control and unmanageable. Josie had no choice: she slapped her to quiet the wildness. She'd never forget the look on Brynn's face. Not just shock. An outrage. As if an entire conspiracy had prompted the slap, rather than just one woman trying to save her life. It worked, in any case, and Josie fisted the two shoulder straps of Brynn's life jacket and hauled the young woman onto the boat, her belly slithering over the gear like a dead body.

Marylou, in the other boat, rowed hard and reached Howard a moment later. Once they let him know they had Brynn, he calmly let himself be rescued, although hefting him into the boat was considerably more difficult. It took all three women pulling, two on his life jacket and one on the waistband of his shorts. He shouted guttural exclamations of pain as they heaved him, inch by inch, on board.

Both boats made their way to the nearest beach. Laurie helped Brynn out of her wet clothes and into a sleeping bag, murmuring reassurances, while the other women hastily made camp. Howard didn't even change out of his wet shorts and T-shirt before hiking downstream to fetch his boat, which luckily spun out in an eddy not too far away, the oars still attached. There was no telling how long it would stay stuck there and so none of the women stopped him, though surely he was hypothermic.

Laurie handed Brynn a bag of Oreos, but Brynn wouldn't eat. She was furious, muttering oaths under her breath and trembling with rage, even as the hot sun and sleeping bag restored her body temperature to normal. Laurie let the young woman seethe. She was more interested in watching Howard's progress as he climbed over massive boulders and even had to wade, waist deep, through one stretch of the calm river. She was relieved when she saw him grab the bowline and drag the boat to a nearby beach, where he tied it up. They could ferry the couple to the boat in the morning. Meanwhile, Marylou and Josie fired up camp stoves to cook everyone a hot meal.

Howard returned, hauling two dry bags containing spare clothes and the couple's sleep kit. He approached Brynn, who still sat on the beach huddled in a sleeping bag, but she said "don't" with such ferocity he veered, continuing into the stand of mesquite at the back of the beach. After setting up their tent, he returned with dry shorts and a T-shirt, both obviously belonging to him, not her. She dismissed him and the clothes with a forceful hand wave. She'd already changed into dry clothes supplied by Kara.

He performed a couple of supplicant head bows, apparently at a loss for words, and then stepped back and looked around, as if for an escape route. The man dance infuriated Brynn.

She leapt to her feet. "You fucking said you knew how to do this! You fucking lied to me, you asshole!"

Howard froze with masculine panic.

Brynn's rage, fueled by a survival-level terror, broke free. She appeared to have lost all control of herself when, speaking in a hot hush, she finished with, "I know who you are, Howard. I know what you do."

Paige grinned, delighted and all too ready to vicariously enjoy a big whopping drama.

Marylou closed her eyes, wishing she could make the couple go away.

Kara searched the cliffs above camp, hoping to see a mountain lion, although she knew the odds were one in a million. It couldn't hurt to keep looking. There'd been so much magic already on this trip.

Like Paige, Maeve stood and watched, although with a sad amusement, as if the behavior of humans never ceased to disappoint her. Still, people were always interesting.

Josie busied herself with cooking and didn't even watch the developing theatrics.

Marylou asked Paige to help her set up the camp chairs.

When Brynn picked up a stone and made as if she were going to throw it at the still statuesque Howard, Laurie stepped forward, sighed loudly, and said, "Put the rock down, Brynn. Howard, why don't you have a seat."

Howard sat.

A moment earlier, she'd intended to gather up all the women and suggest a short walk, leaving the couple to sort out their conflict, but there was really no easy place to walk. Anyway, Marylou and Paige were setting up the camp chairs in a circle that included Brynn and Howard, and Josie announced that a makeshift dinner was ready. Clearly everyone else intended to let the events of the evening swamp over the couple's problems, which after all weren't the women's problems. Fine. They were right. Everyone filled a plate and they ate in silence.

Until Laurie couldn't stand it any longer. "So you're a geology student?" she asked.

Everyone stared at her like she was an idiot. Well, you had to start somewhere, and sometimes the best place to start was with the obvious, with a question that could generate an easy yes.

"He's a fucking geology *professor*," Brynn said.

"I meant you."

"Me? Hell no."

Laurie was confused, which she didn't like to be when it came to relationships.

"They're married," Paige said with an inappropriate grin.

Laurie felt punched in the stomach. Which she knew was a ridiculous response. She didn't know this man, didn't have even a tiny right to his attention. He looked directly at her now, as if reading her thoughts, and for some crazy reason she nodded at him, an absurd affirmation of nothing. He nodded back.

Brynn dropped her empty plate in the sand beside her camp chair and said to Howard, "I'm sleeping out." She marched back across the sand to their tent and yanked out a sleeping bag, which, Laurie noticed, hadn't been zipped together with the other sleeping bag, and then shimmied the plastic ground cloth out from under the tent. She dragged the tarp and sleeping bag far away and laid them out in the sand.

The rest of the women busied themselves doing dishes, stowing food, and setting up their own tents. Laurie stayed right where she was, in the chair next to Howard, weathering a huge wave of grief about her mother's recent death.

"So you two are married," she said.

He rubbed his eyes, blinked hard, as if he could will his vision into focus without his glasses.

"For how long?" she asked, again fully aware that it was neither any of her business nor a particularly appropriate question. But clearly the couple didn't know each other well, and she wanted to understand what was going on, she just did.

"We met six months ago."

"And you fell in love."

He glanced at her, his eyes soft with misery and nearsightedness. "Sort of."

"How do you 'sort of' fall in love? In my experience, falling in love is a full body, heart, and mind experience."

He rubbed his hands back and forth on his quads. Despite the shock in learning he was married, despite how very sad she felt this evening, Laurie apparently couldn't stop herself from admiring the man's good features, and his muscled legs were one of those.

"We both hung out at the same café," he said, further surprising Laurie by being forthcoming. "I was working on an article. She was, just, I don't know, drinking coffee. We were both regulars. So we eventually started talking. She asked what I was working on. It doesn't take much to get me going."

"Apparently."

He grimaced. She thought it was maybe an appreciative grimace.

He said, "I mean about geology. She was really interested in the geology, *is* really interested, and okay, that's a hook with me. It just is."

"But marriage?"

His swimmy blue eyes settled on her face. "It was *her* idea."

"You foolish old man." She spoke softly, saying what she could never say from the chair in her office.

He almost smiled.

"Why?" she asked.

He kept his voice low and glanced around camp, wanting the confessional but not wanting to be overheard. "I've been married three times. Each time it's meant something different. That body and soul thing? That was the first time. You recover from that—actually, you don't, but let's say you do."

Laurie kept herself from interrupting, as she would if she were working, to ask him to stop using the second person, to simply say "I" rather than trying to generalize by saying "you." She did use eye contact and gentle head nods to keep him talking.

"That second time you have this overwhelming feeling of relief, like you've been saved, like you've fixed whatever it was you did to fail so badly the first time."

The phrase "whatever you did" was a huge, hard-blowing red flag. His vagueness, the not taking responsibility by naming it, perhaps the actual ignorance of what "it" was. But again, she was in her own life, not in her chair. She nodded, as if she understood, and the truth was, she did. His guilelessness in telling her this story made him all the more appealing.

"But of course you haven't fixed it," he said. "You just flung yourself desperately."

Ah, so he knew this. She resisted the urge to touch his knee in agreement. Nothing wrong with indulging her crush, silently, secretly, but hands to herself.

Still speaking quietly, he said, "So when Brynn said let's get married, it was like jumping out of a plane with a parachute. A lark. A trip of sorts, a place to go for a while. You asked why. Why not?"

Laurie loved the image of sky diving and felt herself drifting high above Earth with a parachute ballooned over her head. Holding her. Easing the fall. Allowing a magnificent view on the way down. Knowing the whole while, of course, that your feet would return to the mundane earth.

She reached out and, with just two fingertips, touched his knee.

"Brynn is thirty-four and has never been married. I suspect she was worried about that. In any case, it was her idea." Yeah, Laurie thought, you've said that, a couple of times already, almost proudly. "She hinted about wanting to do a Grand Canyon trip, and so I put one together.

Then she just—" The memory of that moment moved him. He paused, almost unable to go on, and his voice turned husky when he finished with, "She just said, 'I want to marry you.'"

His need for full divulgence was interesting. Laurie suspected he knew he'd acted rashly, made a big mistake, in spite of how much Brynn's attention pleased him. "And you said, 'Why not?'"

"I did."

"Do you regret it?"

He looked over his shoulder to the place where Brynn had taken her tarp and sleeping bag, but she was nowhere in sight. "No. She has this amazing eagerness to learn. She loves life so much. I mean, she just wants to do everything."

"She makes you feel young."

The blue of his eyes hardened into a shell and he set his mouth. He felt judged. But he allowed, "I suppose she does."

And what, Laurie silently asked herself, is wrong with that? She forced herself to admit that he made some good points. What if people were more nimble about marriage? Rather than approaching it like sinking an anchor. Marriage didn't have to be on par with death and taxes. It could be a dance. An episode. A stretch of the river!

"I've been married three times, as well," she told him.

He smiled an acknowledgment of their shared experience.

She imagined herself married to Howard. He'd talk too much. His blind spots were obviously vast. But he was gainfully employed. He had a passionate interest in geology, which meant he'd have his own thoughts, his own activities, his own *life*, and wouldn't expect her to supply those fundamentals. He was fit and adventuresome. If he could come to her bed with the ardor he applied to rocks, well, that might carry her around a few bends in the river. She pictured the two of them in the cab of a small camper, the wind blowing through the open windows, driving from one natural wonder to another, camping and hiking.

They could be each other's number four.

She laughed out loud at her preposterousness, and startled Howard.

Thinking she'd been laughing at him, his voice rose to a near bellow. "I *am* foolish. I'll grant you that. But I'm not as foolish as you think. The Grand Canyon blasts your heart open. Have you seen anything so big or bright or deep or storied? The place slices right through time, erasing that elusive dimension altogether. I've been down the Colorado, through the Grand Canyon, many times. You wouldn't know it from how I ran Lava today. But that's exactly why I have a love affair with this place: it's different every single time. The river, never the humans, has the upper hand, calls the shots. In this context, what's marriage? I guess, given how she and I talked about the river and the canyon so much, I sort of thought Brynn was asking to marry the river, not me."

"That's absurd."

"It is," he said, calming down again. "It's absurd. But I like to think of it that way anyway. Is it any more absurd than anyone else's notion of love?"

Probably, Laurie thought, but maybe not.

"I wanted her to fall in love with the canyon. I wanted to watch her do that. I would like, one day, to meet someone who looks here—" He threw out his arms, one toward the north cliff and one toward the south cliff, as if he could touch them with his fingertips. "—for their answers. Not here." He touched his chest, humbled now, grinning like he owned his own foolishness.

Laurie thought she might kiss him. That would make her a foolish old woman. He was right. This place scoured out the plaque built up around your heart, leaving it pink and tender, thumping away over life itself. God, she missed her mother. The grief, mixed with the Grand Canyon effect, catapulted her toward recklessness. It was daft, this feeling, this desire, at her age, to kiss a married man. To kiss a married man, it must be noted, who had married a woman half his age. To kiss a big old fool.

Howard stood. He was done talking. He looked, quite suddenly, as though he wanted nothing more than to walk away. But he forced himself to look squarely at her, as if that would be acknowledgment enough, a kind of thanks for her having listened to him. Laurie saw him see her desire. She saw him recoil. He didn't even say goodnight, just turned and walked in the orange heat of late afternoon back to his tent.

Laurie sat in the camp chair watching the last of the sunlight tinge the rimrock, far above the river, and she stayed there too as the lavender twilight softened the sharp edges of everything.

Kara and Josie walked away from camp into the starry night. The beach was backed by cliffs, and no nearby stream had carved a pathway through the rock, but they found a climbable seam. It wasn't so smart to climb without ropes. If they fell they'd probably hit the sand at the bottom, but they'd get seriously knocked up on the way down. Kara wasn't going to be the one to suggest caution. She climbed, shoving her fingers and toes into the seam, grabbing knobs of rock where she could find them, and they reached their goal, a rough, relatively level ledge. Both tried to control their breathing, pretend that the climb hadn't challenged their lungs, and then they laughed, let go, and just panted. The risk heightened all their senses.

The moon wouldn't rise for another few hours, allowing even more stars to pop against a deep purple sky. Two ravens perched on the smaller ledge above them and vocalized their claim to the territory. Kara cawed back at the birds and Josie laughed.

"I wish I'd been in your boat for Lava Falls," Kara said.

"I wish you had been, too."

"Marylou wanted me to ride with her. I guess for moral support."

"Must have worked. You all didn't flip."

"I didn't do anything other than hold on." Kara paused, wondering if she should say it. "But I did have this secret feeling of invincibility."

"Secret?"

"Secret because I know invincibility is a deception."

"That it is."

"So it was kind of alarming to feel it. Especially given how our boat buckled and spun." Josie just smiled. "You're not afraid of anything, are you?"

"Me?" Josie exhaled softly. "Oh yeah. Sure. All the time."

"Okay, so give me an example."

Josie took a long time choosing one, and Kara knew she was deciding whether to tell her a real one or to just offer up a placeholder. Finally she said, "When I was twelve, my dad tried to teach me to roll a kayak. We were in Puget Sound. My parents had friends up there with a house right on the water. Thing was, the kayak was fitted out for one of their boys, a younger and smaller kid. So my butt wedged way too tight in the cockpit. My dad thought people learned by trial, so he secured the skirt and flipped me."

"With no instruction at all?"

"He gave a verbal description of what to do. Basically, you fold your body forward, so your heavy head is up on the deck of the kayak, and then you do a maneuver with your hips. But it's not intuitive at all."

"So his method of teaching wasn't going to work."

Josie surprised Kara by shrugging, as if she were not quite willing to disagree with her father. She said, "I didn't learn to roll the kayak. Not that weekend, anyway. But you asked about fear. Hanging upside down in the water, completely locked in that too small kayak, that scared me. Shitless."

Kara felt a moment of drowning, as if she were the one trapped upside-down underwater. She nearly gasped the next words, as if breaking to the surface. "What happened?"

"Dad waited for as long as he thought was safe and then flipped me back upright. Of course I thrashed because by then I was totally panicked. It's difficult to right another person in a kayak, especially when they're not cooperating."

"Did he get mad?"

Josie looked up at the stars, and so Kara did, too.

"No. Not mad. He never loses his temper. But he never lets go of a plan, either."

"So he made you try again."

"Again and again and again. I didn't get it until the following summer. I count it as one of my biggest failures."

Kara thought that was kind of intense. "Still? I mean now?"

Josie glanced at Kara and then laughed. "I guess I could let go now, huh?"

Oh, those tawny eyes. Kara had been looking for a mountain lion this whole trip, and here she was, on a ledge with a cougar-eyed woman.

"You love risk." Kara wasn't sure whether her observation fit with the conversation or was a total non sequitur, but if it didn't follow, it might lead.

At first Josie thought Kara had said "You risk love." She unscrambled the sentence in her head and then answered. "No. I don't. It's not risk I love. In fact, I don't like it much at all. I love knowledge that mediates risk. That's why it upset me so much I couldn't master that kayak roll. I knew it'd make me much safer in the boat. It would *reduce* risk."

Kara put a hand on Josie's tanned forearm, let herself pet the blond hairs.

Josie looked at the hand, swallowed audibly. She didn't move her arm away.

"In fact I hate risk." Josie spoke emphatically. "Risk is driving on the freeway. I mean, you can learn the rules of driving, but you're at the mercy of all the bozos also driving, and god knows how many of them are high or drunk or just plain stupid. Risk is letting people interpret your story for you. Risk is—"

"Who's interpreting your story?"

Josie looked at her, the sweetest and rarest expression of confusion on her face.

"I mean it," Kara said. "Who right now is interpreting—or *misinterpreting*—your story?"

"No one. Not now. I'm on the river."

"What you mean is, human beings are fucking unpredictable."

Josie nodded. "Yep. That's what I mean."

"I love how you love the river."

Josie nodded again.

"Tell me your romantic history. With people."

"Nah." But she smiled.

"Why not?" Kara asked.

"*Why?*"

"Have you ever been with women?"

"Sure. I've been with lots of people." Kara didn't like her cavalier tone and pulled away her hand. "But I've never been with a firefighter."

Then Josie, who didn't like risk, who hated the unpredictability of humans, leaned in and kissed Kara, the sunburned roughness of their lips hot and tinged with lingering sunscreen. The women's muscles lengthened with touch and the pain in their bruises deepened against the cragginess. Later they lay on their backs holding hands for a long, long time, Josie feeling as if she were six years old and Kara feeling as if she were twelve, both women alternately feeling solemn and worried, giddy and free. Overhead, the sky darkened to charcoal, the stars tiny fires in the agave roasting pits of ancient time.

Several of the women saw him leave at dawn, long before the sun's rays reached into the canyon. Marylou was making coffee, softly singing Cat Stevens's tune about morning breaking. Maeve was chopping apples. Paige was sitting on the toilet bucket, which had a good view of the river. He left the tent behind, maybe as a decoy or maybe as a humanitarian donation for Brynn.

Clutching a single dry bag, he walked right by Laurie who was on the beach, at water's edge, rinsing out a bandana. She didn't speak to him. After a sleepless night thinking about her cockamamie conversation with the man, she felt exposed and sour. He didn't acknowledge her either, passed on by as if she were invisible and hefted himself over the boulders on his way to his boat. Laurie thought he was getting some food to contribute to breakfast. Or maybe clothes for Brynn. They probably made up last night.

It was Josie and Kara, who'd spent the entire night on the ledge, who saw him untie the boat and push off. The two ravens were back, but now they seemed to accept the pair on their cliffside, pacing on their little black stick legs, as if guarding the lovers. When Josie said, "Look," the birds hopped to a higher vantage point and cawed. They watched Howard in his boat, leaning back with the two oars in his hands. He pulled hard. A moment later, he was gone.

Howard rowed with everything he had, his heart thudding like a stone along the river bottom, thinking only escape, escape, escape. That woman's words, *you foolish old man*, rang in his ears, an endless loop, and he hated her for saying them while simultaneously being grateful to her. Because of course she was right. Not even right—*she* didn't know what she'd uncovered. But she'd broken the spell. The foolish old man spell. It wasn't until after talking with her and climbing into his tent alone that he considered Brynn's revelation. *"I know who you are, Howard. I know what you do."* And still it took him several hours to fully comprehend. Lying there alone, without her beautiful distraction, having witnessed her—yes, call it what it was—hatred for him, thinking back over the last few months, what'd she'd asked for, looked at, insisted on, always while offering herself as a trade, he saw how easily he'd been taken. Worst of all, she'd gotten what she wanted, everything.

Foolish old man didn't begin to say it. He'd fallen into the oldest trap in the book.

That didn't stop him from being hurt, from thinking of her pale thighs with a sorrow far more poignant than the situation called for. Those lit eyes, beseeching him. The open-mouthed laugh, her appreciation of his science jokes, even when he had to explain the punchlines.

That couldn't have all been acting. It couldn't have been. Even so, she'd used him. Played him to harvest all kinds of information. Fool!

Howard rowed. He never stopped rowing, no matter how much his shoulders and back ached. There were no more serious rapids, just long stretches of pools and gentle flow. Some riffles, and he was glad for them, because they helped rocket him along. The pain spiked down his neck and spine, but still he pulled through the water as fast as he could make the big clumsy rubber raft go. How he wished he'd brought along a motor!

He had moments that day when he thought his foolishness extended even to this crazy-paced getaway. Who exactly would make chase? Not her. Couldn't he ease up? Did he really have to run?

Yes. Because she couldn't be acting alone. He knew there were people who would stop at nothing. And so there were other moments, ones that lengthened into hours, when he feared snipers on the clifftops, men lying in wait, ambushes set up in the dark shadows of the side canyons. He felt like a targeted man. She was a scorpion.

Brynn slept in, sprawled on top of the sleeping bag and tarp in the sand, and no one dared wake her. No one wanted to be the messenger about Howard's abandonment. They all watched, from afar, with peripheral vision and quick discreet glances, as she finally jerked awake, stood and stretched, bobbed her head back and forth to crack her neck.

She didn't even look at his tent, at what used to be her tent, as she walked down to the beach where the women were finishing breakfast. Marylou handed her a plate of scrambled eggs, fried potatoes, and apple slices. Brynn took it without thanks. She sat in a vacated camp chair and dug in, as if she hadn't eaten in days. When finished, she stood, washed her dish, and shoved it in the dish bag. By now everyone was silently watching, a little appalled by her nonchalance and also alarmed by what was dawning on them: this brazen young woman now belonged to them.

"Where's Howard?" she asked, as if just now noticing his absence.

It was Marylou who stepped up. "He left."

Brynn's mouth dropped open as she looked back at the tent. She scanned the cliffs as if he might have made his escape that way, and then turned in a full circle, finally staring for a long time at the flowing river, the whole while looking as if she were swallowing back strong feeling. "He took the boat?"

"Yes."

She pressed her lips together and nodded slowly. "Well. What now?"

She obviously was talking to herself so no one answered. They weren't surprised when they saw last night's anger return to her face.

"I suppose you believed what he told you," she announced to the whole group, turning as she spoke to include everyone. "I heard him droning on last night about his heart and the canyon."

Six women stared.

Brynn coughed out a laugh. "Geology prof in Flagstaff. Oh, the magic of floating through time!"

Paige said, "He's not?"

"He's lucky I didn't strangle him. Throw his body onto that blue floating nightmare of a boat and shove his corpse down the river." Brynn threw her arms in the air, raised her face to the canyon rim, and let out a prolonged scream.

Her anger was shocking. It was also clearly genuine.

Kara asked, "Are you okay?"

Marylou couldn't believe this. What now, indeed. They couldn't exactly leave her here on the beach below Lava Falls. They'd have to take her the rest of the way to the Diamond Creek takeout. And then what?

No one knew what to say. So they started loading up the boats. By the time they shoved off, their guest maybe a little contrite as she sat on the stern tube of one of the rafts, the heat had climbed to well over a hundred degrees. It was going to be a very hot day.

"There're some amazing petroglyphs," Josie said, "downstream a ways. Anyone want to stop and see them?"

"Yes!" Kara shouted.

That one word, voiced by a woman who glowed like the moon, caused a shiver to run under Josie's skin, despite the heat.

The two women smiled boldly at each other.

"I'm thinking," Laurie said, "given the circumstances, maybe we should just keep going, get to the takeout sooner rather than later."

"I vote for that," Paige said.

"I'd love to see petroglyphs," Maeve effused.

Marylou shrugged, unwilling to cast the deciding vote.

A few hours later, Josie rowed to shore and tied up her boat, announcing, "Petroglyphs for those who want. We won't be gone long."

Everyone, even Brynn, went on the short hike to see the ancient art. The silence of the morning on the river continued as the women climbed the hill in the stifling heat and even as they arrived at the rock face covered in etched drawings. A snake. A hand. A beast. A human figure. Someone, or maybe several someones, hundreds of years ago, had had urgent stories to tell. Maeve wished with all her heart she could interpret those stories, understand the messages that had been scratched into rock for future humans to interpret. She hovered her hand over each image and closed her eyes, willing the story to transmute from rock to skin.

Josie knew the other women were suffering in the extreme heat, and she was glad they'd mostly had cooler weather over the past two weeks, but just for today she gloried in the swelter. Classic canyon weather. The wrens were singing their hearts out this afternoon, that clear, descending whistle, as they fluttered in and out of the trees, creating their own breezes. Josie ran her fingers through Kara's hair.

Kara could have been looking at petrified rattlesnake shit for all she cared. Just being with this woman. Knowing this rock solid love. Come on so sudden. She thought she could live on this metaphorical river, in the heart of that Edward Abbey line, "Joy, shipmates, joy."

Tears ran down Laurie's face. With the fiction of Howard having been ripped away from her very active imagination, she was left with the unbearable loss of her mother. Yet these pictures. She viewed them as cries of help, screams into some unforeseen future, and here they were, the future. Holding all this pain in her heart was agony, but it was easier—why couldn't she ever remember to apply what she knew professionally to her own life?—than working so hard to push away the pain. Howard was right: This canyon, this river, they blast your heart open.

"Thank you," Paige said to Josie, and everyone knew she meant for bringing them to see the petroglyphs. Paige felt unaccountably happy. She'd endured so many traumas in the past days. And yet the trip had been epic and she'd survived. More, she felt a fresh sense of clarity, like a swift current, and knew that it would guide her next decisions.

Yes, Marylou sang. As the women filed back down the rocky trail to the waiting boats, all of them quietly joined in. *This land is your land. This land is my land.*

Perhaps, had the women known that those minutes viewing the petroglyphs would be the last peaceful ones they were to enjoy for a long time to come, they might have lingered, communed longer with the ancient stories and voices, maybe even prayed.

They found seven ravens perched all over their gear and the rafts. As Josie shooed them, they cawed, their voices hoarse with warning, their flights steeped in urgency. Most of the women laughed. Maeve looked around for what might have alarmed the huge black birds.

Just moments later, as they settled into their ongoing wash down the river, Maeve's eyes were drawn to a spot on the water, not far from the boats, and there she saw the floating body of a dark-skinned girl with the barest swell of a child in her belly. Her black hair fanned on the surface of the water. Her blank eyes looked upward, unseeing, at the torpid sky. The girl had been dead for hundreds of years, and Maeve immediately understood that no one else could see her. The girl who wasn't really there, an apparition.

The canyon widened now and the sky overhead grew so much bigger than it had been in days. One more night's camp, followed by a last half-day float, and they'd be at Diamond Creek where Raymond, the Hualapai outfitter, would meet them, pack up their rented gear, and haul them back to Flagstaff. The heat was insufferable and the women dragged their feet and hands in the river whenever they could, dumping hatfuls of cold water over their heads and shoulders.

In the late afternoon, long after the sun reached its zenith and began arcing toward the horizon, a commercial plane flew into their view, coming from the east. Sunlight glinted off its steel skin, flashing like a welder's sparks, far above the women on the river. At the moment the plane was directly overhead, it did a startling thing. The plane made a U-turn, leaving a huge horseshoe of exhaust streams bloating in the pale sky.

The women made weak jokes about why a plane would turn around so abruptly, so completely, in the middle of a flight. But the heat kept them from thinking too hard, from talking much at all, as they all just wished for the relief of evening, the setting sun, a possible breeze.

A couple hours later, as shadows deepened on the canyon walls, a fleet of fighter jets breached the span of sky, the roar of their engines louder even than the river. Kara, Paige, and Maeve each had seen visions on this trip, and they *knew* they'd seen visions, so they looked around to see if anyone else saw and heard the fighter jets. They did. Everyone craned her neck, all faces turned upward. The lean darts flew in formation, in a big V like geese, but sinister rather than whimsical. Long after the jets were gone, the women stared up at the white streaks, as if they were glyphs in the reddening sky.

The canyon wrens were silent. The ravens too stood voiceless on the shore, their black wings folded against their sides, their obsidian eyes shiny with unease. The women heard only lapping water.

They rowed all night, the dread pitted in their stomachs compelling them to get out as fast as they could. Something had happened. They needed to know what. They needed to know if their families were safe. Maybe what they'd witnessed was just some silly coincidence of airline emergency and military practice. But they needed to know. As they took turns rowing by starlight, the river easy now, the air cool, they talked quietly, recalling each of their camps, agreeing to set up a photo sharing site and telling funny stories about the toilet bucket and failed meals and the night Paige's tent blew away. Sometime in the early morning, a partial moon rose, glossy as a severed pearl.

They arrived at Diamond Creek a bit after dawn. Of course the outfitter wasn't there yet. He wasn't expected until later that afternoon, but at least they'd reached a place with a road, with access to civilization, even if they didn't have a vehicle themselves. Everyone tried her cell phone, but there still wasn't a signal. They found pockets of shade and lay down to wait.

No one came. Afternoon dragged into evening. No other river parties arrived. The outfitter didn't show up. The sun passed from east to west, the heat persisted, and another fleet of fighter jets flew overhead. All this while, Brynn sat at a distance from the other women, her mouth a grim line and her skin a bright red. Apparently she'd forgotten to put on sunscreen today. She looked uncomfortable and nervous.

They didn't set up tents that night. The women lay on their ground cloths and sleeping bags under the glaring stars, wrapped by the hot sky. They talked about that boomeranging commercial flight, followed by the fleets of fighter jets, speculating about what it all could mean.

"Maybe nothing," Laurie said. "Don't make assumptions."

"Nobody's making assumptions," Paige said. "Your generation lives with blinders on. Did you see the planes? Did you see their behavior? Do you need to read it in the *New York Times* to know it happened?"

"Honey," Marylou said.

"Wake up," Paige said.

"My deepest regret," Maeve said after a long silence, "is the way my belief in humanity has shriveled rather than swelled. I want to believe that people are good, that compassion will triumph, but that isn't what I've seen recently."

"What are you talking about?" Laurie said, fear palpable in her words.

"Give it time," Marylou said. "People *are* good. All of *you*, for example. This is just a bad stretch."

"True," Maeve said. "You're right. I love all of you."

Paige, who lay next to Maeve, reached over and took her hand. For a brief period, while Maeve was married to her grandpa, this woman had been her grandma, sort of. A stand-in grandma. Maybe for a year.

"We got this," Paige said. Maeve squeezed the kid's hand, a splash of unexpected happiness soothing her. She knew Paige intended the "we" to mean "young people." Yes, they probably did have this. She squeezed Paige's hand again and said, "Thank you."

Kara and Josie had carried their sleeping kits a long way off, but this was the desert, on a still night, and despite the rumble of the Diamond Creek Rapid not far downstream, the rest of the women could hear them. The faint sound of their lovemaking irritated Laurie, embarrassed Marylou, filled Paige with longing, and made Maeve smile.

"Happiness is not an entitlement," Maeve said into the hot air. "It's an experience. A rare one. So when it's bestowed, pay attention, ride the wave."

Laurie pressed her spine against the ground, made herself not comment on the annoying observation, and wondered whether Howard would have slept with her if she'd made a blatant move. Probably not. She offended herself with such speculation. As if she were desperate. As if she would want a man who wanted someone thirty years younger. She cried softly, thinking she had no business being a therapist, masquerading as an expert on happiness.

No one came for them the next day, either. In the early afternoon, even though it was blazing hot, the women, everyone except for Brynn, wandered up the rocky creek bed that doubled as a road, looking and listening for a truck. Paige held her mom's hand. Kara and Josie walked solemnly side by side, their shoulders bumping, breathing in unison. Laurie silently wept as she walked. The further they got from the river, the more intense the apocalyptic stillness.

Their reconnaissance mission didn't last long and they rushed back to the cold flow of the river where they sat in the sand, under bushes, and waited. One hour. Four hours. They carried on more long speculative conversations. They began to wonder if they were on their own.

Throughout the last thirty-six hours, Brynn had been polite but separate. She joined the women for meals but retreated quickly to her own remote patch of shade once the meal ended. She obsessed about the absence of Howard's truck, which they'd left here at Diamond Creek before being shuttled to the put-in. Had he taken the time to deflate and load the boat? Or had he just put a foot on the rubber hull and shoved it downstream, creating another ghost boat? She tried to ignore the women staring at her from down the beach.

"We need to know your story," Marylou said that evening when they gathered for dinner, which would be chips and one melon, shared seven ways, plus two bags of cookies. They were nearly out of food.

Everyone understood the need in Marylou's question. Alone in the desert, with diminishing hope of rescue, they were morphing into a new kind of community, a tribe. A mysterious member could be their downfall.

To everyone's surprise, Brynn nodded, acquiescing.

"I work for a coalition of organizations, including the Havasupai, Hualapai, and Navajo tribes. Along with some environmental groups I won't name. I'm undercover, gathering information on what the Schmidt brothers have planned. They own most of the potential and working uranium mines in Arizona. We need to know exactly which sites they hope to exploit next, with a focus on saving the Grand Canyon."

Laurie didn't believe her. Maeve grunted her approval. Kara experienced that frisson of clarity she often felt the first moments on a fire. Paige nodded slowly. Josie said, "Wow."

Marylou asked, "Howard works with you?"

"Howard works for the uranium mining lobby."

The women were stunned.

"He is a geology professor," Laurie said. "You can't fake a thing like that."

Brynn gave Laurie a sympathetic look. "Yeah, you're right, Howard is a geology professor. And his knowledge of this geology is invaluable to the Schmidt brothers. Who write him large checks. And who don't give a rip about the purity of the water, the health of the nearby people, or the preservation of sacred sites and archeology."

"I don't believe you," Laurie said.

"Laurie," Marylou said.

"He didn't lie to you." Brynn's voice carried a surprising amount of compassion. "I think he truly loves the Grand Canyon. He probably tells himself that the uranium lobby somehow serves science. People find ways to justify their greed. Without implicating themselves. All the time. People aren't rational."

"That's so cynical," Laurie said.

"I'd say sinister, not cynical," Maeve said.

"Is this true?" Marylou asked, looking up and around, as if she were asking the ravens and cacti, or the river itself.

Maeve said, "If rivers are the blood of a continent, then America is bleeding out."

"Mom," Paige said, "of course it's true."

Josie walked to the river's edge. She dipped in her hand, poured icy water over the back of her neck, like a self-baptism. She crouched there, looking upstream and downstream.

Kara needed more clarification. "You really *married* him?"

Brynn groaned, sounding as if she were nearly vomiting. "What a fiasco. Yeah, I did. My cohorts thought it'd give me more room to play, and it did. It flattered him deeply, which in turn made him trust me. Opened doors. Literal ones. Like to his files." Brynn laughed and then shuddered. "I'd planned a fake justice of the peace, fake papers. We had it all set up with contacts helping, playing the parts. Then he surprised me with a weekend trip to Hawaii." She groaned again. "He called it a pre-honeymoon. And when we got there, boom, he'd arranged every-thing. A real wedding. I could have backed out. Said hell no. Blown my cover. But you know—" Tough, fiery Brynn actually teared up. "I thought, fuck it. I'd find a way out of the marriage later. Small potatoes compared to what the uranium miners are doing. Poisoning the water.

Raping our country. So yeah, I didn't blow my cover and I married the dude."

Paige nearly melted with admiration. "Thank you," she said.

Brynn looked surprised.

"I mean it," Paige said.

"Yeah, well, you can only imagine."

Paige *could* imagine. Fucking that old guy for information. For love of country. As a patriotic act. Wow. Wow. And wow.

"You used him." Laurie didn't know why she continued to defend Howard, but it was wrong to manipulate someone like that.

"For crying out loud," Maeve said to Laurie.

"That's exactly what I did," Brynn said, meeting Laurie's hot gaze. "Howard knows all of the miners' plans, practical and political. I was hired to extract that information from the man just as he was hired to help extract uranium from the Earth. A fair trade."

"We don't know she's telling the truth!" Laurie cried out.

"Yeah, we do," Josie said from the water's edge. "We definitely do."

"Did you get the information you were seeking?" Marylou asked.

"Oh yeah." Brynn breathed deeply. "I got a boatload of intel."

"So where do you think he went?" Kara asked.

In the granular light of dusk, yet another fleet of fighter jets tore open the sky, interrupting everything, including their conversation and the streams of their individual thoughts. Fear swarmed in. The women lay down for the night, but no one slept. They all watched the moon rise in the very early morning, its light throwing all the cacti and stones in sharp relief.

Brynn spent the night at a distance from the women, regretting having told them everything at dinner. She'd made so many mistakes. Losing her cool with Howard, blowing her cover. Then losing Howard altogether. Unburdening herself to these women. It was as if, in those moments, she hadn't believed they would survive, make it out of here. She'd blabbed. Lost control of the narrative in a way she'd never done before. She had so many people depending on her, and she'd messed up.

And yet the truth sometimes moved with the force of a river. You couldn't dam it. The flow of gravity always won eventually. She'd told them the truth because they might *not* make it out alive. They deserved to know.

Moments before sunrise, Brynn heard the faint crunch of big tires on the rocky dry riverbed. It could be anyone, including someone hostile, like a representative of the Schmidt brothers. She had no idea where Howard had gone. He could have made a phone call. In fact, that would have been his best move.

But here was the thing: he did love her. Maybe love was too strong a word. What was it that an older man felt for a pretty younger woman? A deep gratitude laced with a heavy dose of nostalgia? His greed for her, whatever fueled it, was unmistakable. She now banked on his hurt feelings delaying him from figuring out his most rational move. That could even be him driving back here.

Brynn rolled onto her side and looked over at the tribe of women lying stoically on their sleeping pads in the pinking light of dawn. They were lovely women really, entirely innocent. But a liability. They knew everything now because of her big mouth. They were potentially a burden, too. She might be able to save herself, but if she did figure her own way out to safety, could she really leave them to perish? Assuming no one did come for them. Assuming the worst case scenario with the fleets of fighter jets.

Still, was she supposed to lose everything, including possibly her own life, for this group of strangers? If that *wasn't* Howard returning, if he'd gone ahead and alerted his bosses, she was a sitting duck. She should try to disappear into the desert right now, run and find cover, hide, and leave them to deal with the Schmidts' men. They likely wouldn't get hurt. They were innocent bystanders. Maybe they'd even get delivered to safety.

That would be *her* most rational move.

No. She had no time to run and certainly no time to convince the women to keep her a secret. And even if she did run, the goons would find her. Easily. Quickly. Her wits were always her best defense. Brynn got up and washed her face in the river. She found someone's water bottle and guzzled a long drink.

Daylight seemed to attack their camp as the crunching of rubber on rock grew louder. Now she could see a cloud of dust hurtling their way. The sound aroused the motley crew of women, and they all got to their feet, eyes swollen with heat and sleeplessness and fear. They looked at her, as if she were supposed to supply answers. *Fuck this*, she thought. *I*

should *run*. Where though? Miles of desert, just rock and sand, surrounded her. She could throw herself into the river, wash downstream.
It was actually a pretty ingenious idea. A speedy escape, and no one
would think of her on the river without a boat. She didn't though. She
stood facing the storm of dust coming their way until she could make
out a big pickup truck, an ancient colorless Chevy, jouncing toward
them. The driver slammed on the brakes, and the pickup skidded in the
parking area, making a forty-five degree spin. Laughter emanated from
the truck's cab.

The driver jumped out first, still laughing, and batted at the dusty air
around his face. The middle-aged Navajo man was short and stocky
with thick black hair, parted neatly on the right, and he wore fresh blue
jeans and a clean white T-shirt.

"Lionel! Oh thank god," Brynn breathed. She ran to the man and
hugged him tightly.

Backing up from her intensity and looking around, he asked,
"Where's Howard?"

"Ah, man. I've fucked up. He's gone."

"Gone?"

An older woman wearing a red baseball cap over her short gray
hair, a loose pale green shift, and clear plastic sandals, and a young man
wearing a Black Lives Matter T-shirt and a long glossy ponytail, both
also Navajo, emerged from the truck cab. Brynn cried, "Oh, Charlene!
Ross!" She hugged them, too.

"What do you mean 'gone'?" Charlene asked.

"Wait," Brynn said. "Why are you here? I'm so glad to see you, I
can't even tell you, but how did you know?" Tears streamed down her
sunburned cheeks.

"Major shit is hitting the fan," Lionel said. "We didn't want to leave
you in his hands. We decided to intercept. So where is he?"

"Can you get us out of here?" Laurie shouted, startling everyone.
She surged forward and took hold of the older man's arm. "Our outfitter
was supposed to come a day and a half ago. Do you know Raymond?"

Lionel stepped out of Laurie's grip and briefly closed his eyes, as if
summoning patience. Ross pulled the elastic off his ponytail, shook out
his hair, and then tied it back up again, using the gesture to cover his
glancing assessment of the clustered, obviously terrified white women

standing to the side. Charlene nodded at them and held up a hand that said *wait.*

Marylou pulled Laurie back.

"So where is he?" Ross asked Brynn again.

They all listened to her quick account of Lava Falls, how they capsized and how that unraveled her cool, how she lost her temper completely, basically telling Howard who she really was. She told about his early departure the next morning. "I'm so sorry," Brynn finished. "I fucked up."

"Can't say I'm disappointed I won't get a chance to meet the bastard," Ross said.

"Thing is," Brynn said, "we don't know what he's doing, who he's calling."

"We may have to find him and kill him," Charlene said.

The two men cracked up.

Laurie, Marylou, and Paige all gasped.

Charlene walked to the water's edge, kicked off her plastic sandals and waded in, said, "Ahhhh." Then she turned and grinned at her two companions.

"She's joking," Ross explained to the shocked women.

"In any case," Charlene said, "a white man on the lam is the least of our problems now." She tossed her red cap on the beach, bent over, and dunked her head in the river, then stood and shook out droplets.

Brynn shoved aside concern about her own safety, thoughts of what the Schmidt brothers might do to her once Howard confessed. Then she had an insight. There was a chance, a decent chance, he *wouldn't* confess. He'd been a complete idiot in allowing her access to everything, in inadvertently leaking so much intel. His pride would likely keep him from telling them anything about her at all! Then, too, he would lose his lucrative gig if they learned how badly he'd fucked up. Ha! These realizations made Brynn feel almost cocky.

"So what the hell is going on out here?" she asked, waving at the sky.

"Hop in." Lionel held open the passenger door to the Chevy. "We'll tell you everything as we get out of here."

"Hey!" Laurie shouted again, her vocal cords strained with fear. "What about us?"

"Excuse me," Marylou said, wanting to counter Laurie's stridency with a calm, perhaps more effective voice, but she stalled out with the two words.

Lionel, truck keys in his fist, half-turned toward them. "You contract with someone to fetch you?"

"Yes, but—"

"Raymond, right?"

"Yes!"

"He's a good man. If he said he'd be here, he'll be here."

"But he was supposed to be here a day and a half ago."

"Not good," Charlene said, walking back up the beach toward the truck.

"That's Hualapai for you," Lionel said, and the three Navajo laughed.

"Lionel," Brynn said. "They saved my life."

Charlene squinted at the group of women for a long moment before asking, "Where you ladies headed?"

"We have flights out of Flagstaff," Marylou answered. "Later today."

"Probably not anymore," Ross said.

"Hop in the back of the truck, ladies."

"Charlene, no," Ross said. "That's a lot of extra mouths to feed. We can't—"

Charlene reached up and yanked on the young man's ponytail. "What's wrong with you?" She gave him a shove in the direction of the truck cab door, then jerked her head toward the tailgate, and the women quickly climbed in, tumbling onto the hot metal of the truck bed. Lionel waited for them to all to board, giving a hand to Maeve. She smiled at him and said, "Thank you, sir," as if he were doing something as frivolous as helping her into a roller coaster car.

"Where're we going?" Paige asked.

Marylou had no idea where they were going or what they'd be called upon to do once they got there, so she couldn't answer her daughter. But her heart was filled with the intensity of the canyon: sheets of green water punctuated by stupendous sprays of whitewater; hoarse caws of ravens and melodies of wrens; hot blue sky and hotter red rock. For now, these would have to sustain her. It's possible they could sustain her for a lifetime.

Paige sat next to her mom. Her future had busted wide open. There wasn't a single known. It was terrifying. Also exciting. Paige knew she was joining something bigger than she could imagine, perhaps the heart and soul of the resistance, and yeah, she was glad.

As the desert landscape flew by, the truck's hard ride jarred their bones and the wind blasted across their faces. Dazed, they passed around a jug of hot water, grateful and wary both. The three Navajo folks and one pink and blond white girl sitting up front talked heatedly, nonstop, and the women knew Brynn was being filled in about the jets, about whatever nightmare was unfolding in the world at large, and maybe also in the canyonlands all around them. Occasional jokes and shouting laughter punctuated the serious conversation in the truck's cab. Laurie frowned, disapproving of laughter at a time like this. Paige laughed along with them, though she couldn't hear the jokes. Maeve thought laughter might be as important as water, especially now. Kara and Josie leaned against each other, both feeling profoundly lucky to live in their joined skins, despite the unraveling of the world outside their love. As the early morning light filled in the day, each of the women wondered when she would learn about what had happened on the planet.

Marylou, who'd planned and organized this journey, did so because she wanted a new life, one that delivered her beyond her marriage with Joe, one that brought her closer to her daughter Paige, one that would help her understand this crazy human species. Two out of three wasn't bad. So she began singing.

✴

Long after the Glen Canyon and Hoover dams have crumbled and washed away, two young women pick their way through the rocks littering a steep wash. Gar sees that a flash flood recently wiped out the canyon's vegetation, leaving a gray stony swath, perhaps easier to walk than before the torrents of water. She imagines the flood, the trickle growing to a slough, and that gaining volume quickly, until waves reaching far above her own height pounded downhill, clearing everything in their path. Today the sky is blue and the sun shines hard and constant. Walking is difficult, and it would help if her hands were free, but she doesn't let go of her friend, Octavia.

They've been walking for five days, packs on their backs and rifles slung across their chests, and they're out of water. They've sucked the moisture from plants. They've killed game and drunk the blood. They still have plenty of dried fruit and three big sacks of corn kernels. They know how to roast agave. They aren't hungry. But they're very, very thirsty.

The two girls have long heard about the huge green river that runs between majestic walls of rock. Octavia's grandmother drew them a map, as best she could from stories she'd heard. None of the others shared Gar and Octavia's outlandish ability to dream a miraculous future, and so in the end they left alone. Everyone expected them to die in the sand, become food for coyotes. They themselves hadn't known if they'd ever find the green river. But maybe they'd find something else. Who can know what's out there without looking?

Now as they make their way down the canyon recently scrubbed by the flash flood, they begin to hear a gentle din, just under the whistle of the wind. The sound is like a layer of blowing sand, soft and insistent. Then it grows louder, a hot hush. They exchange looks, their eyes bright with thirst and wonder, but they don't dare project their thoughts down the dry riverbed to the source of the sound. They keep walking, their hands grasped hotly, their hearts thudding. The wind stops blowing up the canyon, suddenly, as if in anticipation, and they hear a soft roar. Gar wants to run, but Octavia tugs back on her hand. The last thing they need now is a twisted ankle, a bashed head. So they walk carefully toward the roar and soon it's deafening. They look over their shoulders, suddenly and simultaneously fearing another flash flood in their canyon, but the sound definitely comes from below, not above.

They arrive at the place where they can see the brightness of whitewater, dazzling in the hot sunlight, violent in its speedy course. Just below the rapid, the water calms into shimmering green pools, swirling with eddies, clear to the bottom. Their throats constrict. They do run now, leaping over boulders, falling to their knees on the tiny strip of sand at the river's edge. They plunge their faces into the water and they drink.

The We of Me

with thanks to Carson McCullers

Jim and I are walking together at dusk, and we've wandered far from both of our camps. A light rain is falling, more like a mist, not even enough to catch on an outstretched tongue. But the air is crackling with negative ions. The storms are coming at long last. I want to take off my clothes so I can feel the drizzle on my skin. I know Jim will be uncomfortable because the Second Amenders never remove their clothes in public.

I strip off just my shirt.

I have no idea why we call them the Second Amenders. Roxanne says it's because of their guns, but that doesn't make any kind of sense. What do guns have to do with amends? Jesus says it's because they're descendants of a people who were obsessed with wrongdoing, and so they have to make amends all the time. Sasha says it's their compulsion about rules, which they are constantly amending.

"They can't just leave things be," Sasha says. "They amend everything. They amend and amend and amend. We should call them the Hundredth Amenders."

They call themselves The People. We call ourselves We.

"For goodness sakes, Jim. Have a look," I say. He's a very shy boy and has been trying to avert his gaze. My breasts are just nipples on a couple of swells, but it's more than he's ever seen. I personally can't

220

imagine not looking at something I haven't seen before. Like Jim, I'm only thirteen years old, but my curiosity is fertile.

Jim gives in and stares. He stares and stares, and after a few moments his eyes begin to do a little jig. All at once, he convulses. His waist bends, his mouth opens, and donkey bleats shoot from his throat. They keep coming, louder, harder, and deeper, the sounds now issuing forth from his lower belly.

I watch, fascinated, as he tries to control the convulsions. It seems like the more he tries to stop them, bigger and bigger waves roll through. I know Jim doesn't like to be touched, but I can't help it, I gently pat his shoulder. I let my hand run down his thin arm, smoothing the fine blond hairs to calm him, and then I lay my hand on his chest. I want to feel what's happening inside his body.

My touch scares him too much, though, and the seizure stops. He steps away from me and looks back in the direction of the Second Amenders' camp.

"I won't tell," I say. "I promise."

I should have said that I wouldn't tell *his* people. I can't help telling mine. That night at the campfire, I say, "I think Jim is a laugher."

"Really?" Everyone is interested. "You've seen him laugh?"

"Maybe." I describe his convulsing behavior.

Roxanne says, "Yes. That's laughter."

"How would you know?" Barley gets more annoyed by Roxanne's know-it-all-ness than anyone.

"I've done a lot of research," she says. "I've talked to people who have met laughers. Who have seen laughing."

"I've heard it's very pleasurable," Sasha says. "Like an orgasm. Only it starts in your chest and spreads down rather than starting in your genitals and spreading up."

"Jim looked like he was in pain, not pleasure," I point out.

"That doesn't surprise me," Sasha says. "The Second Amenders probably think laughing is a disease. Jim better hide that shit."

I could talk about laughing all night. There is so much I want to know. According to what Roxanne has told me, all human beings used to have the ability to laugh. Now the trait is rarely found, although she says there are a few communities on the Pacific coast where nearly every-one still laughs. She says it happens when something is very funny or very delightful. I wonder which it was for Jim when he saw my breasts, funny or delightful?

I have so many questions, but Sasha had to go and talk about orgasms, and so Rose and Herbert start fornicating. Jesus and Sasha do, as well.

"If you don't mind," I shout. "Some of us are trying to have a conversation."

Both couples scoot into the darkness just beyond the firelight. But the conversation stops anyway. It's okay. I do want to keep talking about laughter, but I also like listening to the soft animal sounds, the slide of rain-slicked skin. I love Jesus and Sasha. They are the we of me. Roxanne plugs her ears when Sasha kicks up a gear and starts hollering.

Nicholas holds his drum between his legs, and he begins softly, his fingertips barely tapping the tight skin, his eyes closed, testing the acoustics of the night. He can make a composition last seven days, beginning with faint taps and finger slides, his own skin on the drum skin, building to deep, rhythmic thrumming.

It's been a good day. The soft rain. Jim laughing. Jesus and Sasha fornicating. And now me sleeping between them, Sasha's soft breasts mashed against my back and my cheek against Jesus's sharp wing bone.

When I awake in the morning, Jesus is gone. For the past month, he's been sneaking off to the Second Amenders' camp to fornicate with Linda. They don't like our men fornicating with their women, and so he has to steal away in the dead of night, and she has to somehow get out of the women's tent, maybe act as if she's going to the toilet, and they have to do it fast in the sand. Until this time, he's always been back in our camp well before dawn.

Sasha is wild with jealousy. She makes a scene at breakfast, tossing dried dung at the fire and refusing a cup of tea, her eyes all wonky with desperation.

"He's got a lot of nerve, staying the night," Barley says.

"Fornication," Roxanne uses her instructional voice, "is enhanced by danger and secrecy and rule breaking. Jesus is getting a triple whammy."

"Not a necessary comment," Barley says.

I love Sasha and I hate to see her in pain. I want to see her snaggle-toothed smile. I try to think of a way to calm her.

"The rains are coming," I say, holding a hand up to the mist. "It's time to make for the continental divide."

Everyone looks at me and I know why. I've taken it upon myself to speak, both my tone and the content, as an adult. This surprises them.

"Good idea," Sasha says emphatically.

For as long as I can remember, Sasha has rhapsodized about the continental divide. She says there are freshwater lakes and clear-running streams in the mountains. She wants us to make a permanent camp in the highlands. Roxanne, especially, has grown tired of this fantasy. She points out that winter at an altitude of twelve thousand feet would be brutal. She says she doesn't want to live in an igloo. Anyway, lately, everyone thinks Sasha just wants to get Jesus away from Linda.

"The point being," I say, "if there's a rainy season, and it looks like there will be one, we can leave the spring. It'll rain long enough for us to get to the fat alpine lakes and clear-running streams near the continental divide."

"*If* the lakes and rivers exist," Nicholas says in his soft, easygoing voice. His knees squeeze the drum and he takes a deep breath.

Nicholas's caution gives me pause. Imagine dying of exhaustion and exposure in the mountains. We'd be a pile of bones in no time. Gone. Deceased. Extinct.

"Anyway, my dear Sasha," Nicholas says, "it's in-ev-it-a-ble." He taps on his drum, one beat for each syllable in the word. "Our people will braid together. Eventually. You (tap) can't (tap) stop (tap) it (tap)."

Again Barley says, "Not a necessary comment."

Nicholas has given me a new idea. The idea takes hold and grows like a crystal. I can practically see pellucid trapezoid planes intersecting, multiplying. It is inevitable.

"I'll go get him," I say, feeling guilty because my true motivation is seeing Jim, not fetching Jesus.

Sasha storms off. Nicholas's eyes are closed and his fingers are busy on the drum skin. The other adults ignore me as well, and so I leave.

The Second Amenders have been camping near us for months. Roxanne says it's because we're good at finding water. On the face of things, their camps are much like ours. They build fire rings and dig pit toilets. But while we put up open-air tarps, they erect closed tents. They do a lot of things in private. They don't build sculptures or paint pictures. They do sing, though. They sing beautiful ballads that have many, many verses and tell intriguing stories. I memorize them as best I can and hold everyone in thrall at our campfire by reciting them.

I'm tolerated in their camp, allowed to visit Jim because, one, I'm a girl, and two, they think we're children, and three, Jim is not valued. The Second Amenders care very much about what they call bloodlines, and Jim is an orphan. Nobody feels the need to protect him. This allows him a bit of freedom. At the same time, all the Second Amender rules still apply to him, and they are often applied harshly since he doesn't have a bloodlines protector. "I am a stream run dry," he once said to me. It just about broke my heart.

"Greetings!" I call out when I see the armed guards. "Can Jim play?" It's best with them to use the lexicon of childhood although I am no longer a child. The guards wave me past.

Hardly anyone is around, which is strange. All the adults seem to be buttoned up in the tents. Some of the children are roaming about, though. I spot Jim and my heart flip flops. Though we're the same age, he's much shorter than me and he looks like a sprite with his blond cowlick and butterfly blue eyes. "Come on," I tell him. "Can you get away?"

He nods, and we walk right out of camp. We stop at the spring for a long drink. I've never taken him out to see Sasha and Jesus's work. It's a long way, and Jim likes to be cautious. I can't stand cautious today, though. My idea, the one growing like a crystal, is organic and multi-faceted. I want all my senses engaged.

"I'm going to show you something you've never seen before." I swing our joined hands while we walk, pleased that he's allowing contact, and I'm smiling.

"Marvin wants to kill Jesus," he says, and I think my heart stops beating for a minute.

"What?"

"Marvin found him fornicating with Linda. Last night out past the latrine. They've tied him up in the big tent."

"Why?"

"For fornicating with Linda."

"You said that. But—"

"Marvin flew into a rage," Jim says.

I picture Marvin, who I have only glimpsed from afar, airborne and enraged. I think of Sasha's wonky eyes, her dung flinging. Still, I don't understand. "Why would Marvin kill Jesus?"

"He was fornicating with Linda," Jim says patiently. "A schism has torn The People. Everyone has been arguing since well before dawn. Some think we should kill Jesus. They want to put his body in a cave in the cliffs where the hyenas will eat his flesh. Or bury him in the ground where worms will suck his veins dry. Not everyone agrees though. God is against killing."

"Do I know God?" I ask. I don't remember Jim talking about him, or maybe it's a her.

"*God*," Jim says, giving me an uncharacteristically sharp look.

I nod, not wanting to appear stupid.

"It'll be okay," I say. "God's right. They won't kill him."

We've never been afraid of the Second Amenders. Roxanne says that with all those guns, they're mostly a danger to themselves and that they'll likely kill themselves off in the near future. She says that evolution favors love. It favors curiosity, too.

"What's that?" Jim asks, stopping in his tracks.

"Ha!" I cry, delighted. Jim has spied Sasha's biggest painting. It covers a big swath of the lower part of the cliff face. Until Jesus started fornicating with Linda, she loved this camp because she found such good pigments. She's made orange from clay, and green-blue from slate, and yellow, too, from the oxidized residue in dried basins.

Sasha's paintings are so beautiful. I love watching Jim look at this one, the way his pale lashes blink, blink, blink and how I can see a syrupy desire leak into his limbs.

I pull him by the hand around to the backside of the cliff where Jesus has been building. His sculpture starts in an alcove, grows right out of the cliff itself, as if created by the forces of geology, except that the piles of stone spiral away from the cliff, like a long tail, tapering, tapering, tapering, until at the end, Jesus has built a sphere. Three flat stones form the base. Building out and up from there the sphere widens to an equator and then it curves back in again. It's a secret how Jesus has managed to get those rocks on the top of the stone ball.

I can see that Jim loves the sculpture. The size, shapes, and uncanny placement of stones fill him with zeal. His thin, blond paleness begins to quiver. He's going to laugh!

We're all alone, and I'm hoping he won't worry, won't hold back, will let himself go. And he does. He laughs and laughs and laughs, falling to the ground, expelling all the sounds freely. I am so happy he trusts me that much.

When he finally calms, he lies on his back and breathes. I lie down beside him. He cuts his eyes at me to see what I think.

"It's okay," I say. "Laughing is okay." I actually don't know if what I say is true, but I don't want him to be afraid.

"Marvin says there are entire tribes of laughers west of the continental divide."

"I've heard that, too."

"Many of them die that way."

"Die laughing?" I ask.

He nods and begins to look stricken.

I want to reassure him, but in fact it seems entirely possible. Likely, even. When you think about it, that could be why the trait evolved out of most of the human race.

The prospect of dying laughing should put me off my plan, but it doesn't. Instead, Jim's fit of laughter has aroused my desire. An acute and specific urgency speaks in the base of my belly.

I roll onto my side and touch his hipbone. I like the way it juts.

He looks at me like I'm a hyena myself, like I'm about to devour him, maybe stuff him into a cave first. He doesn't move away, though. He waits, not twitching a finger or blinking an eyelid, as I run my hand up his ribcage and then trace his sternum.

"It's going to rain." His voice squeaks.

"I know."

"Will your people move on?"

"Sasha wants to. She doesn't like Jesus fornicating with Linda." I think I'm clever steering the talk in that direction. I roll onto my hands and knees, and then straddle Jim, my pudendum pressed against his bellybutton. "Let's take off our clothes."

I can tell he wants to, but his eyes are full of questions.

"No one will know. Anyway, I love you."

I unbutton his suit jacket and roll him over to get his arms out of the sleeves. I unbutton the fly of his suit pants, too, and pull these off his skinny white legs. He's not wearing underthings. Naked, Jim looks a bit like a larva, his pale whiteness glowing against the scratchy sand. I've never done this before but I've watched enough, so it's no mystery. I'm guessing that Jim has never even watched.

"Are you afraid?" I ask.

He doesn't answer.

I stand up so I can take off my clothes, looking down at Jim the whole time. The skin on his penis is soft and pink, like a baby mouse. I lie back down beside him and wait to see what he will do. I don't want to frighten him, and yet, at the same time, if he doesn't know how it's done, how can he even know if he wants to do it?

Jim knows how it's done. In fact, suddenly I'm the one who is a bit afraid. Watching is one thing. Doing it is another. I concentrate on the laughing genes that I hope he is squirting into me. The chance, the odds.

Jim laughs yet again, only softly now. I do hope with all my heart he doesn't ever die laughing. I stroke his blond hair. I tell him what I know about sex and giving birth. I tell him he doesn't have to be a stream run dry.

"You're only thirteen," he says, and I know he's asking, how would I know any of this, about sex, laughter, and streams?

I shrug. He's right. I'm only thirteen. I don't know anything.

Yet there's a loose happiness between us as we walk the long way back to our respective camps. At the place where our paths split, I kiss him on his red mouth before going my way. I can tell he has liked our day.

All my happiness discharges, though, as I draw near camp. Sasha is keening. Nicholas is drumming, fiercely, angrily. Some adults are arguing, and others are squatted near Sasha, murmuring. The children are huddled under a tarp, for the rain is beginning to fall in real drops, great splats.

"What?" I shout. "What?"

"They've killed Jesus," Roxanne tells me.

"No," I say. "It's only talk. They won't really do it. God is against it."

"They brought us his body." Roxanne gestures at a covered lump under a newly erected tarp.

Sasha is inconsolable. She talks of killing Linda. She talks of killing Marvin. She talks of killing herself.

"We'll go to the continental divide," Barley says, over and over again, trying to comfort her. "We'll go now. We'll make a permanent camp at a sparkling alpine lake with its own clear-running stream."

"I've heard the winters are actually mild in the mountains," Roxanne lies. "We'll have a grand new life there."

We bury Jesus out by the cliffs, right under his sculpture. We have to dismantle a side of it, and some think this is wrong, but I agree that he'd want to be in the heart of his work. Once he's in the ground, I help put the stones back in the exact same configuration. The rain slashes down. Sasha rocks her body back and forth, convulsing with grief.

We leave first thing in the morning, walking west with our full packs, the rain soaking our hair and clothes. I know we'll walk for days, our feet squishing in the wet sand. I cup my tongue and hold it out for a drink.

I am filled with sorrow. I love Jesus. I love Jim. I have lost them both. The we has fallen out of the me.

I am also filled with curiosity. I do want to see the swell of land leading up to the continental divide, the craggy sculptures at the top, and also, maybe one day, what it's like on the other side. I don't care about snow and winter. I'm bursting with curiosity. We all are.

Eventually we'll stop for a campfire, and that's when I'll tell everyone. It's possible that I'll have a baby. It's possible that she'll be a laugher. I can't wait to see what that's like.

Acknowledgments

I am grateful first and foremost for readers, including all the ones I don't know. Friends and colleagues who have read drafts of these stories, and/or participated in the instigating adventures, include Simmons B. Buntin, Suzanne Case, Anne Dal Vera, Paula Derrow, Glenn Fisher, Jane Fisher, Martha Garcia, Allen Gee, Dorothy Hearst, Barb Johnson, Nina Lawit, BK Loren, Raymond Luczak, Peggy Malloy, Cindy Medrano, Pat Mullan, Patrick Perry, Patrick Ryan, Kirstin Valdez Quade, Carol Seajay, and Elizabeth Stark. Thank you.

My agent, Reiko Davis, is smart, hardworking, and kind. Having her in my corner makes all the difference. Thank you. The University of Wisconsin Press has been a perfect home for several of my books, including this one. Thank you Dennis Lloyd, Andrea Christofferson, Sheila Leary, Adam Mehring, Anne McKenna, and Amber Rose, as well as the anonymous outside reviewers. A special dose of gratitude for editor Raphael Kadushin, who shepherds fiction and nonfiction lists at UW Press with courage, heart, and vision.

My parents, Helen and John Bledsoe, chose to raise me and my siblings in Oregon, and the beauty and wildness of that state has shaped me and my stories. When they first moved there at the beginning of their marriage, they started a club called Adventures Unlimited with a group of their friends. The adventures have been indeed unlimited.

I've been fortunate enough to make three journeys to Antarctica, twice on National Science Foundation Artists and Writers fellowships and once with a private expedition led by an Australian group, Peregrine Adventures. So many people in the United States Antarctic Program supported me during these journeys, but a special thanks goes to Guy Guthridge.

Thank you to Yaddo, Jentel, Djerassi, and Playa for the invaluable gifts of time, support, and creative community. Some of these stories were written at these residencies.

Pat Mullan is my surprise companion through everything. One reason it works so well: Pat stays out late Saturday nights playing music at clubs called Piano Fight while I stay home and read; I leave before dawn on Sunday mornings to kayak in the bay while Pat stays home and reads. She also listens to all the minutia, and best of all, provides daily opportunities to laugh.

The following stories have been published previously in slightly different forms: "Girl with Boat" and "My Beautiful Awakening" in *Arts & Letters*; "Life Drawing" in *Roanoke Review*; "Poker" (under the title "Enough") in *ZYZZYVA*; "Wildcat" in *Shenandoah*; "Skylark" in *Jonathan*; "The Found Child" with Shebooks; "The Antarctic" in *Terrain*; "Wolf" in *The Saturday Evening Post*; and "The We of Me" in *The Rumpus*.

While I thoroughly research the places and ideas in my stories, the people come from my imagination.

Lucy Jane Bledsoe is the author of the novels *The Evolution of Love*, *A Thin Bright Line*, and *The Big Bang Symphony* as well as the adventure essay collection *The Ice Cave*. Her work has won many awards, including a California Arts Council Fellowship in Literature, the American Library Association Stonewall Award, and two National Science Foundation Artists & Writers Fellowships. She has rafted and hiked the Grand Canyon, skied Yellowstone National Park, kayaked and hiked in Alaska, and made several journeys in Antarctica. She lives in Berkeley, California. Her website is www.lucyjane bledsoe.com.